SPEAK
NO EVIL

About the author

Born and brought up in Newcastle upon Tyne, Martyn Waites was an actor before becoming a writer. As well as short stories and non-fiction he has written nine novels, several of which have been nominated for awards. He has held writing residencies at Huntercombe Young Offenders Institution and HMP Chelmsford, run arts-based workshops for socially excluded teenagers and recovering addicts and has recently stepped down as RLF Literary Fellow at the University of Essex. He is currently teaching creative writing at Anglia Ruskin University, Cambridge.

Visit www.martynwaites.com

SPEAK NO EVIL

MARTYN WAITES

PEGASUS BOOKS
NEW YORK

SPEAK NO EVIL

Pegasus Books LLC
80 Broad Street
5th Floor
New York, NY 10004

Library of Congress Cataloging-in-Publication Data
is available.

ISBN: 978-1-60598-096-6

10 9 8 7 6 5 4 3 2 1

Printed in the United States of America
Distributed by W. W. Norton & Company, Inc.
www.pegasusbooks.us

PART ONE

BOY CHILD

A room. Two seats. A table. A person either side.

'Just relax. Ignore the recorder.'

She gives a nervous laugh. 'That's easy for you to say.'

They settle down to start. He gets his notes out. She doesn't need any. She waits.

'So where do you want to start?' she asks. 'Prison? Remand home? The escape? The psychiatrists? Fenton Hall? God, there's loads of stuff.' *She pauses, looks away from him. Another drag.* 'Or what I did in the first place?'

'Wherever you like,' he said. 'Wherever you feel comfortable.'

She gave a small laugh, repeats the word, 'Comfortable.'

'I don't think this is going to be in chronological order. But don't worry, I'll do all that at the end.'

'Fine. OK. Whatever you want.'

She sits quietly. He waits.

'You'll have to give me something to talk about,' she says. 'Something to start with.'

'OK. Tell me why. Why you want to do this.'

'You mean talk to you?'

He nods.

'I'm gettin' money for this. There's goin' to be a book.'

'Is that the only reason?'

She pauses, thinks for a minute.

'No,' she says. 'I want to talk. I mean, the money's good. It'll come in handy. I'm not graspin' though. Tryin' to get somethin' I haven't earned. I've earned it, all right. But I just want a normal life. For me. Me partner and son. The money'll help, but so will talkin' to you. I want to get rid of it all and move on. Have a better life. A normal life.'

'If that's the case, shouldn't you be talking to a psychiatrist?'

She becomes angry at the suggestion. 'No. No. No psychiatrists. I've seen them all my bloody life. No. No more. You. I want you to do it.'

He nods. 'OK. Let's start from the beginning, then.'

'Right.' She goes through the ritual of lighting up another cigarette. When she's ready, she begins.

'I used to be a different person,' she says. 'And that person used to lead a different life. She lived in remand homes, went to prison and escaped, did her time and finally got let out. And she used to be one of the most hated people in the country. Mothers would scare their children asleep at nights with my name. That was me. I used to be Mae Blacklock. And I was a child murderer.'

1

The cold kept coming in. And the window couldn't stop it.

Anne Marie Smeaton tugged at the handle, but it just wouldn't settle in the frame. She pulled it close as she could, straining hard to make it fit, get the lock to catch. Then waited, removing her hand slowly, convincing herself that this time she had done it. Then watching, heart sinking, as it crept open yet again. The seal on the ill-fitting uPVC gone, the frame misshapen by years of abuse and neglect. She sighed. The cold never left her, those hard, icy claws rattling the glass, a constant reminder that she could never feel warm, never feel safe. She pulled her cardigan tight about herself, left the kitchen, closed the door behind her.

The living room had all the lights on. Ceiling, wall, standing. Glaring and harsh: making her squint but keeping the shadows at bay. The walls were brightly painted, rich blues and oranges, enthusiastically, but amateurishly applied. She had done them herself, getting bored and impatient with the work, slapping the paint on haphazardly just to be finished. The furniture was cheap, mostly second-hand, but serviceable. The kind of thing she was used to by now. The kind of thing she had always been used to.

The one exception was the gaudily coloured miniature Thai temple on a stand in the corner of the room. The Spirit House, supposedly imprisoning evil spirits, not letting them into the rest of the flat. She didn't believe it but she had bought it, knowing that when people are desperate they didn't believe in nothing they believed in anything. It had travelled with her for the best part of twenty desperate years. It had been battered and repaired but she wouldn't part with it. She didn't dare.

Anne Marie sat on the sofa. In contrast to the brightly coloured walls, she was all in black. Black T-shirt, black jeans, black cardigan, black socks. Her hair was dyed a slightly unnatural shade of red and she was bigger than she would have liked to have been. Like so many things in her life, it was a losing battle.

She looked at the blank face of the TV. There would be nothing on worth watching. Not at this time of night. There used to be quiz shows. She loved them, would sometimes phone in, get herself on air. Sometimes because she had the answers, sometimes just for someone to talk to. But they were gone now. Just foreign films and news. Lots of news. And Anne Marie had had enough of news.

She should be in bed, asleep, dreaming. But she couldn't sleep, couldn't dream. Because, behind her sleeping eyes, the ghosts were massing again. The evil spirits. The ghosts of the dead and the damned, the lost and the left behind. Ready to ambush her dreams, control her mind. Push through to the waking world, dragging their evil and madness with them. Making her do bad things. Wrong things. And she wouldn't let them. She couldn't let them.

They had visited Anne Marie before. She knew the signs. The headaches, niggling at first, building to pounding and smashing the inside of her head, like warring drummers. The blackouts. Coming round, not remembering where she had been, what she had done. Widening gaps in her memory, the voices taunting her with dread possibilities.

She knew why it was happening. The book. But the knowledge didn't help her cope with it. And she couldn't yet stop.

Anne Marie was usually straight down the doctor's whenever the spirits started talking. Cramming all the pills she could down her throat, taking to her bed, the Spirit House beside her, riding the attack out on a wave of numbness. But she couldn't do that this time. Because of the book.

That fucking book.

Anne Marie listened. Outside the flat, the night was quiet. Or quiet for the area of Newcastle she lived in. Not too many police sirens, screams, shouts, glass being broken. Made a change. She listened for sounds inside the flat itself. Jack was sleeping in the next room but as usual he made no sound. Rob did. Her boyfriend sleeping in her bedroom. Or their bedroom, as Rob had taken to calling it. Snoring and farting, his usual night-time symphony. Drunk from a skinful in the Half Moon, back to hers, grunting and falling into bed. At least he had stopped pawing her. That was something.

No, he was good, Rob, she told herself. She could have done worse. She had done worse.

Her heart starting to speed again, she reached for her barley wine. It was warm. Didn't matter. Tasted better that way. She gulped it down, her self-medication, knowing it would be the last one until the next cheque.

She looked from her empty glass to her watch. Nearly 1 a.m. She should try and get some sleep. She had another session on the book in the morning and she needed as clear a head as possible. Get it all taped and over with. Free herself from it and move on with life.

The cold was coming in under the door. It was never wholly gone, no matter how tightly she pulled her cardigan. Her tin was beside the empty glass. She opened it. Just enough for a spliff. She smiled. That would send her off. Deftly sprinkling and rolling, she lit up, dragged down deep. Her lungs clung to the smoke like a drowning man to a life raft, waited for the waves to wash her away. She stared at the blank screen, the garish walls, bright lights, saw no shadows, no ghosts.

The red light on the stereo. Her other defence, music. Perfect with the spliff. The counsellor had taught her years ago to find something she could connect with, that made her feel safe, and give herself over to it. The CD she wanted was already in the tray. It seemed to be always in the tray. She pushed the volume low so as not to wake up Jack, trapped another mouthful of smoke, settled back and closed her eyes.

The music filled the over-bright room. Scott Walker: *Scott 4*. Not the one about Death playing chess with a knight. The one about angels. Angels of ashes. How something good could come out of something bad. At least that's what the song said to her.

The orchestra played, Scott sang in his beautiful voice about being saved by angels and Anne Marie sighed, tried to hold on to those seconds of contentment, stretch them out to minutes, to hours. The angels could lock the bad spirits away forever. She dragged smoke down deep, let the music wash over her, through her, like a huge wave of comforting emotion. Scott's voice told her not to be afraid, that he had been there too, he had come through it.

She took another deep drag, silently mouthing the words to the song like an incantatory prayer, and wished, not for the first time, that she had that disease some people get, that condition where they see emotions as colours. With her eyes closed and her head drifting, she could shut out the cold, the greys, whites and blacks, let the colours of her walls sway to the music, enfold her, keep her warm and safe.

She pulled the spliff down to the roach, stubbed it, clung to the music, kept intoning, imagining. Kept the ghosts at bay.

With another sigh, Anne Marie Smeaton slipped into warm, bright sleep.

'They think I got away with it,' she says, dragging deep on her cig-arette. "Cos I'm out I got away with it. 'Cos I'm not in prison. I was lucky.' She gives a harsh laugh. 'Aye. Lucky. That's me.'

'Who thinks that?'

'The media. An' those that are stupid believe what the media said. They think I'm a liar. A manipulator.'

'Of what?'

'People. The truth. An' I'm not. I'm honest. They think I don't care about the boy. The boy I killed. But I do. I think about him every day. Sometimes I'll be having a laugh, a good time and then bang, there he'll be. And it's like a cloud's come over the sun, you know what I mean? A huge stone in my heart, pullin' me down. Weighin'. Draggin'. Remindin' me. You can't enjoy your-self any more because there's a boy who'll never grow up because of you.' She corrects herself. 'Because of me.'

'And what do you do then?'

She shrugs lightly but her eyes show it's no light thing. 'Just wait for it to pass over. What else can I do?'

'Wouldn't a psychiatrist be better for you? Sort you out?'

'I'm talking to you. This is goin' to sort it. Anyway, I had enough of them inside. They never believed me. No matter what I said, they never believed me. Because I was a liar. A manipulator. I twisted words, I twisted people. Well I didn't. I told the truth. About what I did. About what was done to me.' She pulls deeply once more on her cigarette. Taps the long tube of ash into the ash-tray. Watches it fall.

He allows her to smoke even though he doesn't do it himself. Even though he doesn't like it or want her to. He allows her to smoke. And, he thinks, hopes he isn't being manipulated by her.

'There's been worse things done to children by children since what I did. Much worse. And we never learn. We never make things better. Those two kids who killed that toddler, that . . .' And here she pauses, like she can't bring herself to say the name. Like it'll make it real, make her as bad as them. 'You know. There was a big chance then to actually look at the causes of what made them do what they did. A real big chance. As a society. All of us. Look at families, what they do to kids. How people who are supposed to be looking after the children are really abusin' and hurtin' them. How we can be compassionate and all accept we've got a part to play.' She's starting to well up now, tears forming at the sides of her eyes. She tries to blink them away. They fall. 'But we didn't. The Home Secretary and the media just blamed horror films. Ones the kids hadn't even seen. And then made the kids out to be monsters.'

He looks at her. Not for the first time has she surprised him with her eloquence and intelligence. He wonders whether her words are just to impress him or whether she really believes them.

She stubs her cigarette out. 'We never learn,' she says. 'Kids are still killin' kids. Kids are still dyin'.'

2

The white Fiesta roared round the corner, pulled a hand-brake stop, spinning its rear end as it did so, making the figures standing in the near-deserted corner of the car park scatter as it came to a revving rest. Calvin Bell thought it was the coolest thing he had ever seen.

The scattered kids began to move back, shouting mock abuse at the driver, laughing, their momentary fear now dispersed. Calvin, on the fringes of the group, took this as his cue, joined them.

It was boy racers night out. A near-empty car park on a tattered and battered industrial/retail estate over on the east side of Newcastle. The cars all either small first-buys or twocced joyrides. Halfords-customized to compensate for their size with maximum noise and colour. The bigger kids driving, younger ones and girlfriends as passengers. The cars all parked up at the far end of the car park away from the streetlights, doors open and beams on, sound systems and engines competing for aural dominance. The kids chatting, sharing fags and spliffs, passing round fizzy soft drinks spiked with vodka, nuclear firestorm-bright alcopops, cider and lager. Laughing, joking.

Other kids moving amongst them, slapping stuff into palms in exchange for curled-up notes. The dealers. Keeping the night's highs going, fuelling the drivers.

Calvin so desperately wanted to be one of the gang. Get in one of the cars, drive round with the older kids. His mates Renny and Pez had already done it. They had told him afterwards, laughing and bragging, how great it was speeding round the streets, shouting, singing, draining bottles then flinging them out the window, hearing them smash on the pavements, against the sides of houses. They had made it sound so exciting that Calvin couldn't wait to try it.

He had begged them to bring him down, give him an introduction. They had given in, done so. And now here he was, past one in the morning, waiting. This, he thought with a fluttery pride, was what being grown up was all about.

And something else. The estate wasn't the best place to live. He knew that. Sometimes it felt like a battlefield. And sometimes it actually was. If he was seen with the older kids he might not get picked on so much. His bullies might think he was cool for a little 'un. Safe, even. He just hoped they wouldn't ask him to do something. Some scary initiation rite.

Calvin scanned, recognized some of the faces. He turned to Renny. 'Which one did you go with? Which car?'

Renny didn't answer. He was looking at the Fiesta that had just pulled up.

Calvin kept on. 'Was it that one?'

Renny didn't look at him. 'Aye.'

Excitement rushed through Calvin. If Renny had been once, he could go again. And Calvin could go with him. 'Go an' ask him, then. Ask him if we can all go.'

Renny just nodded. Didn't move. The kid got out of the car, pushed his baseball cap to the right angle, strolled over to the other older ones, walking like some gangsta rapper in a hip-hop video, took a pull on a spliff. Talked to his mates.

Behind him one of the dealers tried to move in. A mate of the driver's pushed him away. The dealer fell.

The drivers and hangers-on formed themselves into a sudden circle. There was no more laughing. Disrespect had been flung. It would have to be answered. Calvin, watching with the others, closed his eyes.

Not knives, he thought to himself, please, not knives . . .

He opened them again, slowly. The fight hadn't started. A peacemaker had intervened. The aggrieved parties were both backing down and saving face, both relieved, although not showing it, that it hadn't come to blades. The atmosphere, although not immediately dangerous, was still tense.

Calvin was getting impatient. He wanted his ride. Before anything nasty happened. He looked at Renny. 'Gan on, then. Ask 'im.'

Renny had been transfixed by what had been happening. He seemed disappointed that there would be no fight. However, he was reluctant to move. 'Doesn't work like that,' he said, not bringing his eyes around to face Calvin.

The would-be combatants were walking away from each other. Someone made a joke. It helped.

Calvin kept looking at his friend. 'How does it work then?'

'Tell him, Pez.'

Pez, smaller than the both of them, clearly a follower where the other two fancied themselves as leaders, looked up startled, as if he had just been roughly woken from a long, baffling dream. 'Eh?'

Renny looked at Pez. Calvin missed the message that Renny tried to send with his eyes. 'Calvin wants to go for a ride. I told him it doesn't work like that.'

'Aw. Right.' Pez nodded. 'Aye.'

Calvin looked between the two. And saw what was going on. 'You haven't been, have you?'

No reply.

'They didn't ask you, you were never in a car. Either of you. Were you?'

Pez looked at Renny. Renny shrugged. 'We just . . . you

know. We didn't wanna . . . look like shites. We thought . . .'
Another shrug. 'Y'know.'

Calvin looked at the other two, at the cars. He was so
near to them. But he might as well have been miles away. In
another country. He felt angry, betrayed. He had sneaked
out of the house in the middle of the night, ran all the way
down here to meet the other two, just on the promise of a
ride. And he wouldn't get one. It was all right for the other
two, their parents didn't care where they went to at night,
Renny's especially. But Calvin's did. It had cost him a lot to
come out. He felt stupid. And angry. He wanted to hit
Renny but he knew his friend's temper would come straight
out and he would end up worse off. He looked at the drivers, at the fear and aggression lurking just below the surface,
waiting for another flashpoint to set it off. And suddenly felt
scared. He had to go home.

'Laters.' He turned round, started to walk away.

'Where you goin'?' asked Pez, clearly confused.

Calvin shrugged. Tried not to make it into a big gesture.
'Home. Not stayin' here with you two little-boy losers.'

He walked away. As he passed the massed ranks of
racers, one of them detached himself from the bunch,
walked over towards him. The same gangsta rapper rolling
gait as all the others used, baseball cap on his head, hoodie
on top of it.

Calvin stopped, looked up. The older kid's eyes were
hidden. Calvin thought his luck was in, that he was going to
be asked for a ride. The kid held out his hand, flashed something hidden in the palm.

'Want some stuff? Some gear?'

Calvin's heart sank. He recognized the boy. It was the
dealer who had been ready to fight. He still looked as if he
was up for it, his anger curtailed but not satisfied. Calvin
always avoided the dealers anyway. This one especially.

He shook his head, tried to walk round him. The dealer didn't move.

'Some blow? E? Get you happy?' The dealer's voice didn't sound very happy.

'No money,' said Calvin, trying again to go round him.

'First taste is always free,' the dealer said, 'an' if it's not your first taste I'll pretend it is. Can't say fairer than that, can I?' He sounded like a salesman in a kid's body.

Calvin shook his head, tried to move forward. The dealer still didn't budge.

'You don't know what you're missin',' he said, trying to sound encouraging, unable to suppress his anger. 'Go on, sort yourself out good.' It sounded like a command.

Calvin tried again. Couldn't get round. He knew the dealer would be armed, that there would be a blade somewhere on him. Calvin was starting to panic. If he kept saying no, the dealer might force him. Or worse—

'Will you fuckin' shift, man!' Calvin hadn't expected the words to emerge so vehemently.

The racers glanced round. Saw what was happening. The dealer still didn't move. Calvin didn't want to stay there a moment longer. He kicked the dealer as hard as he could in the leg. The dealer, unprepared, crumpled to the side. Calvin ran.

There was stunned silence from the racers, then jeering laughter. Calvin didn't look back. Behind him an angry voice started shouting. The dealer. He was called something unpleasant, something that he would have been expected to square up to and fight to make the speaker take it back if it had happened at school or anywhere nearer home. But he didn't stop to challenge, to rise to it, he just kept running. A description was then spat out of what the dealer would do when he caught up to the little kid who had disrespected him in front of his mates. That made Calvin run all the harder.

He ran and ran, not looking back once. Just going forwards. Ignoring the aching in his chest, the pains in his legs and feet. Eventually he could run no more. He found a side street, ran round the corner and dropped to the ground.

On his back, gasping for air, thinking his lungs were too small to cope with the amount he needed to take in. Every breath hurt. But not as much as what the dealer would do to him if he caught up with him. He put his hands to his ribs, hugged himself. Looked around.

He had no idea where he was.

Panicking, he sat up. He didn't know if he had run further away from his home or nearer to it. The place was all rundown factories, old buildings, rubble and weeds. He stood up, trying to ignore the sudden light-headedness that affected him. Scoped. Factories, industrial units. Streetlights. Beyond them, trees. Beyond them an estate. Hope rose within him. Was that the Hancock Estate? If it was, all he had to do was walk through it then at the other side he knew the way home.

Behind him, he heard the roaring of engines. The racers were off.

'Shit,' he said out loud, then chastised himself. He didn't want to be heard. They were looking for him. He knew they were. They had to be. He turned and, dragging his protesting little body, ran towards the trees, the estate.

Anne Marie Smeaton slept. Sprawled on the sofa, Scott Walker whispering to her in the background.

But her face betrayed her dreams. Her features were twisted, contorted, her breathing ragged and quick. She moved her head from side to side, flung her arms around. Her mouth made sounds. No words, just moans, sighs. She was trying to hold them back, but she seemed to be losing.

The bad spirits were breaking through.

*

Calvin was lost. The Hancock Estate was like a maze. He had thought he was on the right track, knew the way. But every time he moved forward in the direction he wanted, the street or walkway took an unexpected twist and left him somewhere else entirely. He had tried to keep track of the corners, keep a sense of direction in his head, but it was hopeless. Now, he didn't know whether he was going forwards or backwards. And the cars were still revving.

They were circling him, getting closer all the time. He was trapped and they were just playing with him, toying with the moment they finally pounced on him, tore him to shreds.

His back was against a wall. He tried to listen, get his bearings that way. The nightly beer screams and responding sirens, the human hyena howls of the estate that he grew up with. Nothing. All he could hear was the pounding of blood round his body, the ragged gasp of his breathing. And the cars.

He wanted to cry. Just sit in the street and cry. But he couldn't. Because Renny and Pez might be in the cars as well. And he didn't want them to see him like that. So he stood up, looked round. Saw a walkway he hadn't been down yet. Or didn't think he had been down. Walked towards it.

There was no light, only darkness and shadows. The streetlights were broken, his trainers crunched glass underfoot. The walls were graffiti-enriched concrete, it stank of bodily emissions. Calvin tried to hold his breath, hurry along. Perhaps this was it. The right way lay just ahead. The opening, lit by the weak orange glow of a streetlight, seemed a long way off. But he made his way towards it, moving as quickly as he could. The wind carried the sound of engines again. He moved quicker and, in his haste, tripped.

He put his hands out to break his fall, felt broken glass,

sharp stone, pierce his palms. Felt his hands connect with other substances that he was glad he couldn't see. As he hit the broken concrete slabs, the air huffed out of his lungs. He pulled himself on to all fours, tried to force air back into his body. Supporting himself with the wall, he got slowly to his feet. Looked ahead. The light didn't seem so far off, now. In fact, he could make out houses beyond it, streets he recognized. He heard a drunken howl going up. His heart leapt. He knew where he was. He knew how to get home.

Reinvigorated, he made his way towards the light. And abruptly stopped.

He had been grabbed from behind, arms tight around his body, pinning him to his assailant, stopping him from moving. Calvin struggled, kicked. No good. Whoever it was had him held tight.

He tried to scream. A hand was clamped round his neck, cutting off the air, trying to make a fist with his neck at the centre of it. He struggled, tried to claw it away. It quickly moved, turned into a fist, punched into the side of his head.

Stars exploded before his eyes. Painful ones. Another punch. More painful stars.

He was roughly thrown to the ground. His attacker said something to him, something unintelligible that he felt he had been expected to know. He turned round, tried to run.

Saw the knife coming towards him.

Calvin didn't have time to cry out, to scream, to feel fear, to think. The knife plunged straight into his chest.

There were other jabs, other cuts, other slashes, but he felt none of them.

The first cut had stopped his heart.

Anne Marie awoke. Daylight seeped almost apologetically round the curtains. The lights were still on, Scott Walker still going on repeat. She sat up, looked round. She was on the floor by the door to the kitchen. Cold all around her. She was frozen.

Anne Marie sat up. Shivered. She pulled herself to a kneeling position, tried to get up off the floor. Placed her hand on the wall for balance.

And stopped.

Where her hand had been, she had left a smear of blood.

She crumpled down again as if she had just been punched.

'No . . . no . . .'

Her hands went to her face, covered it. She felt the blood on them, knew she was smearing it all over herself, knew she couldn't stop it. She looked down at her clothes. Even against the black fabric she could see blood.

'Oh God . . .'

The door opened. Jack entered, ready for school. He looked at her and froze, face a Munch-like tableau.

'Get out!' Anne Marie screamed, aware of the blood mask she was wearing. 'Get out!'

He did so, running for the front door, slamming it behind him.

Anne Marie curled herself into a ball. Started sobbing.

'No . . . no . . .'

They were back. Anne Marie Smeaton knew it.

The bad spirits had broken through.

PART TWO

CLIMATE OF HUNTER

'I'd been on remand for four months when the trial started. I remember it well, considerin'. September 1967. It was strange. I didn't have a clue what they were talkin' about. It was just gobbledegook, you know? All that legalese. I didn't even think they were talkin' about me. They kept lookin' over an' referrin' to me, pointin' an' that. But I still didn't know it was me they were talkin' about.'

'How did they describe you? Evil child? Bad seed, all that kind of rhetoric?'

She becomes thoughtful. 'No. Not really. They never said I was evil. Not as such. It was like they couldn't understand it. I mean, I couldn't understand it, so why should they? But no, not evil, they never used that word. Thinkin' back, they maybe didn't want to. Maybe they thought in those days that if you talked about evil and shared a room with someone you thought of as evil, then that would rub off on you.'

'Not like that now.'

She shakes her head. 'Times have changed. We like to think they've got better but they've got worse. You know, my mother tried to sell the story — my story — to the papers? The Sun? Said that I was out of control, that she could never do anythin' with me. That I'd always been a horrible kid. Had photos to sell to them an' all.'

He frowns. This wasn't in any of his research. 'What happened to it?'

'They wouldn't have it. Wouldn't touch it. Can you believe that? The Sun! Be bitin' your fuckin' hand off if it happened now. Get bloody Max Clifford involved.'

'Was your mother there?'

'Yeah, my mother was there.' She goes through the lighting of the cigarette ritual again. Not speaking until it's fully lit and burning.

'She came every day. Swannin' in and sittin' in the same place. Some days she wore a headscarf done up like Grace Kelly with sunglasses. She would wave to the cameras. Smilin', like it was some Hollywood red carpet. I don't think they knew what to make of her.'

'How was she with you? The same?'

Another short, sharp bark of a laugh. 'Anythin' but. When she looked at me I could feel her sendin' daggers at me. Daggers of hate.'

'Why?'

'Because she did hate me.' Stated like simple fact. 'She did.' She thinks. Drags on the cigarette. 'More than that, though. She'd tried to kill me loads of times when I was little. Push me out of the upstairs window. Give me pills and pretend they were sweets. Loads of times. Tried to give me away. Lose me.'

He bristles at her words.

'It's true. Honest. Loads of times.'

'And did no one pick up on it?'

She shakes her head. 'Not once. Never.'

'So you blame her? For what happened?'

She sucks on the cigarette.

'Well, I wasn't like those two kids in Liverpool. I never saw horror films when I was little.' She sighs. 'I just lived in one.'

3

On Calvin Bell's last night on earth, a lone girl sat in Victoria Coach Station in London. It was busy. The smells of sweat, diesel and cheap fried food giving the place its usual ambience as travellers, thrifty by necessity or design, dragged bulky luggage round the concrete and glass concourse, determined to find the cheapest way to cross the country. She sat on the bench, tried not to be a target for swinging bags, looked up at the board, waited for announcements. The bus would be ready any minute.

She checked her pocket again, losing count of how many times she had done that. The ticket was still there. She checked again. The lifted credit card was there too. She had paid for the ticket with it. She was glad she had watched him at the ATMs, memorized his PIN, filed the information away. Never knew when something like that would come in handy.

Then a pang of guilt. Because it wasn't like her, stealing credit cards and running away from home. It was the kind of thing teenagers in Channel 4 documentaries did, not girls like her. Good ones from good schools and good homes. Supposedly.

She kept one hand in her pocket, the other tightly coiled around the straps of her holdall, stopping anyone running off with it. She had heard the stories, knew what these kinds of places were like. Knew that there would be predators wanting more than her luggage. No eye contact, no conversation. With anyone. She had seen the Channel 4 documentaries.

The board changed. The bus was announced. Newcastle.

She stood up, joined the rest of the people making their way towards the coach. She reluctantly gave up her bag, watched it get thrown into the hold, thinking she would never see it again, that someone would steal it at the first stop. Then she joined the scramble for the door, found a window seat, put her iPod on straightaway, looked away. Not soon enough. A man walked down the aisle, caught her eye, smiled. His grin was predatory. He looked at the empty seat next to her. Panicked, she turned to the window, stared resolutely at whatever was out there. Before the man could speak or sit down, a woman claimed the seat and he shrugged and moved away. She felt his eyes on her all the time.

The woman settled in next to her. The girl kept staring out of the window, no eye contact, no conversation, her face blank. Show nothing. No anger, no pain. No resentment, no hurt. No guilt. Tried not to think about what she was doing. What she had done.

The bus pulled out.

She glanced out of the window into the crepuscular darkness and was shocked to see hurt, wounded eyes staring back at her. She wondered who it was. It took her a couple of seconds to realize it was her.

She cranked up the music, let it flood her brain. The Hold Steady: 'You Can Make Him Like You.' No you can't, she thought. Not always.

She kept her eyes closed. Tried not to think. Tried not to cry.

Early next morning and Joe Donovan sat in the office of Albion at his usual vigil, staring at the screen of the iMac. It was how he started his days and ended them. Sometimes it was how he spent them.

The screen showed a blue front door in a town house. A live feed, channelled all the way from Brighton. It was where he seemed to spend most of the day – and night – just staring at that screen, waiting for something to happen. *Willing* something to happen. Someone to appear, to make contact, to let him know his lonely vigil wasn't in vain. He felt his life couldn't move on until something like that had happened. But nothing happened. No matter how hard he wished, nothing changed.

Sometimes a supermarket delivery van would turn up and groceries would be carried in. His heart would skip and he would jump forward then, playing around with the screen's settings, trying desperately to see inside. Just a glimpse, a quick look. But he never could. It was usually the woman who answered the door and even then she kept out of the way as much as possible, her face hidden, as if she knew she was being observed. Usually the woman. Hardly ever the man.

And never the boy.

The back door of the town house led to a walled, enclosed courtyard garden that was similarly watched round the clock and from which there had never been any movement. So he knew they were in there. They had to be. The grocery deliveries proved it. The curtains never opened and the lights were on day and night. So Donovan watched his screen incessantly. And waited and hoped and prayed.

The not knowing was killing him. Twisting him up inside, turning his insides out. So far away and not able to directly influence the course of action. Impotent and passive when he wanted to be direct and authoritative. If it had been up to him, he would have been to the door, forcing his way inside by whatever means necessary. Kicking up a storm. And getting the boy out. David.

His missing son. Or the boy he hoped was his son.

But it wasn't up to him. And he knew why, even if he didn't like it.

Six and a half months previously, Donovan had nearly died. He had been alone in his cottage in Northumberland, at night, standing in David's room. The boy had never lived in it; it was just a shrine to his memory. Photos of the lost boy covered the walls, some taken from life, some juxtaposed with background images of holidays they had never taken, places they had never visited, things they had never done. Dreams that helped him keep the boy's memory alive. Alongside the photos, files and folders, the investigation and press reaction in full. Donovan had kept everything. And added to it: every sighting or possible sighting logged and investigated. Mainly by him. Every lead and half lead thoroughly exhausted. Files full of paper: maps of every dead end he had walked down.

Gone six years and counting. In a department store, standing behind Donovan, getting a present for Annie, Donovan's wife, David's mother.

There, then gone.

Nothing on CCTV, no witnesses, no cries or screams. Like he had just disappeared. Like he had never existed.

Donovan had searched for years. It had cost him his wife, the love of his daughter, his career and almost his life. But he had never given up, never stopped believing. Never lost hope of finding him either dead or alive. It hadn't been easy. It had consumed him. Sometimes he had doubted that David ever existed, that his own past was a lie, a false construct, a memory implant. And sometimes it felt all too painfully real and he felt himself breaking down, his heart literally aching once more with agony and loss.

In the intervening years, Donovan, a one-time investigative journalist, had pulled himself together and started a company. Albion, an information brokerage, consisted of

himself, ex-policewoman Peta Knight, security and surveillance specialist Amar Miah and Jamal Jackson, a young
mixed-race boy that Donovan had rescued from a life on the
streets. They took a lot of referrals from a lawyer, Francis
Sharkey, who also kept his ear to the ground for any leads on
Donovan's missing son.

There had been false dawns and dead ends. But one lead
had seemed promising enough. A boy answering David's
description had been seen with a young couple at a house in
Hertfordshire. The couple, Matt and Celia Milsom, a TV
producer and his wife, had been thoroughly investigated and
nothing suspicious discovered. Donovan, not wanting to
jump to conclusions even though the resemblance – aged
through computer enhancement – was startling. He had put
an ex-policeman friend and part-time Albion operative, Paul
Turnbull, on surveillance and to try, if at all possible, to get
a DNA sample they could use. Turnbull reported back that
the boy was an HIV-positive Romanian orphan that they
had adopted after meeting him while working on a docu-
mentary over there.

So that was it. Just another dead end. Another one for the
file. Then Turnbull turned up dead and the Milsoms disappeared. And Donovan began to doubt.

That night in David's room just increased his doubts. He
had been alone in the house. Donovan had stood in David's
room, looking again at the photos, waiting to hear a voice
that could guide him, tell him where to look next when he
heard a sound. Someone entering the house downstairs,
making their way up. And Donovan had opened the door to
Matt Milsom.

He hadn't had time to think let alone react before Milsom
hit him with something very large and heavy and he went
down. The next thing he knew he was in pain and being
pulled roughly over the ground. He had opened his eyes:

Jamal and Amar, his friend and co-worker, were there looking down at him, concern and terror in their faces. He had
closed his eyes again and the next thing he knew he had
woken up in hospital.

Milsom had torched his house, leaving Donovan inside.
Nothing was left. If Amar and Jamal hadn't turned up with
booze, DVDs and takeaway food, Donovan would be dead.

So he was alive. But every memento of David was gone.

Donovan threw himself into his work. He hadn't involved
the police because if he did they wouldn't let him near
Milsom. He had learned that previously when he tried to
approach him in Hertfordshire. So it was down to Albion.
But despite their best efforts, Milsom had disappeared without trace. And that just added to the pain and confusion
Donovan carried around with him.

And then, nearly a month later, a breakthrough. Milsom
was spotted in Brighton. An old friend of Peta's from the
police force had tipped her off. Pure luck, she stressed. The
meeting that followed the discovery was predictably intense.

'So what are the police doing about it?' said Donovan.

She sighed. 'Nothing.'

Donovan bristled. 'Why not?'

'It's out of their hands, he said. Apparently the spooks
have told them to lay off. They want him for something
bigger.'

'Fuck them,' said Donovan, getting to his feet. 'I want him
now.'

Peta stopped him. 'Whoa there, hold your horses. We agree.
And I'm on it. Amar's ready and we're off in the morning.'

'Good.'

'But not you, Joe. I think you should stay here.'

He felt anger build up inside him. 'Why?'

'Look at you,' said Peta. 'You're wound up. You're not
thinking straight.'

He started to argue, she held up a hand.

'I know that's to be expected, I'm not saying anything other than that. But think about it. You're too emotionally involved. And OK, fine, but you can't go to work in that frame of mind. And Milsom, if he is there, will be expecting you. And also, it might be a trap.'

Donovan looked at her. As always, her voice carried more authority and strength than her slim frame indicated.

'Let Amar and me handle it.'

The tall, well-dressed Asian man sitting on a sofa opposite Donovan nodded.

'An' me,' said a voice from the corner of the room. Jamal had been sitting there, trying to get his new iMac to work. Or at least play GTA on it. 'I want in on this too.'

Donovan looked between the three of them. Pain was tearing apart his insides. But he knew they were with him, that they wanted the best for him. He couldn't want a better trio of friends.

Peta touched his arm. 'Sit this one out, Joe. Control it from here. You've got a job on at the moment, remember?'

Donovan nodded. He remembered.

'You keep bringing the money in,' said Amar. 'These new offices don't pay for themselves.'

Peta looked him straight in the eye. 'Don't worry. If he's there, we'll find him.'

More than friends, he thought.

Family.

So he sat staring again at the blue door, willing it to open, praying for something to happen. Even something bad because any action was better than none at all. But nothing happened. And the next move, no matter how much it hurt Donovan to realize the fact, was down to Milsom.

The doorbell sounded. He got up from the desk, reluctantly

tearing himself away, and went to answer the door. He knew who it would be. Anne Marie Smeaton.

'Come in,' he said, stepping aside.

She entered. As she walked past him, he could tell something was troubling her. Even more than usual. Then he spotted the bandages.

'What have you done to your hands?'

Anne Marie flinched, instinctively pulling her hands in front of her so he couldn't see. As if she could make them disappear. 'Nothing,' she said, looking at them. 'Just, just . . . a pane of glass come loose last night. Blew in. In the kitchen.' She looked at him, hoped the explanation was enough. 'I got cut gettin' it cleared up.'

They moved upstairs into the meeting room, took their positions on sofas opposite each other, the coffee table in between. They had tried talking at various locations – her flat, a couple of cafés and restaurants Donovan knew – but nowhere made Anne Marie feel as relaxed as this room. It was comfortable and warm, she had said, more like a living room than a meeting room.

He had to agree. That had been done deliberately. Books on the shelves, pictures on the white walls. Movie posters, they were, all old ones. Crime, horror, Sixties British, Woody Allen. Sofas so welcoming you didn't want to get out of them again. Most of the people who came to see them, Donovan had told her, were troubled. The last thing they needed to feel was uncomfortable too. There was even the smell of real coffee wafting through. It was like Starbucks, Donovan had said, but without the world domination overtones.

Anne Marie clumsily put her cigarettes on the table, the bandages inhibiting her, kept her eyes away from him.

'Shouldn't you get it seen to by a doctor? You might need stitches.'

Anne Marie tried to smile. 'No it's OK. It's OK.'

'OK.'

He checked his notes, fiddled with his iPod–attached recorder. 'Fine. Let's get cracking then. You all right to start?'

Anne Marie nodded. He always asked her. And she always said yes. Not because she wanted to, he knew, but because the sooner she started, the sooner it would be finished.

'I thought we'd pick up from yesterday,' said Donovan, trying not to look at her bandaged hands. She tried not to look at them too, instead taking in what he was wearing, checking out what T-shirt it was today. He never wore suits. Instead he had adopted his own uniform of jeans, boots, hoodie and T-shirt, this one bearing the slogan: 'Harlem Heroes – Cut the jive, let's play AEROBALL!' alongside a cartoon image of a helmeted black sportsman from *2000 AD* comic in the Seventies. He caught her smiling at it.

'Right,' he said, switching on the recorder. 'Childhood. Your mother.'

'Oh God.' A shiver ran through Anne Marie.

Donovan tried to forget about the blue door, concentrate on the present. The job in hand, the person in front of him.

He waited for her to speak. The counter on the recorder moved on.

'Right. My mother.' She cleared her throat, shook her head, kept her hands still. 'My mother wasn't an easy person to get on with.' She cleared her throat again. Anne Marie kept her eyes on her hands as they twitched in the bandages. 'There wasn't much . . . she wasn't what you'd call maternal. Not really.'

Donovan watched her, waited, focused, his eyes resting on her face. Just the thing to take his mind off his own problems, he thought, listening to a child killer. Then casti-gated himself for being unfair. Slightly. He was being paid to do a job and he would execute that job as professionally as possible. Then mentally censored himself for using the word execute.

'She was . . . a bitch.' Anne Marie stopped clearing her throat. Her cheeks flushed. 'Yeah, a bitch.'

'Tell me about her.'

'What d'you want to know?'

Donovan shrugged, his voice low, unthreatening. 'What she was like. The kind of person she was. What it was like living with her.'

'What it was like living with her?' Her hands twitched all the more. 'She . . . I don't blame anyone in my life. For what I did.' She put her hand to her throat, as if to ease the passage of the words. 'It was me . . .' Her hands shook. She couldn't take her eyes off them.

She was stressed, thought Donovan. Even more than usual.

'D'you want to take a break? Get a coffee?'

Anne Marie looked up at him like she was drowning and he had thrown a lifeline. 'Yeah,' she said, her voice croaking. 'Yeah, that would be nice, thanks.'

'And then we keep going, yeah?' Donovan reached across and turned the recorder off. He stood up, gave her a smile and went to make coffee.

Checking the screen in the office as he went past.

No change.

'So you've got a son?'

She nods. 'Jack. Nearly sixteen.'

'And is he Rob's son?'

She shakes her head. 'No. Jack was born long before Rob was on the scene. But he's been good, you know. Good to Jack. Been a dad for him, as much as he can.' She nods to herself. 'Yeah.'

'As much as he can?'

She shrugs. 'You know. Boy's not his. These things are never easy. Rob doesn't always seem like a good bloke. But he is. He's got a good heart.'

'How long's Rob been on the scene?'

'Since Hull. Four years, almost.'

'And Jack was born . . .'

'In London.'

He looks at her. 'How long had you been out of prison?'

She tries to smile. It doesn't quite work. 'Long enough to get pregnant. Why you askin' these questions?'

'Background. I have to know these things.'

She nods.

'Right. So Jack's dad . . .'

'Isn't around. Has nothin' to do with him.' *Said with finality, like a huge, old book slamming shut.* 'Jack's dad was . . . no. I won't say it. He might read this. I don't want him back into Jack's life. Or Jack might read this. I don't want him findin' out anythin' about his dad.'

'He might want to one day.'

'Well, that's his choice. I won't be able to stop him then. But I will warn him.'

He tries to get her to say more. She won't. He changes his questioning.

'So Jack. He named after anyone?'

Her face changes. Cracks into a rare smile. 'Yeah. Man I never met. But a man I came to love.'

He's intrigued. He waits for her to tell more.

'My life was saved in Fenton House. In Hertfordshire. It was a special unit for teenage boys. Well, teenage boys and one girl. Me.'

'Really?'

'They didn't know what to do with me. The authorities. They found me guilty of murder and knew that I had to be punished. But they were also curious. Why had I done it? What had made me? So they sent me for therapy.'

He goes to say something.

'Yeah, yeah I know. Therapy. I hate therapists, I hate psychiatrists. And I do. Mainly because of the prison ones, but that came later. But yeah, Fenton. Mr and Mrs Everett. They ran it. Wasn't like prison, not a bit. It was like home. Not a home, home. We were all supposed to have emotional problems that made us do what we did. But they didn't look on us as criminals. They looked on us as children.'

Tears are back in her eyes. She stares into the distance, into the past.

He waits.

'We all lived in the same big house with Mr and Mrs Everett. We all ate sittin' round the big, old, pine kitchen table. We all got help. And it was in Fenton that I met Joanne. Joanne Smeaton.'

'Ah.'

'Yeah. The name. I asked her, she said she didn't mind. Was quite flattered, really. She was an art therapist. Got me paintin' and drawin'. She'd had a husband. A good man, she said. But he was dead. Jack. That was his name. And she helped me so much, she . . .'

She stops talking, unable to hold back the tears.

He waits.

She dries her eyes. Continues. 'Anyway. When Jack was born I called him after her husband.'

'And do you still see her? Are you still in contact?'

She shakes her head. 'No.'

There's a real sense of loss when she says that word. It's the saddest thing he's heard her say. So far.

4

Jack Smeaton had thought things were improving. But he had misread the signs. His mother had been building up to something – another breakdown, another attack – and he had missed it. Her crying, sitting up all night and now finding her covered in blood. Improving. He should have known better than to dare and hope.

No breakfast again and he probably had the wrong books. And because of the new trainers his mother had bought him, the new *expensive*, air-cushioned trainers, he should have been bouncing in to school. But he was so caught up with the tearing, conflicting emotions his mother always unleashed within him that he barely realized he was being herded into the school's main hall along with all the other kids in year ten. Not just his year but the others too. The atmosphere was electric; whispered rumours and attendant gasps zinging through the air like current through cable. Something was up and he had been the last one to spot it.

Trying to ignore the guilty, bindweed tendrils that always pulled at him when he tried to think of something other than his mother's problems, he pulled his focus on to the present.

The hall was its usual rotting self, paint blistered and bubbled where persistent leaks had been patched so often and ineffectually they had eventually been abandoned and left. The familiar smells of damp and mould, anxious sweat and uncontrollable hormones. An undercurrent of whooshing wind, like ghosts trapped behind the crumbling concrete walls, swirled all around them.

He looked at the faces of the other children. They knew as little about what was going on as he did. He absently scanned the crowd, made eye contact with a boy who looked younger than him. The boy, burly with a cropped head, stopped talking to the smaller boy he was with, returned Jack's gaze. His eyes held threat, challenge. He glanced down at Jack's trainers. Jack looked away.

Jack was used to that kind of thing. Every new school he had gone to, there had been someone like that. Sometimes more than one. He looked odd. He was tall, thin and his hair, unlike most of the kids was quite long. He looked like a budding poet in a world of trainee builders. Girls found him interesting – some girls anyway – but he was always too shy to take things beyond the friendship stage.

The doors closed, the head teacher made his way on the stage. Behind him the other staff sat in a semicircle, their faces grave. A woman walked on to the stage, stood in the shadows at the end of the row of teachers, looking out at the children. Jack made her straight away, along with most of the kids in the hall: cop. Plainclothes. That meant something serious. And the way she was looking meant she suspected one of them. He felt the hall tense in anticipation. These weren't kids who welcomed visits by the police.

The murmuring petered out, attention shifted to the front. Mr Heptonstall the head teacher waited for silence. With an approximation of it, he began to speak.

'As some of you may know,' he said, scoping the hall, making eye contact with anyone who wasn't giving him their full attention, 'one of our pupils . . .' He paused. '. . . died last night.'

Gasps. Sighs. Movement, agitation. Heads turned, conversations started. Voices raised. Jack was no different. He turned to the boy at his side, expecting answers, only to see that the boy was doing the same to him. Jack looked at the woman on the side of the stage. She was still staring at the children, blank-faced, trying not to look like she was scrutinizing their reaction.

Heptonstall waited for the statement to embed itself. 'The boy . . .'

Their voices dropped in anticipation. They waited.

'The boy's name was Calvin Bell.'

Another murmur. Heptonstall rode it, continued. 'Calvin Bell. Many of you knew him.' The murmuring rose. Heptonstall talked over it. The hall fell silent, guessing what he was about to say next. 'He was thirteen. Year eight. And his death was no accident. He was stabbed. Murdered.'

He stood back, giving the children their chance to take it in. More gasps, shouts, some sobbing.

He's really milking this, thought Jack. Even in the short time he had been at the school he had grown to dislike Heptonstall. His performance now was doing him no favours. Jack looked round again. He didn't know whether any of the other kids shared his feelings. Most were too busy looking shocked.

'Now,' Heptonstall went on, 'I want to introduce you to someone who's here to help us.' He gestured to the woman standing at the side of the stage. 'This is Detective Inspector Nattrass. She's here to help. She's got something to say to you all and I'd like you to listen.'

DI Nattrass made her way to the centre of the stage. Heptonstall stepped back. Jack watched them both. Heptonstall, he noticed now that the man had stopped speaking, looked visibly shocked. Nattrass stepped up to the podium. She was dressed in usual plainclothes cop uniform, thought Jack. Cheap suit, shoes with sensible heels, no-nonsense haircut. She looked round the packed hall. Jack could feel the mistrust and animosity directed towards her. He was sure she could feel it too. As he watched she sighed, looked slightly sad. The action made her seem more human. But Jack wasn't fooled. And neither, he imagined, would anyone else be.

'When something like this happens,' Nattrass said, eyes roving round the hall, 'it's tragic. Not just for Calvin but for his family and friends. For everyone. All of you.' She gestured at the teachers behind her. 'Even the teachers up here.' She smiled. 'Because teachers are human too.'

'Fuckin' social worker,' someone close to Jack muttered under his breath. Someone else stifled an explosive giggle. It threatened to get out of hand until Heptonstall walked to the front of the stage and stared out. The giggling stopped but the silence that replaced it was more like an unspoken threat. Heptonstall sat down. Nattrass continued.

'Calvin Bell was killed last night on the Hancock Estate. He was stabbed to death.'

A girl sobbed. Eyes darted towards her, telling her not to show weakness in front of the filth. She didn't sob again.

'Now. One of the things I have to do is make sure whoever did this gets caught. Because if they don't they may well do it again. And it could be one of you next time.' Another scope of the room with her eyes. 'But I can't do it alone. I need help. Your help. So if anyone knows anything, please come and see me. I'm going to be in the school with my team all day today. We're setting up a mobile station on the estate near to where it happened. Please . . .' Her voice sounded desperate, like there was real emotion behind her words. 'Please, if you do know anything, or even if you think you know everything then come and talk to me or one of my team. We're not the enemy. We're not here to hurt anyone. We just want to catch whoever killed Calvin. So they can't do it again.' She gave a small, sad smile, thanked them, thanked Heptonstall then stepped away from the podium.

Heptonstall spoke for a while longer but everyone was getting restless. Eventually the assembly was broken up and the pupils, including Jack, were told to return to normal lessons.

The children were still buzzing but there was a weary edge to it, like they were all coming down after a collective adrenalin high. Jack followed the rest of them out. The boy who had stared at him earlier walked past him, made a show of bumping into Jack's shoulder, the smaller boy following behind. Jack didn't rise to it. He was the new kid, the one who spoke funny, the one who had to find his place in the pecking order. Again. But he didn't want to think about that now. Because he was thinking of the murdered boy. Of the policewoman. But most of all, of his mother. Her hands covered in blood, crying in the flat. Again.

He tried not to think of her, to focus on getting through the day, trying to fit in, make friends, attempt to put down roots. But all he could think of was his mother and her hands.

The image upset him. The more he thought about it, the more it became some kind of snapshot, printed not on paper but on stone or concrete, weighing him down every time he picked it up to look at it.

With an effort, he tried to push it out of his mind, get on with his day.

Hoped he could.

The girl stood outside the building, checked the address again on the piece of paper in her hand. Summerhill Terrace, just off Westgate Road. Behind the second-hand stores and motorbike shops. This was it, no doubt about it.

Except it wasn't. The building was lying dark, empty. Weeds grew freely in the small front garden, junk mail stuck out of the letterbox. An estate agent's board attached to the front gate: FOR SALE.

Albion had gone.

She looked round as if someone passing by might be able to help her, tell her where Albion had moved to, where she could go next. But there were no passers-by, and she doubted that they would know.

Rage and helplessness built up inside her. It was a stupid idea coming here. Really stupid. She had spent a night on a coach, staring out of the window, scared of everyone around her. Especially the creepy guy who had sat behind her. She was sure she had seen him since she got off the bus. Was he following her? She hoped she was imagining it.

She had spent the morning walking round Newcastle, avoiding unwanted attention, trying to get her bearings, and all for nothing. But she couldn't go back. Not yet. Perhaps not ever. So she had to do something about it, find a way out.

She hefted the bag on her shoulder, wondered if she had enough money for some food. And maybe a hotel for the night. No problem, just use an ATM. But she couldn't. Because that would give her location away. Oh God. She sat on a stone and brick wall and felt tears well up inside her, impotent, helpless tears that she couldn't allow out. Because once she had, like a genie uncorked from a bottle, she would lose all control.

Oh God, if she had just thought first, not said anything. If he hadn't responded in that way. If she had just kept it in . . .

Stop it, she told herself. Don't give in. It won't help. Think. Think.

She stared at the property, her mind fighting to be rational, constructive.

She could phone them. If they had moved premises they

might have taken the same phone number with them. It was a possibility. But then *he* might answer. And she didn't want that. Didn't want any warning.

There must be another way . . .

The board. The estate agent's board. They might know. If they were selling the place they would know where they had moved to. Worth a try. She took her notepad and pen from her bag, wrote the address down then stood up, pulling the bag back on to her shoulder. It seemed to have doubled in weight since she left London.

Sighing, she went back on to Westgate Road and headed towards the city centre, hoping that she was walking towards a happy ending but somehow doubting it.

Unaware of the figure watching her from inside a run-down sex-shop doorway. He waited until she had gone far enough down Westgate Road, then stepped out, following her from a discreet distance.

'Fenton Hall was the last time I was happy. Well, until Jack was born.'

'Tell me about it.'

'I've said. It was this big old house in Hertfordshire. Mr and Mrs Everett ran it. And it was like they were family, you know? We'd all eat round this big old kitchen table and they'd even let us make the meals, teach us to cook to take responsibility for ourselves.'

'So you're a good cook, then?'

Another draw on another cigarette. 'Used to be. But if you don't keep workin' at somethin' you stop bein' good at it. Like a lot of things.'

He gives a smile. 'Very wise.'

She looks at him, unsure whether he's laughing at her or not. 'Just 'cos I've been in prison most of my life doesn't make me thick, you know.'

'I know,' he says. 'I've seen your report. I know how high your IQ is.'

She sits back, pleased with this.

'So,' he says, 'Fenton Hall. What kind of activities did they do there?'

'There were lessons. But some of the boys couldn't read or write so they were pretty basic. I'd always liked books so they just used to give me somethin' to read while the rest were catchin' up and I'd be away. Loved it. Especially if it was summer, then I could sit outside and read. Just perfect. Felt really alone and at peace then. Really safe.'

'What kind of things did you like to read?'

'Well, there wasn't much choice. Most of the books were for the boys, and the boys, like I said, couldn't read very well. So I used to read Mr and Mrs Everett's stuff. They didn't mind. I read Graham

*Greene but he could be a bit complicated. Agatha Christie. Loved
Agatha Christie.' She smiles.*

'What was it about her that got to you?'

*She thinks. 'There was murder. But that didn't really matter, it
was only there to get things goin'. And they always happened
somewhere like Fenton Hall, so I could relate to it like that, you
know? But the thing I really loved about them was, that no matter
how bad things got, there'd always be someone there to sort it out.
Make the world safe and everything would be all right again at the
end. That's what Mr and Mrs Everett did. That's what Fenton
Hall did. And that's all I ever wanted. Someone to make it all right
at the end. But it didn't last. Nothin' good ever does in this life.'*

'What happened?'

She sighs. Stubs out her cigarette.

'I got moved to prison. And that's when things really went bad.'

5

Jack Smeaton sat on the wall outside the school canteen, looked around again. Police were onsite and journalists were camped outside. Floral tributes at the huge metal gates were increasing. News of the dead boy had gone round the school like several Mexican waves, each time with a different aspect. From initial shock, horror and loss, to a desperate need for news of the killer being caught, then, when no news was forthcoming, filling the void with prurient, lurid speculation. Some of the kids seemed to enjoy that part of the process the most. That and hurling abuse at the police. But lessons had been suspended and counsellors brought in. All over the school, children from all years were coming together, talking in little groups. They would talk so much, get so involved they would be overcome with emotion and then the counsellors would have to step in.

Jack just tried to keep his head down, concentrate on getting through the day. He hadn't made many friends yet so, although he had joined in with some of the others on the only topic of conversation, he spent his breaktimes alone. He didn't like a lot of the other kids and the feeling seemed to be mutual so far. He was sensitive to emotions and environments and this place was no exception. He could feel fear in the school round the estate. Even without the events of the day. And where there was fear, violence wasn't far behind.

So engrossed was he in his own thoughts, he didn't hear them until they were on him.

'Where'd you get them from then?'

Jack looked up. The boy who had stared at him that morning was standing in front of him, his runty sidekick at his right. The boy was pointing at Jack's new trainers.

'Present.' Jack knew he should say as little as possible. Sometimes greetings like this meant they wanted to be friends. But most of the time it meant the opposite. Also, he didn't want them to hear him speak. His lack of a Geordie accent, as much as his longish hair, already marked him out as strange. He didn't know if he had become infected with the fear bug too or whether it was just self-protection.

The boy persisted. 'Where from?'

Jack wanted to walk away, be left alone. But that was impossible. He shrugged. 'Friend.'

The boy kept staring at him. Jack tried to look away. He didn't know if that made it better or worse.

The boy kept staring, Jack kept ignoring him. It was time for the boy to make a move. Either that or walk away. And Jack didn't think that was about to happen. The boy was a couple of years younger than Jack but that didn't count for anything where meanness and rage were concerned. Jack tensed, expectantly.

'Gis them.'

Jack looked up, caught the boy's eye for the first time since he had spoken. 'No.'

The word was spoken calmly and quietly but with force behind it. Jack's hair might be long and his accent strange. But he knew how to fight. He had moved around so much in his short life, he had learned the hard way.

The other boy, not wanting to lose face in front of his follower, stood his ground. 'You better gis them. Now.' The words were growled, but Jack could detect the fear behind them.

'No.' More forceful this time, his eyes meeting the other boy's.

'You'd better do as he says, like.' The runty boy spoke from behind the bigger one.

'Shut up, Pez,' said the bigger boy, clearly embarrassed by the outburst. He turned back to Jack. Jack knew the signs. The boy was looking for a retreat that would save face.

'I'll see you after school,' he said. 'I'll have them then.'

Jack said nothing, just stared at him.

Anger clouded the boy's vision. Jack hoped he wasn't going to try to hit him. He wasn't a coward and he was no stranger to fear. It was something he could use, turn outwards into violence. But he didn't want to. He wouldn't fight back, not because he was scared of being hurt, but because he didn't want trouble at this school. Trouble was something that followed him around.

Instead the boy turned away and walked off, his sidekick trying to keep up in the slipstream.

Jack watched them until they disappeared round the corner of the building.

He looked at his hands. They were shaking.

He thought about his mother's hands again, closed his eyes. Wished he was somewhere else. Someone else. Leading a better, happier life.

Knew it was never going to happen.

The bell rang. Break was over. He welcomed it.

Donovan turned away from the screen, the blue door still unmoving, and stared out of the office window as a Metro train went by on the viaduct overhead. When he had first moved Albion into the building he had thought their regular rumblings would have been a distraction but now he found them quite reassuring. The habitual rhythms gave him a sense of people going somewhere, of lives moving forward. At least that was what he told himself. Really, he probably just liked the sound.

Anne Marie had gone home. It had been a difficult, distressing day. Donovan knew that it would be hard to get her to talk honestly about her mother but he hadn't realized just how hard. Anne Marie had fretted, procrastinated, found displacement activities, in fact done anything but confront the memories of her mother head on. Donovan couldn't blame her. Anne Marie's childhood was the stuff of nightmares. And if he'd had a mother like her, he might have ended up the same way.

Monica Blacklock should never have been allowed to have children. Forced into prostitution at a depressingly early age by her father, she had grown up working the only way she knew how. By selling her body. Anne Marie, or Mae as she had been known then, had been born when Monica Blacklock was only seventeen and already her looks were fading due to years of abuse, her body tired and exhausted. But she still needed to earn so she had begun to specialize. S & M. Those punters cared less about looks and more about attitude. If she still had a bit of strength in her arm and a nasty way with her mouth they went away happy. Or at least satisfied.

But there was one thing she hated even more than herself. Mae. Because the older her daughter became, the more she reminded her of how much she was ageing. And Mae's increasing prettiness just contrasted with Monica's increasingly haggard appearance. She began to feel like the child was sucking what life she had out of her.

So Monica had tried, unsuccessfully, to give her away for adoption. When that failed she had, in desperation, left her with a childless couple and ran away. But Mae had been returned and Monica seemed to be stuck with her. So she resolved to kill her.

She made the acts out to be accidental: pills that resembled sweets left lying around, a first-floor window left fully open where she was playing. Neither worked. So, with nothing left to lose, she had put Mae to work servicing punters. The S & M ones.

Looked at in that context, the fact that Mae had, at the age of eleven, killed a toddler wasn't surprising.

Donovan had been presented with all these facts before he had started working with her. A literary agent had presented him with a report.

The call was unexpected but timely. Peta, Amar and Jamal were in the process of leaving for Brighton. There was no one else in the office so he answered it.

'Hi. Can I speak to Joe Donovan, please?' A woman's voice.

'Yeah, this is me.'

'I'm sure you don't remember me,' she said. She was well-spoken, confident-sounding. Professional but enthusiastic. She clearly enjoyed her work and it showed in her voice. 'My name's Wendy Bennett. I'm a literary agent with, well, you'd know them as Morgan and Rubenstein. I'm sure that rings some bells for you.'

It did. The words transported Donovan back to a time before Albion, before David went missing. When he still had a wife and family. A career. An agent for his freelance writing.

'God. The last person I expected to hear from.'

'I'm sure.' There was warmth in her voice too. 'I was just an office assistant in those days. Too junior for you to bother with then, probably.' She laughed.

She was right. He couldn't remember her. She continued.

'Are you still in the market for freelance work?'

'What makes you ask?'

'Well . . . we had an approach. A job. And I thought of you.'

'After all this time? You've got no one else?'

She laughed. 'It's a very specialized job. Would suit someone with your talents down to the ground. Let me tell you about it and you'll see why.'

She told him. And he did see why. Wendy Bennett was on the next train to Newcastle to discuss it with him.

The Living Room on Dean Street was a modern, stylish restaurant. Attached to a boutique hotel, it catered to an aspirational, urban, hip clientele. And – which was why Donovan had chosen it – expense accounts. The sleek, modern décor had been designed to complement the high-ceilinged Georgian architecture. It felt, he thought, catching glances of the ways in which the other diners surreptitiously managed to get themselves noticed, exactly like it was supposed to.

Wendy Bennett was, Donovan assumed, in her early thirties. She had brown hair, brown eyes and a wide, confident smile that showed perfect teeth and had engaged him immediately. She was full-figured, curvy in a way that he suspected could tip over into unwanted pounds if she wasn't careful. Not that something like that would ever bother him. She was also filled with an energy, joy and life that was positively stimulating. She had an appetite, he had discovered in conversation during the course of the meal, not just for food and wine, but for life itself. It was, he thought, hard not to be swept along by her.

They spent the ordering time and the first course talking about his old literary agent. Donovan had forgotten she existed. When Wendy talked of the agency and the world he had once been a part of, it seemed like she was talking of events in a foreign country that he had once enjoyed visiting and meant to return to, but because other things had got in the way had never got round to it.

'Morgan and Rubenstein,' he said, watching the way the

light caught the red wine as he swirled his glass. 'Names I never thought I'd hear again.'

'Well,' said Wendy, leaning forward, 'it's not exactly M and R any more. Susanna Rubenstein's gone.' She smiled, savouring her next words. 'It's Morgan and Bennett now.'

'Right. Well done, you.'

She raised her glass. 'Thank you.'

The waiter cleared away the start plates and they looked at each other. There was that smile again. It was hard not to return it. So he did.

'So,' he said, reaching for his wine glass, 'tell me about Mae Blacklock. And why I'm so crucial to the job.'

Wendy Bennett bent down, pulled out a folder from her bag. 'It's all here. Mae Blacklock obviously isn't her name now. When she was eleven she killed a little boy. Trevor Cunliffe. Huge scandal at the time, big media circus.'

'I remember.'

She looked at him and he was suddenly conscious of the gap in years between them. It wasn't huge but it suddenly seemed that way. 'Of course,' she said. 'Anyway, she was released about twenty years ago. Given a new identity, sent somewhere far away. She met a man, got pregnant, had a baby. A boy. Then she moved. And she moved again. And again. And now she's back in Newcastle. And she wants to tell her story.'

Donovan frowned. 'Why? Why now?'

Wendy shrugged. 'Who knows? But she came to us. And we didn't have anyone we thought could do that. And then someone thought of you.'

'Someone?'

'Well, me, actually.'

Donovan smiled. 'Thank you. And I have to say, I'm interested. But I'm not a journalist any more. I don't do that kind of thing now.'

'Oh I know,' said Wendy. 'I know exactly what you do. I've been keeping tabs on you.'

'You?'

She blushed slightly. 'I meant we. The agency. We never forgot you. You did some good stuff. Back in the day.'

Donovan smiled again, loving the way young, middle-class professionals had appropriated aspects of urban culture to give them what they thought was a hip edge. 'It was a blast,' he said.

'Good. Well, let's hope this will be too. Are you interested? Will you do it? We've got a publisher lined up ready to pay the advance. I know that's unusual without actually seeing anything, but this is an unusual case.'

'What's the money like?'

She told him. And he thought of the new Albion offices and the wage bill. And something else — how this might be just the thing to take his mind off Brighton.

He said he was in and asked for more details.

'Right. Well, she now lives in Newcastle on the Hancock Estate in Byker.' She was going to continue. He stopped her.

'Please don't do the Byker Grove thing.'

She looked slightly put out. 'Why not?'

'Because it's not funny any more. And because you'll mark yourself out as a southerner and you might get a smack in the face for it.'

She looked round. 'What, even in here?'

He smiled. 'Even in here. City hasn't been gentrified that long. Ancestral race memories and all that. Anyway. Please continue.'

'Right. Well, she's up here now. She's moved about a lot. She's got her son with her, like I said, and a partner.'

'And do they both know who she used to be?'

'The partner does. The boy doesn't.'

'Right. What's she like?'

'Very bright, very sparky, highly intelligent,' said Wendy.

'Self-educated, obviously. Did all sorts of studying inside. But, needless to say, that hasn't translated to a steady job or a happy life since then.'

'Sure. High IQ doesn't always equal high self-esteem. Especially not when you've had her background.'

Wendy smiled. 'You've met her boyfriend, then.'

Donovan raised an eyebrow.

'Oh he's all right, I suppose. I'm sure he loves her. She's always saying how good he is to her. I'm sure he is.' Wendy took another mouthful of wine, looked at him, her face suddenly serious. 'Do you think you would have a problem talking to her?'

'Why? How d'you mean?'

'She killed a little boy. And you . . . y'know.'

Donovan nodded, took another mouthful of wine. 'I know,' he said. 'Well, I don't know. Honestly. But I'd give it my best shot. Give her the benefit of the doubt. She was only a child herself when she did that.'

Wendy nodded. 'I agree. I think everyone deserves a second chance. Well, most people, anyway.' She smiled again. 'But that's good. In fact, that's exactly what I was hoping you would say.'

'Good.' Donovan returned her smile.

The main courses arrived. They ate. He asked more questions about the job. What did they hope the book would achieve?

'We don't want it to be sensationalist. Not the usual true crime kind of thing. Not just a ghosting job. More like what Gordon Burn did with the Yorkshire Ripper and the Wests. Your voice is just as important. That kind of thing. I'm sure that's right up your street.'

Donovan agreed it was. They worked out a rough schedule and working method. Interview Mae – Wendy still wouldn't tell him her new name at this point – wherever she felt comfortable. Start generally, work in deeply. Mae knew what to expect. She knew how emotionally challenging the questions would be. She was prepared. She was ready.

They finished their mains. The waiter cleared the plates away.

'That was brilliant,' said Wendy. She leaned back in her chair. 'Man, I'm stuffed.'

As she leaned back, her large breasts strained against the low-cut dress she was wearing. He tried not to, but couldn't help his eyes from dropping down there.

She sat forward again. Another smile. 'This is so great to have you on board. I can't tell you how excited I am.'

'Good. I hope I can do a good job for you.'

'I'm sure you can.'

Was she coming on to him? He didn't know. But he didn't mind. She was very attractive. And he was unattached.

'So . . .' he began. He was so out of practice. 'What about you. Tell me about you.'

She looked slightly taken aback but a smile played round the corners of her lips. 'I'm thirty-four, I work in publishing. I'm a literary agent. I love my job.'

Donovan was smiling. Enjoying himself for the first time in ages. 'Anything else?'

'Like what?'

'Married? Kids?'

She blushed slightly. 'There's . . . someone. We're not married, though.'

'Is he in publishing?'

'God no. Local government. Couldn't do that. Get enough of writers all day.' Then she looked at Donovan. 'Sorry.'

'No problem. I'm not a writer any more.'

'But you will be again, I hope.' She smiled, but some of the sparkle seemed to have dissipated from her.

At the mention of the boyfriend, Donovan decided that

pursuing interest in her was, unfortunately, a dead end. He brought the talk round to work again. 'Trevor Cunliffe's mother's still around, you know,' he said.

Wendy frowned. 'How d'you mean?'

'She pops up on TV now and again. Whenever there's a murder involving kids they trot her out for a quote. Whether she knows anything or not. Gets her face on TV, in the papers, radio. Everywhere.'

'Is she an expert?'

Donovan shrugged. 'I don't know. Her son was murdered. And she's had a lifetime of bitterness and pain to contend with because of that.'

'Right.' Wendy's smile faded.

'Grief does affect different people in different ways.'

She nodded. Her smile disappeared completely.

'Well,' she said, 'it's been a great meal. Thanks. I—'

'Are you rushing off?'

She pointed towards the hotel next door. 'Staying overnight. Got to head off in the morning. Early. Need some sleep.' The smile returned. 'Thanks for a great time.' She signalled to the waiter for the bill.

'Would you like to stay and have a drink?'

She looked genuinely torn. 'Maybe next time.'

Donovan nodded. Tried not to feel too sad. 'OK, then.'

She charged the meal to her room, stood up and looked at him. 'Thanks. It's been great to meet you. Any problems or questions, give me a ring.'

And she was off.

Donovan had gone back to his flat, read the report, made notes. Readied himself to start work.

Put Wendy out of his head.

Donovan poured himself a coffee, sat down on the sofa, checked his watch. Too early to go to the Cluny. Even if he was going to eat there too. He picked up his notes from the session, thought of listening to the tapes. Decided against it. Not enough there worth transcribing. He would do it tomorrow when hopefully there would be something more to add.

He picked up the remote, flicked on the TV. Local news. A boy had been killed in Byker. The *Look North* anchor had on his serious face for relaying it. The scene switched from studio to live outside broadcast, where a reporter wearing a similarly serious face was standing outside the gates of a school in Byker. She told the camera what had happened. A thirteen-year-old boy had been stabbed in the early hours of the morning on the Hancock Estate.

'Not surprised,' said Donovan under his breath.

The boy was named as Calvin Bell and his family were appealing for witnesses.

Good luck with that, thought Donovan, quickly castigating himself for being so cynical then reasoning to himself that it wasn't cynicism. Who else would be out at that time of night apart from the killer? And who would come forward from the Hancock Estate?

The scene jumped to a police press conference where a female detective was making an appeal for information.

'Hi, Di,' said Donovan, waving to the screen when he saw DI Di Nattrass. She and him had history. Mostly good, or tolerable at least, but not always.

She finished and the story was filled with images of a more general nature. Knife-crime stats swirled and danced. A voiceover told of rising violence among the young in such apocalyptic terms that Donovan wouldn't have expected a single teenager to still be alive by the time *EastEnders* came on. They went for a quotation to a talking head – and Donovan was taken aback.

There was Sylvia Cunliffe. He remembered his conversation with Wendy once again.

She was a grandmother now, heavy and solid, her brow furrowed, her face permanently twisted. She looked like an angry Easter Island head. Donovan knew from experience how easy it was to allow just one, horrific event to define a life. She had parlayed her rage and grief into a media career, never forgiving, never forgetting.

He switched off the TV, picked up the mug, took another mouthful, drained the mug empty. He took it into the kitchen, placed it on the draining board. Albion House. He couldn't resist it. If ever there was a place and a business made for each other, this was it.

Situated on Stepney Bank in the heart of the Ouseburn area of Newcastle, the area's claim to fame was that it used to appear in the credits of *Whatever Happened to the Likely Lads?* as a symbol of the region's run-down industrial past. It was now rapidly redeveloping as a base for newer, smaller, more dynamic businesses. Artists' studios. Theatre companies. Galleries. Printers. Publishers. The Seven Stories children's literature museum. And pubs like the Cluny, a reclaimed bonded whisky warehouse now turned into bars, restaurant, live music venue and art gallery. And Donovan's local. Almost his second office.

Albion House was a great location, he thought. And the mortgage was cheaper than on the old place. Business was starting to pick up and the place had been renovated and redecorated. Things were going well.

He thought of the screen downstairs in the office showing the unchanging blue door.

Most things were going well.

He checked his watch once more. Yes, he wouldn't look too desperate if he turned up at the Cluny now. He was just about to leave, moving towards the front door, when he noticed an envelope on the floor. A brown manila. He picked it up. No postmark, no address. Just his name printed on the front.

He opened the door, looked up and down the street. Saw no one, nothing except streetlight-cast shadows in the late November evening. It could have been delivered any time since Anne Marie left. He closed the door, entered the office, opened the letter. Read it.

You're working with that child murdering bitch. She's probably giving you the sob story. Well here are a few things you don't know about her. Check these. Guy Brewster. London. Adam Wainwright. Bristol. James Fielding. Colchester. Patrick Sutton. Hull. Now go to work.

Donovan no longer wanted to eat or drink at the Cluny. Or anywhere. He wanted to do what the letter said. Go to work. He sat down at his iMac.

Did just that.

'So what were you found guilty of?' He knows the answer to the question but asks it anyway. For the recorder. For the record.

'Manslaughter. On the grounds of diminished responsibility.'

'And how did you feel about that when it was read out?'

She sighs. She reaches automatically for a cigarette but stops herself from taking one. Her bandaged hands stay on the table, fingers moving like small electric shocks are being administered.

'I didn't know what he meant at first. I didn't know whether that meant I could just go home or not. I knew that if he said murder then that meant prison.'

'How did you know that meant prison?'

'I'd seen it on the telly. Murderers were caught and went to prison. Sometimes they were hanged. That's what really scared me. That they would hang me.'

'They wouldn't have hanged a child, I would have thought. Not even then.'

'They would have done if they could have got away with it. But they gave me manslaughter because of the psychiatric report.' Her fingers reach for the cigarette pack on the word 'psychiatric'.

'What did that say?'

'That I had a psychopathic personality. That I didn't know right from wrong. That I had no concept of death.'

'And did you?'

'Which one?'

'Any of them.'

She thinks for a moment before speaking. 'Back then I probably didn't know right from wrong. No. Lookin' back I can say that now. But then I only had the things that had happened to me up till then to go on. But death . . . no. I thought Trevor would get up again. And play.'

'Trevor was . . .'

'The boy.' She nodded. 'That I killed.' Her voice shrank away from the words as she spoke. 'No, I didn't know what death was. Not really. I used to love police shows. Cops and robbers. Couldn't get enough of them when I was a kid. But like I said, when they caught the baddie they put him in prison or murdered him. And then next week he was back, in some other cops and robbers programme. So he wasn't really dead, was he? I mean, now I know they were only actors. That it wasn't real life. But not then.'

He starts to ask another question but she hasn't finished. 'That's the only question they should ask, I think. Well, only two. To kids in murder trials: Do you know what death is? Real death? And do you know right from wrong? The only two.'

'What about the other thing you said?'

She frowns.

'A psychopathic personality? What do you think about them saying that?'

She looks at him, away from him, down at the cigarette packet. She takes one, lights up, exhales. Again. Looks at him once more, then looks away, head slowly shaking.

'And you wonder why I fuckin' hate psychiatrists?'

6

'Hey kid, what's your name?'

Jack Smeaton looked up. He had been in his own world, head down, trying not to walk home too quickly, fearful of what kind of mood his mother would be in. The woman before him was dressed casually: leather jacket, jeans, .trainers. Dressed for a quick getaway. Hair dark and straight. London accent. Cocky, confident grin, the kind that was verging on arrogant. The kind Jack wished he had.

'J – Jack.'

'Yeah, Jack. Terrible this, don't you think? This kid getting stabbed. You knew him?'

Jack made her now. Journalist. On the hunt. He looked round, taking in the scene properly now. How had he missed it before? There were TV cameras pointed at the school gates, still cameras flashing all the time. He recognized a couple of the faces talking to cameras from the local news. Word of Calvin's death had spread.

Jack looked back. The journalist was still in front of him, waiting.

'N – no, I didn't know him. Not very well, anyway.'

'Sure?' She gave him a kind of come-on look, eyes locked on to him like heat-seeking missiles. He stepped back, frightened. 'Could be a bit of money in it for you. Get yourself a new PlayStation. Nintendo Wii. Whatever. Good bit of money.'

A new PlayStation sounded great. In fact, any PlayStation sounded great. It was something they had never been able to afford. In the other schools he had been to he had been so jealous of the kids who did have them. Which seemed to be all of them. It had just been one more thing that had stopped him fitting in.

But he hadn't known the dead boy. So it didn't matter.

Jack couldn't answer. He shook his head and walked away. The journalist didn't waste time calling after him, just went up to the next child leaving school.

Jack was disappointed. A journalist was one of the things he quite fancied being when he left school. He liked the idea of standing at the sidelines, reporting on what was happening. Knowing what was going on, but not getting directly involved. Trouble was, every journalist he met put him off the idea. They all seemed to be like the one at the school gates. Male or female. They saw people just as excuses for stories, not real living, breathing people, just things to use up and drop once the stories were wrung out of them. And he didn't want to be like that. No way.

As he rounded the corner at the far end of the school fence, he looked back again. The two boys who had spoken to him earlier were coming up to the journalist. The smaller one, Pez, seemed happy to talk, nodding and gesturing.

Jack walked away, left them to it.

Wondered, with fear and trepidation, what home would be like when he got in.

'Hey, kid, what's your name?'

'Pez.'

'That your real name?'

The kid shrugged. 'S'what everyone calls us, like.'

Jesus, she thought, they were thick up here. She kept smiling at him. 'Right, Pez. How'd you like to make a bit of money?'

The boy's eyes lit up. 'Aye. Great.'

'Good man. The kid who died, Calvin. Was he a friend of yours?'

'Aye, 'e was. Me best mate, like.'

'Your best mate.' Where had she heard that one before?

'Aye. He was. An' I was with 'im the night 'e died.'

Bullseye. Tess Preston was still in her twenties, probably still had a lot to learn, and the best way to do that, she always said, was on the job. And that was what she lived, ate and breathed. The job.

Theresa Preston-Hatt was her full name. She was the youngest of two daughters – her father, a colonel in the army, wanted sons. He never came to terms with the fact that he had ended up with two girls instead. Her sister was a qualified doctor and, to please her father, Tess enrolled at Sandhurst to train as an officer. Unfortunately she left during the first month. Her father never forgave her. Especially after she became a journalist. So she dropped the parts of her name she didn't need any more, except when she ran out money or needed bailing out of something unpleasant, and became Tess Preston, ace reporter for the People's Paper, the *Daily Globe*.

She was fiercely ambitious. For the job itself, she told herself, the rewards. Not to show her father, her family how good she could be at something. That wasn't the reason at all. No way. She was on the way up. Tess Preston was going all the way to the top.

That's what Calvin Bell represented to her. The next rung on the ladder. The only thing she knew about the victim was that he had been stabbed and the only thing she knew about the area was that Cheryl from Girls Aloud came from somewhere near. Looking round she could well believe it.

But all she was interested in was her work. A big exposé of the crime-riddled inner cities and what it was doing to the kids. Correction: *our* kids. Because she had the readers at heart. And, if she was telling the truth, this mouth-breathing midget in front of her could be her way in to the story.

'You were there? Great. So, Pez . . .' Tess Preston allowed herself a smile. She never forgot a name. Prided herself on the fact. And she knew how dazzling that smile could be to the opposite sex. Even kids, she didn't care. She practised it in front of the mirror. Shame to waste it. 'Why don't you tell me all about it?'

Pez frowned. 'What about the money?'

Sharper than he looked, thought Tess. But then he'd have to be. He couldn't look any less sharp. 'We'll get that sorted, don't you worry.' She slipped her hand into her jacket pocket, thumbed her recorder on to record. She noticed Pez's eyes being drawn to her chest. She stuck her breasts out a bit more to keep him beside her. 'Just tell me what happened that night.'

Pez, transfixed by her breasts, opened his mouth to speak.

'Who the fuck are you?'

Tess turned round. There was another boy standing next to Pez. Slightly taller, harder-looking. Pug-faced with cropped hair and a dirty, torn school uniform. Angry.

Time for a charm offensive, thought Tess. Keep the natives onside. 'Hiya. My name's Tess. Just chatting to your friend Pez here.'

'Haway, Pez, man, divvent talk to her. She's a fuckin' journalist, man. Haway.'

'Aw, but she's nice . . .'

The new boy started to walk away, tried to drag Pez with him. Pez looked conflicted but also looked used to doing what this other boy said. He turned to go.

'See ya.'

Tess didn't want to leave it there. She couldn't, not when she'd just had a way in. And if Pez wasn't talking . . .

'Hey,' she called to the other boy. 'What's your name?'

The boy turned. 'Renny.' Spoken like it was an act of defiance.

'Well Renny, how'd you like to make some money?'

'Fuck off.'

That wasn't the answer Tess had been expecting. She would have to try harder. Turn on that old Tess charm. Would work even on him.

'No need for that, Renny. Pez was just telling me how great a mate Calvin was. And I bet he was a mate of yours too.'

'So?'

Jesus. Arguing with a schoolkid. 'Well, his two best mates? Telling the story of what happened to their poor friend that night? Together? There'll be a lot of money in it for you. A lot.'

Renny frowned. Tess had him, she knew. 'How much?'

'Well, that depends on what you have to tell me. Pez said he was there last night when Calvin died. If that's the case, and you were there as well, then we're talking thousands. Thousands.'

Some of the anger fell away from Renny's face. But wariness remained. 'What do we have to do for this?'

'You tell me. Take me to where you all were. Show me round. The spots you hang out, the place where he died. All that.'

'When?'

Tess shrugged, smiled. 'No time like the present.'

Renny said nothing, his brow furrowed in concentration. When he spoke a smile played on the corners of his mouth. 'Later.'

'What?'

'Now's no good. It'll have to be later. When it's dark, like.'

'Fine. You're the boss. Whatever you say. When and where?'

Renny looked around, considering it. 'Here. Nine o'clock.'

'It's a deal.' Tess could already see the headlines and, more importantly, the byline.

'How much?'

'What?'

'How much you payin' us?'

She thought of a figure she could get away with. 'A grand.'

'Fuck off.'

'Each.'

'Fuck off.'

Tess tried not to let her exasperation show. These people were the first to complain about chequebook journalism and trading on misery to sell papers, but they complained all the harder if they didn't think you'd paid them enough.

'Two grand, then.'

'Each.'

'All right, two grand each.' Her editor would be well fucked off. 'But it better be worth it.'

Renny grinned. It wasn't entirely pleasant. 'It will be. And bring the money with you. Cash. If you don't you can fuck off. An' we're takin' you nowhere.'

'OK. What if I bring half the money and when you've given me the guided tour and I've interviewed you both you get the other half?'

Renny furrowed his brow again. Nodded. 'All right.'

'Deal.'

Tess extended her hand. Thought that would be the kind of thing the locals would like. Renny shook it.

'Nine o'clock,' she said and the two boys walked away.

Tess watched them go, smiling to herself. Not bad, she

thought. Not a bad bit of business if they came up with the goods.

Then another thought struck her. Shit. She would actually have to pay this time.

Or at least, pay half.

Jack Smeaton turned the key in the lock, pushed open the door as slowly as possible, his hand away from the edge as if expecting it to slam shut and take his fingers off. It swung open. He looked down the hallway. No sound. He didn't know if that was a good sign or not.

He had been expecting another row. Rob shouting at his mother. Drunk and angry. Or Anne Marie tearfully screaming that he didn't understand her. The usual thing. Then things being thrown around. Then silence. Then, eventually, laughter as they come down, cuddle up with each other. Her telling him she was lucky to have him, he was the only one who understood her and had stood by her. He telling her how much he loved her and how they would get through this. What a great family they made. What a lovely lad Jack was. By which time Jack was usually in his room, headphones clamped to his ears, trying to block it all out.

He knows Rob loves his mother. And he's grateful to him for taking some of the pressure of looking after her off his young shoulders. And he's good to Jack too, in his own way. But he gets depressed and when Rob gets depressed he drinks. And that's when his problems start.

He put his school bag down, walked towards the living room. Pushed open the door. His mother, Anne Marie, was sitting on the sofa. Hands bandaged, head back, eyes closed. Mug of tea beside her, cigarette burning in the ashtray. Scott Walker singing softly from the corner of the room. The one about angels again. The Spirit House had been moved too. Brought further into the room.

Jack breathed out, relieved. She was back to normal. Calm. For now. He felt a stab of guilt at his earlier actions, at his anger over her situation. She was his mother. And he loved her. He just wanted to feel happy and safe. Knew that she did too.

She heard him approach, opened her eyes. Smiled.

'Hello, love.'

He said hello in return.

She kept looking at him, long enough for Jack to start feeling uncomfortable. She did this often. It was usually the prelude to something. But it was never predictable, never the same thing twice. She patted the seat next to him.

'Come and sit here, son. Sit with your old mother.'

Reluctantly he went over and sat next to her on the sofa, perching on the edge, not committing himself to full relaxation.

Your old mother. She was just coming up for fifty. Not that she ever mentioned it, but he knew her age. Had seen her date of birth on an official form and he never forgot things like that. But she looked older. As if she had experienced more of life, the wrong sort of life, than should have been allowed in her years.

She looked at him, smiled. Draped her arm around him, the bandaged hand flopping down over his shoulder.

'Good day at school, son?'

He grunted, unsure of what to say. She got like this all the time. Soppy-happy. Usually after a crying or screaming fit. Her way of saying sorry, he supposed.

'Good,' she said. 'Good.' She took another deep draw of her cigarette, let it go. Watching the smoke dissipate, smiling like she had just released white doves into a clear blue sky. She looked at the ashtray. Sighed. 'I'm feelin' better now. Your old mother's feelin' better now.'

Jack said nothing.

'I've cleaned up the broken glass in the kitchen. The pane fell out. That's how I got these.' She raised up her bandaged hands. 'How I got these . . .' She trailed off again. 'I've put some cardboard in . . .'

Jack nodded, listened to the music, that strange mix of beauty and strangeness she found so compelling. He knew she wouldn't have done a good job, knew he would have to replace the cardboard.

'Yes, I'm feelin' better now.'

He felt her hand on his shoulder shake. Knew the sign: she was building up to another crying fit. He had to do something, head it off.

'The police were at school today,' he said.

Her hand stiffened. 'What did they want?' Her voice hard, anxious.

Jack continued. No going back now. 'Some kid got knifed last night. On the estate.'

She took her arm away. 'What happened?'

He shrugged again. 'Dunno. Just got knifed.'

'Did you know him?'

Jack shook his head. 'We got our lessons cancelled. They brought counsellors in. Police are all over the place. Journalists an' all.'

Her hand was fully withdrawn. She put both of them in her lap. Her breathing quickened. 'They didn't talk to you, did they?'

'Who? The counsellors?'

'No,' she said quickly, 'the journalists.'

'There was this woman standing at the school gates, tryin' to get kids to—'

She turned to him, grabbed his shoulders. Her hands must hurt, he thought. She must be ignoring the pain. 'What did she say? What did she say?'

Her fingers dug into him. 'Nothin' . . .'

The fingers dug harder. 'What . . .'

'Nothin'! There was a few of them. They wanted to know about the kid who died. Offered money, an' that.'

'Did you take it?'

'No . . .'

She looked at him, her eyes wide and wild, pleading with him. Desperate for him to be telling the truth. Deciding he was, she relaxed her grip. 'Good. Never talk to them. They're scum. All of them. Have nothin' to do with them. Ever. You got that?'

He had that. It wasn't the first time she had said that to him. He nodded. She took her hands away, sat back.

'Good.' He watched her face contort as she struggled to find a smile. 'Right. Well. I'd better start thinking about the tea, hadn't I?'

Jack gave a small sigh of relief.

'What shall we have, eh? I haven't been able to cook, I've been out all day.'

A cloud passed over her face. Some troubling memory, Jack thought. Her brow furrowed, her lip trembled. Oh no, he thought. Here it comes. She looked at Jack. Dredged up a smile.

'You don't want that,' she said, looking at him but seemingly speaking to herself. 'I don't want that for you. Not you.'

Jack said nothing.

'Anyway,' she said, struggling for brightness, 'what shall we have? Fish and chips? Pizza? Kebab? Your choice.' She reached for her purse.

'Whatever,' he said. 'Whatever you like.'

Anne Marie nodded, handed him a note. At that moment, the front door opened. It was a lot noisier than Jack's entrance, smacking loudly off the hall wall. A stumble, followed by an angry, guttural noise. Anne Marie and Jack stood up quickly, exchanged a glance. Scott Walker was singing about the old man being back again.

Rob entered. 'Who the fuck left that bag in the hall? Almost broke me fuckin' neck.'

He had been good-looking once but a life lived on the bottom had worn those looks away. Now he had a beer gut, a ponytail to compensate for what was thinning on top and was red-faced and angry at anything. Mainly himself. Black leather bike jacket, jeans, T-shirt and boots. He looked like an ageing, pensioned-off roadie who after years travelling wondered why he was stuck in one place. He looked like exactly what he was.

'S – sorry,' said Jack.

Rob looked at him, as if about to get angry, but the fight went out of him. Suddenly tired, he slumped down on the sofa. 'Where's me dinner?'

'Jack was just goin' down to the chippie, weren't you, son?' A desperate edge was back in Anne Marie's voice.

Rob grunted. Whether from satisfaction or displeasure, it was hard to tell.

Anne Marie sat down next to him. 'What have you been doin' today, then, love?' Jack noticed she used the same kind of bright, false voice she used with him.

'Down the bookies. The pub.' He shrugged. 'You know.'

'Did you win anythin'?'

Another grunt. 'Nearly.' He appeared thoughtful for a few seconds. 'We've got money, though. While you're bringin' that in we don't need worry.'

Anne Marie said nothing. Rob looked at her.

'What?' he said.

'I didn't say anythin'.'

'Nah, but you were thinkin' it. What?'

'Well, this money won't last forever. I just think—'

'Then you'll get some more, won't you?' His voice was

building up to anger. Jack wanted to be out of the house.
'You should. They owe you. Fuckin' *owe* you, man. Don't
they?'

She sighed. 'Yes, Rob.'

'Well then. You'll get some more. Won't you?'

Anne Marie said nothing.

Rob gestured towards Jack. 'And you shouldn't go
spendin' it on fuckin' trainers for him.'

Anne Marie and Jack exchanged a glance. Anne Marie
gave a silent shake of the head. Jack said nothing.

Rob sat back, argument apparently won.

'Now. Where's me tea?'

Jack took that as his cue to leave the flat. As he did so he
stuck his headphones deep into his ears, turned the sound
up. Blocking out everything around him, even stopping his
thoughts.

My Chemical Romance: 'The Sharpest Lives' from *The
Black Parade* album. The voice in his ear told how the
sharpest lives were the deadliest to lead and how he wanted
a shot to take all the pain away.

He walked to the takeaway. Hoped there would be a
queue.

'So how did it feel to be branded a psychopathic personality?'

'How d'you think it felt? Like Christmas had come early?' She stubs the cigarette out as hard as she can. 'Sorry. That wasn't called for.' She smiles nervously. 'Must be my psychopathic personality.'

'Did the court describe you as that?'

She nods. 'Best thing they could have done, in a way,' she says after thinking hard for a while. 'Sort of.'

'Why?'

She puts her head back, searching for words. 'It was . . . I'm tryin' to remember the full phrase. A psychopathic personality disorder that impaired my mental responsibility. And they said it was treatable.

'Basically they said I was the way I was and I'd done the things I'd done because of no fault of my own. And so if I had treatment rather than punishment, I'd get better.'

'Right.' He nods.

'But they didn't know where to send me. There wasn't a secure hospital or treatment centre that knew what to do with me. Not at my age. Not with what I'd done.'

'So that's where Fenton Hall came into it.'

'Right. But they didn't know they were going to send me there. I think it was the last resort.'

'And they . . . what? Gave you therapy? Cured you?'

She looks down at the packet of cigarettes. It's been joined by a mug of coffee. Steam rises from the coffee. She watches it curl up into the air and disappear.

'They can treat me,' she says, then looks up. He sees sadness and loss in her eyes. 'But they said they can't cure me. Ever.'

7

Jamal Jenkins leaned over the railing and looked along the beachfront. The wind coming in off the Channel was cold, harsher than he had expected. His Avirex jacket was getting old and worn now, but he was glad he had put it on. He pulled it round him, collar up, the thick leather doing its best to keep out the chill, pushed his hands deep into the pockets and tried to stop his teeth chattering.

Brighton in November and it could be worse, he thought. At least it wasn't raining. Yet.

The pier was still lit up even though there weren't many visitors, the amusement arcade all but deserted, the fish and chip restaurant nearly empty. The waves lashed the side of the pier, crashing and breaking. Jamal could taste the salt in the spray that made it to the seafront. It carried the smell of fried food and diesel fumes, alcohol and whatever dead things the sea brought with it. Behind him he could hear the throb of the bars, the weather not deterring the drinkers, the alcohol acting as their topcoats. He wished he could have joined them.

The white earbuds of an iPod were in his ears, the wire running under his jacket. But he wasn't listening to music. He was working.

'How you doing?' Peta said in his ear.

'Man it be freezin'. I'm gettin', like, hynothermia from standin' here.'

'Hypothermia,' Peta corrected. 'Won't be for much longer now, don't worry.'

'Man, I ain't worried. Just cold. An' there's nothin' happenin'. I've done a circuit, peeked in through the back way. Nothin'.' Another look round, then he spoke again. 'Know what?'

'What?'

'This is, like, the first time I ever been to the seaside, you get me?'

'Really?' Peta was incredulous. 'What, ever?'

'Well . . .' He thought for a moment. 'I went to Southend once with some of my mates from the home I was in at the time. Bunkin' off for the day. But it wasn't like proper seaside. Just Tottenham with a waterfront.'

Peta laughed. 'Well. That's Albion. We get all the glamorous jobs.'

'Nah, man,' Jamal said, suppressing another shiver, 'you can keep it. Gonna be strictly urban from now on.'

'Won't be much longer.' Peta cut out.

Jamal looked along the length of the seafront, first one way then another. He checked the bar behind him. Nothing. No movement. He shivered, pulled the jacket close to him once more. Did what Peta instructed.

Kept on working.

'Thanks for coming,' Donovan said. 'Good to see you again.'

Wendy Bennett smiled but it was frayed at the edges. 'Well, I had no choice. Not after the way you sounded on the phone. What's happened?'

'First things first. Can I get you a drink?'

She asked for a gin and tonic. He went to the bar to get one, adding another half of wheatbeer for himself.

He was waiting for her in the Cluny. He had stood up from the battered, worn leather sofa when she entered, waved her over. She was dressed more casually today – jeans, boots, jumper and jacket – as if she hadn't expected to be going somewhere after work. Which she hadn't. Certainly not three hundred miles away.

He had read the note, then hit the internet immediately, entering some specialist sites that the general public didn't have access to but that Amar had ensured they did. Once he realized what the names and locations meant, he knew he had to phone in help. The rest of Albion were too far away and working, and as he was deciding what course of action to take, the phone rang. Wendy Bennett asking for a progress report. He told her about the latest development and she insisted on coming straight up. So, straight from the office via Stansted, there she was.

He carried the drinks back over to her. She had sat down, taken her jacket off, made herself comfortable. She looked up at him as he approached, and there was that smile again. Tighter than the last time he had seen it, but there all the same. And it made him, despite everything, feel good.

He set the drinks down, sat next to her. She spoke first. 'So tell me. What have you discovered?'

He took the note out of his pocket, handed it over. 'Read that.'

She did so, put it down. Looked at him, frowning. 'What . . . what does it mean?'

He leaned in closer. He could smell her perfume. 'It arrived a few hours ago. I got straight on the internet to do some research.' He smiled. 'Sites that no mere mortal knows about.'

She looked impressed. Despite everything, he liked the look she gave.

'These names,' he said. 'And these locations. Guy Brewster, London. Adam Wainwright, Bristol. James Fielding, Colchester. Patrick Sutton, Hull. They're all kids, boys, between about seven and twelve, who died.'

'How?'

'They were murdered.'

Wendy sat back, visibly shocked by the news. 'Oh my God . . .'

'I know,' said Donovan. 'And it gets worse. I checked them against the report you gave me on Anne Marie. The boys were killed in places she lived in, while she lived there. And another thing. Every place, she left soon afterwards.'

Wendy sat with her mouth wide open, her eyes roving the bar. It was clear that this was totally out of her world of experience.

Donovan took out another sheet of paper. 'I made these notes. Look.' He put them on the table. They both leaned forward. 'London. She lived in West London from her release in 1989 up until 1993.'

'By which time she's had Jack.'

'Right. Now during this time, 1992 to be precise, Guy Brewster, a kid who lives right near her is killed. In 1993 she moves to Bristol.' His finger moved down the list on the page. 'In 1996 Adam Wainwright is killed. He lived in a children's home nearby. From checking your report and the stuff I found out tonight there were some connections between her and it. Social workers, I think. Then after that she moves again. Colchester. And there's a bit of a gap here. It's not until 2000 that there's another killing. James Fielding this time. A boy from the same estate as her. So she moves again. To Hull. Where in 2004 Patrick Sutton is killed. And then finally here.'

Wendy sat back. 'Oh my God . . .'

'I know. And there was a murder here last night. On her estate. A teenage boy knifed to death.'

'You don't think . . .'

'I don't know what to think at the moment. I'm going to have to look further into it.'

Wendy gulped her gin and tonic as if she was dehydrated.

She put the glass down. 'Are the methods of death . . .' She couldn't finish the question. She looked horrified that she had even thought of it.

'I checked that too. All the same. Strangled then slashed.'

Wendy looked very queasy. 'Just like she did with . . .'

'Yes. Sorry.'

'No, no, it's just . . . God . . . Didn't . . . didn't anyone notice this going on?' Wendy said.

'No. The boys were either from children's homes or dysfunctional families. There was a history of abuse or neglect behind all of them. They were lost boys. The kind of dead kids that don't sell papers.'

Their stories, Donovan had discovered, made the local papers for a couple of days, a week at the most, but then the trails went cold, interest petered out. Occasionally there would be a follow-up piece by some diligent journalist six months or a year later reminding people what had happened, but nothing ever came of them. No new leads. No breakthroughs.

'What about . . . DNA? CCTV?'

Donovan shrugged. 'Nothing.'

'So . . . what do we do now?'

Donovan thought for a moment. 'I don't know. Keep doing what I'm doing with Anne Marie for the present, hopefully get confident enough with her to ask about them. But for the meantime . . .' He looked at the list. 'I think I'll have to make a phone call.'

He looked at Wendy. She was still reeling from the news.

'Sorry,' he said. 'You coming up here like this. But I had to tell someone.'

The familiar smile made a slow return to her face. 'That's OK.' She frowned. 'But should we not tell the police?'

'About what?' said Donovan. 'We have no proof that it was her. Just some anonymous letter. No, I think the best thing would be to look into it ourselves. Like I said, I'll make a phone call. Get some of my team on it.'

He liked the way she smiled at the words 'my team'.

'We might have something bigger on our hands than just Anne Marie's life story.'

Her eyes widened again.

'I know it's awful about those boys, but at the same time . . . this is all quite exciting, isn't it?'

Donovan smiled. 'Welcome to my world.'

They talked some more. Wendy wondered whether Donovan thought it would help to talk to Anne Marie in the morning. Donovan advised caution, told her to wait and see what Anne Marie came up with. Wendy said she would stay in Newcastle, see what developed.

'Don't you have to be getting back down to London? Meetings and contracts, that sort of thing?'

There was that smile again. 'Nothing that needs my urgent attention in the next couple of days. I checked before I came up. Besides, we have email and mobiles and hotels with wifi. So it's not like I'm exiled to Alaska. Although the weather out there feels like it.'

'There'll be people out there with bare legs, in mini skirts and vest tops.'

There was that smile again. 'I didn't know Geordie men were so in touch with their feminine side.'

Donovan laughed. And they stopped talking about work and instead talked of other things. About the literary agency she worked for, the world Donovan once used to be a part of. For his part he told her about some of the work Albion had been involved in. Playing down, rather than bigging up his own involvement. Trying to relax, recharge.

Last orders came. They had one more, then it was time to leave.

'Did you manage to book into a hotel for the night?' Donovan asked.

She nodded. 'Grey Street. Same as last time.'

'Good.'

Silence fell between them.

'Look,' Wendy began, 'last time when I was here, I made a bit of a hasty exit.'

'No problem,' said Donovan. 'You were tired, you said. You wanted to get up early the next morning.'

She nodded, but that clearly wasn't it. He waited.

'The thing is, I wanted to keep drinking with you that night.'

'Right.'

'But . . .'

'Your boyfriend.'

'Not just that.'

Donovan waited.

She looked down at the empty glasses, a smile forming on her face. 'You see, I remember you from before.' She laughed. 'Sorry. I shouldn't even be saying this. Must be the gin. Very unprofessional of me. But yeah. When you were with us before. I remember you. And it was me who thought of you for this job.'

'Thank you.'

'You're welcome. But you see . . .' She looked away from him, an uncertain smile on her lips. She looked back at him. 'Well, I used to notice you. A lot. I . . .'

Donovan knew what she was trying to say. He wasn't sure how to respond so he said nothing.

She looked embarrassed. 'Well, I suppose I liked you. I must have done. I mean, I did remember you after all those years.'

Donovan smiled. 'And have I changed much?'

There was no mistaking what the expression on her face meant. 'Only for the better.'

Their eyes locked. He felt their bodies moving towards each other along the leather sofa.

'You rushing off tonight?' he said.

She was just about to answer when his phone rang.

He tried to ignore it, couldn't. It kept ringing. 'Sorry,' he said reluctantly pulling away from her, 'I'd better get that.'

He tried to answer but the person on the other end, clearly distraught, wouldn't let him. He listened, looked again at Wendy who was now staring at him with a look of concern. He turned away, tried to lower his voice so she couldn't hear. He closed the phone.

'Work?' asked Wendy. 'One of your Albion team?'

Donovan shook his head. 'Worse. Family.'

'Oh. OK.' She couldn't hide the disappointment in her face.

He sighed. 'I've got to go.'

'What, now?'

'Right now. Sorry.'

She nodded. Clearly disappointed.

'I really am sorry,' he said again, holding eye contact with her. 'I'll make it up to you. Good job you got that hotel room.'

He arranged a cab for her and left as soon as he could.

He would call Peta from the car. But right now, this was his priority.

Jamal pulled his jacket around him. He really had had enough now. The bars were emptying, even the kebab shops were slowing down. And still there had been no movement.

He opened the channel, spoke. 'Had enough now.'

'You're right. Come on in and get warm. Joe's been on

the phone. Something's happened with what he's dealing with. We've got to talk about it.'

'Right. Over and out.'

He detached himself from the railings he had been leaning against and began to walk off. Looking forward to getting in the warm.

'So tell me about Jack.'

She sits back, folds her arms across her chest like a breastplate. 'What d'you want to know?'

He shrugs, tries to put her back at ease. 'What sort of boy he is. What he's like. That kind of thing.'

She relaxes slightly but still keeps her arms crossed. 'He's a good lad. A really good lad.'

'He doesn't know . . .'

She leans forward. 'No. He doesn't. And that's the way I'm goin' to keep it. Poor lad.'

'Why poor lad?'

She thinks for a minute before responding. 'When I think what . . . when I think about my childhood, if you can call it that . . . my upbringing. When I think about my mother . . .' She waves her hands at him, sits back. 'I don't know. I can't explain.'

He leans back, at ease. 'Take your time.'

She nods, tries again. 'A mother's love is the strongest of all. Or it should be. Mrs Everett told me that. Joanne taught me that. The art therapist. She had a son. A stepson really, he wasn't even properly hers. But she loved him and brought him up and she was, to all intents and purposes, his mother. And I used to think about that. About her. And my mother. My biological mother, the woman who gave birth to me. She . . .' Her hands go to the table. The bandaged fingers start knotting and unknotting. She doesn't look at them. 'She . . .' She sighs. 'I just want him to have a good life. I don't want him to go through what . . . what I had to go through. He didn't ask to be born. But he's my responsibility. I've got to raise him right. Make him feel safe. Make him proud.'

He nods. Knows there's more. Waits.

'It's not a sickness, what I've got. What I did. It's supposed to

*be because of my psychopathic personality. And that's not somethin'
you're born with, I don't think. It's somethin' that happens to
you. But it feels like a sickness. Like somethin's not right, in there.'
She points to her head. 'Like the bad spirits are there just waitin'
for their chance to break through. Lookin' for weaknesses, lookin' for
holes . . . I tell meself that it's not that. It's something psychological and treatable.'*

*She sighs. He waits. She looks down at the table, at her band-
aged hands, continues without raising her head.*

*'But sometimes, the dreams, the voices . . . the bad spirits.
They're there. I know they are. I can feel them. Hear them.'*

'And what do these spirits tell you to do?'

She keeps looking at the table. He waits.

'They're angry with me. Want me to do, to do bad things.'

'What kind of bad things?'

She looks at her hands. 'Just . . . bad things.'

'Hurt people? That kind of thing?'

She nods.

'And do you listen to them? Ever?'

*She shakes her head. 'I keep them at bay. Whatever it takes, I
keep them at bay. Because Jack's there. And I have to protect him.
I have to protect him no matter what.'*

She keeps looking at her hands. He waits.

8

'Is it much further?'

'Keep your voice down, knacker, they might hear you.'

Tess Preston closed her mouth, said nothing more. Renny led the three of them through the estate. Tess had started out trying to keep track of where she was headed but Renny had taken them this way and that, navigating through silent, shadow-laden cut-throughs, over-exposed patches of scorched earth grass and through a dingy, unlit, tunnel-like maze of streets and walkways, some of which looked so familiar she was sure she had been led through them at least three times. She had thought her army training would come in handy. If their plan was to disorientate her it was working.

She had met them down the road from the school gates, away from any other lurking, predatory journos or paps. This was her lead. Let them get their own.

'Right,' Tess had said, looking between the two of them, 'where we going?'

'Money up front,' said Renny, his eyes hard, his features studiedly blank, a next-generation inner-city recidivist in waiting.

'Sure . . .' Tess had hoped they wouldn't mention it or be fobbed off with waiting for later but she knew from the boy's expression that it wasn't worth risking. She covered her irritation with a smile. It didn't matter really. If they came up with a story it would be worth so much more than that.

'Will you take a cheque?' she asked.

The scowl she received in return answered that question.

'Thought not.' Tess dug into her pocket, opened up her work wallet. She had been careful to move her own money to another pocket so they would think she didn't have any more. She counted out the bills into her hand. 'A thousand. Now I need you to sign this . . .'

She produced a form, handed it to Renny along with a pen. Renny took his eyes off the money in order to frown suspiciously at it. 'What's this?'

'A release form. An invoice. To say where you got the money from. Standard procedure.'

'I'm not signin' anythin'.'

Tess began to re-pocket the money. 'Then thanks for your time.'

'Wait.' Renny watched the money disappearing. 'Gis the pen.' He took the pen, filled in his name and address details, handed it back. Tess pocketed the form, brought out the notes again.

'All yours. This better be worth it. If it's not I'll be after you. I've got your details.' She patted her pocket.

'Try it.' There was defiance in Renny's eyes but also fear. Tess doubted that Renny's parents – if he had parents – would see any of the money. So the threat of an appearance by a journalist at his house would keep the kid in order. She had him. There would be no more trouble tonight.

'Let's go, then,' said Tess, gesturing for Renny and Pez to lead.

They had done. And now Tess was totally lost.

Broken glass and cracked cement underfoot. Dark, threatening shapes cast by haphazard lighting. Everything lit by sickly sodium orange or lurking in black shadow: graffitied walls, rusted handrails, stinking skips. And the triple-S cacophony – screams, shouts and sirens – bleeding in and out of the night.

Tess kept her voice quiet. 'So where is it we're going again?'

'Shut up,' hissed Renny. 'We're nearly there.'

Anne Marie looked round the corner of the block of flats, scanned the open space in front of her, tried to make out shapes, movement, anything. Or anything resembling Jack.

He had gone to the takeaway hours ago and not returned. She had been arguing with Rob and hadn't noticed at first. Jack did this often, just quietly slipped out of the flat, usually when Rob turned up. Anne Marie knew he wasn't the best of men but he was certainly the best she had ever had. He had been good to her. Better than some.

But if he ever laid a finger on Jack he was out. And he knew it.

When it had looked like becoming serious with Rob she had dropped some hints about her past life. A childhood in prison, abuse in her past. Just enough to be honest, not enough for him to walk away. That had happened too many times in the past and she had learned from it.

It hadn't been enough. He had asked more questions. Eventually she told him. Not everything but near enough. And he hadn't judged her. More importantly, he had stayed around. Became protective of her. He wasn't bad. But he had his own demons. She just wished he didn't drink so much.

She had wanted him to be another father to Jack but it hadn't worked out that way. Rob had accepted that if he wanted to be with Anne Marie then Jack was part of the deal. Jack, for his part, had been mature enough to realize that his mother had needs that only a partner could meet and had accepted Rob. But it was always uneasy. And just lately with her bringing in the money and Rob incapable of finding, or unwilling to find, any work his moods had become blacker, his drinking heavier. She had better wrap the book up as quickly as possible and move on to something else.

Moving on. Her life was a constant moving on. For one reason or another. She tried not to dwell on it too much. Don't give the bad spirits a reason to stay.

At the thought of bad spirits her hands began to shake, her legs felt weak. The wounds on the palms of her hands beneath the bandages felt sticky. She tried to push the thoughts from her mind, concentrate on looking for Jack.

She walked around the corner of her block, the geography not yet imprinted in her mind, still having to think where she was going. Crossed the main forecourt. No one about. A murder on an estate tends to have that effect, she thought. Just lights on behind curtains, doors firmly closed on landings.

She moved cautiously, watching for any sudden movements. She felt scared on the estate, as she had on most estates she had lived on. If she had been housed there, she often thought, then who else was there? She knew kids shouldn't carry knives, but in a way, she didn't blame them. She might have done if she was their age.

She reached the row of shops where the takeaway was. An array of graffitied metal shutters and grilles. The off-licence was still open, dispensing cheap, sugary alcohol and cigarettes to the local kids over a counter in the window behind a metal cage, the Indian owners no longer taking chances. Next to it was the takeaway. It didn't really have a name just an illuminated sign advertising what it sold: pizzas, burgers, kebabs, fried chicken, fish and chips. There were photos stuck to the glass of the supposed food, full colour, unattainable; wish-fulfilment of a level the food dispensed there could never reach.

No, that wasn't true, she thought. The pizzas were quite nice.

The lights were on, it was still open. She walked to the doorway, stepped inside. Immediately the smell of hot, dirty frying oil hit her. She didn't find it unpleasant. Years of exposure had made it a comforting smell to her, the nearest thing to a happy memory of home cooking that she had.

The two men behind the counter looked up at her approach. Dark-skinned, but she couldn't place their ethnic origin. Could be anywhere from Greece to Iran for all she knew. One of them gave a weary half-smile as she approached the till, the other turned his back, busying himself with cleaning down surfaces.

'Hiya,' she said. 'Have you seen a lad?'

'We see a lot of lads in here.'

'Well, he's about this high . . .' She gestured with her hand. 'Tall, skinny. Long hair. Wearin' a black jacket and jeans. New trainers. And he was supposed to be gettin' some tea from here. She thought for a moment, couldn't remember what he had actually gone to get. 'Pizza or somethin'. Kebab. Have you seen him? Has he been in?'

The man behind the counter shrugged, clearly disappointed at not making a sale. His eyes went to her bandaged hands, the dressing now loose and dirty. She put her hands behind her back, kept talking.

'You haven't seen him, then? He's new around here. We haven't been moved in long.'

Another shrug, a shake of the head.

'He has long hair?' The second man spoke without turning his back, his hand still cleaning the work surface.

'Yeah, that's right, long hair,' said Anne Marie, suddenly nervous over what might have happened to him.

'Listening to music?' The man pointed to his ears.

'Yeah.'

'He was in earlier. Couple of hours.'

A couple of hours . . . Had she really been drinking and arguing with Rob for that long? A shaft of guilt ran through her. Sort yourself out.

'D'you know where he is now?' She realized how stupid the question was as soon as it left her lips. 'I mean, did he say where he was goin'?'

The first man shook his head. Anne Marie looked from one to the other, waiting as if for Jack to appear or for them to tell her where he was. The second man stopped cleaning, turned and spoke.

'After what happened to that boy last night everybody worries.'

Anne Marie nodded, thanked them and, her hands unclasped from behind her back, left the shop. Panic was rising in her chest. She tried to tamp it down, calm herself with the deep breathing exercises she had been taught. She had to think.

Where was he? Where would he have gone?

She didn't know. She looked round again, chose a direction and walked towards it. If she had believed in God she would have prayed that Jack was at the end of it.

As it was she just hoped.

'Here.' Renny stopped walking, dropped down behind a brick wall. Tess stopped walking as Renny spoke, did exactly what the boy did. Pez too.

'What am I looking at?' said Tess, risking a glance over the wall.

Renny pulled her back down. 'Fuck off, man, if they see wuh, they'll fuckin' have wuh.'

'Right.' Tess stayed where she was.

As she had looked up, she saw a flash of a Tesco sign, an industrial estate, a car park. There were cars in the car park. Revving up, lights full on, the drivers, passengers and hangers-on clustered round, drinking, smoking, talking, laughing.

'None of them seem too worried about a possible murderer,' said Tess.

'That's because one of them did it,' said Renny.

'Right.' Tess felt that shiver of excitement when she knew she was on to something. She nodded. 'Which one?'

'Dunno,' said Renny.

'Then how do you know it's one of them?'

''Cos we were here last night,' said Pez. 'Aye, an' we saw them—'

A kick from Renny shut him up. Too late, Tess had heard.

'You were here last night?' she said. Renny reluctantly nodded. 'With Calvin?' Another reluctant nod. 'What happened?'

'Calvin went home,' said Renny. 'We were down there with the drivers an' that, an' Calvin wanted a ride an' they wouldn't give him one. So he went home.'

Tess looked between the two of them. 'And that's it? He went home?'

'Aye,' said Pez. 'You gonna give us the rest of the money now?'

Tess ignored the question. 'Did you see anyone follow him? Did he argue with anyone?'

'He bumped into someone, I think,' Renny said. 'I think they might have followed him.'

Pez looked at Renny, clearly wanting to speak and wanting permission. Renny stared at the other boy, silencing him. Pez's head dropped. He said nothing.

'Who was this person that he bumped into then?'

'Dunno his name, like,' said Renny. 'But he's a dealer. Off the estate.'

'Would you recognize him again?'

Renny shrugged. Affected a look of disinterest. 'Dunno.'

Tess risked a glance over the wall. She saw individuals on the periphery of the group who made no attempt to join in, who only spoke when spoken to and who, from the way their hands were moving about faster than a street-corner card shark, were dealing.

Tess felt excitement rise with her. She sensed she was on to something here, an aspect none of her colleagues or rivals – and they were all her rivals, really – had discovered yet. This could be the break, her entrance into the big time. She tried not to let her excitement show, tried to remain professional.

'So which one is he?'

'The one in the baseball cap,' said Pez.

Tess took another look. 'They're all wearing baseball caps.'

'Well, he's one of them, then,' said Renny, smugness in his voice. 'So where's the rest of our money?'

'Aye,' said Pez, shuffling about as if he had worms, 'where's wor money, like?'

'You'll get your money, don't worry,' said Tess.

'Good,' said Renny.

'As soon as you tell me which one followed Calvin.'

Anger flashed in Renny's eyes. Even in the dark Tess saw it, catching in the streetlight, shining like a blade.

'That wasn't the deal,' said Renny. 'You bitch.'

'Deal's changed, boys,' said Tess, thinking quickly, trying to make the situation work for her as smoothly and cost-effectively as she could. 'You held out on me. Didn't tell me the whole story, did you? Now if you'd said all that at the beginning we'd have had a different deal. But because you didn't tell me the truth, well . . . that changes things.'

'Bitch,' said Renny again, and at that moment Tess felt sure that, boy or not, he could do her some serious damage.

Negotiate from a position of strength, Tess thought. No matter what. 'Deal's a deal,' Tess said, hoping there was no fear in her eyes. The boy was beginning to unnerve her. 'Take it or leave it.'

Renny said nothing. Pez looked between the two of them. 'Well, gentlemen,' said Tess, making to move, 'if that's everything, then thank you for a wonderful evening—'

'Stay where you are.'

All three of them looked up. Four figures stood over them, the outwardly pointed flashlight beams rendering them nothing but dark outlines, hulking with menace.

Tess was the first to speak. She stood up. There was no need for secrecy now. 'Who the fuck are you?'

'Detective Inspector Nattrass,' the speaker said, holding out a warrant card. 'And you are?'

'Tess Preston, the *Globe*. These boys here were just giving me a tour of the area, Detective Inspector.'

'Well, your tour guides have just led you right into a police surveillance operation. So I suggest you ask them to show you some other sights.'

Tess felt that familiar thrill run through her again, the one she felt when hunches were played out and everything started knitting together. 'Would this surveillance operation have anything to do with the murder of Calvin Bell, Detective Inspector Nattrass?'

'Just go back to your hotel room, please, Ms Preston. Better still, take yourself off home.'

'But Detective Inspector—'

'There will be a press conference in the morning. If you're still here, we'll see you at that. But for now I suggest you leave. Or my men will have to escort you.'

Tess realized she had no option but to do as she was told. She looked at the boys. 'Well, boys, gonna show me back to civilization?'

The three of them trudged off. It didn't matter whether Renny came up with a name or not. Tess was on to something.

She knew it.

Losing a child. It was the worst thing that could happen to a mother. Anne Marie knew that. It was something that she carried with her every second of the day. Something that, no matter what she did with the rest of her life, she could never fully atone for. Because there was a part of her that would never allow it.

As she searched the estate for Jack and felt that panic rise once again, she knew, not for the first time, what it must feel like. She had to find him. Get things sorted out. Once and for all. Sort it and move forward.

And then she saw him. Or someone she thought was him. In the only quiet spot on the estate. Sitting on a bench at the top of the hill, looking down over the Tyne as it slopped along to the North Sea, the lights of the tall riverside apartments twinkling, throwing fairy-tale reflections into the water, making that kind of life look unattainable from where Anne Marie stood.

She walked up to the bench. Jack was sitting there, legs pulled up to his chin, arms wrapped round his calves, MP3 player clamped to his ears.

She sat down next to him. If she didn't know better, she could start believing in God again.

'Hello, son,' she said.

He looked up, startled, turned off the music. He gave her a look that said he was pleased to see her but that gradually became fearful.

'I've been worried sick about you,' she said. 'Where've you been?'

He shrugged. 'Just walking. Here and there.'

'Why didn't you come home?'

He sighed, rocked backwards and forwards slightly. 'You were fighting.'

'No, we weren't.'

'You were going to fight.'

Anne Marie's turn to sigh. 'I was worried about you.' She looked at the empty wrappers beside him. 'Is that my dinner?'

He looked fearful again. 'He'll kill me.'

Anne Marie caught the hurt in his eyes as, having spoken his words, he looked away. Her heart broke. She remembered her training, her counselling. She kept her voice calm. 'No he won't. I won't let him.'

Jack rocked.

'I won't let him hurt you ever. I won't let anyone hurt you ever.'

They sat there in silence. Eventually, Anne Marie gently placed her arm round Jack, her bandaged hand resting on his shoulder. He moved into her. They sat like that for a while, neither speaking, neither moving.

'Come on,' she said eventually, 'let's go home.'

Jack nodded. Got up and followed her.

Nothing's sorted, she thought. Nothing's different. Just another ceasefire. Another little piece of peace. Maybe that's it, she thought. Maybe that's all you can expect.

They walked back to the flat in silence.

'Look.' It was Pez who spoke. He was pointing across the open forecourt, stopped moving to do it. The other two followed his gaze. Tess saw a skinny teenage boy, hair perhaps a little too long for the area, and a woman, presumably his mother. Dressed like an ageing goth or rock casualty on her night off. Heavyset, long-haired.

'It's that kid from school,' said Pez. 'The new kid. The weird one that wouldn't give you his trainers.'

Renny just nodded, clearly not happy to be reminded of that loss of face in front of a stranger. Tess tried not to smile. She looked again at the mother and son. They moved beneath a streetlight and her face was suddenly illuminated. She jumped. Thought for a minute she knew her.

'She just arrived, you said?' said Tess.

'Aye,' said Pez.

'Where from?'

'Dunno. The lad talks funny like.'

Probably talks properly and you can't understand him, thought Tess. 'Has he said anything about where he's from? Dropped any clues?'

'Nah.' Pez again. Renny clearly found the subject of the boy uninteresting. 'We don't have that much to do with him.'

Tess nodded, not really listening. She was watching the mother. Even in this light and from this distance, she thought, there was definitely something familiar about her. Her looks, the way she walked. And the boy. Something connected to the boy . . .

It was like spotting an actor on TV and not being able to place what they had appeared in before. She thought it was something important, though. She would give it some thought. Hope an answer came to her.

Renny stopped walking. Pez did likewise. Tess joined them.

'Money,' said Renny, sticking his hand out in as threatening a manner as possible. 'Now.'

'Whoa there, partner,' said Tess. 'Remember what I said. Deal's a deal. You come up with the goods, I come up with the money. Might even be something more in it for you both if you come up with enough.'

Renny moved in closer. 'And if we don't?'

Tess swallowed, hoped the boy-thug couldn't sense her

fear. 'Then I've got your details,' she said patting her pocket. 'Like I said, would whoever's at that address like to know you're holding out on them?'

Renny took a step back. Tess's words had clearly jolted something in him. There was someone at that address that the boy was clearly scared of.

Tess took that as her cue to leave. 'See you tomorrow, lads.'

She walked off, thinking. The police, the boys, that woman. Plenty going on, if she could just join up the dots . . .

She smiled to herself.

Not a bad night's work.

'Family,' she says. 'Toughest bond in the world. Or should be.'

He agrees with her.

'But I've learned somethin' over the years. Your family isn't what you were born with. It's not biological. It's what you make it.'

'True.'

'I mean, Fenton Hall, Mr and Mrs Everett, Joanne . . . they were like family to me. I mean, I even took Joanne's name and she was pleased about that. Really pleased. I got a good feelin' about it too. Felt connected, you know?'

He does.

'But we weren't related. Not really. Blood, an' that. You know what I mean?'

'I know exactly what you mean.'

'Sometimes you don't choose your family. Sometimes your family chooses you.'

'You're right,' he says. 'Dead right. And it's a good feeling to be part of something like that. To belong.'

She nods, looks out of the window while she answers.

'Mostly,' she says. 'Sometimes.'

9

Donovan drove fast, hoping he wouldn't be pulled over for speeding, hoping he didn't have enough alcohol in him to matter if he was.

The phone call had been completely unexpected. Of all the people it could have been, his ex-wife Annie was the last person he would have thought of. There was no greeting, no attempt to find out how he was or what he was up to. Just pitching straight in, her voice frantic, desperate.

'Don, it's Abby. She's . . .'

A sick sense of déjà vu overtook Donovan as he immediately feared the worst. 'What? She's what?'

'She's gone.'

Donovan's legs began to shake. He felt like they were about to give way. 'Gone where?' Disappeared?'

There was a pause as Annie realized what he was thinking. When she spoke again the heat in her voice was slightly lower. 'No, not like that. Gone. Left us.'

Not *me*, Donovan noticed, *us*. He didn't think the phrasing was accidental.

'OK. She's gone where?'

'She . . . there was an argument. She . . . she walked out.'

'Has she been in touch? Have you heard from her?'

'No.'

Donovan sighed. 'Shit.'

'She took Michael's credit card, though, when she left.'

'And has it been used? Have they traced it?'

A stifled sob down the phone. 'Yes.'

'Where?'

'Newcastle.'

Wendy Bennett had been sitting opposite him while the call was going on. He had turned away from her once he realized who was calling; no matter how much he liked her, this conversation wasn't for her. He gave his full attention to Annie.

'Newcastle. So she was looking for me.'

'Well, who else does she know up there?'

Donovan felt anger rise as an initial response to her outburst, wanted to reply in kind, but swallowed the response down. It wouldn't help. But after all these years, he thought, they still knew which of each other's buttons to press.

'Have you tried calling her?'

'Of course I've tried calling her. Her phone's switched off. Just goes to voicemail.'

'OK. Let's think rationally. If she's looking for me she'll have gone . . . does she know about the house? What happened to it?'

'What? I don't know. Yes, I think so. I told her.' Another sigh. 'Oh, I don't know.'

'I'll have to assume she doesn't, then. I'll try there first. Then the old work address.'

'Just, just . . . do something . . .' It sounded like the fight had gone out of her. Donovan could imagine her standing there, the worried expression on her face. How her forehead would crinkle when she frowned or was upset. Klingon brow, he used to describe it as, back when they still found things like that funny, when they could laugh as a couple.

'I will. Don't worry, Annie, if she's there I'll find her.'

'You'd better,' she said angrily.

She knew he would do his best. He knew her anger was not aimed at him, merely displaced impotence.

'What were you arguing about?'

'What?'

'Why did she leave home?'

Silence, then a sigh. 'I don't think we need to discuss that now. It's not important. Just find Abby. Please.' Her voice choked off as she hung up.

Donovan had then pocketed his phone. No matter how disappointed he was at the way the evening had turned out with Wendy this had to take precedence. He waited until her cab had pulled away then ran to his car and drove off as fast as he could.

He drove up the A1 to Northumberland, pushing the Scimitar as fast as it could go. He knew the car was a classic and was fast for its time, but there were times when he wished he had bought something more contemporary. More practical.

Donovan pulled up outside the remains of his cottage and looked at the boarded-up, blackened shell. It was so different from the place he and Jamal had renovated and decorated, made habitable. Now he would have to start all over again. If he had the strength to do so.

But that was something for another day. Right now he had more pressing things on his mind.

He turned off the engine, got out. Because he was so far out in the country and there was no streetlighting, he used the car headlights for illumination.

'Abby . . .' He shouted, heard his voice echoing off into the darkness. He tried again. 'Abby . . .'

Nothing. No response of any kind. No movement, no reply.

He shouted again and did a circuit of the house. No sign of her. She wasn't there. Wherever she was, she wasn't there.

He took out his mobile, scrolled through the numbers, looking for Abby's. Although Annie had said she had tried calling and the phone was switched off, she might pick up if she knew he was calling her. If she was actually here and looking for him.

He found her number, called it. Waited.

Voicemail.

'Hi, Abby, listen it's . . .' It sounded so strange saying the word after so long. 'It's Dad here. Your mum says you're up here. Looking for me. Well, guess what? I'm looking for you. Give me a call when you get this and hopefully we can meet up.'

He finished the call. Best to keep it light, he thought, try not to scare her off.

He gave a final look around. She definitely wasn't there.

He got back in the car, headed for the city.

Wondering where to try next.

Hoping she would turn her phone on so he could trace her.

Hoping she was OK.

'So Jack's important to you.' Not a question, a statement.

'He's the world to me. And I'll do anythin' to protect him. Anythin'.'

He nods. Understands.

'D'you know what it's like? D'you know what I mean?'

'I do.'

'You've got kids, then.'

He nods.

'How many?'

He doesn't reply straightaway. He doesn't know what answer to truthfully give. 'A couple,' he says eventually.

She doesn't notice his hesitation, keeps on talking, looking at her hands all the while. 'Then you know what I mean. You'll take any amount of shit for yourself to see them all right, won't you? Put yourself through anythin'. Because they're the world to you. Your world.'

He doesn't reply.

'And you'll fight for them,' she says. 'I'll fight for Jack. Tooth an' claw. I'll do anythin' to make sure he has a good future. Anythin' to make sure he doesn't end up like me. Anythin'.'

She looks up at him.

'An' you'd do the same, wouldn't you? For yours.'

'Oh yeah,' he says. 'Yeah. Course I would.'

She becomes thoughtful once again. He waits for her to speak. 'I saw that Sylvia Cunliffe on TV. I didn't recognize her. She looks rough, doesn't she?'

'She's been through a lot.'

'Is she famous? Why were they askin' her?'

'Because of her son. Because of Trevor.'

She sits back, thinks. Then nods again. 'I didn't even know that was his name, you know. Cunliffe. I just knew him as Trevor. It

*wasn't until the trial that they started talkin' about Trevor Cunliffe.
I didn't know who they were talkin' about at first. Is she often on
the news?'*

'Time to time. When there's been a teenager or a child murdered.'

She frowns. 'Is she an expert?'

'Only from experience.'

'So because I killed her son she's fuckin' Yoda?'

'She's carrying a lot of grief and anger. When people have that,
they work it out how they can.'

'Should have asked me,' she says. 'But then they wouldn't ask
me, would they? Some opinions are worth more than others.'

'That's not true.'

'Really?' She looks at him then straight in the eye. 'You've got
children?'

He nods. 'Yes.'

'How d'you think you'd feel if one of them—'

'Was murdered? You mean, would it make me an expert?'

She jumps slightly, taken aback by the sharpness of his answer.
When she speaks her voice is soft. 'I was going to say, was a killer.
How would you feel if your son or daughter was a killer?'

He doesn't answer straightaway. 'Depends on the circumstances.'

She nods, not believing him. 'You'd have opinions, though. On
what had happened. Do you think anyone would want to hear
them? Or would they listen to the victim? Or the victim's mother?'

'OK then,' he says. 'What about that boy? Calvin Bell.'

She looks up sharply, answers quickly. 'What about him?'

'He lived beside you. He got stabbed. Have you heard anything?
D'you know why? What happened there?'

Her arms are folded against her chest again. Her face is set. She
glances down to her bandaged hands then quickly back to him.
'How should I know?' Her voice is a monotone. 'What are you
askin' that for?'

He shrugs, tries to keep it light. 'I want your opinion. You're the
expert from experience.'

He's angry now and he doesn't know why he did that. There are more things he wants to say, more questions he wants to ask about other dead boys but he's gone about it the wrong way, let his anger dictate the pace. So instead he says nothing, waits. Catches the timer on the recorder out of the corner of his eye, counts off the silent seconds.

Anne Marie looks at him, says nothing.

10

James Dean and young Elvis looked down on her like unattainably handsome angels time-trapped in a faraway world. Marilyn Monroe smiled from the far wall, the smile telling her life had its heartache and dark secrets and made her weary beyond endurance but, baby, wasn't it just great anyway? Her plate sat in front of her, the food mountainous and oil-laden enough to give even older Elvis pause, and the creepy guy who had sat down opposite was really starting to scare her.

The Stateside diner on Pink Lane was one of the few places in the city centre still open well after midnight that didn't involve drinking, dancing or pulling. Retro-fitted in an approximation of an American Fifties diner complete with red vinyl booths, chrome-edged Formica tables, black and white checked floor and rock 'n' roll jukebox, it was open almost twenty-four hours catering from early breakfasts to post-clubbing munchies and everything in between. Naturally it attracted more than its fair share of dispossessed, transient souls who, for one reason or another, couldn't or wouldn't go home.

She had seen him before. He had sat behind her on the coach. In his thirties as far as she could tell, dressed in the accredited casual chav about town uniform of long-sleeved shirt and jeans accompanied by spiked, gelled hair and a range of cheap, flashy, chunky finger and neck jewellery so extensive that it spoke of a personal account at Elizabeth Duke. The waitress behind the counter kept glancing over, clearly concerned, but not enough to actually intercede.

'Well, well, well,' he had said when he sat down opposite her, 'fancy bumping into you here. That's a coincidence, isn't it?'

Abigail doubted it.

'I really like girls with long brown hair. And you've got lovely hair. Needs a wash, though.' He gave what he probably thought of as a smile. 'So what's yer name, then?'

She kept her attention on her food: a burger the size of a child's head with a pile of fries large enough to host a colony of gerbils. Beside that a token clump of salad fought and failed to make its presence felt. Comfort food. And she needed comfort right now. More than anything.

She gave a quick glance round: there were other people at the tables, some just stopping in on the way to their, or hopefully someone else's, homes, some who were on the way somewhere else for the evening and a few who seemed to have no intention of leaving, whose vacant expressions spoke of some kind of fatal flaw in their brains' hard-wiring. At least her unwanted dining companion didn't fall into that category. Although, knowing that he had probably been following her for a whole day and night just for the opportunity to sit next to her, she thought that maybe he was something worse.

She speared a chip into her mouth. Chewed, swallowed. Not bad. She couldn't remember when she had last eaten and it almost fell into her with a resounding, ravenous echo that suddenly rekindled her appetite. She forked in two more. Then two more.

'Hey,' the gold-plated chav said, his smile souring unpleasantly at the edges, 'I asked you a question. It's not polite to ignore people. What's your name?'

'Abigail,' she said automatically, then instantly regretted it.

He sat back, smiling once more in triumph. He had made her speak, his smile said. She was his now, he owned her. Abigail kept her head down, concentrated on eating.

She had walked round the city all day. Looking, unsuccessfully, for the Albion offices. The estate agents wouldn't release the information without first checking that she was who she said she was. That was no good: she didn't want him warned. He might contact *them*, make them take her back. So she had just walked.

She had found the Stateside diner and sat inside, wondering what to do, where to go next. She didn't want to use the credit card again in case they found out where she was. It had been a risk to use it the first time. She couldn't use it in a hotel for the same reason. If she went to sleep she would wake up with *them* at the end of the bed. Or worse. The police, even. But on checking her phone she found a message from her father. A recent one. Her first response was to panic, delete it. They had got to him. He knew. He was looking for her on their behalf. But instead she listened. And to her relief, it didn't sound like bad news at all. In fact, his words had given her hope.

She should call him back. But it was still a big step after everything that had happened between the two of them. And, reluctant though she was to admit it, she needed his help. But she also needed food. So she ate.

'Abigail,' he said. 'That's a nice name. Really pretty. D'you want to know mine?'

She kept her eyes on her food.

'Gavin. Can I have a chip.'

'Get your own,' she said, the words surprising her, finding a strength she didn't know she had.

He sat back, shocked. The smile disappeared momentarily to be replaced by a hard-edged anger.

'No need to be like that,' he said. 'We can be friends, you and me. I'm a kind man. You'd like me. Why don't I buy that for you? Eh? Your dinner.' He glanced at her bag. 'Now I've gone to a lot of trouble to find you. Because I thought you looked lost. And I was right. I can give you somewhere to stay for the night too. Come on, it'll be fun.'

Clearly he had his mind made up. Her or nothing. And he wasn't going to settle for nothing.

'No thanks,' she said, picking up her burger and biting into it. She could barely get her mouth round all of it and had to press it down.

He leaned forward over her plate, watched her lips as she ate. 'That's not polite. That's not very nice.' His voice was wheedling. He made another attempt at a smile. 'Come on, be nice.'

Emboldened, she found her voice. 'Get away from me or I'll tell the management and they'll have you thrown out.'

He thought for a few seconds, digesting her response, then laughed. 'I see. Like that is it? You little whore. Who do you think you are?'

Abigail was scared now, really scared. She was a polite, good-natured middle-class teenage girl from a comfortably well-off area of North London. This was so far outside of her experience that she didn't know how to handle it. She even wished her dad were there. Things must be bad, she thought, to want that. Then mentally corrected herself. They were.

'I'm going to tell them,' she said, her voice sounding as unsteady as she felt.

'They won't do anything,' he said, leaning in closer and hissing in her ear while still maintaining the smile, 'they'll think you're just my girlfriend and we've had a fight. Or I'm your pimp and you won't hand over the money you've made to me.'

The breath left her body. She was shaking, like she was about to faint.

'So you get me thrown out. Then what? I'll be waiting for you. Because you've got to leave sometime. So what's it going to be?' He then sat back and opened his arms expansively. 'Come one, I'm not such a bad guy. And you'll have somewhere to stay for the night.' He leaned forward again, placed his left hand over her right. 'Could be a lot worse. A lot worse. Come on. It'll be fun. You know you want to.'

Without pausing to think or question her actions, she picked up her fork and, channelling her fear and anger into strength and force, she slammed it down into the back of his hand.

At first he didn't react. Then the pain hit. He jumped back, staring at his hand with the fork still sticking out. Blood was starting to pump out, dripping on to her half-eaten burger. That was the end of her meal.

He then realized what she had done and his face rapidly changed. All pretence of friendliness was gone, in its place just feral hatred.

'Bitch! Fuckin' bitch!'

He lunged at her over the table. Abigail was aware of the rest of the diner reacting in shock as his hands, now balled into fists, were flung in her direction. She tried to shrink back into the booth. As she tried to dodge the blows he was inexpertly swinging at her her drink and the plate went flying.

'Help me . . .' Abigail didn't know whether she had screamed or whispered those words. 'Please . . .'

She felt rather than saw him looming into her vision and screwed her eyes tight shut in anticipation of the hail of blows that were about to fall.

But they didn't come.

Slowly she opened her eyes. Gavin was being restrained round the neck. He was attempting to fight off his assailant but without much success. Abigail heard a familiar voice shouting, gasping out angry words.

'Good at picking on girls, are you . . . see how you get on with me . . .'

She looked closely at the assailant. Jeans, T-shirt, hair slightly greying, slightly too long. Her dad.

Joe Donovan.

She sat up straight.

Donovan was dragging Gavin from the booth, one arm locked round his throat, the other twisting his left arm up behind his back. He tumbled him on to the floor. Kneeling on him as he did so. He pulled Gavin's left arm up further. Gavin screamed.

Behind him, people were gathering. Staff hovered, nervous about interceding. From the doorway came two burly, suited men. Bouncers from the club down the lane. Someone must have gone to get them.

'It's OK,' Abigail shouted as they approached, ready to haul Donovan off, 'he's my dad. He's come to pick me up. This guy was attacking me.'

They stood off, pumped for a fight, clearly unhappy at the thought that there would be no initial violence. Donovan looked up.

'If you'd like to take over, gents, I'd be more than happy.'

Donovan loosened his grip, stood up. The bouncers moved in, picked Gavin up from the floor. Looked between Donovan and Abigail, the waitress, as to what to do next.

'He called me a whore!' shouted Abigail. 'He wanted to, to do things to me. Take me back to his. I'm only fourteen, for God's sake.'

That was all the incentive the bouncers needed. They dragged him out of the diner, while he whimpered. She didn't want to think about what would be in store for him. She looked at her dad. He smiled.

'Hey,' he said.

She smiled in return. Felt like crying. 'Hey, yourself.'

She ran to him. He opened his arms. She hugged him and the floodgates opened, tears streaming down her cheeks, body wracked by sobs. Eventually she pulled away from him. Looked at him, puzzled.

'How did you find me?'

'You left your phone on, thank God. We've got a GPS tracking system at Albion. Highly illegal, but I bet you're glad we have.'

She smiled.

He broke the embrace, turned to the waitress, gave her his card. 'Any damages, give me a call.'

The waitress, clearly fearful of a lawsuit, returned it unused, hurriedly telling him there wouldn't be, that she was sorry for what had happened and that under the circumstances Abigail's meal was on the house.

Donovan picked up her bags and they moved towards the door.

'Well,' he said, 'this is a pleasant surprise.'

No matter what she had said to him in the past, how she had treated him and what she thought about him, she was so glad to see him now. She smiled again.

'Let's go home,' he said.

They walked off into the night.

Together.

PART THREE

SONS OF

'That first place they sent me to, when I got out, in eighty-eight, that was horrible. Horrible.'

She stubs her cigarette out in the ashtray as hard as she can for effect.

'The Powell Estate in Paddington?'

She nods.

'In what way?'

'Just . . .' She thinks for a few seconds. 'It was where they sent the people they couldn't deal with, that they didn't want to know. Sweep them under the carpet, like. I'd been all over the place by then and I was looking to settle down somewhere, you know, find some roots.' She gives a harsh, fag-enriched laugh. 'Like I'd want to put down roots there.' She falls silent again, thinking. 'It was no better than prison. People were frightened to leave their homes at night. Or during the day, some of them. Awful. Mind you, they say it's not like that now. That it got better when I left.' Another harsh laugh. 'Typical.'

'And that was where Jack was born?'

She nods.

'And . . . conceived?'

She nods again. Looks out of the window while she talks. 'But I wasn't there for long. I moved soon after that.'

'Why?'

She shrugs. 'Wanted a change.'

'Was Jack's father with you?'

'I told you, I'm not talkin' about him.'

He tries something else.

'You were there when that boy died? Guy Brewster?'

'Dead boys.' A small note of irritation in her voice, threatening to get bigger. 'What is it with you and dead boys?'

He chooses to regard her question as an outburst and ignores it.

'What happened to Guy Brewster? Can you remember?'

She keeps looking out the window. 'A boy was found dead. Murdered.' She sits silently.

'That's all?'

She folds her arms. 'As far as I'm concerned.'

'So you didn't know the boy? Didn't have any contact with him?'

She stares at him. He doesn't know whether it's defiance or fear. She says nothing more. He waits. Eventually she speaks.

'They kept tellin' me I was one of the lucky ones there. 'Cos I had backup. Social workers. Well, I wasn't lucky. Not a bit.'

He frowns. This isn't what he was expecting her to say. 'What d'you mean?'

She keeps staring out of the window. A Metro train rumbles past. She barely notices. Her eyes are on something she can see. Eventually she looks back at him.

'I've got Jack, though. So some good came out if it.' She smiles. 'Yeah.'

11

Anne Marie's screams woke her up. The nightmares were still clawing at her, trying to claim her, pull her back. She had escaped from them.

For now.

They were getting stronger. There was no denying the fact, no trying to ignore it or pretend it wasn't happening. They were getting stronger. The bad spirits had faces this time.

Trevor Cunliffe looking up at her. Smiling, trusting, big mouth, missing teeth, head full of curls. Her hands on his neck, choking, pressing. His face changing colour, the fear in . . .

His eyes. She couldn't see his eyes.

Sylvia Cunliffe standing there next to him, watching. Angry face. At the other side of her, a man. She knew who it was. Trevor, grown up. Trevor denied. Watching himself as a boy die. Watching Mae Blacklock kill him.

Behind them another man. She could only see an outline but she knew who that was. A shadow with a razor-slash mouth, blood-red lips, blade-white teeth. Laughing.

She screamed, opened her eyes again. Nothing. No screaming or shouting. No grinning shadows. Just grey November light creeping round cheap curtains. Rob snoring.

She breathed deeply, trying to get settled again. Closed her eyes.

Saw Calvin Bell's smiling face. The one from the papers, the TV.

Saw him cry out in agony.

Blades slicing . . .

The grinning shadow . . .

Calvin . . . Trevor . . .

The others . . .

She opened her eyes again.

'Oh God . . .'

She breathed heavily, like her chest was about to burst. Despite the cold, sweat covered her whole body. Her head was spinning, the room sparkling before her eyes.

'Oh God . . . I'm . . . oh God . . .'

Her tablets. They were in the bathroom. She needed her tablets. Slowly throwing the covers off her body, she pulled her body upright, trying to ignore the pounding and swirling in her head, and put her feet on the floor. Slowly, she got up. Put her hand out to steady herself. Saw a trail of blood on the wall.

She looked at her bandaged hands.

There was fresh blood on them.

She moved as quickly as she could to the bathroom to take her tablets.

And to throw up.

Trellick Tower dominated the landscape. The neo-brutalist Sixties tower block had survived sour times, including women being raped in the lifts, children being attacked by heroin addicts and squatters trying to burn the building down from inside, to become something of a landmark. Modernism's last gasp.

It stood in West London, straddling the border between the gentrified Notting Hill and the much less genteel Kensal Town. Once the domain of social housing, its three-bedroom flats were now going for nearly half a million.

Amar Miah and Peta Knight stood at the base of the

tower, staring up at it in the harsh, autumn morning light. Amar was in his early thirties, Asian, with a trim, gym-worked body. He was dressed in his usual working uniform of parka, jeans, T-shirt and trainers. All either designer labels or high-end high street. Peta, her blonde hair pulled back into a ponytail, had on her jeans and trainers, a fleece-lined jacket covering her top. They both looked fit, like they could handle themselves.

'Listed building, you know,' said Peta, shutting and locking the door of her Saab soft-top.

'Looks straight to me,' said Amar, a smile playing on the corners of his lips.

Peta shook her head. 'God save us from terrible jokes this early in the morning.'

Amar persisted. 'You know the guy who designed this was called Goldfinger? Like in James Bond? Apparently Ian Fleming hated the tower so much he named a villain after him.'

'Am I paying for this guided tour?'

'Sorry.' Amar became mock-hurt. He pulled his padded jacket around him, hitched up his jeans, polished the tops of each box-white trainer on the back of his calf. 'Just trying to be entertaining.'

'Find the directions to where we're going. That should be entertainment enough.'

A few hurried phone calls had been made the day before and they had driven up from Brighton first thing in the morning. It felt to Peta like lunchtime, they'd been up so long, but it was not yet nine o'clock. London was waking up, going to work.

'It's this way,' Amar said, consulting a printed page of A4 and an A to Z of London and pointing up a street. He began walking. Peta followed him.

Until the previous night they had been tracking Matt

Milsom in Brighton. They had given the house he was in a round-the-clock vigil, as well as setting up a live feed that went to their rented flat and to Joe back at Albion. And, beyond taking deliveries of food from supermarket vans, there had been no movement in or out. There had been a light on in the flat at all times and only the faintest of movement glimpsed behind the pulled curtains. They had waited. Nothing.

'He must have a secret tunnel,' Amar had said, several days previously in the rented apartment in Brighton where they were then based. 'Where he can come and go without us spotting him.'

'Prob'ly goes to the pub an' back,' Jamal had said. 'Or comes round here to laugh at us watchin' him.'

Peta had smiled at her colleagues. Despite the seriousness of the job in hand, she enjoyed working with them. Recently there had been a real chance they would not be working together again at all. Or that not all of them would even be alive. But they had prevailed. They had survived. They were Peta's closest friends, as close as family. Closer, in fact.

The last few months had been traumatic for Peta. She had discovered the true identity of her biological father only to have him taken away from her before she could get to know him properly. She had promised her mother they would spend some time together to come to terms with it all, but found she didn't want to talk to her. She couldn't come to terms with her mother's deceit. Perhaps in time she could, but not quite yet. And then this happened. Donovan's near death and the hunt for Matt Milsom. She had been so relieved. And as soon as she had started looking for him she had realized something. *What happened in the past isn't important. This is who I am now. These are the people who are important to me.*

Closer than family.

She looked at Amar, walking up the road, trying to read both things at once. He looked fit and strong, healthy. Barely a trace of the pain a bullet had caused him over a year ago. He had kicked the drugs, controlled his drinking. Started working out again, looking after himself. And he had started dating again, not just casual bar pick-ups, but proper dates. And dating safely now, which, for a gay man who had once been as promiscuous as he had, was a weight off her mind.

They had argued about who would do what. Jamal had been adamant.

'Nah, man,' he had said back in Brighton. 'It's best if I stay here. Really.'

Peta had looked at him. He was seventeen, streetwise beyond his – and probably her – years but still just a boy. He was growing into a handsome young man. And he had joined the two of them in the gym, started to work out. With his mixed-race, light-skinned features giving him lean and attractive good looks, accompanied by his increasing taste in high-end urban fashionwear, he resembled a professional footballer, with the confidence but without the attitude or arrogance. She was proud of the part she had played in his upbringing. They all were.

'No,' she had said. 'Milsom's dangerous. We know that. What if he spots you? Finds you? What if he tries to do to you what he did to Joe?'

Jamal had smiled. 'He won't though, will he? He'll be lookin' for, like police an' proper tails an' stuff. He won't be expectin' me. I'll be like a ghost. Slippin' in an' out through the cracks in the pavement.' Jamal smiled, pleased with the analogy.

'OK ghost,' said Amar. 'Supposing you do stay.'

Jamal started to speak. Amar held up a hand for silence.

'And I'm not saying you do. Just supposing. What then?

What are you going to do if he's on the move and you have to follow him?'

'I've got my scooter.'

Donovan had bought him a scooter for his seventeenth birthday. Jamal had tried to pretend he didn't like it, that it was wussy and underpowered, but he was secretly thrilled with it. He had even insisted on bringing it down to Brighton in the back of Amar's battered old Volvo estate.

'I think he might move faster than a scooter,' said Peta. 'He might get on a train or move out of the city.'

'Then I'll follow him. Whatever. Leave your car here, man. I been takin' lessons.'

'My car?' said Amar.

'Not like it's a good one.'

Peta had hidden a smile at Amar's shocked face. Unsuccessfully. His taste for designer gear didn't extend as far as his car. Once he had calmed down, the two of them exchanged a glance then looked back at Jamal.

'Look, man,' Jamal said, his hands out, imploring. 'Just trust me, yeah? I ain't no kid any more. I can handle a job like this. If he does anythin' or goes on the move, like, I'll be on the phone like lightnin', you get me?'

Peta studied him, making up her mind. What he said sounded reasonable but she sensed there was something else, something he was avoiding. His eyes gave it away. They were going on the trail of missing boys, lost boys. Boys from horror-film families and uncaring care homes. Boys with pasts like Jamal. He didn't want to be reminded of it, she thought, didn't want his past dredged up again.

Another glance at Amar. He knew what she was thinking. He nodded. That sealed it.

'OK,' she said. 'But on one condition. My friend who's on the force here. The one who spotted Milsom. I'm going to ask him to come down and check you're OK. Work with you.'

'Ah, man, you don' have to do that.'

'I do, Jamal. Or you're not staying. This is serious. He's a professional. Consider him one of us for the duration.'

Jamal wanted to argue. But it was clear he had no choice. 'OK,' he grumbled.

'Good. Amar and I'll get on with this other thing. You stay here. But be careful.'

'You know me, man. Careful is my middle name.'

'After Mouthy and Tosser,' said Amar smiling.

Jamal looked hurt. 'No need to be rude, man. Just 'cos I dissed your car. An' you know it's true.' He smiled to show no offence. 'Look, peeps, I'll be good, yeah? I'm strong. I'll laser lock him like a heat-seekin' missile, man. Won't let him out of my sight.'

'I know,' said Peta.

Peta had made her call, everything was agreed there. They had left almost immediately.

'Here it is,' said Amar, trying to match the real coordinates with what his A to Z said.

'You sure?' Peta said. 'Your map-reading skills are worse than mine. Last time I asked you to find somewhere you confused Leamington Spa with Leaming Bar. You'll be telling me the Dogger Bank is in Jarrow next.'

'Dogger Bank? Isn't that outside Tynemouth? Didn't the police raid it last month? I think I've been there.'

She sighed. 'You can tell you don't listen to Radio 4.' She looked at the building before them. It was part of a low-level estate, social housing built as a response, and an antidote, to tower blocks like Trellick. There were signs that it had been the target of a recent overhaul. Replacement windows, unvandalized streetlighting, new front doors. Clean roads. It wasn't utopia but it wasn't the sink estate they had been expecting.

'This is the house here,' said Amar, consulting his paper once more. 'This is where Guy Brewster used to live.'

Guy Brewster. The first boy to have gone missing. The first boy to turn up dead. Anne Marie had lived in the area, in the street Amar and Peta were now standing in, for four years. It was, by her own account, where her son, Jack, had been conceived and born.

'Do we know who the father is?' asked Amar.

Peta shook her head. 'Apparently she never said. Even the birth certificate doesn't say.'

Peta and Amar had read Donovan's research. Guy Brewster had been nine years old. Already a lost boy, he had only been seen sporadically in school and spent most of his time roaming the estate and nearby railway line, committing acts of petty vandalism – throwing stones at windows, that kind of thing. He had been disruptive and violent in school so his teachers hadn't been too bothered when he stopped turning up. Since his mother's departure shortly after his birth, he had lived with his father, an alcoholic who had been violent and abusive towards him.

'Going nowhere, really,' Amar had said on reading the account.

'Nowhere good,' Peta had replied.

He had come to the attention of social workers but their reactive approach had ensured he wouldn't be looked after until something serious had happened to him.

'And something serious did happen to him,' said Peta. 'He was murdered.'

It was hard to pinpoint with any accuracy when he had actually gone missing since he spent most of his short life not being noticed. Even his death didn't invite much attention.

His body was found at the side of the main railway line in an old, disused, concrete tool store. Some children had been playing there and kicked down the semi-rotted door to find

Guy's decomposing body. He had been strangled then slashed with a blade. There was very little forensic evidence since the playing children had contaminated the scene of crime, and it was an era before CCTV cameras.

The police had conducted door-to-door enquiries but nothing had come of it. It wasn't the kind of area to be forthcoming. Guy's father had been hauled in for questioning and, despite being as unpleasant as possible, was clearly not guilty.

Guy's killer was never found. Eventually the police were needed elsewhere and the investigation was wound down, an open verdict recorded. An unpopular child was dead. Everyone agreed that, with his background and disposition, it had not been a question of if but when. The fact that it had been sooner rather than later was a little shocking, but there you go. Hardly unexpected.

But then something strange happened. Voices began to speak up on the estate. People were tired of living the way they were. In an area where semi-feral children could grow up and be murdered and no one was the slightest bit interested. Pressure groups were formed. Community action organizations took shape. In the absence of any real police presence, citizens' committees took matters into their own hands. Drug dealers and other undesirables were made unwelcome. Councils were pressed into doing repairs that they had ignored for years. Collective responsibility was taken. A sense of community was engendered. And the estate became a better place to live.

'Well, some good came of it,' Peta said.

'Wonder what Anne Marie made of it,' said Amar.

Peta looked up the street. 'I think we may be seeing someone who can provide the answer.'

Amar followed her gaze. A man was coming towards them, middle-aged, small, round. Grey hair bouncing with each step, stubbled, red cheeks. Wearing an anorak and jeans. He saw them, smiled.

He reached them. 'You the two I'm supposed to meet?'

Peta smiled, stuck out her hand. 'Tom Haig? I'm Peta Knight. This is Amar Miah. Thanks for arranging to see us at such short notice.'

'No problem.' He shook hands with her, nodded at Amar. He looked small and cherubic, with a face that seemed always ready to smile. Unapologetic London accent. 'So, what can I do for you?'

'You were Anne Marie Smeaton's probation officer, is that right?' said Peta.

He gave a small shrug. 'Probation officer, counsellor, therapist, call it what you like. I was her one-stop shop for keeping her on the straight and narrow.'

'Is that usual?' asked Amar.

'Pretty much. In cases like hers when they're given new identities, new lives. They have a guardian angel with them, or at least on call, pretty much twenty-four seven.'

'So you knew her well?' Peta again.

Another cherubic smile. 'I did. For a time.'

'And this area?' asked Amar.

Tom Haig looked round. 'Lived here all my life. Changed a bit in the last few years, I must say. Used to be really bad.' He nodded. 'Really bad.'

'You were around to see the change?'

'I like to think I was part of it. Well, the probation service, not just me.'

'What happened?' asked Peta.

'There was a boy murdered. Everything changed after that.'

'Would that be Guy Brewster?' asked Amar.

Tom Haig's eyebrows raised. 'It would.' He smiled. Peta could imagine him propping up the bar in a local folk club, pint of real ale in one hand. 'You've done your homework.' His brow furrowed. 'What is it you wanted, exactly?'

'Just a couple of things,' said Peta. 'Like I said on the phone, we're working with Anne Marie's solicitors. Just a background check, that kind of thing. Here when she said she was, story checks out, blah blah, you know. And while we were doing that we found out about this unsolved murder. Just interested us.'

Another smile from Tom Haig. 'So you're going to solve the crime, that it?'

Peta smiled. 'Sadly not. But I'm ex-police. Old habits die hard.'

He laughed. 'Know what you mean. I'm ex-probation. Same thing. You can't stop banging them up, I can't stop trying to keep them out.'

He laughed, Peta joined in. Amar smiled.

'Anyway, long time ago,' said Tom Haig. 'Nothing to do with Anne Marie, either.'

'She didn't know the dead boy or his father?'

Tom Haig shook his head. 'Not that I know of, no.'

Peta looked at the house where Guy Brewster had lived. It had new windows, a well-tended patch of lawn in front. A shining front door. 'I think we can assume Brewster Senior no longer lives here.'

Tom Haig followed her gaze. 'He doesn't. When the clean-up operation took off, so did he. No one's heard of him since.'

'And when did Anne Marie move?'

'Let me think.' He closed his eyes.

'Around about the same time?' asked Amar.

Tom Haig opened his eyes. 'Might have been.' A wary look came over his features. 'You're not suggesting she . . .'

'No,' said Peta quickly. Perhaps too quickly. 'Not at all. Like I said, just interested.'

'Right.' The wary look hadn't disappeared from his face.

'How was she at the time?' said Peta.

'How d'you mean?'

Peta shrugged. 'You know. Mentally, emotionally. That kind of thing. We're just trying to build up a picture of her.'

Tom Haig didn't look entirely happy, but he continued. 'Fine, for the most part. As well as could be, you know.' He thought for a few seconds. 'Mind you, thinking about it, when that boy died, it changed her.'

'In what way?' asked Amar.

Tom Haig gave his words careful consideration, like he didn't know whether to trust them. Peta and Amar said nothing, waited.

'She said she couldn't live here any more. It was giving her nightmares. Said the boy's death had triggered something.'

'What?'

'I don't know. She wouldn't say. But she felt she would do something awful if she wasn't moved. And she was pregnant by this time.'

'So you moved her.'

Tom Haig nodded. 'To Bristol. And that was when my involvement with her ended.'

'There is something that puzzles me, though,' Amar said. 'If there's a boy been murdered, and someone living nearby has just come out of prison for murdering a child, wouldn't the police look at her first?'

'I believe they did at the time,' said Tom Haig. 'Found nothing. Which is a good thing. For her. I mean, she's done her time. What's to be gained by persecuting her? She hadn't done anything wrong.'

Amar nodded, said nothing. Tom Haig looked between the pair of them then at his watch.

'So has this been any help? Only I've got to dash. Might

be ex-probation but I still do consultancy for them. Still sit on their committees.'

'No problem,' said Peta. 'Thanks for your time.'

They shook hands.

'What's it for, by the way? All these questions? You writing a book, or something?'

Peta smiled, aimed for breezy with her answer. 'You could say that. Anne Marie's collaborating on a book of her life. We just have to do the leg work, check out what she says is true.'

Tom Haig nodded, taking the information. 'So how is she? Anne Marie.'

'She's . . . well,' said Peta. 'Doing well.'

'And her boy? He must be . . . God, sixteen now?'

'Nearly sixteen, yes.'

'Jesus. Tempus fugit, ay?'

Peta agreed.

'So where is she?' he asked.

'Sorry. Can't say.'

'No, course not.' He laughed. 'Well, never mind.'

He turned and made his way back up the street.

Peta and Amar watched him go. 'Well, that was pointless,' he said.

'You never know,' said Peta. 'You have to do these things.'

'What he said,' said Amar. 'About looking into the boy's death. We're not really doing that, are we?'

'Not really. If we find out it's her that did it, though, we've got them all solved.'

'True. But it's still a shame, isn't it?' He looked round. Some people live or die and no one cares.'

Peta nodded.

Amar seemed aware that his introspection was spreading so quickly snapped out of it. 'Right. So where next?'

'Where d'you think?' she said. 'Bristol.'

'Why did you move away from the Powell Estate?'

'Have you been there?' She gives a weak smile.

He shakes his head. 'You know I haven't.'

'Well, you wouldn't ask if you had. Like I said, it was awful. No place to bring up a kid.'

'No other reason?'

She shakes her head.

'Anne Marie's shaking her head,' he says into the recorder. He leans back, wondering how to pose the next question. 'What about Guy Brewster? Did his death have any influence on your leaving?'

'Should it have done?'

'I don't know. I'm just wondering whether that was what made you decide to move. A boy dies near to where you're living. Murdered. If people knew you lived there they might put two and two together.'

'And come up with six.' She spits the words out.

'I'm just speculating. That's all.'

She breathes in deeply through her nose, her nostrils flare as she does so. 'I had nothin' to do with that boy's death. Nothin'. I didn't even know him, right?'

'OK. I had to ask.'

She nods her head. 'I know. An' I said I would be honest. An' I am bein'. It's just . . .' She sighs. Heavily. 'You've got no idea. You're a nice bloke an' that, but you've got no idea.' She sighs again, reaches for the cigarettes. Her hand shakes.

'Next question,' she says.

12

Abigail looked out of the window. She saw a river, hotels, a huge, rounded concert hall made of shimmering, undulating curves. An art gallery in an old flour mill. Landmark bridges. She saw a city she didn't know. Yet she felt safe.

She turned back to the living room she was in. The flat seemed like a hotel suite that a long-stayer had made himself comfortable in. It wasn't homely — there were very few books or CDs and nothing on the walls, things she measured homeliness and comfort by — but it seemed lived in. Like there was a real, warm human presence. She put her arms round herself, hugged. The borrowed T-shirt she had worn to sleep in had an image of the first issue of the X-Men on it. She looked at it, smiled. He hadn't changed.

She looked out of the window again. Sighed. Her heart felt heavy, her head confused. She had slept soundly last night, exhaustion claiming her to a near comatose degree, the stress of the last few days taking its toll, working its way out.

She was here now. She had made it. But she still didn't know what she was going to do next.

She heard movement behind her, turned.

'Sorry,' he said, making his way into the room. 'Didn't mean to wake you.'

'That's OK,' she said, suddenly aware of herself to an awkward degree. 'I was awake anyway.'

He nodded, stayed at the other side of the room, keeping his distance, giving her space. 'I phoned . . .' He paused, the word he wanted unfamiliar to him. 'Mum. Told her you were here.'

'What did she say?' Quickly, suddenly alarmed.

He gave her an appraising look then his face broke into a reassuring smile. 'Told her you were here. That everything was fine.'

She listened, nodded, said nothing. Then: 'Did she . . . did she say anything?'

'Not really. I said we'd talk later. When you'd rested. When we'd had a chance to talk properly.' He became suddenly tongue-tied. 'Listen, Mum hasn't said anything yet. Do you . . . do you want to talk yet? About why you're here?'

She thought for a moment, deciding. 'No. Not yet.'

'OK,' he said, 'that's fine.'

She saw the relief on his face, guessed his parenting skills were somewhat rusty. Relieved as well, she sat down on the sofa. 'What happened to your house?' she said. 'Why are you here?'

He scratched his ear, looked uncomfortable. 'That's a long and boring story,' he said, aiming for offhand.

'Well, make it short and interesting,' she said.

He gave her a direct look, slightly taken aback. Then laughed. 'That's my girl.' He sat down at the other end of the sofa. 'It burned down.'

She sat forward, looked alarmed.

He spoke before she could. 'Well, it's OK, I'm OK. No damage done. Well, books, CDs, stuff like that. Stuff that can be replaced. But no real damage done.' He tried not to think of his son's face. Wondered whether he would ever see it again.

'How did it happen?'

He didn't speak straightaway, as if rehearsing words in his head before letting them out. 'Just . . . an accident. One of those things.'

'So why didn't you tell us?'

'I told your mother. She mustn't have mentioned it.'

'She's had a lot on her mind recently.' The words said bitterly, an undercurrent of anger.

Donovan noted it, decided the time wasn't right to press further. 'Anyway,' he said, 'no real harm done. Jamal and I were OK.'

'Who's Jamal?'

'The lad who lives with me.'

She felt a seismic shift beneath her. She didn't know this man at all. 'What? What d'you mean, lives with you?'

'What d'you think I mean? He's seventeen, he had nowhere to live, so I took him in and gave him a job.'

She looked around. 'So where is he now?'

'Brighton. With the rest of the team. Working.'

'Why aren't you there, then?'

'I'm working on something here.'

She shook her head, not sure if she was taking everything in. He looked at her. 'Problem?'

'Well, it's just . . . your house burns down and I don't get to hear about it, plus you've got a boy living with you. A Muslim boy from the sounds of it.'

'No, he's not.'

She stood up, exasperated. And if she was honest, a little bit afraid. 'I just . . . I don't know you. A *boy* . . .'

'OK.' His voice was calm. 'When I met him he was living on the streets. Being bought and sold by perverts. He came to me because he needed my help. So Peta and Amar and I got him out of there. He's one of the bravest people I've ever met. So we gave him a home. And a job. And he's doing fine now. Fine.'

She looked out of the window again, struggled for words. 'Well. You should have let us know. That's all.'

'Abigail, are you angry at me or your mother?'

'Both.' Plosively spat out, as only a teenager could. 'Why didn't you tell me? Never mind her, why didn't you tell me?'

'Well, the last time we met, you didn't exactly make me welcome.'

She felt anger rising again within her. 'Can you blame me? You turn up at the house six months ago, I don't know why you're there or what you've been doing, you tell me you'll soon have news about . . .' She couldn't say his name. 'Then nothing. Next time you call you behave like you never said anything, like nothing happened. And now this . . .'

He sighed. 'Sorry. It didn't work out the way I thought it would.' He snorted a harsh laugh. 'Story of my life.'

Her anger subsided at his words. She fell silent.

'Right,' he said, standing up, 'that's the air cleared. Let's concentrate on the present. You're here now. So what can we do with you today?'

'Are you going to send me back? To Mum?'

'Do you want to go back?'

She thought of what awaited her if she did. What had made her leave in the first place. 'Not . . . right now.'

'OK. Fine. Then you're welcome to stay.'

'Thank you. How long?'

He smiled. 'Long as you like. Treat it like your home. Or home from home. Your mother can contact your school, sort it with them. Don't worry.'

'Right.' She looked out of the window again.

He started to walk away then turned back to her. 'Hey, Abigail.'

She turned. 'Yeah?'

'Good to have you here.'

She smiled and felt relief and relaxation in that smile. She only nodded again, not trusting her voice to speak. She turned back to the window, looked out again.

'Right,' she heard her father say behind her. 'Breakfast . . .' He went into the kitchen.

Missing the tears that sprang into her eyes. Good. She didn't want him to see them.

She kept looking out of the window at the new city.

She smiled.

'Thanks for coming. Short notice, really appreciate it.' Tess Preston had polished up and trotted out her best estuary accent in the hope it would impress. She was desperately trying to lose the Posh Bird tag the guys in the office had given her.

'No problem, Posh Bird.' Well, that was a waste of time.

Tess looked at the man. Ray Collins looked like a street-fighting gnome. He was a seasoned old Fleet Street hack in his forties, with long, greased back shoulder-length dirty grey/blonde hair and matching beard, an oily, mottled complexion, wearing jeans, work boots and a battered leather jacket that, like its owner, had seen plenty of action in super soaraway skirmishes and various tabloid warzones over the years. He was, Tess knew, one of the best photographers she could get. Or get from the office at short notice.

'What's the story, then?' Ray Collins's voice was authentic cockney geezer, gravelled and roughened by years of Benson and Hedges, whisky at all hours and screaming from the terraces at Upton Park.

They walked through the front doors of the hotel to the car park, Collins hefting his camera bag on to his shoulder, towards Tess's Golf. She was proud of her Golf. Not the biggest, best or fastest car but a damned good place to start. Unfortunately it also had dreaded Posh Bird connotations, but she couldn't manage everything.

They got in the car. At close range, Tess noticed Collins smelled of tobacco and old leather. Tess didn't mind. To her it was the smell of success. And success was what she was about. Especially now. She was so excited by what she had discovered she was practically buzzing.

'What's it all about?' she said, heading the car east along the quayside. 'I tell you. This is going to be the biggest story of the year. Huge.'

Collins nodded, said nothing. Took a cigarette out of the pack, stuck it in his mouth, lit up.

Tess grimaced immediately. She hated smoking. She wasn't that keen on drinking, but she knew they were things that had to be tolerated if she was to make it in this racket. Her fingers went to open the window but she stopped herself. That's not what a pro would do. A pro would grin and bear it. A pro would join in.

'You got a spare one?' she asked.

'These aren't Posh Bird fags.'

Collins exhaled. Tess found herself momentarily driving through fog.

'You were sayin'. Biggest story of the year an' all that.'

'Yeah.' Tess hadn't been able to get the woman she had seen out of her mind so she had spent the night going through her scrapbook. She carried it with her everywhere she went. It was her diary, how she measured her life. Proof of who she was and what she had achieved. If her house were on fire it would be the first thing she would save. It would be the only thing she would save.

She had leafed through it, hoping to find the story that went with the woman's image. She knew it was something big, something important, but she couldn't place exactly what. She went all through the book, left to right, right to left, open at random pages, nothing. There was no story. That got her doubting. Maybe it was someone off the TV after all. She thought even more. Went through her notes, her phone, her laptop.

And eventually she found it. The story. And she was right. It was a big one.

She had phoned her editor. She didn't care that it was the middle of the night, or that she wasn't senior enough to have her mobile number. This was news. Big news. She would thank her for it.

Once her editor had finished bawling her out for calling in the middle of the night, she said: 'This better be fucking good. Or you'll be looking for another job in the morning.'

Tess assured her it was good. The best. 'Remember a few years ago, that child killer?'

'Which one?'

'The female one. When she was a kid she killed another kid. In the Sixties.'

'Mae Blacklock. As was. What about her?'

She swallowed hard, tried to keep the tremble out of her voice. 'I know where she lives.'

'Good for you. So does everyone. You'll get your P45 in the morning. Good night.'

'No wait . . .' This was it. Make or break. She swallowed again, started. 'That's right, yes. Someone found out where she was living. We all went down there. I can remember it because it was one of my first stories. I was a trainee at the time. Then there was this court injunction stopping us from printing. Because of her son, or something. He didn't know who she really was.'

'That's right. So what?'

'The kid's nearly sixteen. Or turned sixteen. They moved her but I've found her again.'

Her editor was interested, but she felt that interest could go either way.

'And listen to this. There's been a murder. Right on her doorstep. A boy. Stabbed. Coincidence? I think not.'

She had her full attention now, she knew it.

'Go on,' she said.

'Well, I checked up on it. Where she last lived, in Hull, when she was nearly outed, there was a murder there, too. A boy. Knifed to death. She moved straight afterwards.'

'Fuck . . .'

Tess allowed herself a small smile. 'You see what I mean?'

'You got a photographer with you?'

'No, we're using agency for this.'

'I'll get one sent up.' She paused. She could guess what she was thinking. 'You sure about this? Definitely her?'

Tess thought of seeing the woman the night before. Was it coincidence she was on a part of the estate journalists wouldn't venture into? 'As sure as I can be.'

'Get some corroboration. And some photos. They got any floral tributes up? Any of that shit?'

'Plenty at the school gates.'

'See if you can get a snap of her beside them. Killer's guilt, or something.'

Tess felt a ripple of excitement running through her. Not a ripple – more like a wave. 'Will do.'

She thought again. 'Tess, the last time this fell apart because of the boy. Because the Press Complaints Commission said it wasn't in the public interest. So we couldn't publish. I don't want that to happen again. It needs to be airtight.'

'What would you suggest?'

'Get me photos, a story, someone close to her going on record. A testimony. "I let evil killer babysit my kids." Something like that. Get me airtight, get me overwhelming public interest and we're good to go.'

'How soon?'

'Soon as. Airtight and legal can do it on the run.'

Tess grinned. 'Got it.'

'And Tess?'

'Yeah?'

'Don't ever phone me in the middle of the night again. For whatever reason. Or I will fucking sack you.'

She put the phone down. Tess danced round the room.

'Biggest story of the year, an' all that.'

Ray Collins was irritated that Tess hadn't answered him.

'Yeah, sorry. I'll tell you.' She told him.

Another plume of smoke, another grunt. 'So she's gone for it an' sent me up.'

'That's it.'

Collins sucked the life from his fag, threw the butt out of the window. Tess hoped he would leave it open, air the car out a bit but he closed it straightaway. She would have to have it fumigated after this job. But the money she would make in bonuses would be worth it.

'I think the kid's nearly sixteen,' said Tess. 'Or sixteen now. We can move on it straightaway. Get some shots, reaction, that kind of thing. I'll try to find someone to talk to on the record. And there's something else.' Tess grinned. This was the part she had kept until last, the part that would, even if it wasn't true, make her reputation. 'The story I came up here to cover. A kid's murder. Happened on the estate she lives on.' She assumed an American accent. It was as unconvincing as her estuary one. 'Coincidence? I think not.'

The accent was wasted on Collins. 'So what? I get some photos of the kid? Of her?'

'Yeah. That kind of thing.'

'So you know where she lives?'

'I know the area. But not the flat itself.'

'We gonna find out?'

'That's where we're going now.'

'Bit risky all this, innit? Legal been on to it?'

'She says if we make it airtight it'll be of overwhelming public interest. We can get round it that way. So let's do it.'

Another grunt from Collins, another cigarette. Not the response Tess had been hoping for. Tess also thought that now wasn't the time for a lecture about the health risks of passive smoking.

Now was the time to break the story of a lifetime.

'So tell me about Jack.'

She lights another cigarette, takes a mouthful of coffee. A large one. Uses both actions to think before answering. 'What d'you want to know?' she says eventually.

He shrugs. 'About him. His life. His upbringing. Has it been difficult for him moving around the country, not being able to settle in one place for too long?'

She shrugs this time. Again it's a cover for her thoughts. 'S'pose so.'

'Has he ever said anything? Acted in a certain way about it? Tell me about him.'

She sighs, knowing the questions aren't going to go away until she answers them. 'He's a lovely lad. A really lovely lad. I think the sun shines out of him. I do.' And she does. He sees it in her wistful smile, in the summery glaze creeping over her eyes. 'He's my world.' She stubs her cigarette out as she gets talking. He's noticed she does this as her defences come down. 'All those years, in prison an' everythin'. I just wanted somethin', someone. To . . .' She pulls back, takes a mouthful of coffee, gives an apologetic half-smile. 'Sorry,' she says. 'This sounds wanky when I say it out loud.'

He smiles, encouragingly.

'But . . .' She shrugs again. 'It's true. I did want somethin' like that. Someone like that. I used to have lots of time on me own, I was always kickin' off. I wasn't what you'd call a model prisoner for a lot of the time, I mean I even escaped once. But yeah. I used to think that. If I had somethin' to love or someone waitin' for us when I got out. An' when I got out I had Jack.' A smile splits her face. A true one this time, no half measures. 'An' he's my world. My big, beautiful boy.'

'Is it tough on Rob knowing you think that about Jack?'

She shakes her head. 'He knows. That was part of the deal when I met him. An' he was fine with it. But Jack . . . he's a bright boy. Really. Reads all the time. He deserves the best. The best I can do for him.' She sighs. 'That's why I'm doin' this, isn't it?'

He senses there's more to come. He waits.

'But I do worry about him.'

'Only natural. Don't all mothers worry about their children? All parents about their sons?'

She leans forward, wanting to make sure he understands what she means. 'Not all mothers did what I did when they were eleven years old. Not all mothers spend the rest of their lives payin' for it one way or another.'

'No, I just meant—'

'No, it's all right. I know.' She sighs again. 'I just worry. I worry that whatever was in me is in him. Maybe it's somethin' psychological. Maybe it's hereditary. Maybe it's . . . I don't know. A bad spirit, or something.' She tries to laugh but it sounds hollow and unconvincing even to herself.

He says nothing.

'I mean, I know it can't be. But I just worry. That it's in the bone.'

'What is?'

'It. The bad shit. It's supposed to be psychological, because of my upbringing, an' that. Because of my mother. Like they said. But I worry that he's like me. That he's too much like me.'

She reaches for another cigarette.

'I worry that she's put somethin' in me an' I've passed it down to him. I worry that he's goin' to turn out like me.'

13

'How. You. Aye, you. What are you lookin' at?'

Jack's head came up sharply from the hardback library book he had been reading. *The Boy in the Striped Pyjamas.* He was completely engrossed in it. He was unaware that he had been looking at anyone. He recognized the voice straight away. Renny. The little, stocky, shaven-headed kid who was quickly becoming obnoxious.

Jack had hoped his day at school would go OK. Put everything that had recently happened behind him, just get on with his life. The reporters were still hanging round the school, along with police. Floral tributes to Calvin Bell were piling up at the gates and in the alley on the estate he had died in. Plastic-wrapped mostly, some with little teddy bears attached or Newcastle United scarves. Hand-written cards talking about what a loss he is and asking God to put him with the other angels. Jack wasn't a cynic, but he doubted that angel was a word Calvin Bell had often been described with. Or any kid round here.

He could see a reporter standing in front of the school gates, instructing his cameraman to get a good shot of the flowers before delivering his speech to camera, his face mournful as if he's personally upset.

'I'm talkin' to you. Fuckin' weirdo. Fuckin' spazz.'

Renny moved closer to Jack, Pez trailing behind him. Jack hadn't made many friends and spent most of his break-times alone, reading. He loved getting lost in books, having other worlds open before him. So much better than the real one. Even the one he was reading about. Concentration camps, the Second World War.

Renny stood over him. Jack ignored him, tried to keep reading.

'Saw you last night. Out with your mother. Holdin' hands, weren't you? Fuckin' weirdo. Fuckin' paedo mother.'

Jack's hands started to shake as he gripped the book even harder. He refused to rise to it, just kept his head down.

'You ignorin' me?'

Jack was doing exactly that. He stared at the words, not understanding them. All he could see was the shadow of the other boy.

'How. I'm talkin' to you.' The boy's voice had taken on a harder edge. Nastier. Much nastier.

It was no good. He had to look up. And widened his eyes in surprise. Renny was sporting a black eye, cuts and bruises on his cheeks. His eyes were aflame, angered, like he had been stopped in the middle of a fight and wanted to finish it. With whoever he could find.

'What happened to your face?' Jack asked, closing his book but keeping his place with a finger.

Renny was taken aback. He hadn't anticipated that question. His mouth moved but the words were slow in emerging.

'Never . . . never . . .' His anger overtook him again. 'What the fuck's the matter with you? Eh? You a fuckin' puff? Eh? What's the matter with your face. Puff. Paedo mother an' a fuckin' baby for holdin' her hand an' a puff. That it?'

Jack frowned. He couldn't follow the words but he knew the boy was building up to something and he knew it wouldn't be good. For him.

Renny stood his ground before him, balling and

unballing his hands into fists. Snorting through his nostrils.
Jack knew that it would only take one more word, one
more sentence. He knew that whatever came out of his
mouth next would be the excuse Renny needed to take a
swing at him. Jack was shaking, his legs vibrating inside his
trousers, his hands holding the book unable to keep still. He
hoped it didn't show.

It was clear to Jack that Renny had his agenda of aggression and that now it was no longer a question of if but
when. He would have to be ready for him. Or get up and
walk away. That was what he tried to do. Renny blocked his
way.

'You startin', eh?' Renny pushed into Jack. 'Eh? Eh?'

Renny pushed him backwards. He stumbled on the wall
he had been sitting on, angling his legs for balance, putting
out his arm to keep upright, not letting go of his book, or
his place in the book. Renny moved in. Jack waited for the
punch.

'Fuckin' puff, fuckin' puff . . .'

Renny swung his arm back, telegraphing his intent.
Jack moved to the side as he did so, hoping to dodge the
blow that he knew would be aimed at his face. It connected with his shoulder, sending shockwaves of pain all
the way down his left arm. He let out a gasp, tried to move
out of the way.

'Bastard . . .'

Renny was coming for him again. Not trusting himself to
get away so quickly this time, Jack brought his right hand up,
still holding the library book. He removed his finger, no
longer bothered about marking his place, and held the book
round the spine. Then, summoning up as much rage as he
could manage, brought it down sharply on the bridge of
Renny's nose.

Renny howled in agony. Blood began to pump from his

left nostril. Playing the advantage, Jack smashed the spine of the book underneath Renny's nose, along his top lip. It was a move someone had taught him years ago. There was a cluster of nerve endings there and if they were hit hard enough and sharp enough the blow could make the biggest opponent crumple.

Jack hit him hard and sharp. Ignored the blood that spattered the book, just watched the other boy reel backwards in pain, his hand to his face, and fall to the ground.

Jack looked at Pez who was standing there as if struck by lightning. He was about to say something to him but didn't get the opportunity.

'You!'

Jack turned. Mr Heptonstall, the head teacher, was striding across the yard to see him. The other children had stopped what they were doing and turned to look.

'Yes, you. In my office now!'

As he walked he was glancing to either side. Keenly aware of the film crews around, Jack thought, eager not to get any more bad publicity for his school.

On the ground, Renny was trying to get up.

'And you. Both of you. Now.'

Jack didn't bother to look behind him, just followed Heptonstall to the office. As he walked he looked at the book in his hand. The spine was dented, the plastic cover blood-splattered.

He hoped it was still readable.

'That behaviour, as I have said before, would be unacceptable in my school at the best of times. However, need I remind you that this week is not the best of times.'

Heptonstall stopped pacing, looked at the two boys. Jack returned his gaze. He didn't go seeking violence or trouble but when it came he was ready to stand his ground. He

always had been. But he had a temper, though. He knew
that. And he found it hard to let something go once it had
started. That was the main reason he tried to avoid con-
frontation as much as possible. Because he hated to feel that
way.

'And don't look at me like that, Smeaton.'

Jack held his gaze. Heptonstall tried to do likewise but,
despite his anger and authority, couldn't. The teacher
turned away. Jack saw doubt behind his eyes. And fear at
the new boy, the boy who had the arrogance and temer-
ity to stand up to him. Some would have considered that
a personal victory. Jack didn't. It would, he knew, be
something that would make him feel sad once his anger
had subsided. But not yet. Not when it still burned so
brightly.

'Disgraceful.' Heptonstall turned to Renny. The boy had
cleared the blood from his face as best he could but that,
together with the earlier cuts and bruises, made him look
like he had just been pulled from a car wreck. 'Renwick,
you're well on the way to being excluded from this school.
Permanently. And don't think it's something I'm not looking
forward to.' He turned back to Jack. 'And Smeaton . . .' He
sighed. 'I don't know what to make of you. You seemed a
different kind of boy to' – he gestured towards Renwick –
'the usual kind we get here.' He shook his head. 'I don't
know what's happened.'

Hentonstall stopped pacing, turned and faced them both.
'What did happen?'

Neither boy spoke.

Heptonstall looked from one to the other. 'Well?'

Neither spoke. Jack knew that the proper thing to do
would be to tell the truth. Say he was provoked. That it
looked worse because of the blood. And that most of
Renny's facial injuries had been inflicted before the fight.

And not by him. But he knew better than to say anything. He had no love for Renny and didn't want to get himself into further trouble but he knew that if he sided with the teachers, once word got round Renny, Pez and others could make his life at this school intolerable. And he didn't want that. Not here. He wanted to stay here, keep his head down, live his life in peace.

So he said nothing.

Heptonstall, realizing he was going to get no further, sat down behind his desk. 'You are to go home and stay there until the end of the week. Letters will be sent to your parents. Although, Renwick, with yours I doubt that will make the slightest bit of difference. Now.' He waved towards the door. 'Out.'

Renny turned and walked out. Jack looked between the door and the head teacher. Nothing like this had ever happened to him before. His anger was subsiding and he was beginning to realize just how serious this affair could be for him.

Heptonstall looked at him. 'You too, Smeaton. Out.'

Jack closed his mouth again. Left the office.

Outside, Renny was standing there.

'Thought you'd squeal your fuckin' head off in there,' he said.

Jack just looked at him, saying nothing. Letting him have the last vestiges of his disappearing anger.

Renny nodded. 'Good lad. But I still fuckin' hate you.'

He turned and walked away. Rolling his shoulders as he walked, aiming for dignity with a sneer on his face, sporting the victory that only comes in defeat, the knowledge that comes when you've been branded as society's refuse. The unwanted. The unloved. The ultimate outsider.

Jack waited until he had left the building and, not wanting

to be seen with him, walked out of the building and out of the school grounds.

No idea where he was headed, just as long as Renny wasn't there.

'So after West London . . .'

She rolls her eyes at the memory of the place.

'It was Bristol?'

She nods.

'For the record.'

'Bristol, yes.'

'And were you happy there? Or happier?'

She thinks about the question. Hard. Like she is rehearsing which answer to give and can't decide how much of the truth should be in it. 'Happier,' she decides on at last. I don't think you can ever be truly happy. I think you'd be some kind of gimp if you were.'

'Anyone in particular, in general, or just you?'

'Anyone. I think anyone who says they're happy is just lyin'. To themselves.'

'So what do you believe in then, if not happiness?'

She thought again. 'I think you can get pockets of happiness, of contentment, like. But you don't get many. And they don't last long.'

'Is that what Bristol was for you? A pocket of contentment?'

She thinks again. At least, he notices, she doesn't go for the cigarettes or the coffee or any of her usual props. She just takes her time thinking, leading him to believe he'll get a truthful answer.

'Up to a point,' she says.

'What happened then?'

'It stopped bein' happy.'

'You'll have to give me more than that.'

She sighs. Looks at the cigarette packet. He can see she wants to take one out but she stops herself. She thinks again, makes a decision. 'I was happy. With Jack. Really happy. Bristol was all right. St Paul's, it was. I mean, it wasn't the best of places and they looked at us strange because I talked funny. Well, to them. They talked funny to me. But we were, I suppose, happy there. We had a nice house, I had a part-time job in a shop, we had nice neighbours, I had friends. You know, I don't make friends easily. I'm sure you can understand that. But I had friends there that I really liked.'

'Were you still having difficulty with your new identity? Or had you settled in by then?'

'No, I was doin' all right. Once we'd escaped from London—'

'Escaped? Why d'you say escaped? From what? From who?'

She looks at him, then away, deciding whether to say more.

'I just mean from London. From the Powell Estate, an' that.' Her voice was high, unconvincing. She was lying, but he couldn't call her on it.

'OK. Go on. Your new identity. Were you settled in it?'

'Well, occasionally somethin' would happen and I'd be reminded of the past, but not often. I was all right. It probably doesn't sound like much to you, but when you'd been through what I'd been through, a normal life was the only thing I wanted.'

'So what happened?'

She sighs. 'Somethin' always comes along to spoil it.'

'Something?'

She nods. 'Or someone.'

14

'You know,' said Peta, looking out in front of her, eyes squinting against the late autumn sun, 'when people say they like Bristol I don't think they really mean that. I think they just mean here. Not that horrible, concrete city centre, just here. Clifton.'

Amar was standing next to her, the span of the Clifton Suspension Bridge over the River Avon and Downs in front of them. The weather had held out and the view was beautiful. The trees around them held falling brown and red leaves and behind them Georgian terraces and townhouses stretched and wound, continuing the picture postcard prettiness. It was the kind of view that made Peta forget what she did for a living, that even threatened to restore her long-lost faith in humanity.

'I doubt Anne Marie lived round here.' Amar looked at the papers, the map, the scene in front of him. 'Doubt she even came here. Or the boy who was murdered.'

Peta turned to him, his words breaking the spell. A cloud obscured the sun rendering the buildings a dull grey. The trees were just denuded brown stumps, the bridge iron and brick. 'No,' she said, 'you're right. Probably lived somewhere horrible and concrete. And the same for the boy.'

Bristol was the second place on the list of places Anne Marie had lived and also the site of the second boy to die.

'What was his name?' asked Peta.

Amar checked the papers in his hands although he knew the name off by heart. 'Adam Wainwright.'

Amar had printed off everything Donovan had sent them about the cases. He had read them aloud to Peta in the car as they had travelled, bringing her up to speed as she had attempted to do the same by flooring the accelerator. They had reached the city from West London in less than two hours.

Adam Wainwright's death differed from the first in that he hadn't lived at his family home but had been in care. A difficult, angry and inarticulate boy of nine. Hard to love and he found it harder even to find love. They had found a photo in an online news archive. It showed a boy with close-cropped hair and angry eyes too scared to show vulnerability. He had willed his features to be as hard, cold and impervious as concrete.

His mother had been a heroin addict, his father unknown. When she died of AIDS, and with no other relatives claiming responsibility, Adam had been moved to Beech House, a state-run children's home on the outskirts of the city – the horrible concrete side – that had eventually been investigated for allegations of abuse.

'Apparently his murder was the catalyst for getting the home closed down,' said Amar. 'The home was investigated as part of the murder inquiry and a few inconsistencies came to light.'

Peta frowned. 'Inconsistencies?'

Amar shrugged. 'That's what it said in the report. Inconsistencies. I remembered it because it seemed so . . . incongruous to everything else going on.'

'Incongruous inconsistencies,' said Peta, an involuntary smile playing on her lips. 'Get you.'

Amar didn't rise to it. 'Let's walk while we talk.'

They turned away from the bridge that had now lost its allure to Peta. The sun had made a re-emergence as if to apologize for breaking Peta's feel-good spell but it was too late, she thought. The damage had been done.

'So the home gets closed down and the abuse allegations investigated. Anything turn up? Any prosecutions?'

'Don't know. Nothing involving the guy we're going to see; he came out of it clean. Although he may be able to tell us more.'

A name stood out from the reports: Martin Flemyng. He had been Adam Wainwright's social worker at the time of the boy's death. He was reported as being horrified by what had happened and left social services soon afterwards, apparently horrified that he hadn't been able to stop either Adam's death or the abuse. His name hadn't come up in connection with the Beech House investigations.

Amar had phoned him on the way. He had been wary at first but once Amar had explained that he and his colleague were looking into Adam Wainwright's death once again his tone changed and he said he would be delighted to meet them. He told them he still lived in Bristol, Clifton, to be precise, and arranged to meet them in a nearby café.

Amar and Peta walked down the main street through Clifton village. It seemed as if the word 'boutique' had been coined for it. Designer clothes shops, bathroom shops, stores that sold nothing but chi-chi frou-frou and made Peta wonder how they made a living. Then she saw the price tags. Even the pubs and cafés were hip and designer, even the charity shops, come to that.

Adam Wainwright's body had been found on a patch of abandoned ground by the old docks that had been earmarked for redevelopment. New flats.

'Same pattern as before,' Peta said. 'Wasteground. Away from home, houses, anything. Cause of death?'

Amar consulted his papers once more. 'Strangled.'

'That's all? Nothing about stabbing?'

He scanned the paper, didn't find what he was looking

for, leafed through to another. Sighed. 'I don't see why I had to carry all this. Why couldn't you? I'm a man of action. I deal with computers, surveillance. Not . . .' He rifled the papers. '. . . this stuff.'

Peta suppressed a smile. Badly. 'Come on, man of action, less of the queeny fits and more facts, please.'

Amar shook his head, kept scanning. He almost collided with a student coming the other way. He sighed, found what he was looking for. 'This should tell us. The coroner's report on the death.' He scanned it, stopping still to do so. 'Here we are. Death by strangulation.'

'Hands or an object?'

He scanned again. 'Ligature marks . . . fibres . . . plastic . . . they've speculated on a length of clothes line. Something like that.'

'Not hands. Right. Knife marks?'

'Yep. Here we are. Slashes to the stomach and genitals.'

A woman gave him a look of terror as she passed. He gave a weak smile in return.

'Come on,' said Peta, 'keep walking.'

He did so. 'The marks were thought to be done post-mortem.' He stopped, looked at her. 'Same as the last one.'

Peta nodded. 'Or before that.'

He knew what she meant. Right back to Mae Blacklock's original crime. The same MO. Exactly.

'Come on then,' said Peta. 'Nearly there.'

They reached the end of the parade of shops, kept walking. Peta gave one last look behind her as the road took them downwards, a regretful look that said goodbye to the chocolate-box beauty of Clifton. Then she turned and, along with Amar, went to keep their appointment. Preparing to rejoin the real world.

Their real world.

*

'Hello, boys. What have you got for me?'

Tess Preston sat in a moulded plastic chair attached to a Formica table in a local greasy spoon. In fact, she thought, it wasn't just the spoon that was greasy it was the whole place. She could even feel her skin becoming oleaginous. Long bath in the hotel tonight. In front of her she had a mug of tea that looked strong enough to go six rounds with Ricky Hatton. It was undrinkable. But she had persevered, taken a few mouthfuls. Because she felt it was the kind of thing a posh bird wouldn't have done. And because Ray Collins, as impassive as Iron Man in the seat next to her, had downed his already.

At the other side of the table were Renny and Pez. The bigger boy looked like he actually had gone six rounds with Ricky Hatton. His nose was swollen and red, the blood hastily wiped away, his eye blackened and enlarged, his cheeks nicked and cut.

'So what's the other bloke look like?' said Tess, smiling.

Pez started to laugh in his usual snorting, braying way, but a look from Renny silenced him. Renny then stared at Tess, leaning forward threateningly, scowling. Tess involuntarily moved back, then checked herself. This was a boy. She shouldn't be scared of a boy. A twelve-year-old. But she was scared of this boy. And plenty more she had seen on the estate. Beside her, Tess felt Ray Collins move. There was no change in his face but there was a light in his eyes. Enjoyment at Tess's discomfort, perhaps? Boredom? She didn't know. She felt her cheeks reddening, looked back at Renny.

'So,' she said, clearing her throat and trying to remain in charge, 'what have you got for me?'

Renny and Pez looked at each other. Tess waited. She knew what their answer would be. And she didn't care. She had something else for them to do.

Pez looked expectantly at Renny, waiting for him to speak and tell him what to think. Renny said nothing, just appeared to be deep in thought. Renny eventually spoke.

'Aye, those dealers . . . we've got names.'

'Names? How many?'

Renny shrugged. 'One or two.'

'And what are these names? And what do they have to do with Calvin's death?'

Renny looked down to the right, scratched his neck, tells that telegraphed the fact that his next words would be lies. Tess struggled to keep her face straight, tried not to smile. But she couldn't deny it. It felt good to have control over the boy.

'They're . . . they were there that night. Aye.' He nodded, as if confirming it to himself.

Tess waited.

Renny continued. 'How much we gettin' for tellin' you this?'

'Nothing,' said Tess.

Renny's eyes were lit by sudden, red angry jets. 'Fuck d'you mean, nothin'?'

'Nothing,' said Tess, 'because I'm not interested in them any more.'

Renny looked anxious, like he was about to lose something big and would do anything not to let that happen. Pez leaned across to him.

'Hey, Renny,' he said in an approximation of a whisper which his naivety rendered indiscreetly loud, 'we need that money. Yer dad took the last lot off you last night, didn't he? Gave you that black eye—'

Renny grabbed him by the collar, pushed him back in his chair. 'Shut up . . . Shut the fuck . . .' He began spitting and hissing, his words inaudible.

Pez looked terrified. Tess gave a glance towards Collins

who was watching the whole thing with surprised and bemused detachment. There would be no backup from him. Tess was scared that Renny would do something to the other boy. It was up to her to stop it.

'Renny . . .' Tess's voice seemed smaller than usual when it should have been bigger. She cleared her throat, tried to remember her Sandhurst training, had another go. 'Renny . . .'

The boy turned. His face was twisted, contorted with rage. He looked like a horror-movie vampire furious at being denied its prey.

'I've got some other work. If you want it. Paid work.'

Renny stared at her, a struggle clearly going on within him. Reluctantly regaining control, he dropped the terrified Pez and gave Tess his attention. 'What?' he said. It came out like a harsh bark.

'There's a kid I want you to follow.'

'Who?'

'The one we saw last night.'

Renny thought. A smile played at the sides of his mouth.

'Hey,' said Pez, 'that's—' A punch from Renny silenced him. Pez looked sad, rubbed his arm.

'What about him?'

Tess tried to appear nonchalant. 'Just follow him. See where he goes, what he does. Where he lives. He goes to the same school, right? Should be able to get plenty on him.'

'How much?'

'Depends on what you come up with.'

Renny looked at her, deciding whether to push it further. An easy decision. 'Money up front. Now.'

'You'll have to wait until—'

Renny's expression hardened, his eyes blazed. 'I said now.'

'Do your job and you'll get your money.'

Renny fell silent. So did Tess. Ray Collins had spoken. Renny looked at the man, ready to argue but something in his eyes stopped him. Perhaps a stronger, fiercer personality, thought Tess? Perhaps recognition of a kindred spirit? She didn't know, but she was grateful.

Renny nodded. 'OK.'

'And make sure you find out where he lives. And quickly.'

Renny seemed about to argue but one look at Ray Collins changed his mind.

Collins gestured to the door. 'Go.'

The boys got up, left.

Tess looked at Collins who sat watching the boys leave. Silence fell between them. Tess felt she had to break it.

'Remind you of yourself at that age?' she said, smiling. 'That it?'

Ray Collins stood up, walked towards the door. 'Get the bill, Posh Bird,' he said.

Tess, the relief of a few moments ago turning to disappointment, did as she was told.

'So how did the pocket of happiness come to an end in Bristol?'

She says nothing.

'Who came along this time?'

She sighs, shrugs, her face contorts, like the words are going to have to be torn from her. 'A friend. Or he said he was. And at first he was. But then . . . things started changin'. People never stay good for long. Not in my experience, anyway.'

'When you say people, do you mean men?'

'I mean people. Women can be bitches as well. But men, yes. Especially in this case.'

'What happened?'

'He was someone . . . who was supposed to help me. Look after me. But it got to be a bit more than that. Y'know what I mean?'

He nods. 'So what happened? How did he turn nasty?'

Another sigh, another longing look at the cigarette box. She doesn't reach for it, though. Watching, he chooses to regard that as progress. 'Him an' me . . . we were lovers. Not just a shag, but lovers. But then I found out some nasty stuff about him. And I didn't feel safe with him round. Round Jack.'

'What kind of nasty stuff?'

She sighs, split between being honest and not wanting to dredge up unpleasantness from her past. Unpleasantness that can still damage her in the present. 'There was a big case at the time. A children's home. Big scandal. You might have heard of it?'

'Tell me more, I don't know.'

'Well, they were abusin' the kids. All ages. Little ones as well.' She shakes her head. 'I mean, I know what I did once was horrible. Really horrible, with no excuse.'

'Apart from . . .'

'*Leave her out of this, you know what I mean. But this lot did it deliberately. They made a choice. Targeted the kids, got their trust, groomed them. Bastards. An' not just the men, it was the women as well. It didn't come out at the time, but I knew.*'

'*How?*'

She pulls back. She's said too much.

'*How?*'

'*He told me.*'

'*He was one of them?*'

She nods, her hand snaking towards the cigarettes.

'*Yes?*'

'*Yes. He was one of them. He told me about it. Laughed when he said it. Said he knew who I was, who I'd been. Thought I would like that kind of thing.*'

'*How did he know who you were?*'

She sits tight-lipped for a few seconds. '*He just knew. I can't say how, he just did.*'

He senses she won't say anything more in that direction so starts on a different track. '*So what did you do when he told you that? Did you go to the police?*'

She gives a harsh laugh. '*Me an' the police haven't always seen eye to eye in the past, have we? Why should anythin' have changed?*'

'*So what did you do?*'

'*I did what they do in the old cowboy films. I got out of town. Well, got them to shift me.*'

He nods, takes it all in. '*So where is he now?*'

'*I don't know. But I just want him as far away from me as possible. He's evil, that one. Real evil.*'

'*He wouldn't be able to find you up here, surely?*'

She looks right at him, her eyes boring into his. She's been crying. She looks like there are more tears to come.

'*He can find you anywhere. Anywhere. If he knows where you are, you're not safe.*'

15

The café was on Park Street. Sweeping up from the water-front and the cathedral to the huge, imposing university Wills Building, it consisted of the kinds of shops the inhabitants of Clifton liked to be seen in and that the rest of Bristol liked to be seen in if they wanted to be considered inhabitants of Clifton. Peta didn't blame them. If she had lived here she would have done the same. In fact, if time permitted she might just join them.

She had seen some T-shirts she liked and even a dress, although she didn't know when she would get the chance to wear that. Amar had seen loads of things from suits to T-shirts to trainers. But then, as she never tired of reminding him, he was a vain, shallow, self-obsessed clothes horse. He took that as a compliment.

The chrome, fake leather and Formica made the café as part Fifties diner, but the broken mosaic walls gave it away as part boho chic student hang-out. The menu, with its blue-cheese burgers and Ben & Jerry's milkshakes reflected that. Martin Flemyng sat at the opposite side of the booth, a coffee before him. Both Amar and Peta were hungry and had ordered burgers. Amar had even ordered a milkshake and tried to justify it on nutritional grounds. Peta hadn't been impressed but had secretly wished she could join him.

There were so many things in life she couldn't have. Alcohol being the most serious one, serious enough to send her to AA, and into a lifetime of recovery. But the milkshake didn't come with those kinds of associated problems. Just calories. She tried to work out how many hours she would have to put in at the dojo and the gym if she had that and lost count. She looked at Martin Flemyng, concentrated on the job in hand.

He sat opposite them open-faced, bland-featured, with a slightly curious smile. He seemed friendly enough but Peta knew from experience that the wrong question to a person could bring down a guard that might never be opened again. He was in his mid to late forties, she imagined, his sandy hair greying at the sides. Of medium height, he had kept himself in good shape and was comfortably dressed in jeans, trainers, sweatshirt and suede jacket. Peta quickly noticed he had a habit of intently peering forward and making eye contact with her when she spoke. She didn't know whether she found that unnerving or attentive.

'OK,' said Peta, taking Amar's papers from him and placing them in front of her on the small table. They had agreed in advance that she would do most of the talking. 'First of all, can I just say that we're really pleased you could meet us at such short notice.'

He smiled at her, crinkling his eyes at the sides. The smile came so quickly she couldn't decide whether it was genuinely warming or the expected response. 'No problem. You caught me on a slack day. I don't have a class this afternoon.'

'You teach at the university?' asked Amar.

Martin Flemyng nodded. 'In the Humanities department. Social Care. I just hope none of my students are seeking me out.'

'Do they do that?' asked Peta.

'They do. Questions about their courses, that kind of thing. I always tell them the same thing. Try turning up to lectures. The answers are generally there.'

He laughed. Peta joined him although she didn't find it particularly funny.

She smiled, continued. 'Well, as my colleague' – she gestured to Amar – 'said on the phone, we've been asked to look into the death of Adam Wainwright again and your name came up in the inquiry.'

Flemyng's smile faded. He became serious, businesslike. 'By whom?'

Peta and Amar exchanged a glance. They had agreed a cover story for this, partly truthful, partly fabricated. Just enough to be plausible yet fanciful enough to quell suspicion.

'There have been a series of murders around the country all bearing similarities to Adam Wainwright's. The police seem to discount this, so we've been asked by one of the families to investigate.'

Flemyng became interested, leaning even further forward. 'Whereabouts? What murders?'

'That's confidential, I'm afraid. Client privilege. Sorry.'

'Please.' He leaned forward intently. 'Just tell me where.'

'Not round here,' said Amar. 'Nothing to worry about. These are further afield.'

'Where?' Urgency had entered his voice. 'Tell me.' He sat back, and in a calmer tone said, 'Sorry. I can remember it well. Still upsetting.'

Peta and Amar surreptitiously exchanged a glance. They had picked up on the change in his tone, so tried to ease back. Stick to the cover story. 'OK, we'll tell you. But this is strictly between ourselves, right?'

Flemyng held up his hands in mock surrender. 'Absolutely.'

'Right. Rotherham. Oldham. Taunton. Carlisle. Don't say another word to anyone.'

Flemyng sat back. Peta might have been mistaken but he seemed relieved. 'Thank you,' he said.

'No problem. Can we get on now?'

He nodded.

'Good. As I said, we're looking into Adam Wainwright's death once more. Which is why we're talking to you.'

'In what respect do you want to talk to me? Should I have a solicitor present?'

'Oh no, nothing like that. Sorry if we gave that impression. It's just that you were his social worker at the time, is that right?'

He nodded, giving nothing away. Waiting to see what she was going to come out with next before committing himself to a full response.

'Can you tell us a bit about him, then?'

Flemyng frowned. 'In what way?'

'Just general. What kind of boy was he, who his friends were, the progress he was making, that kind of thing.'

Flemyng nodded again, looked thoughtful. And relieved once again, Peta thought. Give the man a break, she thought. The boy was murdered when he was in his care. It's only natural he should be defensive.

'He was . . . bearing in mind this was a long time ago, and if he had been anyone else he may not have sprung so quickly to mind.'

'Sure.'

'Adam was . . . difficult.' He smiled. 'But then what child wouldn't be in his situation? Mother dead from drugs and AIDS, father unknown . . . you try to encourage the best of humanity to flourish but in that job, in that situation . . . it tends not to happen too often.'

'Why d'you do it, then?' asked Amar. 'The job?'

Flemyng took a mouthful of coffee, turned to him. 'I don't do it now. Haven't done it since then.'

'So he was difficult,' said Peta, keeping the interview on track. 'In what way?'

'The usual. Pushing the boundaries. Swearing, behavioural

problems, violence. You know the kind of thing, I'm sure. Better a bad reaction than no reaction at all.'

'Better to feel something bad than feel nothing at all. Isn't that from a Warren Zevon song?' Peta said, noting how thoroughly Donovan had indoctrinated her with the work of obscure American rock singers.

'I wouldn't know,' said Flemyng.

'Right.' Warren Zevon or not, it was a sentiment Peta could appreciate. She looked down at the papers before her. They were largely props, but she wanted to give Flemyng the impression that her questions were based on them and not the ones they had worked out in advance. 'It says here that the police did a very thorough investigation both of you and the workers in the home and found nothing that pointed towards either you or the staff being the murderer. Is that correct?'

He nodded.

'You must have been relieved when that happened?'

He smiled. It seemed genuine. 'You can't imagine. That was one of the things that led to me leaving the profession. Seeing your colleagues' faces all the time, looking at you. Especially since the murderer was never found.'

'Quite. Then who did they think did it? The police. Who do they believe murdered him?'

He shrugged. 'I have no idea. You'll have to ask them that one. I'm afraid they didn't take me into their confidence.'

'They didn't say anything? Run any theories past you?'

He sat back as far as the booth allowed, appeared thoughtful.

'Come on, they must have said something,' said Peta. 'You were a social worker, you must have had a good relationship with the police or at least contacts.'

He thought again. 'Well . . . yes, I suppose . . . They thought that maybe he was a rent boy, operating down by the old docks, that was one of them . . . killed by a client . . . that he was involved in drugs or gangs, or both.' He sat forward again. 'Not very helpful, I'm afraid. I mean, anyone could come up with those ideas.'

'Still, it's something,' said Peta. 'Thank you.'

'Did they say Adam had befriended anyone before his death?'

Flemyng frowned, leaned forward once again. 'How d'you mean?'

'Just that. Had someone come into his life . . . I don't know, taken him out to places, shown an interest in him, anything like that?'

'Not that I know of.'

Amar kept going. 'Anyone at all?'

Flemyng's cheeks became slightly flushed. 'What are you suggesting?'

Amar shrugged, tried to appear as open as possible. 'Nothing. Just asking. Male or female? No? Nothing?'

Flemyng's attitude changed slightly at that remark. Peta didn't know if he was relaxing or thinking. 'As I said. Not that I know of.'

Amar leaned back, shrugged. 'OK.'

'What about Beech House, Mr Flemyng?' said Peta. 'Did you have any idea about the abuse going on there?'

The shutters were coming down again. 'Did I have . . . What d'you mean?'

Peta's turn to look as open as possible. 'Just that, really. The scale of it. The people involved. That sort of thing.'

'Well . . .' He looked down at his coffee cup. 'I suppose in hindsight it's easy to be wise. You know, you might have had suspicions but you wouldn't voice them because, well, because you know these people. They were friends, some of them. You don't expect that from friends. You think it must be outsiders.' He gave a shrug. 'Although I don't know why

I should think that. As a social worker there seemed to be no end of horrific ways for adults to inflict pain and suffering on children. And other adults, I suppose.'

'I can imagine,' said Peta.

'I hope you can't. For your sake.'

Peta looked down at the notes in front of her. 'Can you think of anyone else we should talk to? Another social worker? Police? Perhaps one of the children from the home, grown up. Anyone like that?'

Flemyng frowned again, thinking. Or an approximation of it. 'No, not off the top of my head . . . but if I think of anyone I'll be sure to let you know.'

'Thank you.' Peta handed him a card. He looked at it.

'Hold on, this is . . . Newcastle. You didn't mention Newcastle on the list of places.'

Peta was aware of Amar's eyes on her. 'That's just where we're based,' she said. 'There's been no murder there. Well, none we can connect to Adam Wainwright.'

He looked between the pair of them, eventually nodding, seemingly satisfied.

'Well,' Flemyng said, standing up to leave, 'if that's everything . . . thanks for the coffee.'

'Oh,' said Amar, 'there's just one more thing.'

Flemyng stood, waiting.

'Have you ever met someone called Anne Marie Smeaton?'

Flemyng's face changed. It was like he had been hit by an electrical charge. He struggled hard, forced his features to recompose. 'Anne Marie Smeaton?' Another pretence at thinking. 'I don't think so.'

'Not to worry,' said Peta smiling, 'we just wondered.'

'Who is she?'

'No one,' said Amar. 'Just a name that came up in the investigation at one time. If you don't know her that's fine.'

He extended a hand. 'Thanks for taking the time to meet us.'

Flemyng shook both their hands. 'Glad I could help,' he said, and hurried out of the diner.

Amar and Peta sat back down again and looked at each other. Their blue-cheese and mushroom burgers arrived at that moment. They smelled and looked delicious, exactly as they would have expected from a top-end American diner with a bohemian wholefood ethic.

But suddenly neither of them felt hungry. Nor did they want to go shopping for designer clothes. They had they felt, been given some insight into Anne Marie's background.

Now they just had to discover what that insight was. And how to use it to take the investigation forward.

'So he's never bothered you again?'

She sighs before answering. 'I've always managed to get away from him.'

'Always? You've seen him again?'

She plays with the cigarette pack. Still doesn't take one but it can't be far away now. 'No,' she says, her head still down, looking at the pack. 'No.'

He waits. She doesn't look up.

'I've got enough in my life without him,' she says. 'Enough to worry about.'

He nods, wondering whether to pursue it or not. Decides not to.

'So,' he says, 'tell me about—'

There's a noise from downstairs.

'Who's that?' she says, getting up from her chair. 'We're supposed to be alone here. Who's that?'

He thinks he knows. When he speaks it's in his calmest, most reassuring voice. He doesn't want to spook her.

'Don't worry,' he says. 'It's only—'

'—my daughter.' He shouted down the stairs. 'Just up here, be down in a minute. Put the kettle on.'

Anne Marie looked at him warily. Unsure whether to believe him or not, body tensed for fight or flight.

He sensed her unease, smiled. 'Shall we have a coffee break? I can introduce you if you like.'

Anne Marie sat back down in her chair. Realizing there was no imminent emergency, she relaxed, reached for the cigarettes. 'Fag break?' she said.

Donovan smiled. 'Why not?'

He stood up, moved towards the door. As he crossed the room he thought, once again, how proud he was of the Albion offices. He knew in a sense that it wasn't much to be proud of, but the place was his and it worked. He was looking forward to showing Abigail round. He wanted his daughter to be proud of her dad for something.

He walked downstairs to the reception. More white space, an iMac on a desk, Abigail sat behind it. Swinging on the chair, hands between her legs. Donovan couldn't get over how she had grown. She wasn't the baby daughter he carried with him in his head. She was a teenager, tall and slim and from a distance looking much older. But, as she had already proved in the diner, capable of dealing with any unwanted attention. Dressed in teen uniform of skinny jeans, Cons, tight-fitting T-shirt and short jacket, with her brown hair stuck into some kind of elaborate knot that would have taken Donovan hours to master but which

Abigail had probably done in seconds. He was proud of her but guiltily so – he had been absent for much of her upbringing.

He felt his emotions being torn, tried not to dwell on them. Let actions dictate the way forward. He smiled at her.

'You need a receptionist,' she said.

'I'll bear that in mind. Kettle on yet?' he said.

'And the kitchen is where?'

'I'll show you.'

He led her through the main office, once again with pride. Three desks, again sporting iMacs. Filing cabinets and more film posters. Michael Caine in *Get Carter* dominated the back wall. Donovan's idea of a joke.

'This is the main office,' he said.

'Bit quiet,' said Abigail.

'As I said. They're all away working.'

One of the iMacs was on, the screen showing images. Abigail stopped to look. 'What's that?' she said. The image was of a doorway. Big and closed, in daylight. Nothing seemed to be happening round it. Faint sounds of traffic, pedestrians talking, moving past.

Donovan stopped walking, crossed over to join her.

'A live feed,' he said.

'Where from?'

'Brighton.'

Abigail watched the screen. Nothing happened. 'Bit boring. If you were setting up a webcam you could have picked somewhere with a bit more action going on. I mean, Brighton's got more going for it than an old door.'

'It's work. That's the house we're watching.'

She looked at him quickly then back to the screen. 'Oh. Right.'

Donovan looked at it, not wanting to let her in on his thoughts, then straightened up, smiled at her. 'Right. Coffee?'

He walked into the kitchen through a door at the back of the office. Abigail followed him. He filled the kettle from the tap, began to spoon coffee into the cafetiere.

'There, see. Water, kettle. Coffee. Simple, really.'

Abigail gave him one of her patented teenage sarcastic smiles. Then she looked at what he was doing, frowned. 'Why don't you just use instant? I thought that's what you were supposed to drink in offices. Drink instant coffee then spend all morning complaining about it.'

'I think you've just answered your own question,' he said. 'I never drink instant coffee. There isn't much I'm fussy about, but coffee's one thing. And it has to be the right coffee too. Java or Italian. Nothing else. And warm milk, preferably steamed.' He smiled. 'If your grandma and grandad could hear me now . . .'

She gave a polite smile in return, nodded. Her grandparents had been dead for several years. Living down south they had got together as often as they could, but they had never truly connected, not on a close familial level. They had been proud of their son, he knew that, being the first in the family to go to university, taking up a career they could never have dreamed of, moving successfully to London, with beautiful wife and gorgeous children. His dream life. He was, in a way, quite relieved that they hadn't been there to see it all fall apart.

And now he was back in the north-east, in Newcastle, his hometown. As far away from that dream life as ever.

'So how do you take it?'

'White. Sugar.' She looked at the amount of coffee he was spooning in. 'Not too strong.'

'Comin' right up,' he said with a terrible American accent. He busied himself with the coffee. 'So how was Seven Stories?'

She shrugged. 'OK. Interesting, you know, but . . .'

'You're a bit too old for it.'

She smiled. 'Maybe. A bit.'

He had sent her to the children's literature museum while he was working with Anne Marie. It was just down the road and, although expensive to get in, he had enjoyed it. But he knew what she meant. And he knew that since he had given her the money for it she didn't want to seem ungrateful.

'No problem.'

'But I enjoyed it. Thanks.'

'Good. Then it was all worthwhile.'

The kitchen door opened, hesitantly. They both turned. Anne Marie entered, stopped when she saw Abigail. Eyed her warily. Donovan knew that this was inevitable. Anne Marie was revealing her innermost feelings and unloading her most difficult memories in this space. It was understandable she felt territorial. He had better not exclude her or she might stop talking.

'Anne Marie,' he said, again using his most open and unthreatening voice, 'this is my daughter, Abigail.'

Anne Marie stepped into the room, shook hands with her. Smiling, but still unsure. 'Hello,' she said, putting her cigarettes away. She turned to Donovan. 'I just went for a smoke outside. Bit of fresh air.'

'That's fine.' He smiled. 'It's allowed. Coffee?'

She said she would. Donovan busied himself making it.

'Abigail's just up for a few days from her mother's. Visiting.'

'Ah.' Anne Marie looked between the two of them. 'You're not together then. You and your . . .'

'We're not, no.'

Anne Marie nodded. As she did that, Donovan realized that although he had been probing this woman's background and getting her to open up, she barely knew anything about him. He knew this was a professional arrangement and it shouldn't matter, in fact it was better that way, correct, but with Abigail standing in front of him and his own background being revealed, he felt slightly uncomfortable.

The coffee was ready. Donovan suggested they go upstairs to drink it. They did, Anne Marie still slightly wary of letting someone else into the space.

'So,' she said to Abigail, sitting down on the sofa, 'what are you goin' to do with the rest of the day?'

She shrugged. 'Don't know. Go round town, maybe. See if—'

Anne Marie's phone rang.

Jack slid the key in the lock, cautiously opened the door. He didn't know whether he should do it fast or slow. He suspected Rob would still be around, sleeping off his hangover from last night. He wasn't pleasant to be around at the best of times but when he was hungover, Jack believed he was about as bad as humanity got.

He settled on edging the door open slowly, hoping that it wouldn't creak or squeak, or that no one would go past on the landing shouting something. He was lucky. Neither thing happened. He closed the door behind him as silently as he had opened it, stood in the hallway, listening.

No sound. He had expected snoring – Rob's usual daytime noise – but he heard nothing. Jack breathed a sigh of relief and walked into the living room.

Where Rob was sitting on the sofa.

He looked up. The cup of tea he had balanced on the arm of the sofa threatened to decorate the floor. His hair was sticking out at impossible angles, his face looked red and puffy, as if the previous night's alcohol had settled beneath his skin and was getting hot and sweaty trying to force its way out. A creased and folded tabloid lay on the arm of the chair, a pen in his hand. Studying form. His mood of initial shock at Jack's entrance was soon replaced by his default setting – anger.

'What you doin' here?'

Jack stared at him. What did he say? The truth or a lie? Another decision. He hated making decisions.

'I'm . . . I just . . . I forgot something.'

Rob thought about that for a second. It must have sounded plausible and didn't involve him so, thought Jack, he found it acceptable. He turned away from Jack, took a mouthful of tea.

Jack stayed where he was. He couldn't believe that was the end of it. No argument, no fight. Rob noticed he was still there, turned to face him again.

'What you standin' there for, then? Go an' get what you want.'

Jack didn't reply, just moved straight into the bedroom. He shut the door, sat on the bed. Sighed. This was his safe house, the place where he could be himself. Whatever else Rob was, he respected Jack's privacy. He never came in without asking first and never stayed longer than was absolutely necessary. Jack should have respected him for that and it was a credit to him, but there were too many things in the debit column that more than counterbalanced it.

He had decorated it with the things he recognized as his own. His posters, his music, his books. My Chemical Romance. Bowling For Soup. An old Kurt Cobain poster. His shelves of books, mostly all dark fantasy: Darren Shan, Scott Westerfeld. They may have all been made by someone else, but they all expressed his worldview perfectly.

He wanted to get changed, wondered whether he could risk it with Rob in the living room. Not that he was a stickler for uniform, but he may notice something if Jack went past dressed differently. Jack decided to risk it.

He stripped off his uniform, replaced it with jeans, a T-shirt and his jacket. Kept the trainers on. Couldn't change them. He checked himself in the mirror, relieved to see no real damage to his face, played around with his hair. He wasn't too bad-looking. Not really. Not that he had ever had a girlfriend, but he had seen some looking at him. At least he hoped that was why they were looking. Anything else, his stomach flipping, was unthinkable.

He walked through the living room. Rob didn't look up. He was out the front door and away.

The elation he felt as he walked down the pavement towards the end of the estate was short-lived. The reality of the situation fell on him like a sudden cloudburst. He had been thrown out of school. He had nowhere to go, no one to talk to, nothing to do.

He sat down on a wall, heart as heavy as a stone lodged in his chest.

He took his phone out. He thought long and hard before dialling. But there was no one else to turn to, there was nothing else he could do. She would be angry but hopefully would listen to his side of the story. He knew she was busy – he didn't exactly know with what – but she would understand. He hoped she would understand.

He pressed speed dial. He didn't need it, he knew the number by heart. Waited. She answered.

'Hello, Mum,' he said hesitantly. 'Listen . . . I've got something to tell you. You're not going to like it . . .'

'Excuse me.' Anne Marie answered her phone, listened. Her eyes widened, shock crossed her face, then anger. 'What? What d'you mean you . . .' She listened again. The anger gradually subsided. 'Right. Fine.' She listened further, anger all but gone, replaced with resignation. 'Right.' She sighed, looked to Donovan then at Abigail. 'Yeah. You'd best come here then.'

Donovan frowned. Anne Marie ended the call. She looked at the other two, gave a weak smile.

'I think I've found you somebody to go round town with,' she said.

'That the kid you want?'

Tess Preston risked a glance round the corner. The boy was sitting on a low wall, talking on his phone. God, didn't any of them go to school round here?

'Yeah, that's him.' She turned back to the two boys. 'You've done well on this one, lads. Earned your money. And quick, too. You'd only been gone, what, ten minutes? Good work. I'm impressed. And I'm not a woman who's easily impressed.'

Pez looked pleased with himself. Even Renny seemed to be allowing himself a slight loosening in the tension of his features.

The next line, Tess knew, would be the make or break one. 'Course, I can't pay you just yet. Not just for this.'

Renny's features tautened. His angry, pinched face bore straight into Tess's. 'Why not? We found him like you asked, we showed you where he is, like you asked, why the fuck can't you pay us, then, eh?'

'Aye,' said Pez, tentatively, anger making him find his voice, 'we did what you asked us to do. That's not fair.'

'Yeah,' said Renny picking up the theme and developing it with more menace, 'it's not fair. You owe us, you southern bitch. So fuckin' pay up.'

Tess looked round. Collins had elected to stay in the car. She risked a glance over. Collins was studiously ignoring her. She was on her own. She couldn't back down, she knew that. At least not yet.

She tried to brazen it out. 'All you've done is point him out to me. I still don't know where he lives, who he lives with, anything like that. That's what you've got to find out before I pay you.'

'Fuck off. We want payin' now.'

Tess had had enough. 'And what will you do if I don't?'

Renny actually growled. Tess couldn't believe her ears, she had heard nothing like it. She flinched, expecting sudden violence. None came. Instead Renny had regained his composure and was now smiling, a look of animal cunning in his eyes.

Tell 'im,' he said.

Tess swallowed. 'What?'

'That's what I'll do. Tell 'im. That kid. Tell 'im you're lookin' for 'im. Tell 'im you wanted us to spy on 'im. Aye, that's what I'll do. Tell 'im. An' see what 'e says.'

'You wouldn't.'

Another unpleasant smile from Renny. 'Is that a dare?'

Tess backed off. She knew she had no choice. She couldn't risk the fact that Renny might do what he intended. He was certainly unhinged and angry enough and, since he hadn't been paid, had nothing to lose. Tess had underestimated him.

'All right,' said Tess. 'I'll pay you. And that's it, right? You're off the clock. That's the end, OK?'

The boys looked at each other, nodded.

Tess slid her hand into her coat pocket, brought out her work wallet. The two boys' eyes never left it.

'There's fifty quid. Thanks for your time.'

'Each,' said Renny, looking at the rest of the money going back into the wallet.

'For pointing out a boy? I don't think so,' said Tess.

'Fuck you, then.' Renny turned and started to walk towards the kid.

'All right, all right . . . fifty quid each.' She took her wallet out again, counted off more bills.

'Now that's it. Finito. No more. You got that?'

Smirking, Renny and Pez slipped away.

Tess turned and, keeping one eye on the kid, walked back to the car, got in. Collins was staring straight ahead, practising his smoke rings. Tess got behind the wheel, slammed the door.

Collins exhaled a particularly elaborate circle of smoke.

'That went well,' he said, without looking up.

Tess felt her cheeks burning. 'I'm never having fucking children,' she said, her voice suddenly high, dry and raspy. 'But we've got the kid. It's down to us now. Let's follow him.'

Collins said nothing, just puff, puff, puff.

'So back to work, then,' he says. He puts the recorder on the table between them, switches it on again.

'Yes, back to work.'

She smiles but it still seems as if a cloud has appeared over her. A cloud she can't shift. Or won't be able to shift until her story has been told.

'OK. We were talking about Bristol. How you left there quickly. Faster that you intended.'

She nods, volunteers no more information.

'So . . . why?'

She shrugs.

'You mentioned a predator?'

She sighs. That's got nothin' to do with . . . with anythin' you want to know about. I don't want to talk about him.' She sounds adamant.

'Right. OK.' He has filed that away, he will try again later. 'So where was it next?'

'It's all about protection,' she says suddenly.

'You mentioned that before.'

'Well, it is. I mean. If you can't protect your family, what's the point? What's the point of havin' one? What's the point of me talkin' to you now?'

'Right.'

'I mean, look at Jack. He's a good lad. A really good lad. I couldn't have that, that . . . thing gettin' ahold of Jack. Hurtin' him. Twistin' him. The poor lad's got enough to go through without that. So I ran. That's why I ran. To protect my son.'

'Right. And you couldn't go to the police.'

'No.'

'There were other outlets, other things you could have done. The newspapers, the TV . . .'

She sighs. 'You don't get it, do you? What if I had gone to them? With my background? Bein' who I am? Who I was?' She glances quickly down at her bandaged hands. He catches her do it. 'Look, I know it's supposed to be secret, but he knew. What if he tells them? That would be as bad as him comin' after you. No. I did the right thing.'

'OK.'

'You'd do the same.'

'I probably would.'

She smiles then. It's unexpected and it takes him off guard. It lights her face up in way he hasn't seen before. 'Your daughter's lovely.'

'Thank you.' Not knowing what else to say, he laughs.

'She's a credit to you.'

'I didn't have much to do with her.'

'Well, you say that, but she's here with you now. So you must have done somethin' right.'

He shrugs. 'I suppose so.'

The smiles leaches out of her face like colour from a sun-faded painting. 'But you see what I mean. Think of her and see what I mean. How would you feel if you had a predator comin' after her? What would you do then?'

'Well . . .'

'See? What if it was your son that you had to save? Or daughter? What would you do then?'

'I'd do everything I could to save them.'

She sits back. 'Exactly. I didn't just run away. I saved him. I saved Jack.'

He nods.

'Right. So where did you go next?'

17

'So, uh, so what kind of music d'you like?'

Jack realized how dumb and lame that sounded even before the words had left his mouth, his cheeks reddening accordingly. He expected Abigail to point and laugh at him at the very least. But she didn't. Either she was too polite, which was possible, or genuinely interested in the question, which he very much doubted.

'Oh,' she said, putting the straw back in her smoothie and licking her lips, which Jack pretended not to notice, 'you know. Just stuff I hear. Alphabeat are good to dance to and I like Brandi Carlile. She's good. Fall Out Boy. Bowling For Soup, you know, the usual. But I've been listening to some really old school stuff too like Nirvana? You know them?'

'Yeah,' said Jack smiling. Who didn't? And she liked them too. Result.

'What about you?'

She was asking him. What did he do? Tell the truth and risk ridicule? Lie and be caught out? He looked at her. She had big brown eyes and straight, bobbed brown hair. She was wearing make-up but it had been expertly applied. And she had a great, slim figure. She looked way older than four-teen. She looked way older than him.

'Oh, you know . . . Nirvana, yeah course. I like some of the usual stuff too. My Chemical Romance, but I think I'm growing out of them. That whole emo thing. Just a phase I was going through.'

She laughed, a little giggle. Was that funny, what he had said? Was that a joke or was she ridiculing him?

'You're so right,' she said.

It was a joke. He had made a joke and a girl had laughed. And not just any girl, but this one. The kind he never thought he would meet let alone talk to. The kind who was laughing at his jokes. Perhaps this was going to be a good day after all.

They were in a smoothie and juice bar in Eldon Square shopping centre in the heart of Newcastle. The view from their table was of Eldon Square itself, the statue of St George slaying the dragon, flanked by bronze reliefs of Justice and Peace fronted by a stone lion. It was certainly peaceful out in the square, with the usual drinking schools lying around on the grass even in November, goths, emo trainee wannabe goths and social outsiders who had no particular badge of allegiance all clustered round, taking companionship from each other but mainly from their cider and Special Brew, the cans and bottles giving most of them a warmth and comradeship no other person could.

Jack had sought out his mother at Albion. He had been introduced to Joe Donovan who seemed OK, a big guy in his early forties, Jack thought, wearing a T-shirt that someone at least ten years younger would usually be seen in. Donovan, however, managed to pull it off without looking either old or ridiculous. It suited him.

He had a charisma about him, like he was used to asking questions and getting answers or telling people what to do. However he didn't seem cruel with it – it was a natural, easy thing he had. Jack could imagine that people liked him. But for all that, there was something else about him. Something dark. Something damaged. Jack only glimpsed it when he was talking to him – a look in the eye, a stray thought passing across his face, but it was unmistakably there. Or maybe Jack recognized it because he felt he carried something similar within himself.

And then there was Joe Donovan's daughter, Abigail. He had stopped dead when he looked at her. Stunning, way out of his league. But there she was saying hello and shaking his hand. And there was Donovan telling the two of them to go round town together, get to know each other since they didn't know anyone else in the place. Jack thought she wouldn't go for it but she had said yes straight away. He thought he would have been elated. But his troubles had only started then. Because once he was with her, he had to entertain her. He had to make her like him. Or at least make her think he wasn't a complete dork.

Her laugh brought him back into the present. It was a beautiful laugh. He smiled at her, tried to find something to say that would keep her laugh going.

'Yeah,' he said, 'no more emo for me. Didn't really like it much. I don't look good in eyeliner.'

She laughed again.

'And I can't stand the sight of blood. Especially my own.'

She laughed again. What was going on?

'I kept the hair, though.'

She didn't laugh, just smiled. 'It looks nice. Suits you.'

He reddened, put his face down, concentrated on his smoothie. She had got him again. He didn't know what to say next. While he was searching, she beat him to it.

'So, that's your mum, right?'

'Yeah,' he said, nodding.

'So what's it like living round here? Newcastle?'

'Erm . . . don't know. Haven't been here long.'

She looked surprised. 'Really?'

'Yeah. We moved here not so long ago. I hope . . .' He

tried not to think of the kids at school, at the morning he had endured. At his mother's bloodied and bandaged hands. 'I hope we're going to be living here for a while. That everything's OK. Goin' to be OK.'

She nodded, frowning. 'Where did you live before?'

'Hull.'

'That's in Yorkshire, isn't it?'

'Yeah. It's at the end of Yorkshire. Last bit before you fall into the North Sea. Sometimes it felt like the end of the world.'

She laughed again. He didn't think about it, just enjoyed her reaction.

'Fish town, they called it. When the wind was in the wrong direction all you could smell was rotting fish.'

'Lovely.'

'I'm just telling you the good bits.'

Another laugh. 'You're funny.'

He felt something in his chest. He didn't know whether it was good or bad but it certainly went deep.

Her laughter subsided to a smile. 'So why did you move from there to here? Don't you like fish?'

His turn to laugh now. It felt good. 'Not any more.' He stopped laughing, trying to answer her question seriously. 'I'm not really sure. My mother . . . she has problems. Emotional problems. I don't want to make a big thing about it but . . . I don't know. It means we can't stay in the same place for too long.'

'So how long are you here for?'

He shrugged. 'Don't know.' He thought of the episode with her a few days ago. Her hands covered in blood. Tried to shake the image from his mind. He had been trying to forget about that. 'Hopefully a while but . . . you never know. I think your dad's helping her, though. So that's good.'

She nodded, went back to her smoothie. He had said more to her than just about anyone. He didn't want to lose the connection, had to find some words to bridge the gap.

'So . . . why are you up here? With your dad?'

The smile slipped from her face. Jack felt he had said the wrong thing and opened his mouth to say something else, backtrack, make it OK again. Before he could do that, she spoke.

'Oh,' she said, playing with her straw, 'I had . . . a few problems at home. I had to get away for a few days.'

Jack leaned in closer. She was opening up to him. Why? No girl had ever done that before. 'What kind of problems?'

She looked up. Saw him looking intensely at her. Straightened up and pulled back. Damn. He'd lost her. He'd been trying to be nice and he had lost her.

'Well,' she said. He hadn't lost her. She was answering. 'Just . . . stuff, you know.' She ran her fingers through her hair before continuing. He watched her do it, watched the way the strands fell down into place again, how the light caught it as she did so. How that act transformed having a smoothie in a juice bar on a November afternoon into something special. 'My dad and mum are separated, as you know. And my mum wanted to . . . well, she wanted to move on. Without dad. And I thought fine, you know? He's never been my number one favourite person since . . . since he moved out. Fine, do it.'

She sighed. He waited.

'So . . . so what happened?' he said eventually.

She sighed, looked into her smoothie that, beyond the slow falling froth on the inside of the glass was empty. 'I don't know,' she said, still looking into the glass. 'I just thought about it and why he left and how things were before and . . .' She shrugged again. Jack felt it covered a lot of emotions. 'We had a row, I walked out and I really wanted to see him.'

'So you came up here.'

She nodded. 'Mum wanted to marry again. And she's never divorced dad. So, you know, you always think, you know . . .'

He nodded. He thought he knew what she meant.

She sighed as if shifting the weight of the world. 'But I guess not. Oh, I don't know. I just wanted things to be like they used to be. With Dad there, and . . . and . . .' Another sigh. 'Never mind. I do go on. Sorry.'

'No. That's all right. Don't say sorry.'

She looked at him. Their eyes locked. Jack felt panic pulse through him like an electric current. They looked away.

'You're sweet,' she said.

'Er, thanks. Is that a good thing?'

Another smile from Abigail. 'I think so.' She looked at her watch. 'Where shall we go next?'

'I don't know.' He knew he didn't want to go home but he didn't know his way round well enough to show her the sights. 'I don't know the city very well.'

She stood up, put her bag over her shoulder.

'Let's go and discover it together, then, shall we?'

Jack smiled. That sounded like a great idea.

Tess was bored. All the excitement she had experienced earlier at tracking down Mae Blacklock and preparing to expose her was wearing off. This was what it had come to. Following two teenagers round the shops.

They had walked all afternoon, stopping for smoothies and to windowshop CDs. It was clear the girl wanted to look in the clothes shops but she didn't want to offend the boy. Aw. How sweet.

She followed them to the Gate where the girl took out

her mobile and made a call. Since the Gate had restaurants, bars and cinemas, she could safely bet that they were going to get something to eat and see a film. She didn't need to shadow them for that.

Phoning Collins, she decided to go back to the estate and wait for Mae Blacklock to put in an appearance. The boy would have to come back sooner or later.

'I'm coming back,' she said, 'there's nothing doing here. Let's go back to the estate. See if we can find out which flat they live in.'

Collins grunted in reply. The daylight had gone by the time Tess picked up a cab from the Haymarket and started to make her way back to the east side of the city. The driver was either avoiding rush-hour traffic or, more likely having heard her accent, giving her a scenic tour of darkened back alleys and estates. Tess was about to say something when someone caught her eye.

'Wait up a minute, slow down,' she said.

They were going down an alleyway under what looked like a flyover or viaduct or both when she saw two people standing on the pavement underneath a streetlight, outside a building, the word Albion written on the front.

She couldn't believe her luck. There she was. Mae Blacklock.

Talking to some other guy, big, longish hair, leather jacket. Boyfriend? No. Body language was all wrong. Must have been close, though, the way they were talking.

She had an idea.

'Go round this corner, please, and pull over.'

'What for?' The driver didn't sound very pleased.

'Just do it, please. I'm paying for this trip.'

The driver muttered something under his breath that Tess didn't catch, although she was sure the words 'southern' and 'cunt' were in the mix somewhere.

Once the car had stopped she got out and took a small digital camera out of her pocket that she carried for occasions like this one. She was sure Collins wouldn't be pleased with her, any more than she would be happy if Collins tried to write an article, but she didn't have time to think about that now.

She hid round the corner of an old building and risked a peek round it. Mae Blacklock was still saying goodbye to the other guy. Neither of them had seen her yet so she risked a couple of shots. Hoping the streetlights provided enough light because she couldn't risk the flash. And another one for luck. Great.

Mae Blacklock said goodbye to the man and started walking towards her. Tess thought quickly. She could just step out now, confront her, tell her she knew who she was, what she had done and get her side of the story. Promise a lot of money for an exclusive.

But then she might run. She might lose her. It might never see print. She might be wasting her money. She might lose her job. Her promotion. Scratch that.

She would wait. Yeah, that sounded like a plan. Wait, follow her back to the estate, see where she lived.

She jumped back into the car. The driver said nothing, waited. Tess said nothing, just watched Mae Blacklock walk by.

'So you ganna tell us where I'm goin' or is it ganna be a surprise?'

'Yeah, yeah, just a minute . . .'

Tess thought. She could just go straight back to the estate and wait. But what if Mae Blacklock wasn't going back to the estate? What if she was going out? What then?

'Look, it's your meter that's runnin', but I've got a livin' to make. You're not the only fare around, you know.'

'I know.'

'You gettin' out?'

Tess thought again.

'Yeah.'

She paid the cab driver and got out. She had no idea where she was. But it didn't matter. She was going wherever Mae Blacklock was going. She waited until she was a discreet distance ahead then began to follow her.

Back to the estate. Tess had been right all along. She mentally awarded herself some brownie points and the promise of a treat later. She approached the block of flats Tess knew she lived in. Good. She followed her up the stairs.

It stank of piss — canine, human and possibly others — and was decorated with fast-food debris, old, wind-deposited tabloids, and other detritus that crunched and squelched underfoot that she would rather not put a name to. She had never felt more out of place in her life. Or more scared. She didn't know how people lived in these conditions.

She waited until Mae Blacklock had reached the correct floor before running up behind her to see where she went. She listened, heard her footsteps going along the landing. She walked almost on tiptoe, risked a glimpse round the corner.

Mae Blackock had met a man coming out of a front door. The same one she had been about to enter. They didn't go inside. They stayed on the landing, talking. Tess ducked back round the stairwell, listened. It was indistinct, but it was clear they were arguing.

'Well, I'm sorry,' she heard a woman's voice say, echoing along the landing and round the stairwell. Presumably Mae Blacklock. 'But I've just finished and got home. If you were hungry you could have made something to eat. In fact you could have made something for all of us.' She sounded so tired. Like she was ready to drop.

The reply was male and angry. 'That's not my job. My job's to work or find work. Not do bloody housework. That's what you should be doin'.'

Ah, thought Tess with a wry smile, the age-old battle of the sexes.

They continued in this vein, she sounding increasingly more tired and imploring him for help which she clearly wasn't going to get, he getting more and more angry until he told her he was going out, that he would get something to eat in the pub and that she would see him later. Much later.

Footsteps told Tess that the owner of that angry male voice was heading towards her. She looked round for somewhere to hide, ran quickly upwards, hoping he wouldn't look there for eavesdroppers. She flattened herself into an alcove and hoped that no one else would see her and ask what she was doing there. Her luck held.

She heard footsteps go past, head towards the ground floor. She waited until she was sure their owner had left the building before following. She had changed her mind while listening to the argument. Mae Blacklock was in for the night. This guy, obviously her partner, was off out. One of the things they had argued about was money. They were clearly short of it.

Tess felt that tingle. She had just found the key to unlock the story, and with it, the entrance to the magic kingdom. Promotion. Front-page bylines. Money.

Her editor's words niggled at the back of her mind: *Overwhelming public interest. We can't publish unless there's overwhelming public interest.*

She would cross that bridge when she came to it.

She reached the bottom of the stairwell, waited until

the bloke, big with a ponytail of grey hair, black jeans and an aged leather jacket, was ahead and began to follow him.

Tess was confident that whatever this guy's price was, she could match it.

Or get away with paying him less.

'I think I've had enough now.'

'In what way?'

'For today.'

'Right. Look, Anne Marie, there's loads we haven't covered yet. And if we want this to work, we have to step up a gear.'

She sighs again. 'I know . . .'

He waits. She looks like she's about to speak then stops herself. She sits silently a while longer. He thinks she's not going to say anything else and is going to turn off the recorder when she starts again.

'I still think of him, you know.' Her voice is thin, fragile and breakable. Like a robin's eggshell. 'The boy. Trevor. I still think of him.'

He says nothing, waits.

'I still see him. In my dreams. Yeah . . .' She nods slowly.

He waits, expecting more. Nothing comes. He gently prompts her. 'As he was then? Or now?'

She thinks before answering. He is aware of the darkness outside, the cold seeping into the room. Shadows surround the light. Night is prematurely here.

'Both. I see him as a little boy. As he was before I . . . before he . . . His face. But sometimes there are bits missing. Like I can't see his eyes. I can remember other bits, his hands, his hands are pumpin' open and closed, open and closed . . . but I can't see his eyes . . . I know they're starin' at me but I can't see them . . .'

She trails off. The darkness grows. He waits.

'And then I see him now. He's . . . not alive but he's angry . . . he tells me he should have had a life, that I took his life . . . he's bad, a bad spirit, he's . . .'

Her voice wavers. He keeps pressing her.

'Is he alone?'

She looks at him, shock and fear in her eyes. 'What d'you mean?'

'When you see him, is he alone? Or are there others with him?'

She looks like she wants to answer but can't find the words. He sits forward, willing her to speak. Her head drops to the table, then comes up again. She looks at him. There are tears in her eyes and her thick, tar-enriched voice is clogged when she speaks.

'I want to go now. Please. I want to go home.'

18

The pub was called the Half Moon. It was situated far enough on the edge of the estate to attract locals, but not far enough on the main road in Byker to attract attention to itself. The kind of local pub that, through surliness and unfriendliness, actively discouraged outsiders from entering. The kind of pub that could keep its mouth shut and hold its secrets. The kind of pub that, Tess could see, Rob had quickly made himself at home in. And because of that, the task ahead of her was made even more difficult.

But not impossible.

The pub was old, high-ceilinged, with mostly original features. Something that would have been desirable to many developers but had been ignored in this pub. The regulars and owners liked it the way it was. It felt cavernous, old. Functional. Yet its walls held ancient ancestral race memories, like a meeting hall of legend and history where once-mighty tribal chieftains had gathered. Now their descendants gathered in their places, sat round playing pool or darts, or watching Sky Sports, drinking heavily, a clan of unacknowledged underachievers, their comradeship keeping the outside world at bay.

Tess felt as out of place and conspicuous as a BNP candidate trying to win Muslim votes at a mosque.

But she could take that, work with it. In fact, she had no choice. She had to hope that, even if they wouldn't speak to her they wouldn't hurt her. But it wasn't the kind of pub — or area — that could guarantee that.

In a way, working at the newspaper was exactly the same. She didn't fit in. There were a lot of posh boys working there, ambitious ones too, and posh birds. But the posh birds were expected to play a different kind of game to succeed. And it wasn't one she really liked. Not with those boys, anyway. She wanted to make it on her own terms. She hoped she could.

The man was leaning at the bar, pint before him, paper spread out. Studying form. The pathetic hope of the perpetual loser, Tess thought. Backing horses. It made doing the lottery look like sound financial planning. But, Tess thought, suppressing a smile, it meant he needed money. And he might be more inclined to open up to a woman than a man.

Tess was thankful that she was wearing her dress–down clothes. Leather jacket, jeans, boots. Casual clothes helped in her line of work, in places like this. All the same, she pulled the front of her T-shirt down, exposing a bit more cleavage. She didn't mind playing up to targets, just not co-workers and bosses.

She walked up to the bar.

'Pint of . . .' She surveyed the pumps. Something matey but not too strong. After all she was working. But nothing that would make her look out of place. 'Lager, please.'

The barmaid wore a white blouse and black leggings. She was middle-aged, careworn. A diet of bad food, housing and luck combined with a life spent doing more work for less money had left her looking lumpen and tired. She didn't smile at her. To Tess, she looked like Les Dawson in drag. She smiled at the thought, at her. The barmaid didn't return it.

She glanced along the bar, saw the newspaper the barmaid was reading. One of hers. She should have felt a glow of pride. She was with her people. But there was one thing she had in common with her fellow journalists – the punters were for exploiting, not for befriending.

She glanced along the bar in the other direction, saw her target leaning over his paper. He didn't look up. On the wall overhead, Sky Sports News was pumping out, its headlines scrolling across the screen. Most of the drinkers ignored it. Tess listened, tried to catch what was being discussed, hoped that something she saw might give her an in for conversation. She didn't understand a word of it. She would have to try another approach.

However, she felt eyes on her. Her presence hadn't gone unnoticed. She didn't feel the attention was entirely positive, either. She had to think quickly. Come up with a strategy. She thought for a few seconds. Got it. She wiped all trace of a smile from her features, necked nearly half the pint and, trying to ignore the rush to her head, leaned on the bar next to him.

'Been lucky?' she said, trying to be aware of her cleavage.

The target looked up. The man looked tired, thought Tess. Tired and worn down. With a hint of anger at the edges. Tread carefully.

His face was guarded, giving nothing away. He shrugged. But she noticed his eyes dart to her chest. Good. 'Bit. Here an' there.'

'Can't win all the time, eh?' Tess erased any note of cheer from her voice, said it like she meant it. She had sized the man up: loser. She would match him accordingly. That was the way to get him talking. That was the plan. 'Although once might be nice.'

With a sigh, Tess heaved herself on to the stool next to the target.

'Tell me about it,' he said, looking up.

'Yeah,' said Tess, at a loss to follow it with anything else. But she had his attention. He thought she was coming on to him. Good, use it, work with it. This was it. Now or never. 'Bad do the other night, wasn't it?'

He frowned.

'That kid who got stabbed. Bad do.'

Angry recognition began to form in his eyes. And a certain disappointment. The poor sod really thought he was in with a chance, thought Tess. But now he had realized perhaps not who Tess was, but certainly what.

'You're a journalist.'

Tess sighed. 'Yeah. I'm a journalist.'

He went back to his paper. 'Then go talk to someone else.'

Tess sighed again. Was she overdoing it? She didn't know. Best to play it down, though, just in case. 'Thanks. I've heard that a lot. Hell of a lot. No one wants to talk round here.'

He turned away, studiously avoided her. 'Then take a hint.'

Tess continued. 'I can understand why. I mean, if I lived round here and some flash Londoner came round opening her cheque book . . .' Another sigh. 'I don't want to be here either.'

Tess was sure his head had perked up slightly at the mention of the cheque book. Tess noticed his glass was empty. 'Can I get you another?'

He stared at her, said nothing.

'Please, I'm not trying to . . .' Another sigh. 'I've been here three days now and no one's talked to me. Let me get you a drink. Have a conversation. Then I'll go. I don't care whether you knew that kid or not.'

He tried to maintain his stern expression but Tess noticed his eyes flicker towards his empty glass. She smiled inwardly.

'Stella,' he said.

Tess drained her glass, ordered. When the drinks were

bought and the first mouthfuls taken, Tess smiled. 'Tess Preston.'

'Rob. Rob Hutchinson.'

Tess stuck out her hand. Rob took it. And gave another appreciative look at her breasts.

Bingo, thought Tess. Got him.

Donovan looked at the menu and was suddenly very hungry. It happened every time. The Flatbread Café on High Bridge in Newcastle city centre was fast becoming one of his favourite places to eat. Far Eastern mixed with Middle Eastern mixed with Mediterranean food made it, he thought, something a bit special. He felt his usual over-order coming on.

The restaurant was richly coloured in purples and aubergines, the décor design Moroccan/Persian. Cushioned sofas lined one of the walls, which were inset with candles and lanterns, Moroccan lamps hung from the ceiling. It was a place to relax, kick back. Not discuss business.

He looked over the top of his menu across the table. Wendy Bennett was giving her menu close scrutiny. She looked as stunning as ever, wearing a simple dark-brown suit with a mauve raw-silk blouse underneath. The ensemble complemented both the colour of her eyes and the walls of the restaurant. Light from the lit candle on the table between them danced on her flawless skin. Donovan would have been lying if he had said she wasn't having an effect on him.

She looked up. 'I've chosen.'

'Me too.'

The waiter came. They ordered, Donovan having trouble with some of the pronunciations but he knew what his favourites were none the less. As long as he had khoresh and ceviche and plenty of it he didn't mind what else he had.

Wendy Bennett ordered wine, asking him first. 'You fine with that?'

'Absolutely. Whatever.'

The waiter left the table, returned with the wine and water. They poured.

'So,' said Wendy, holding up her glass, 'a toast? Here's to . . .'

'Me apologizing for standing you up last night.'

She smiled, cast her eyes down. 'No problem.' She looked at her glass. 'Toast?'

'Right. Erm . . .'

She locked her eyes on his. 'To a successful partnership.'

'We're a partnership now, are we?'

She smiled, shrugged. It was impossible not to return the smile.

They clinked glasses. Drank.

'So,' Wendy said, leaning across the table and giving Donovan a generous glimpse of her cleavage, 'was everything all right last night? Your family emergency?'

'Everything's fine.'

'Good,' she said, sitting back. 'Shall we talk business now?'

He sat back, looked round. Trying not to be too taken with her. Or taken in. 'Not the kind of place where you come to talk shop,' he said.

'Then let's get the shop talk out of the way first and enjoy ourselves,' she said. 'You can tell me what's happening, then we can relax.'

He had phoned her during the afternoon, setting up the meeting and apologizing for the night before. Donovan had then contacted Peta and Amar, got an update from them. He spoke to Peta. She told him of their two meetings with Tom Haig and Martin Flemyng and her suspicions concerning the latter. Nothing definite, she said, just a feeling that he wasn't telling the truth.

'Or the whole truth,' she had said.

'In what way?' Donovan had asked.

'I don't know exactly,' she said. 'Just a feeling. We're looking into him further. Amar's staying behind for a bit to do some more asking round, I'm off to Colchester tomorrow to look at the next one.'

'Nice. Britain's oldest town.'

Peta didn't sound so impressed. 'Been before. Chose the wrong time to try and leave. Got stuck in Britain's oldest traffic jam.'

Donovan laughed. 'Never mind. Have a lovely night.'

'What are you doing?'

'Tonight? Wendy's still up here so I'll be taking her to dinner. Flatbread Café, probably.'

There was a pause on the line. 'Oh, it's Wendy, is it? Not her full name or Ms Bennett? Wendy. Very cosy.'

'Oh shut up.' He was glad she couldn't see him blush. 'You jealous?'

'Why would I be jealous? Of who exactly?'

Donovan found himself smiling again. 'I don't know. You said it.'

'No. I'm not jealous. You go out and enjoy yourself with *Wendy*, don't worry about me sitting in some Travelodge somewhere outside Brentwood with only chicken and chips, a glass of Coke and some drunken travelling salesman trying to get off with me for comfort.'

'What a great night.'

'Really? Want to swap?'

'Nah. You're all right.'

Peta was silent for a moment then returned to business. 'Anyway. Amar's doing a bit more digging. Let's see what he turns up.'

'Right. Heard from Jamal?'

Peta laughed. 'As I'm sure you have.'

So keen was he to prove himself, Jamal had reported in to the office every other hour. Peta's friend was there, supporting him when his shift was over. They felt fine about him. He could handle himself.

'Well, I'll let you go,' said Peta. 'Think of me when you're out enjoying yourself.'

'I will.' And he was.

'Penny for them?'

'Sorry?'

Wendy Bennett was leaning over the table, looking at him expectantly.

'Sorry. I was miles away.'

'Then come back. I'm over here. Work then play, remember?'

'Right.'

'So after you dropped that bombshell last night, how's it going? Has Anne Marie said anything yet?'

'About the dead boys? No.'

'Right. So what kind of things has she talked about so far?'

Donovan thought for a moment. 'Not sure. Not much so far.' He told her some of Anne Marie's stories regarding Fenton House and Jack.

'Anything else?'

'Well, she's made references to men in her past, how they've taken advantage of her. That kind of thing.'

Wendy Bennett sat forward. 'Really? How?'

'Don't know if I can say yet. I'm not sure she's told me anything about them yet.'

The food arrived. They ate.

'I saw the news. They haven't found that boy's killer yet,' said Wendy through a mouthful of flatbread.

'I know.'

'Oh God. It's exciting doing this, isn't it?'

'Sometimes.'

'But it's . . . I don't know. These are people's lives you're playing with here.'

'I know. So that's why we tread carefully.'

They ate.

'So your family emergency . . .'

'The fire's are out. Everything's fine.'

'Oh. Good.' Wendy looked nervous about asking the next question. 'Was it . . . your son?'

'No,' said Donovan, 'my daughter.'

Wendy's eyes widened in surprise. 'I didn't know you had a daughter.'

'I don't think we know each other very well at all, do we?'

She smiled, the candle lighting up her eyes. 'Not yet.'

Donovan didn't reply.

'So where is she now, this daughter of yours?'

'She's out for the evening.'

'On her own? In Newcastle?'

'With Anne Marie's son, Jack. They've gone to see a film.'

Wendy put down her fork, her eyes widening. 'Seriously? Are you sure about that? Are you happy for your daughter to . . . go out with him?'

'Why not? Yeah, she's done something awful in the past but that was when she was a kid. And this is her son, not her. You can't judge him on what his mother did when she was eleven.'

'Yes, but, all those dead boys . . .' Wendy shuddered.

'I know.' Donovan smiled. 'But he seems like a nice lad. And him and Abigail got on well too.'

Wendy's turn to smile. 'You're a very noble man, Joe Donovan.'

'Don't talk bollocks.'

'I mean it. You practise what you preach. That's rare.' She picked up her glass. 'Here's to you.'

Donovan didn't join her.

They finished their meal, talking all the while. They finished the bottle of wine, ordered another. Donovan found her easy company. Warm, funny, charming. And the fact that she was beautiful to look at didn't hurt either.

The bill arrived.

'I'll take that,' said Wendy, tossing down the company credit card. 'Business expenses.'

'Thank you.'

She fixed him with another killer smile. 'Not at all. I've thoroughly enjoyed it. You're worth it.' She didn't drop eye contact after her words. Neither did Donovan.

He could feel stirrings within him the more she looked at him. She was beautiful, she was available and she had made it clear just what she felt for him. He had known this would happen and no matter how much he had tried rationally to argue himself out of it, there was an inevitability about what was going to happen next.

'So,' she said.

'So.'

'Your place or mine?'

He laughed. 'Do people still use that line?'

'People will use anything that works. So?'

'What about your boyfriend?'

'He's not here.'

She leaned forward again. Fantastic cleavage, he thought.

'I asked you a question.' Suddenly she seemed very assertive.

'Mine,' he said.

They got up and left.

Hurriedly.

*

'Thanks,' said Abigail, 'I've really enjoyed tonight.'

Jack gave a smile as if no one had ever said anything nice to him before. She smiled in return. He really was a sweet boy. And good company too.

She had been wary of him at first, if she was honest. When he turned up at the office to see his mother who was some kind of ageing goth, and told her he had been sent home from school for fighting, she knew he wasn't the kind of boy she wanted to spend time with. But he had insisted it wasn't his fault, that he was just trying to sit and read and the other boy had picked on him and started it so she had given him the benefit of the doubt. She asked him what he had been reading and when he told her *The Boy in the Striped Pyjamas*, and that he had been really enjoying it and they had a discussion about it, she changed her opinion of him. Maybe he was telling the truth.

So when her dad suggested they take a look round town together she didn't mind as much. And he knew as much about Newcastle as she did, so they were even. And she had really enjoyed herself. The film wasn't very good, a teen comedy about a geek getting a hot-looking girl pregnant, but that was OK. They had fun. And when he walked her back to Donovan's flat they aired their impressions of the movie. He had thought the same as her and they enjoyed sharing deprecating remarks about it that were actually funnier than the actual film had been.

He walked her to the main entrance of the block of flats, stood there on the doorstep.

This was awkward. She liked him, he was sweet, but sweet didn't always translate into anything else. He was fun to be with. But she didn't want to spoil it by making it something it wasn't. Or something she didn't think it was.

'I've had a really great time today,' he said, looking at his trainers. 'Thanks.'

'You too. It's been fun.'

He smiled shyly, kept his eyes downcast. 'Erm, look, I . . . I don't know what's happening tomorrow, if I'm, you know . . . back at school or anything . . .'

She waited. Here it comes, she thought.

'But, erm . . . if you're around and you've got nothing to do . . . well, of course you're around and you've got nothing to do, sorry that's . . . well, anyway, should I . . . you know, call you?'

He really was sweet, she thought. And quite good-looking too, in his own way. And intelligent. And funny. In fact, she could do a lot worse. Certainly worth spending another day with.

'Sure,' she said. 'Let's swap phone numbers.'

He looked as though he couldn't believe his luck. They swapped numbers, then he stood back and looked at her. Oh God, she thought. He's going to try and kiss me.

But he didn't. He smiled at her, catching her eye, this time. 'Thank you. I've . . . thanks.'

She smiled. 'Get home safely.'

'I will.'

He looked relieved that the kiss hadn't happened. So was she. She thought. Probably.

He turned, walked away. She watched him go. He got a way down the street, turned and, when he saw her still there, smiled and waved. She waved back. He walked off, a spring in his step.

She let herself in with the key her dad had given her, made her way up to his floor. He had told her he wouldn't be back until late and to let herself in. And not to tell her mother that he had allowed her to be out so late with a boy. She smiled at that. Maybe he wasn't as bad as she had thought. Maybe she would be able to talk to him. Get things sorted.

She let herself into the flat.

It had been a good day.

'Hello.'

She answers her phone without thinking. Not knowing who it might be but hoping there will be no more talking tonight. She cannot talk any more.

'Hello, babe.'

She hears the voice and freezes. She doesn't answer. She can't answer.

'I hear you've been a naughty girl. I hear you've been talking. That's a no-no, isn't it? Remember what we agreed? What would happen the next time you felt like doing that?'

Her mouth moves but nothing comes out. She wants to ask so many questions, but she doesn't want to hear any of the answers. She wants to put the phone down, pretend she never answered. Pretend she's somewhere else. Someone else.

'You know what I said would happen, what you'd have to do . . .'

She nods.

'Speak up, I know you're there.'

'Yes . . .'

'Then do it.'

'No . . . no . . .'

'You've got no choice. You broke the rules. You know what to do. Do it now. Now.'

He tells her where.

'Alone.'

He hangs up. She stares at the phone. She wants to scream her lungs raw, throw herself at walls, slice her skin down to the bone. Anything but what he wants. She sobs. She knows he's right.

She wipes the tears and snot from her face with the back of her hand, gets up, walks to the door. Her heart is like concrete.

She leaves the flat.

19

'Yeah, it's a pisser, I mean, what isn't? The way they've got it, fuckin' government's got no respect for the workin' man. Have they?'

Tess agreed that indeed they didn't.

Rob continued. 'You've got to make money where you can these days. How you can.'

Tess spotted her cue. 'And how are you doing it?'

Rob gave a smile that he probably intended as cunning and clever but came over as more feral and vicious. 'We've got a plan. Me an' the missus. A plan. An' a fuckin' good one too.'

Rob then excused himself to go to the toilet. Tess watched the drunken man weave his way across the barroom floor and stifled a smile. She had him right where she wanted him. The man was drunk and, he had revealed, skint. A perfect combination for what Tess was about to propose.

Tess had fed him drinks all night. She had tried to maintain the illusion that she was keeping up with him, matching him pint for pint, but when his back was turned she had been returning them to the barmaid for her to pour away. She knew exactly what she was doing and it only increased her sour-faced appearance but she didn't tell Rob. Probably because Tess had included her in every round she bought. However, Tess still felt the effects of the alcohol and knew she shouldn't have much more. Which meant it was time to move up a gear.

Rob returned from the toilet, resumed his seat.

'So,' said Tess. 'You were saying.'

Rob looked blank.

'Your missus and you have got a plan.'

Rob remembered. As the memory of his plan returned, his face split into a venomous grin. 'Yeah. Get our own back. She's fuckin' suffered, my missus. Fuckin' suffered loads. 'Bout time she got her own back. Got what was comin' to her.'

'You mean money?'

'Oh yeah,' said Rob, 'money. Plenty of it . . .'

'And what about you? Do you get it as well?'

Rob frowned. 'Yeah . . .'

'You don't sound so sure. Will you get it? Or will she?'

Rob frowned further. He didn't answer. Tess pressed on.

'Because I've got a proposal that could make you a hell of a lot of money. A hell of a lot. In no time at all. Say yes and the money would be with you tomorrow.'

Rob's eyes were once again alight with feral cunning. He was listening.

'You see . . .' Now or never, thought Tess. She leaned in close, reminding Rob of her breasts, took a deep breath, dived right in. 'I know who you are, Rob. I know who your missus is too. Or rather was. And I know what she did to that boy.'

Rob stared at her, suddenly sober, too stunned to speak.

'And there's been another boy killed right where you live. You can put two and two together . . .'

Rob still said nothing, just stared at her.

'So this is my proposal. Talk to me. Give me an exclusive about her, what your life's like together, all that. We'll get some photos and in return all your money worries will be over. You might even get your own book out of it. Get you on *Richard and Judy.*' She smiled what she assumed was her most winning smile. 'What d'you say?'

Rob looked at her, slid off the bar stool and stood up slowly. He said one word.

'Cunt.'

And threw a punch that knocked Tess right off her stool and sent her crashing to the floor, drinks spilling, glass breaking. There was a blinding flash.

Tess opened her eyes, saw Rob standing over her.

'Fuckin' cunt.'

She closed her eyes expecting a kick that she knew would shatter ribs. It never came. But there was another blinding flash. Then she heard quick footsteps – Rob running away. There were gasps and shrieks from around the pub. Tess ignored them. She groaned, touched her face. Brought her hand away wet and red.

'God . . .' It hurt. It hurt so much . . .

Tess opened her eyes. She wanted to cry, but Collins was standing over her. She tried to pull herself together, be professional.

'Did you . . . did you get the photos . . .?'

'Yeah,' said Collins, animated for the first time since Tess had met him. 'Got a couple of great ones as he hit you. Another of him standing over you about to do some more damage. Good stuff.'

Tess managed a weak smile. It hurt even more.

'Come on then . . . let's get after him . . .'

Collins pulled her roughly to her feet. The pain was so intense as he did so that Tess feared she would black out. She didn't realize a punch to the face would affect her whole body this way. Her head was spinning, she thought she might be sick. Then tried to get a grip once more. Focus. Concentrate.

'Public interest, my fucking arse . . .'

Collins dragged Tess to the car, looked at her as she sat down.

'You did good, Posh Bird. We'll make a reporter out of you yet.'

They set off for the estate, Collins's endorsement ringing in her ears. It almost made the pain worthwhile.

Almost.

Pez was upset. Renny was his best friend no doubt, the best he had ever had and ever would have, but sometimes he upset him. Like tonight.

They had been to the off-licence with that journalist's money, bought enough sweets to send them to Haribo heaven, two packets of cigarettes – which surprised Nihal because they only ever had the money for singles usually – and some WKDs and cider. Sorted for the night.

Sitting on the bench watching the world get dark. Nothing else to do. Sugar-rushing from the sweets, mellowing out from the cider. They couldn't open the WKDs. They talked, laughed. Sat for long stretches in silence.

The sugar comedown hit Pez hard, he kept eating and drinking to keep on the high. Renny went into one of his angry moods, twitching and jumping around, mouth moving worldlessly, having imaginary conversations with whichever demons were plaguing him. Pez didn't interrupt, knew better than to do that when he was in one of these moods. Just sat next to him, happy just to be beside his friend. His best and only friend.

And then Renny, after necking the last of the cider and lobbing the plastic bottle as far as he could, had started. They had this money left, their heads were loaded, they should go somewhere, do something. And Pez, like always, agreed. It was too early to go and see the cars and the police were in the area, watching for Calvin's murderer after Calvin's death. So they couldn't go there.

Renny had been on edge a lot the last few days. Ever since Calvin died, Pez thought, but he didn't say it because it just might make Renny angry. So he said nothing. He was good at saying nothing.

So he and Renny had walked round the estate. They knew every centimetre of it, had walked it so many times. Knew which bits were usually safe, which were best avoided. But it wasn't happening tonight. The booze, the sweets, the cigarettes had all promised something but failed to deliver. There was something more happening, something better, but Pez didn't know what and didn't know where. So Pez told Renny he was going home.

And that's when the trouble started.

Renny turned on him. Nought to sixty in seconds. 'Go then, fuckin' go, you fuckin' cunt. Go on then, see if I care. Do I care? I don't fuckin' care. Fuck off. You can do what you fuckin' want. I don't fuckin' care . . .'

And on and on. Pez was hurt by the words; even for Renny they were unkind. When Renny was unkind to him Pez usually forgave him. But the look in his best friend's eyes when he was ranting at him told him it was best to leave him alone for the time being. So Pez left him.

But Pez didn't go home. He couldn't. Renny's words had upset him. So he walked round, on his own, thinking. It took him a long time to think. So it took him a long time to walk.

He bought more sweets, another two cans of cider.

Lost all track of time.

'Here. Just here . . .'

Collins pulled the Golf up on the Hancock Estate, opposite the block of flats that Mae Blacklock lived in. Tess, curled up foetally in the passenger seat, turned to look out of the window. Arrows of pain shot up through her as she did so. 'Jesus Christ . . .' It hurt so much. So fucking much. .

Her first reaction after Collins had given her that rare note of praise and the comedown had hit, was to want to cry. Scream, shout and bawl. She didn't want this any more. Being hurt, sitting in cars all night, trying to destroy people's lives just to sell papers. She wanted to go home. Not her little flat in Dalston but her real home. Back to her parents in the country. But she got a grip. It was just the pain talking. She would be all right once they got moving.

Yeah. She'd be back to normal.

'We must have . . . have . . . beat him back . . . let's, let's wait . . .'

Collins took out his camera, attached a telephoto lens. He was like a different person from the one he had been all day, Tess thought. Focused, alive. Now she could see why he was so highly rated.

They waited, watched. One of the kids Tess had been using staggered past, Pez, she thought his name was. He looked wasted. Probably on my money, she thought, curling down so she couldn't be seen, head spinning once more.

Pez disappeared round a corner. Tess and Collins kept watching the flats.

Eventually they saw movement.

'That her?' asked Collins.

Mae Blacklock was coming out of the stairwell, hurrying across the square.

'That's her,' said Tess.

Collins adjusted focus, started snapping.

'Look.'

From the opposite side of the square Rob appeared. He looked out of breath, as if he had ran the whole way. He saw her, summoned up some remaining energy and ran towards her.

'Round two . . .' Tess said.

Rob started talking to her, loudly, waving his arms round, pointing back the way he had come. They couldn't hear what was being said but Tess was sure she knew what Rob was saying. Mae Blacklock looked suddenly terrified. She fell into Rob's arms. He held her tight. Collins kept snapping.

'Ah, isn't love sweet . . .'

Then she abruptly pulled away. Rob looked surprised. She was saying something to him, pointing off in another direction. He grabbed hold of her arms. She bent forward, pleading with him to let her go. He shook his head. She pleaded some more. Tess wished she could hear what they were saying.

Eventually she broke down in tears and Rob let her go. She hugged him, clinging like she didn't want to let go until she reluctantly pulled herself away. Just as reluctantly he let her go.

'You getting all this?'

'Crisp and clear.' Collins kept snapping away.

Suddenly Rob looked over, anger in his face.

'Fuck,' said Tess, 'he's spotted us.'

Rob was striding over to the car, hands balled into fists. He stopped on the way to pick up a length of pipe that was lying in among the debris of someone's front garden.

'Move,' said Tess, 'move . . .'

Collins dropped the camera with its heavy lens on Tess's lap. She gave a start, let out a grunt of pain. Collins started the car, put it in gear, drove off before Rob could reach them.

He drove out of the estate, didn't stop until he was sure there was no danger. Turned the engine off. Tess let out a huge sigh of relief. It hurt but she didn't mind.

'Fuck me . . .' She laughed. 'That was close . . .'

'What should we do now?' said Collins, picking up his camera again, checking that Tess hadn't damaged it with her lap.

'Let's wait,' said Tess. 'She seemed like she was off somewhere. Let's give her time to do what she has to do and get back. Then we'll go and keep watch.'

Collins nodded.

'So what d'you reckon then?' asked Tess. 'Have we got overwhelming public interest yet?'

Collins looked at Tess's ruined face. 'I think we're getting there.'

Tess managed a mangled smile. 'Fantastic,' she said.

She hoped she meant it.

Pez walked. Because he didn't know what else to do.

He shook his head, tried to clear it. Those extra cans of cider had been a mistake. Instead of making things clearer they had just made them murkier. He didn't know why Renny behaved the way he did. He knew things were bad at home, that his father hit him and hurt him, sometimes in horrible ways, in fact it was partly why Pez was friends with him. Because he thought he would appreciate someone being nice to him. But it didn't always work out that way. Renny didn't always appreciate it. Or if he did, he didn't always show it.

But at least Renny had a dad. Pez had lost his. To lung cancer. He remembered when he used to be a big bloke, the life and soul. Always laughing, with a drink in one hand and a fag in the other. He can't think of his dad then without smiling. But not later. When he had a lung removed and needed a canister of oxygen in the front room just to get up and make a cup of tea. He didn't laugh so much then. Or when the cancer really got him, when it stripped him down to his bones like that monster off *Doctor Who*. He was a walking skeleton. Well, not walking. Just lying there.

But he missed his dad. Wished he was there. His mother tried her best but when he died she seemed to as well. Or a part of her did. The happy part.

He closed his eyes. He shouldn't drink. It always made him sad eventually.

Pez looked up. He was in a part of the estate he hardly ever came to. He didn't know anyone here and no one knew him. Not good. Time to go home. He didn't even have a blade on him. He could see Renny tomorrow, hope he was in a better mood. Do something fun together to put him in a better mood.

He turned round. And stopped.

Someone was blocking his way in the alley. Someone holding a very large knife.

Pez tried to scream, to shout for help, but a hand was clamped round his neck. The hand squeezed, twisted. The other hand held the blade. Brought it closer. He tried even harder to scream but when the blade opened the veins and arteries in his neck it also sliced through his vocal cords. By the time he had crumpled to the ground, his intestines spilling out from the slashes the blade had made in his stomach, he could do nothing but lie there. A darkness that was blacker than the night crept into his vision and he knew he was dying. He closed his eyes, too surprised even to cry.

The blood bled out of his body. His heart stopped. His final thought:

I hope I see my dad.

Tess checked her watch. Nearly an hour had gone by. Time, she thought, to resume their position.

Collins drove back to the estate, parking in a different position from the previous time since Rob may still be on the lookout for them, but still with a view of the entrance to Mae Blacklock's block of flats.

'Ready for a long night?' said Tess.

Collins looked at Tess and she saw some small amount of concern in his eyes. 'Shouldn't you go and get that nose checked out? Might need a bit of surgery to push it back into place. Don't want you ruinin' your good looks.'

Tess was stunned at the words. She didn't know what to say. Instead, she pulled down the vanity mirror on the sun visor, checked herself out. Collins was right, she looked a mess. Hardly a night for pulling. But there was nothing she could do about it now. With the money she made from this she could get it surgically reconstructed. Christ, she could probably get her whole face reconstructed. And a boob job as well, if she wanted.

She flipped the visor back up. And saw Mae Blacklock walking over the square.

'There she is.'

Collins reached for his camera, stared snapping. 'She looks exhausted,' he said.

'Wonder where she's been?' said Tess. She checked her watch. Coming up for two in the morning. 'Late to be out for a stroll.'

Collins snapped her all the way into the stairwell.

'That's her for the night, I guess,' said Tess. 'What should we do?'

Collins shrugged. 'Wait.'

Tess attempted a smile. 'Fine.' She shifted in her seat. Felt shafts of pain lance through her. 'I find it of overwhelming public interest that we sit here and wait.'

She tried to settle back into her seat. She was exhausted,

experiencing pain like never before and about to sit up all night watching a stairwell where she doubted there would be any movement.

Tess hoped it would be worth it.

PART FOUR

WAIT UNTIL DARK

'Right. We've got to step up a gear.'

She doesn't answer.

'Hello? Did you hear me?'

She looks up at him. She's clearly been crying and more – she has black circles under her eyes and her clothes are creased. She looks like she hasn't slept. Her eyes are unfocused, like she can't hear what he's saying or there are other things clouding his words out.

'Yeah . . .'

He decides to carry on. 'What you've given me so far is OK but it's not enough. I need much more than that if this is going to work. And more depth too. We've only skimmed the surface.'

'I can't do this today.' She picks at the bandages on her hands as she talks.

He waits.

'Look, I just . . . things have changed. Thing have happened. This might not be finished. I might not be here much longer. I might have to go away again.'

'Why?'

'Because . . .' She wants to answer but stops herself. 'Because it's all changed. I can't say any more.'

'You can talk to me. What's happened? Why have you got to go?'

'I just have.' She shakes her head. 'I shouldn't be here now. I should be off.'

'Where?'

'Anywhere. Just . . . as far from here as possible.'

'Again, why?'

'Because . . . things have happened. Bad things. You thought I was making it up? The bad spirits and that? Rubbish. It's not safe for me here any more. Or Jack. I've got to get away.'

'If things are that bad, you need help.'

'I've got to get away . . .'

'Why?'

'I just have! That's why!' She stops, looks at him. Knows he's only trying to help. Tries to calm down. 'Sorry.'

There are things he wants to say to her, questions he wants to ask. But he is unsure whether they will pull her closer to him or push her further away. 'You need help. You need to confront whatever's gone wrong and put it right.'

'That's easy for you to say. But I can't get help, don't you understand? I can't. It's beyond that now.' She looks around. 'I've got to run.'

He has to be direct. 'What have you done, Anne Marie?'

She doesn't answer, just closes her eyes.

'Please,' she says eventually, 'will you help me?'

He looks at the distraught, fragile woman before him, sees the state she is in. He won't let her run, he knows that. There is too much at stake. Too much he needs to know.

'I'll help you,' he says.

She looks about to burst into tears.

'But I won't help you run.'

'But . . .'

'You want to leave but you haven't gone,' he says. 'You don't want to talk but you're sitting here in front of me right now. You say you want to run and hide, but you didn't. You came to see me.'

She looks at him, says nothing.

'I think there are things you want to tell me. And that's good, because I'm here to listen. So here's what we'll do. You talk to me. Tell me everything that I need to know. Tell me honestly. Don't hide things, don't embellish, don't try to make your—'

'I'm not a liar. I'm not manipulative.'

'Good. Then just be honest and talk to me.'

'And then will you help me get away?'

'I'm making no promises. But I will help you.'

She looks at him, says nothing.

'It's either that or nothing, Anne Marie. And no one else is queuing up to help you. So what d'you say? Deal?'

She sighs. And the weight of the world moves slightly.

'Deal,' she says.

'Good,' he says, knowing this could well be the breakthrough he has been working towards. He is also aware that he needs to know everything but thinks it best to do so in order. 'Right,' he says, making a decision. 'Let's start at the beginning. I can't understand the present without going back into the past. You're eleven years old, Anne Marie. Tell me everything.'

20

Abigail opened her eyes and for a few seconds was disorien-
tated. A strange room. A strange view. Then she
remembered. And smiled. Her dad's flat. And a good day out
with a nice boy. Almost enough to make her forget why she
came here in the first place.

She stretched, arms above her head, threw back the duvet
and got off the sofa, stretching again once she was upright.
She walked over to the window, pulled back the curtains.
The weather wasn't great but the view was. She had never
realized just how attractive the quayside of Newcastle could
be. For a girl whose friends, socializing and attitude were
avowedly North London, that, she considered, was quite an
admission.

She smiled, closed her eyes, slowly rotated her head on
her neck. She felt relaxed for the first time in days, weeks
even. She was enjoying herself. And, surprisingly, her dad's
company. She had heard the shower go, in fact that was
what had woken her up. So she knew he was awake.
Deciding to surprise him with some coffee, she walked into
the kitchen.

And stopped dead.

'Who are you?'

There was a woman, dressed in a suit which looked a day
old, standing with her back to the sink, leaning on it, drinking a glass of water. She looked as surprised as Abigail.

'Oh,' the woman said. 'You must be Joe's daughter.'

'Yes. And who are you?'

'I'm . . . a friend of your father's.'

The woman looked as embarrassed as Abigail felt. But she hadn't moved, her hand clasped round the glass, poised against the sink in an attempt to regain her composure. Abigail felt her cheeks reddening.

'A friend.' She seemed uncomfortable in saying even that much.

She nodded, tried for a smile. 'I'm Wendy. What's your name?'

'Abigail.' She could feel her lip curling and with it, the sourness entering her expression. She couldn't help it. She felt that her good mood, the morning itself in fact, was curdling.

'Abigail,' the woman repeated. 'Nice name.' She smiled. 'Well. This is a bit embarrassing, isn't it?'

Abigail said nothing.

Wendy put the glass down on the draining board. 'I'll just finish up here and be off, I think. Sorry.'

She walked out of the kitchen, past Abigail, leaving a scent of perfume in her slipstream. Abigail looked round the kitchen. The woman's presence seemed to be everywhere.

She didn't want to make coffee any more. She didn't want to speak to her dad. She felt betrayed. She didn't know why because rationally it was none of her business, the fact that he hadn't mentioned he had a girlfriend. And so what? He was entitled to have one. Just like her mother . . .

She sighed. That was the problem.

'Hey,' a voice said behind her, 'didn't hear you get up.'

She turned. There was her father. Standing there in his regulation T-shirt, jeans and boots, hair still wet from the shower. He smiled at her, looked genuinely pleased to see her. She couldn't return the smile. He caught her mood, frowned.

'You OK?'

She turned away. 'Yeah. Fine.' She tried to busy herself with making coffee, a bowl of cereal, anything, but didn't know where anything was so just stood there looking helpless.

'Erm . . . I'll be off, then.'

They both turned. Wendy was standing in the living room. Donovan looked between the two and guessed immediately at the cause of Abigail's mood.

'You two have met, then?'

'Just now,' said Wendy. She looked at Abigail, gave her a smile that tried to be dazzling but was hindered by embarrassment. 'Nice to meet you.'

It didn't sound like it had been, thought Abigail.

Wendy then turned to Donovan. Gave him another smile. 'Will I see you later?'

'Where are you going?'

'Back to the hotel.'

It was clear to Abigail that they wanted to have a conversation without her being there. She resolutely stayed where she was.

'I'll call you,' said Donovan. Wendy made her way out.

Donovan looked at Abigail, his face that of a naughty schoolboy, caught out doing something he shouldn't have been doing. 'Not the best way for you two to meet, I suppose.'

Abigail turned away again, looking for phantom kitchen implements. 'Nothing to do with me,' she said, head down, addressing the sink.

Donovan said nothing. Waited.

'Why the bad mood? Because Wendy spent the night?'

Abigail shrugged, didn't turn round.

'Sorry, Abigail. Yes, I'm your dad, but I'm not with your mum. You know that. She's got someone else. He lives with you. You're good with that.'

Am I? Abigail thought but didn't trust herself to articulate it. Instead she said nothing. The things she wanted to say to him, discuss with him, seemed as distant as the planet Jupiter.

'She your girlfriend?' was all Abigail could manage to mumble.

Behind her, Donovan shrugged, grimaced. 'Well . . . it's kind of complicated.'

Abigail said nothing. She didn't trust herself to speak.

He sighed. 'What's worse? If I tell you she is or I tell you she isn't?'

'Nothing to do with me.' Mumbled at the sink again. 'Your life.'

'Look, Abigail. Wendy's somebody that I . . . she's a work colleague. That's the first time we've . . . that she's ever stayed over. She lives in London. I don't know if she's my, my girlfriend. She's . . . We'll have to talk about that. Her and I.'

Abigail said nothing. Emotions whirred through her, ricocheting round like an apple in a wind tunnel.

'What?' said Donovan. 'Why are you so upset? You wouldn't be upset if it was Mum and her boyfriend.'

Abigail turned to him, hot tears threatening in the corners of her eyes. 'How would you know? Ey? How would you know what I think or what would make me upset? How would you know?'

'Well . . .'

'You don't know anything . . . anything . . .'

She couldn't look at him any more. She ran past him, grabbed her stuff from the living-room floor and made for the bathroom, locking the door behind her. Trying to ignore the tears that were now streaming down her face and the wracking great sobs issuing from her body, she turned the shower on as hard as she could, stripped off and stood underneath it.

She could hear the faint sounds of her father knocking on the door, muffled solicitous words. She ignored them. He would give up and go away at some point. She knew that. He had to go to work. So she wouldn't get out until he had gone. Just stand in the shower.

Stand in the shower all day if necessary.

Peta woke to the sound of ringing. At first she thought it was in her head, a flashback to her drinking years. She expected, as usually happened, to become aware of her kidneys throbbing then try to roll over only to discover her arms and hands were dead with pins and needles.

But it wasn't like that. Not any more. She blinked twice, allowing her memory to catch up with the rest of her body. A Travelodge in Essex. She was clean and sober. And the ringing was her phone.

She reached out, answered it.

'Peta Knight?' a voice asked.

'Yes.'

'Tom Haig here. We met yesterday.'

She cleared the sleep from her mind, concentrated on the call. Tom Haig. Ex-probation officer. West London. Anne Marie's one stop shop. 'Yes, Tom. What can I do for you?'

'I hope you don't mind me calling you like this . . .'

'Not at all.'

'Only you got me thinking once you'd gone. About Anne Marie. And . . . well, I don't know. I'm just, I may be speaking out of turn here . . .'

'No, you go right ahead. If you think it's important, let me know.'

'Thanks. Well, it's probably none of my business, and I shouldn't even be telling you this, but she once told me about someone. Someone she was seeing. And how it all went wrong.'

'Who?'

'She didn't give a name. But he was a social worker.'

She was sitting upright now. He had her full attention. 'A social worker.'

'Yeah. This was after my time, though. After she moved. Bristol, I think.'

'And this social worker, what was the matter with him?'

'Well . . .' He seemed reluctant to commit himself.

'In strictest confidence, Tom.'

'Right.' He cleared his throat. It became a coughing fit.

'You OK?'

'Yeah, just . . . just a bit of a cold. Be . . . all right in a minute . . .' She waited while he regained his composure. He continued. 'He was . . . she told me he seemed fine to start with. But then he turned on her. Became nasty.'

'How d'you mean?'

'I don't know,' he said. 'That's all she told me. We lost touch soon after that. Wasn't really supposed to be talking to her. Home Office rules, and all that.'

'So why were you?'

'Well . . . you're not supposed to have favourites, but you know what it's like . . .'

He talked a little more but didn't offer any further information. Peta hung up on him, thinking that maybe he was just lonely and wanted someone to talk to. Wanted to feel useful again. She hoped she never ended up like that.

She played the conversation back in her head. There was something odd about it. Something he had said that didn't fit. But she couldn't think what it was . . .

Her phone rang again and when she answered it all thoughts of Tom Haig were knocked from her head.

'Flemyng's gone.' Amar.

'Gone where?'

'Don't know. I phoned the university to speak to him, said I was following up on a few things and they told me he hadn't come in. Asked if he was sick, they got a bit cagey. Same as when I asked whether he was coming back.'

Peta got out of bed. Her mind was whirring in overtime. Could Flemyng have been to Newcastle, left that note, come back to Bristol, met them . . . could he have someone working with him, could he . . . 'Has he been at work all week?'

'They wouldn't say. They're not very forthcoming with information.'

'Right. Have you been round to his house?'

'I'm there now. Going to do a spot of B and E.'

'OK. I'll phone Joe, bring him up to speed. Let me know what happens.'

'Consider yourself looped.' Amar hung up.

Peta speed-dialled Donovan straightaway. Told him what had happened along with her suspicions and suppositions. Told him what Haig had said. There was only one person he could have been alluding to. Donovan seemed initially distracted, as if he hadn't wanted to be disturbed but once she told him what had happened she got his full attention.

'Think you'd better get back here right now. I don't think you need to bother with Hull or Colchester, it sounds like he's our man.'

'Unless she's our woman,' said Peta.

'I should know soon enough. Look, I've got to go. Just get back here soon as. If it's him, and it sounds like it is, we can consider him very dangerous.'

'Right.'

'By the way, how was last night?'

Taken aback by his sudden change of direction in his questions, she managed a smile. 'Brilliant. Time of my life. You should have been here. Although on second thoughts, it's probably good you weren't.'

He gave a tight laugh. 'No. I hate to see a grown woman cry.'

She laughed. 'Piss off.' Hung up.

The smile disappeared from her face as she tossed the phone into her bag. She was back to business.

'Oh God . . .'

'Eleven years old. Tell me what happened. Tell me everything.'

She sighs. She is without her props. No coffee, no cigarettes. Nothing to hide behind but an assumed name, which she has used for so long it has become more real than her birth one. She thinks, her mind reluctantly travelling back in time.

'So was Trevor Cunliffe the first child you'd attacked? Or had you done something like that before?'

She thinks again, face twisted as if in pain. She closes her eyes. 'No. There were these girls. In the street. Skipping. Clean, pressed frocks. Laughing, smiling. Enjoying themselves.' She sighs, eyes still closed, back there. 'I hated that.'

'What did you do?'

'I went over to them. Grabbed one of them. Round the throat. Hard. I said, I could kill you, I could kill you . . .' Her hands grip hard on air at the memory. She lets go. Opens her eyes. 'She ran home. I laughed.' She sighs. 'But not because I was happy.'

'And this was how long before? Weeks? Days? What?'

'I don't know. I can't remember . . .'

'Right.' His voice drops to just below a whisper. 'D'you know why you did that? Why you grabbed her?'

'Because I was angry. I was always angry. All I had was anger. Rage and hate. My two best friends . . . My mother, she . . . and, and my grandad . . .'

He has heard this before, knows this. 'Your grandad? He hurt you as well?'

She nods. He doesn't ask her to articulate it for the benefit of the recorder.

'He used to . . . like my mother's clients used to . . . They gave *me to him when my mother was . . . when she couldn't look after me for a while. He was supposed to care for me. He didn't.'*

'He abused you? Sexually?'

She nods. 'I couldn't help it. Couldn't stop him . . . I had no control, no control . . . They all controlled me . . .' Her eyes are closed again. Tears run down her cheeks. 'He called me filthy. A whore. His whore.'

'So what did you do?'

Her voice a whisper. 'I stabbed him.'

'You stabbed him?'

Another nod.

He hasn't heard about this. 'With what?'

'Scissors.'

He nods. 'Was it fatal?'

She shakes her head. 'Barely made a mark. He just laughed. Said he liked it rough.'

He says nothing.

'But when I picked those scissors up, I knew I'd found another friend. A third one. I had no control over my body, over anything. All I had was rage and hate. And the scissors. Now I had the scissors.'

'And what did you do with them?'

She opens her eyes, blinks as if emerging into the light after being underground for a long spell. 'Nothin' at first. But I knew they meant power. I knew they meant control. I knew they could give me somethin' I'd never had before.'

'So what did you do with that control?'

She thinks, searches for what he believes is the honest answer. 'I played with the kids. It was the little kids I mainly played with. The ones my own age were too . . . they didn't like me. I didn't like them. I couldn't relate to them. But the little ones . . .' She smiles and it looks almost like a happy memory. For a second. 'I could boss them around. Order them. Have control.'

'Bully them?'

She is torn between the honest answer and the acceptable one. She goes for honesty. 'Yes.'

'Hurt them?'

She thinks again. 'Yes.'

'And it escalated until . . .'

She sighs. 'I started hurtin' them more an' more. Bein' more aggressive. So if you wanted to talk like a psychiatrist or a therapist I suppose you could say what I did next was an escalation. A progression.'

'We're talking Trevor Cunliffe.'

'Yes.'

'You killed him.'

'Yes.' She gives another sigh, wipes at her eyes and cheeks. 'Quite a progression, isn't it? Biggest one of all.' Her eyes mist over once again and what Donovan can only describe as a kind of sick fear moves into them. 'It's awful. It's what people who have no power do. They hurt the powerless ones. To make themselves feel better, more important. They kill kids to make them feel big. They make . . .' She pauses, struggling with tears once again. ' . . . helpless people do what they want. Just because they can.'

She struggles to hold back another wave of tears. Struggles to hold herself together.

Donovan watches her. No longer sure she's talking about the past.

21

The news of Pez's death broke that morning.

The body was discovered by a Polish immigrant on her way to do the early shift as a cleaner in a city centre office block. She was walking towards the bus stop to catch the first bus of the day when she came upon the body. She called 999 and went no further.

The police arrived and took a statement from her, quickly discounting her as the murderer. DI Diane Nattrass was informed as she was already looking into the murder of Calvin Bell on the same estate. The immediate assumption was that both deaths were connected.

Nattrass was soon put in charge of the investigation. The boy was quickly identified: John Pearson. A preliminary cause of death was given: strangulation and stabbing. A full post-mortem would reveal which came first, which provided the death stroke. But for now it didn't matter. The next of kin would be informed. The SOCO unit would start combing the area. Uniforms would go door to door. A mobile incident office was already on the estate; it would be moved to the scene of this new murder. Nattrass would coordinate, push.

The investigation into the murder of John Pearson, aka Pez, was now in full swing.

The press conference had been hastily convened. The school hall, where not so long ago Heptonstall the head teacher had informed the children about the death of Calvin Bell, was now given over totally to the police. On their orders, the children had all been given the day off.

On the stage were hastily erected Northumbrian Police fold-out screens and before them a table with microphones and water, chairs behind. Ready for the press conference.

The hall was crowded, buzzing even more than when the schoolchildren had been informed of Calvin Bell's death. Because this was big news. Bigger. This was when the professionals moved in.

Tess Preston sat near the back. She had tried to get a seat at the front but been beaten away in the scrum, mainly by photographers wielding lenses so large and heavy that if wielded incorrectly could rightly be classified as offensive weapons. So the back it was. But she didn't mind much. She felt like some old-time gold or oil prospector who knew they were sitting on a fortune, just biding their time to make the first strike.

Her face was starting to bruise up and she imagined she looked a sight. She would have been in a lot more pain too, if Collins hadn't given her some extra-strength 'painkillers' he just happened to have lying around. Tess had gobbled them down. She didn't know what was in them but she felt she could go one on one with the Hulk now.

As soon as she had heard about the murder of the boy she had started making connections. She had seen Mae Blacklock walking round the estate late last night. Very late. Arguing with her partner. Looking like she was going somewhere, or coming back from somewhere weighed down by worry, looking anxious and agitated. Put two and two together . . .

She looked up. The press conference was starting. A detective walked on, sat down behind the desk, introduced as Detective Inspector Diane Nattrass. She introduced the person on her right. The mother of John Pearson.

Tess looked at her, decided that the boy hadn't had much to look forward to. Prematurely aged, with poor clothes, a bad haircut and a bad complexion, she looked worn away, shrivelled by life. She would have guessed her age to be late forties, early fifties. She was genuinely shocked to hear that she was in her mid-thirties.

John Pearson's mother spoke. Her face was red from crying, her voice small and wavering. 'Someone took my little lad ...' She had to stop, compose herself again. 'Someone ...'

She broke down.

I hope Collins is getting all this, thought Tess.

Nattrass spoke. As she did, copies of a photo of the dead boy were circulated round the room. Tess took one, glanced at it briefly. Did a double take. She knew him. Renny's silent partner. Pez.

Tess felt like she was actually levitating, so fast was her brain whirring, making connections. Pez. Dead. And Mae Blacklock walking round the estate at night . . . as was Pez. She had seen him stagger past the car, ducked down to avoid him. This was brilliant. Brilliant. It couldn't get much better.

Nattrass was talking. She knew she should have been writing all of this down, making notes to turn into a full article, but she couldn't concentrate. The story in her head was so much bigger.

Nattrass finished talking. She was allowing questions. Tess had one, stuck her arm eagerly in the air. She pointed to her, waited.

'Tess Preston, the *Globe*,' she said proudly. 'I just wondered if you could give us a specific time of death yet.'

'Well, as I just said, the post-mortem hasn't been carried out yet so I wouldn't like to hazard a guess until we know more.'

She moved her attention away from her.

Tess wasn't going to let it go. 'Could you hazard a guess, please?'

She looked at Tess, clearly irritated by her persistence. She seemed to be deciding whether it would be better to ignore her in the hope she would go away or give her an answer. She decided on the latter.

She sighed as she answered, betraying the fact that she had probably been up all night and wouldn't have been so accommodating if she had had more sleep. 'After midnight. Sometime in the early hours. Probably, and this isn't confirmed yet, probably between 1 and 2 a.m.'

Tess thanked her graciously. Nattrass turned away from her to answer another question.

Between 1 and 2 a.m. Just the time Mae Blacklock had been on her night-time wander.

Perfect. She was tingling with anticipation.

After what seemed like an interminable few hours but was actually nearer half of one, the press conference eventually broke up. Tess was first out of the door, out of the school.

As she walked through the gates the same old woman she had seen interviewed on the news was back again. Red-faced and angry, she was shouting to the camera about children who kill children. Tess managed to pick up snippets of her rant that no doubt would be on every news bulletin for the rest of the day. Knife crime. Lawless teenagers. The breakdown of society.

She had asked a local journalist who she was the day before and been told that her son had been murdered by Mae Blacklock. Since then she had never missed an opportunity to get on TV and work out her angry grief in front of a camera. They kept her on because she provided good content and a faint whiff of authenticity.

Tess smiled to herself. She opened her mobile while she walked, and phoned her editor.

'Listen,' she said, once she had got past various people her editor had put in the way of taking calls directly, 'the story I'm working on. The child killer, there've been developments. You want public interest? I'll give you public interest. Rock-solid, copper-bottomed public interest.'

She talked and fifteen minutes later had been given an unequivocal go-ahead.

She snapped the phone shut, felt like her heart was about to burst it was beating so fast. Although that could have been the painkillers. She had to find Collins. There was work to do. She looked around. The mad old woman was still shouting at the camera, railing by the railings, she thought, mentally noting that one down for future use.

And then an idea occurred to her. Instead of walking away she turned, went back to Sylvia Cunliffe. She was just finishing up, being thanked by the TV reporter. Tess waited until the TV crew had moved away before approaching her.

'Mrs Cunliffe?'

She turned. Now that the cameras were off she looked, older, frailer. As if the only thing that kept her going was her hatred.

'What happened to your face, pet?' Her voice betrayed a lifetime of nicotine addiction. She sounded like she could beat Tom Waits in a gargling contest.

Tess had almost forgotten about her face, her rearranged nose. She had patched it up as best she could – sticking plaster and even a bit of make-up – but she still looked as if she had been on the receiving end of a particularly vicious night out. Still, she gave her her best smile. The one that was supposed to charm little old ladies. Or old ladies of any size, she mentally amended, taking in Sylvia Cunliffe's bulk.

'Was it a man?' said Sylvia Cunliffe.

'Yeah,' said Tess, spotting an in when she heard one. 'Boyfriend?'

She gave a small, calculated laugh. 'Don't have time for a boyfriend, not in this job. And looking like this I doubt I'd get one.'

'So who are you, then?'

'I'm a journalist. Tess Preston, the *Globe*. I was wondering if you had time for a quick interview?'

She wheezed, it became a cough. Tess waited. 'I've given all me interviews for the day, pet. These lot are waitin' to take me back home now.'

'I could do that,' said Tess. 'It would be no trouble. And we could have a little chat on the way. Does that sound OK?'

She sighed. 'What d'you want to talk to me about? The little lad what was killed?'

'Sort of,' said Tess. 'But something else. Mae Blacklock. I'm sure you remember her.'

It was like she had been attached to a power supply. Sylvia Cunliffe drew herself up to her full height. Her eyes were lit by a dark, nasty sparkle. 'What about her?'

Tess led her to the car. 'Let's talk on the way,' she said.

'Oh my days . . .'

Jamal stared at the screen on the laptop in his hotel room in Brighton. There was movement. Things were happening.

He watched. The front door, the one he had been keeping vigil on all week through the hidden webcam, was opening. Pulling up close to the monitor screen of the laptop he saw figures emerge. He could barely contain his excitement. There before him was the person they had been sent to find. Matt Milsom, instantly recognizable from the photos with his floppy black fringe and black-framed glasses, was the first to emerge. He was followed by a woman who looked nervously around as if expecting someone to jump out on them. And then came the third person. And that was when Jamal felt his legs begin to shake.

It was the boy. The one they claimed was an HIV-positive Romanian orphan. The one who Donovan believed was his son, David. He was still with them.

'God . . .'

Jamal watched them go, checking in which direction they were going. His mind went into overdrive deciding what to do next. He knew what he should do. What he had promised to do. Phone Peta's mate, get him down here straightaway. But he was working.

'Shit . . .'

'Right. Phone Donovan and tell him what was happening. Or Peta. Or Amar. He looked around, then back at the screen again. If he stopped to do that, they might get away and be lost again. He couldn't take that risk.

Watching the figures on the screen, he made a decision.

He grabbed his crash helmet and made for the door. The flat was near to their quarry. Near enough for him to be able to run out, get onto his scooter and be after them before they had gone too far.

That was what he did. As he ran he thought: he could phone Donovan or Peta's mate on the way. Once he knew what was happening. Yeah, that's what he would do. .

He ran out of the flat, slamming the door behind him.

Unaware he had left his mobile sitting on the table by the laptop.

'So. Trevor Cunliffe.'

She sighs, closes her eyes. Just before she does, he gets a glimpse into them and sees – just for a second – the struggle, the everyday war for survival raging within her. And in that second he is glad – even with everything that has gone wrong in his own life – that he is not she.

'Why him? Why then?'

Another sigh. 'I don't know. I've asked myself that over the years. Tortured myself with it. I don't know. It was just . . .' Her eyes, closed, were screwed even tighter shut. '. . . everything. Everything came together. Everything came to a head. I don't know. Because . . . because he was there. Because I was angry.' She sighs. 'I don't know.'

He sits, leaning forward. Trying to catch every word she says, interpret it as it leaves her mouth, dissect it for every layer of possible meaning it might contain. Apply it to her but simultaneously applying it to himself. Searching for reason, for understanding.

She continues, eyes still tightly shut. 'I was bored . . . I remember bein' bored . . . I watched the kids, the little kids playin' in the street . . . I remember feelin' the blade in my pocket, feelin', I don't know . . . safe when I touched that. Comfortable. No, not comfortable, powerful.'

She stops talking. He waits, knowing she will continue.

'It was just waste ground. They were pullin' down all the old houses, the slums, they called them, replacin' them with tower blocks. They were meant to be the future. No more slums. Look how they turned out.'

He wants to keep her on track. 'Go on.'

'The kids were playin'. Chasy, or somethin'. One of the kids called over. Asked me to join them. So I did.'

'*And this was Trevor?*'

She nods. He doesn't ask her to articulate.

'*And when he looked at me, I knew . . .*'

'*Knew what?*'

She shakes her head, slowly, like she's dislodging thoughts. '*I just knew. It was him. It was goin' to be him.*'

'*Your victim?*'

Another nod.

'*So what did you do?*'

Another sigh. He notices her hands are shaking. Her eyes are still closed. '*I said we'd play hide and seek. I said I'd shut my eyes, count to a hundred. But I didn't. I kept my eyes open. I watched where he went. Into this old, half-demolished house. I went after them. After him. I went up the staircase, found him upstairs. Told him to be quiet, that we were still playin', that this was still part of the game. Told him to lie down. Lie down like he was a statue. Or like he was dead. He did.*'

Tears crept from the corners of her screwed-up eyes. The shaking spread up her arms.

'*I got on top of him. Put . . . put my hands round his throat . . . and . . . and . . .*' She opens her eyes. '*Killed him.*'

He keeps looking at her, waiting, expecting more. It seems nothing more is forthcoming. The spell was broken when she opened her eyes.

'*Killed how?*'

'*Strangled him,*' she says, although it's clear she's not going to elaborate.

'*What about the scissors? The cuts?*'

She sighs, closes her eyes again. Opens them. '*I need a coffee.*'

'*What about the scissors?*'

She screws her eyes up tight again. '*Leave me alone . . .*'

'*The scissors, Anne Marie, tell me . . .*'

'*All right . . .*' She shouts. '*I slashed him. Got the scissors out and slashed him.*'

'Where?'
'Can't remember.'
He leans forward. 'Where?'
'Here . . .' She points to her groin and stomach. 'Here . . .'
The sobbing starts again. He looks at her. Gets up.
'Thank you. I'll put the kettle on.'

22

Amar rang the bell of the house, stood back, waited. No reply. He rang again. Same thing. He looked round. No one watching. Oh well, he thought. Time for a little B and E.

The house was on Royal York Crescent in Clifton. Probably the most desirable address in the whole area, if not the whole city. But Martin Flemyng's house wasn't in the desirable part. Near the shops and without any of the Georgian adornment that made the rest of the crescent so attractive, it looked less like a desirable town house and more like a terraced house that would have been given over to servants quarters. It was now the kind of house that only university students, or their teachers, could afford.

He checked the windows on either side of him. No one there. He took out a lockpick tool that he always carried. Peta had showed him how to use it. She was very adept with it and had tried to teach the rest of them how to use it. But he had never had the patience to master it as well as she had. As he inserted it into the lock, he was wishing he had paid more attention to what she had said.

But he remembered more than he had realized. It wasn't as hard as he had thought. He felt it move within the grooves, felt the levers click into place. A couple more moves and turns, gentle turns . . . nearly there . . .

'Can I help you?'

He looked up, startled. A woman was standing next to him, looking at him with suspicion in her eyes. Lots of suspicion. She was in her thirties and, from the look of her clothes and appearance – a long skirt, striped cardigan, cord jacket with scarf and lots of dark, wild hair – he guessed she was probably another university teacher.

Amar straightened up, weighed up his choices. He could run, which apart from immediately marking him as suspicious wouldn't help get him the information he wanted, or he could brazen it out. He decided on the latter.

'Do you live here?' he asked.

'No,' she said, 'do you?'

He smiled. 'No I don't. Can I ask if you know the person who lives here?'

'Can I ask why you want to know?'

He smiled. He admired her spirit, even if it was making his job more difficult. Maybe she just wasn't used to seeing Asian men trying to break into houses in broad daylight, he thought. Good job it wasn't Jamal in his place.

He came to a decision: he would tell her the truth, see what she said then.

'My name's Amar Miah,' he said. 'I'm a private investigator working for a solicitor in Newcastle. I've got a letter in my pocket I can show you if you like.' He made a mental note to thank Donovan for insisting on that piece of paper at the start of every job. Made his life so much simpler.

She was taken aback by his words, not expecting this, but recovered quickly. 'Show me please.'

'Can I ask who you are?'

'I'm a neighbour.'

'Called?'

The woman was getting rattled. 'Why d'you need to know that?'

'Because you're stopping me doing my job. And my job, in this instance, is very important. Your name, please?'

'Elizabeth. Elizabeth Galloway.'

He took the letter out, showed her. It was a standard letter their lawyer, Sharkey, had composed for just such a situation. While she was reading he continued. Just go for it, he thought. 'Well, Elizabeth, I believe this is the home of Martin Flemyng. We had a meeting with him yesterday in regard to some irregularities in statements he made regarding abuse at a children's home several years ago.'

She put the letter down, looked at him, eyes wide. 'What?'

'We tried to contact him again today and were told he hadn't turned up for work. I came round here to see if he was in.'

'Oh my god. You mean Martin . . . I work with him . . .'

So his assumption had been correct. 'Well, you never know. Sometimes, and I'm not saying this is the case, but sometimes if people have done something horrendous and think they've got away with it, when their past catches up, they might be tempted to do something drastic.'

'Oh my God . . . you'd better come in. Come through my house, we can go through the back way.'

She led him through the house next door. From the fleeting glimpses he had of the décor it was how he would have expected a university teacher's place to be. Comforting, warm. Intelligently and culturally decorated. They went through to the back yard, skipped over the fence. There were double-patio doors at the back of Flemyng's property.

'I've got the key,' Elizabeth said, and opened them.

Amar stepped inside. Elizabeth followed. 'Don't touch anything,' he said to her. 'Just in case.'

She immediately put her arms by her sides.

Amar stepped into the back room. It too was quite comfortably furnished, but messy. He checked all the downstairs rooms. No sign of Flemyng. He gingerly made his way upstairs, taking his own advice, keeping his hands off the banisters. He checked the bedrooms. Nothing.

He thought quickly. There were dirty dishes in the kitchen, the remains of a hastily eaten breakfast. The bed was unmade, the wardrobe doors open, empty hangers showing he had packed quickly. Downstairs in the back room that Flemyng clearly used for an office, there were papers all over the dining table, a laptop still open. Flemyng had clearly left in a hurry.

Amar went back downstairs, sat in front of the laptop. Made a mental note to clean his prints off it afterwards.

'How well do you know him?' Amar asked.

'Quite well,' she replied.

'Did he have a girlfriend? Boyfriend?'

She thought for a moment. 'Not . . . usually . . . but he did say there was someone once, a girlfriend and a little boy. They were like a family, he said . . .'

'He mention her name?'

'Anne, I think. Talked like the boy was his own . . .' She looked down at Amar. 'What are you doing?' she said, still keeping her arms at her sides.

'Checking something. He's not here and it looks like he left in a hurry. Must have been something I said. If he's left in that much of a hurry, he might have left a trail . . .'

He powered up the laptop, waited for it to come on. 'Right . . .' He opened the internet connection, checked through recent history. 'Here we are . . .' He opened the relevant screens. 'Ah.'

'What?'

'Martin Flemyng made a reservation on the eleven-thirty from Bristol Temple Meads to Edinburgh. Bit stupid not to cover his tracks.' He checked his watch. 'I've just got time to catch him.'

He looked at Elizabeth who was standing there, her eyes

wide. So far out of her comfort zone she didn't know how to react.

'Have you got a car?'

She nodded numbly.

'Good.' He gave his most winning smile. 'Then could you give me a lift to the station?'

The tea was milky and watery but Tess took the proffered bone-china mug with a smile of gratitude. She had known she would get into Sylvia Cunliffe's house. Journalism, she often thought, was a mixture of charm, tenacity and saying the right things to the right people at the right time.

'Thanks,' she said, looking at the unappetizing, thin liquid. 'Just what I fancied.'

Sylvia Cunliffe grunted and sat down in an armchair opposite Tess leaving her perched on the sofa. She looked round. The house was in a late-Sixties estate in Grimley, five miles out of Newcastle. The room was as she had expected. A widow living on a budget, the furniture and fittings weren't the newest or the best quality. She had done what most women would have done in her situation, filled up the remaining space with pictures of her children and grand-children. Most of the pictures were recent, or fairly recent, with one exception. Some black and white shots of a grin-ning, curly haired boy. Taken on a run-down housing estate, he looked like something out of an old Ken Loach film.

'Is that Trevor?' Tess asked, pointing to the photo.

'Aye, that's him.' She slurped her tea. 'All I've got left of him. His sisters got married an' that, had kids so I've got grandkids, like, an' I love them, but that's all I've got left of him. That's all she left me of him.' The statements were matter of fact, dry, without emotion or elaboration, but Tess doubted that meant there was none. Time had crusted over her memories but not healed them.

Tess nodded, gave what she hoped was her sympathetic look. It usually worked. If not, she had other methods. 'So you live here alone?' she said.

She nodded. 'Me husband died a few years ago. I don't think he ever recovered from losin' Trevor. I don't think our marriage did either. But he stayed with me. That's somethin', isn't it? Not many would do that these days, is there?'

Tess agreed that there wasn't. She studied her as she took another mouthful of tea. Her eyes were hard with either anger or fear, she didn't know which. Perhaps both. Whatever, it was what drove her, kept her alive.

Sylvia Cunliffe placed her tea on a coaster with a picture of a Scottish piper on it and took out her cigarettes. She didn't offer her one, just lit up. Once the smoke had escaped her lungs, she seemed to relax slightly.

'The doctor says I shouldn't be doin' this, says it's bad for me. An' it is, I know it is. That's how I got the emphysema. But what else can I do? It's me little bit of joy, me luxury. I can't give that up otherwise I'd have nothin'.'

'Quite right,' said Tess. 'We all need a bit of luxury.' She wondered when she herself had last had any and placed her mug on a similarly tartaned coaster on the coffee table, her eyes going to a scrapbook sitting next to it. 'What's that?'

'That's me,' said Sylvia. 'That's all my clippin's. Stuff from the papers, magazines, everythin'. I've got some new stuff as well, from this week, but I haven't got round to puttin' them in yet.'

She reached for it. 'D'you mind?'

'Course not, pet, that's what it's there for.'

Tess took the scrapbook, placed it on her lap, opened it. Some of the clippings went back years, the paper yellowed and brittle, the glue and tape thick and congealed. She started from the beginning. The first few showed Sylvia as a young woman, the same picture of Trevor in the articles.

Even then, Tess thought, she had a sense of the self-regard-
ing, the dramatic. She found that quite calculating,
deliberate. She thought of her own scrapbook and recognized something kindred in her.

The articles went through the years. The same picture of
Mae Blacklock that had been used around the time of the
trial. The one all the tabloid editors had trotted out over the
years to accompany a story about her. In its way it was as
iconic as the photo of a blonde Myra Hindley. Tess skipped
forward. There was Sylvia railing against . . . well, anything
really. The Bulger case had a quote from her. Ian Huntley.
The Wests. Everything and anything to do with premedi-
tated violent death and she was there. Tess read some of the
quotes.

'Well, he's just evil, isn't he? I mean, I'd call him an
animal but that's an offence to animals, isn't it? My dog's an
animal and he wouldn't behave like that.' That was about
Fred West.

'Well, they say you can't believe it but you can. You can.
And they always think that it'll never happen to them but it
will. Look at me, I used to say that. It happened to me.' The
two boys in the Bulger killing.

'They should just lock them up and throw away the key.
Let them rot.' The Bulger case again.

Tess looked up. Something dark, sad and conflicted had
stirred in her while reading the pieces but she quickly
pushed it out of her mind. 'It's a very impressive collection.'

Sylvia almost smiled. She nodded as if to confirm her
impression. 'It is. It's a lifetime's work. And it's still goin' on.'

Tess nodded.

'So what did you want to talk to me about?'

'Well, it was about the two boys killed this week.'

She nodded, as if ready to dispense her wisdom.

'Who d'you think killed them?'

She thought for a moment. Tess surreptitiously slipped her hand into her jacket pocket, switched on her tape recorder. 'Well,' she said at last, 'these kids on these estates these days have got no respect. I mean, you can't blame them for everythin'. Just look at the parents.'

'Right. So you think it was other kids that did this?'

She nodded, took a drag on her cigarette. 'Who else? I mean these days you've got drugs like you never used to an' they bring their own problems. Dealers, an' that. An' then there's no jobs or nothin' for them to do. Nowhere to play. An' the parents don't care. They're just as bad.'

Tess nodded, expression blank, biding her time. 'Absolutely. Now. What if I told you it might not be kids. What if I told you I had another theory?'

Her brow creased. 'Like what?'

'What if I said that living on the estate, right now, was someone who had been released from prison and given a new identity.'

'What?' Syliva went into a coughing fit.

Tess waited until she had regained her composure. She took another drag on her cigarette, exhaled and she was listening again.

'Now this killer with the new identity. What if I told you this killer had killed children?'

Sylvia waited. Tess, the dark conflict of a few moments ago now completely banished, could barely contain her excitement as the words left her mouth.

'In fact what if I told you that this killer was responsible for the death of your son? Had killed Trevor?'

Another coughing fit. This one so severe, Tess thought she might expire. She looked round frantically for something, anything, that would help, a glass of water – wasn't that what they gave them in films?

It wasn't necessary. Svlvia rode it out. As she regained

composure, Tess got a sense, from the look on her face, of what her life had been like, what kind of struggle she had gone through just to keep going. She was the last person to judge her about the choices she had made to help her keep going.

'No . . . not Mae Blacklock . . .'

Tess nodded. 'The very same. We're running a feature on it in the paper tomorrow. Just wanted your reaction before you saw it. Thought it only right that you should be the first to know.'

She nodded, the nasty light back in her eye. 'Aye. You're right, pet.'

'So what d'you think about that?'

'I think . . . I think . . . it's too much of a bloody coincidence, is what I think. She turns up an' . . . an' those bairns get killed. Well, what would you think? What would anyone think?'

Tess nodded, struggled to keep a triumphant smile off her face.

Sylvia continued. 'It's a bloody disgrace. She should have been locked up for the rest of her life where she couldn't do any harm again. Except to herself, mind. But that doesn't matter. Anyway, they have it cushy in prison these days, so it wouldn't be much of a punishment, would it?'

'Quite,' said Tess, wondering whether she had actually been in a prison lately. Or ever. 'So you think it's her then? Up to her old tricks?'

Sylvia was sitting bolt upright again now, feeding off her own anger. 'Well, who else could it be? When you say that, it's got to be her, hasn't it?'

'Right. So what should we do about it then?'

'Get her out,' she said with no hesitation, no doubt in her voice. 'Get her out. By force if necessary. I mean, how long before another one gets it?'

Tess nodded. Bingo. This was gold dust.

She let her go on but she had the quote she wanted. She nodded sympathetically, fake-matched her anger and told her, with all the sincerity she could muster, that her words would be the centrepiece of her article and she was to look out for it tomorrow.

'I get your paper every day. Think it's a great paper.'

'I'm glad to hear it,' she said, smiling.

She left as quickly as she could. She felt like she was about to faint, she was so excited. That or the painkillers.

Elizabeth's car, an anonymous Renault Clio, pulled up in front of Bristol Temple Meads Station. Amar had the passenger door open before Elizabeth had put the brake on.

'Hey,' she said.

'Sorry,' he said, getting out, 'but I have to catch him.'

'Look,' she said, grabbing his arm, 'I have done the right thing, haven't I? Helping you? You're not some kind of con man?'

He quickly reached inside his pocket, took out a business card. 'Phone this number if you've got any worries. Or if you want to see what happens.'

She gave him a shy smile. 'Will you be at the end of it?'

He gave her a sad smile in return. 'I'm sorry,' he said, 'but I'm on a different bus to you.'

He got out of the car, ran into the station concourse, checked the monitor. He had minutes to board the train. He ran to the gate, went straight through, holding up a Metro transport pass and shouting to the startled female member of staff that he was police. Flustered, she let him through. Once there, he ran down the steps, along the underpass and up on to the platform. The train was still there. Without hesitating, Amar jumped on.

The door slid shut behind him. He looked up and down

the carriage, with no idea where Flemyng might be, only hoping he was on this train. He started his search.

It didn't take him long. The aisles were full of people taking off coats, storing luggage, checking reservations. Amar managed to blend in perfectly, looking like a lost traveller checking for his seat number. He moved up the train, and found Flemyng in coach C. Sitting by himself in an airline seat on the far side, looking out of the window, biting his nails. The seat next to him was free. Amar sat down in it.

Flemyng glanced at him, then, once he had realized who it was, did a double take that under other circumstances Amar would have found comical. Flemyng immediately tried to get out of the seat.

'Going somewhere, Martin?' said Amar. 'You've booked all the way to Edinburgh.'

Flemyng was trapped. He looked round frantically for a way of escape, but like a claustrophobe in a broken lift knew it was hopeless. Eventually he slumped back down in his seat. Sighed.

'How did . . . how did you know where I was?'

'Checked your laptop. Always cover your tracks. You've been so good at it for so long, but you're getting careless now, aren't you?'

He frowned. 'My laptop? How . . . have you been in my house?'

'I have.'

'You broke in?'

Amar shook his head. 'No your neighbour let me in. Elizabeth. Lovely woman.'

Flemyng sat back against the seat. Hard. 'Why? Why would she . . .?'

'Because I told her I wanted to question you in relation to a series of child sex offences that you were involved in a few years ago. Couldn't let me in quick enough after that. Even gave me a lift to the station.'

Flemyng covered his face with his hands, groaned.

'So. You and me are going to have a long chat. We've got hours to do it in. It's a long way to Newcastle.'

'But . . . but I'm going to Edinburgh.'

'You were going to Edinburgh. Now you're coming to Newcastle. With me.'

Another groan.

'Right,' said Amar, settling back, 'let's start. Anne Marie Smeaton. You can tell me all about her.'

'Now I want you to tell me about the boys.'

'The boys?'

'The other boys. The dead ones.'

She holds her face in her hands once again. 'Oh God . . . no . . . don't make me. Please, don't make me . . .'

'Anne Marie, you have to.'

'No . . . I don't know anything about them, please, I don't . . .'

'I don't believe you.'

She stands up. 'That's it. I'm goin'. I've told you about Trevor, that's enough. That's all I'm sayin'. This was a bad idea, stupid. I haven't got time to stay here. I'm goin'.'

'Sit down, Anne Marie. Come on, you've got to keep going . . .'

'No. I want Jack. I want to see Jack . . .'

He gets up, crosses to her, looks her straight in the eye. 'Come on, Anne Marie, please. I'm trying to help you. If you run, what happens then? I can't protect you.'

She is listening. She says nothing. He continues.

'I can help you. But you have to talk to me. Please. Sit down. And we'll keep going.'

She looks at the sofa, at the door and at him. Makes up her mind. She sits down again. He does the same.

'Thank you. Now. Those boys. Tell me about those boys.'

'No . . . Don't make me, please don't make me . . . I don't know about them . . .'

'I think you do, Anne Marie. I think you know about them. And you've got to tell me about them, you've got to. It's important.' He puts his hands in front of him, imploring her. 'Come on, face it, Anne Marie, whatever went on then you have to face it. Then start to get over it. Face it. Tell me.'

She keeps her face covered, starts rocking back and forward where she's sitting. He keeps pressing her.

'Tell me . . .'

She makes a strangled sound in the back of her throat. It sounds like a wild animal caught in a trap, dying slowly.

'You have to face it, you have to tell me . . .'

'I don't have to face it, I don't . . . you don't tell me what to do. That's what he does, you're just like him, just like him . . .'

He leans forward, aware that some kind of breakthrough has taken place, but not sure what. He tries to keep his voice even when he talks, swallowing down his excitement. 'Just like who, Anne Marie? Who?'

She pulls back, aware that she has said too much.

'Who? Tell me.'

She doesn't reply.

'I'm not like him, whoever it is. I'm honestly not. I'm trying to help you. Please, just tell me about him.'

'I can't . . .'

'You can. Come on, Anne Marie, you're doing really well, getting really strong. Just tell me.'

She doesn't reply.

He decides to take a chance. He has to do what he can to keep her talking. Whether she is guilty or not he has to do everything to keep her talking. 'Look, I know you didn't kill all those boys. I'm sure you didn't. I never for one minute thought that. But I do think you know who killed them. So tell me. And I can help you.'

'Help me to do what?'

'Find whoever's done this. Turn them in.'

She looks at him, her broken face trying to find truth in his words. She's distraught, he thinks, carrying the knowledge of the killer's identity is obviously a burden to her, on top of everything else she has to go through. She opens her mouth to speak, thinks better of it.

'Anne Marie . . .'

'No. I can't. You don't know. The bad spirits. He's one of them. The worst one. He's the one who talks to me. Tells me I'm a bad person. He's there even when he's not. I see him in my dreams and he won't let me go . . . He tells me how I let these things happen. How I can't stop them . . . I can't stop them . . . I can't stop him . . .'

'Anne Marie, look. It's not you doing this. Any of it. I believe that. What does he do to make you think that?'

The tears start again. She seems to be sobbing her heart out. 'I black out . . . an' when I do, things happen. Things I can't remember . . .' She holds up her bandaged hands. 'I hurt myself. I could hurt other people . . . I can't remember . . . And then he calls me, tells me these things . . . these horrible things . . .'

'What horrible things? When does he call you?'

'Last night, he called me last night. Told me . . . reminded me about the deal . . .'

'The deal? What deal?'

'The deal. The one I made with him, all those years ago.'

'What kind of deal?'

'If . . .' She sniffs, wipes her nose on her sleeve. 'If . . . he knows. I have to do what he tells me. Or he'll tell everyone what I did. Who I am. When I try to get away from him somethin' happens. Somethin' . . . bad.'

'Something bad? Like killing all those boys?'

She nods, crying too much to speak.

'Why? Because you try to get on with your life and he doesn't want to see you do that?'

She nods again.

'So he kills a boy? Why?'

'He tells me what to do . . . sometimes when I black out, I don't know . . .'

A cold chill goes through him. 'What are you saying? He kills them? Or what? He makes you kill them?'

'The bad spirits . . . I . . . black out . . . I don't know . . . I *could hurt myself or other people, those I love . . . I don't know . . . he tells me . . . he tells me I have to keep quiet, but it hurts, hurts so much I black out . . . But it's Jack he wants . . .'*

Jack? Why?'

'He says, he says he's just rehearsin'. It's juh — just to prove his power over me. That he can get me to do what he wants . . . That . . . that wuh — one day when I'm l-least expectin' it, one day he'll come for Jack . . .'

'And, what? Tell him about you? About what you did?'

'Wuh — worse than that . . .'

Donovan lets the words sink in. 'Oh God . . . You mean he'll . . .'

Jack . . . he'll get Jack . . . or make me do it . . .' Another fresh bout of sobbing.

'Oh God . . .'

23

Jamal was glad he had thought to get on the scooter.

Milsom, the woman and the boy had gone straight to the car that was parked round the back of the flat he was in. An Audi A4. He had zipped round on the scooter, careful not to be seen, and watched them load bags into the boot.

His heart was hammering in his chest. They were off. Leaving. He had no choice but to follow them. He pulled the scooter up behind a wall, killed the engine, risked a glance round. Definitely getting ready to move out.

While he was watching, he reached into his pocket, getting his mobile out to call Donovan. But the phone wasn't there.

'Shit . . .'

He checked every pocket, trousers, jacket, even ones he knew he never kept it in. It wasn't there. And then he remembered. He had left it on the desk, just beside the laptop.

'Damn . . . fool . . .'

Angry with himself, he thought quickly. As he saw it, he had no choice. If they were leaving, he had to follow them. He might never get another chance like this again. None of them might.

Milsom slammed the boot down. The other two were already inside. He got behind the steering wheel, turned the ignition on. Jamal readied his scooter.

The car sped off.

Jamal followed.

*

Countryside flew by outside the window. Being unfamiliar with this side of the country, Amar had no idea where he was. Countryside changed to urban, changed to countryside again, to urban. It didn't matter. He wasn't interested. All he was interested in was the man sitting next to him.

The ticket inspector had been round, Amar, knowing expenses would be picking up the bill for this trip, had paid the full fare. He had checked Flemyng's ticket.

'Edinburgh Waverley,' he had said, marking it and handing it back.

Amar had given him a smile. 'I think he may get off before that.'

'That's quite all right, gentlemen. As long as you don't stay on afterwards that's no problem.'

Flemyng, crushed up against the window and unable to move, turned pale, looked like he was about to be sick. Amar kept smiling, giving the impression to fellow travellers that nothing was wrong.

'So,' said Amar, settling back into the cramped seat and stretching out his legs, another disincentive for Flemyng to make a dash for it, 'are you OK? D'you want anything?'

'A coffee.' He looked round desperately as he spoke. 'I'll go to the buffet car and get it.'

He made an attempt to rise. Amar gently, but firmly, pulled him down again.

'The trolley will be around soon. Might even treat you to a sandwich then. If you're a good boy. If you tell me what I want to know.'

'I need to go to the toilet.'

'Then I'll come with you.'

Flemyng looked at him, aghast.

'Don't worry,' said Amar, smile in place, 'you're not my type. Believe me, it'll be more harrowing for me than it will for you.'

Flemyng said nothing. Amar could see his mind whirring, trying to find a way out of his present situation. He was clearly used to worming his way out of trouble, he thought. That's how he had survived this long.

'So,' said Amar, 'I think it's time for you and me to have a little chat.'

'I don't have to talk to you,' he said making one last, defiant stand. 'You're not even police. Before I say anything I want my solicitor present.'

Amar shrugged. 'Fine. I'll call the police. Have them waiting for us at the other end. I'll tell them you went on the run when we tried to ask you about abusing children. As well as some other stuff we want to put to you. Now I'm no expert, but that kind of thing means you're guilty, doesn't it? I'm sure they'll think so.'

'This is kidnapping.'

Amar looked round at the rest of the people in the carriage. No one was taking any notice of them. 'Then tell someone. See what they say.'

Flemyng looked round also.

'Go on, tell them that I kidnapped you. Tell them to get me off you. Go on.'

Flemyng sighed. He was finally accepting that there would be no escape for him. He settled back into his seat, resigned to whatever might happen to him next.

'That's better. Now. Time for a chat. I asked you yesterday if you knew Anne Marie Smeaton. You said no, very unconvincingly, I might add, and ended our chat pretty quickly afterwards. And then legged it. So I'll ask you again. And this time I want the truth. Did you know Anne Marie Smeaton?'

Flemyng sighed. 'Yes. I did.'

'Good.'

'But not very well.'

Amar rolled his eyes. 'Oh, here we go.'

'I . . . I didn't. We . . . I came into contact with her as part of my job. As a social worker. That's all.'

'You and her were lovers.'

'That's not true.'

Amar stared at him, anger in his eyes. But he kept a smile in place and his voice low so as not to arouse the suspicions of the other travellers. 'Now listen. There are certain kinds of people that I don't like. Paedophiles are one lot. Liars are another. So are people who think that all gay men like Shirley Bassey. Now I know that you're at least two out of three. And that's enough to make me really angry. And like the Hulk used to say, you wouldn't like me when I'm angry. So stop fucking me about. Right?'

Flemyng realized he had pushed things as far as he could and relented. 'All right. All right. I'll tell you the truth. Anne Marie. Yes, it's true. We were lovers for a time. She came to Bristol and we met through work. Things got a bit . . . personal.'

'Do things always get a bit personal with you and your clients?'

Flemyng blushed. 'No. She was . . . I liked her.'

'And presumably you knew who she was. Who she used to be.'

Flemyng nodded.

'And that was, what? A turn on for you?'

'It did add a certain . . . frisson, yes.'

Amar digested Flemyng's words. 'A certain frisson. Right. If you say so. So how did it work out, this relationship? What was in it for you?'

'I . . . I liked her. She was a, an interesting woman.'

Amar folded his arms, pretended to think. 'Right. You sure you didn't like her son better?'

Flemyng looked scared, as if he had been caught out in a lie. 'What? I . . . no, I . . .'

'Oh come on. Don't fuck me about.' Amar tried to keep his voice quiet, his face from betraying his anger. It was a struggle. He turned in to face Flemyng, cutting him off from the rest of the carriage. 'What kind of appeal could a grown woman have for a bloke who gets his kicks from abusing kids? Unless this woman was a child killer and had a boy of her own. Get in with her, wait until the boy's the age you like them at and bang. You're in. Christmas has come early for a sick little fuck like you. How'm I doing so far?'

Flemyng covered his face with his hand. 'Oh God . . . oh God . . .'

'Is that a yes?'

Flemyng, without raising his head, nodded.

'Good. Well, now we're communicating. What about the dead boys?'

Flemyng looked up, frowned. Dead boys?'

'Oh don't start all that again. The truth, remember? The dead boys. Everywhere Anne Marie went there's been a dead boy. He was one of yours in Bristol. Adam Wainwright. James Fielding in Colchester. Patrick Sutton in Hull. And, of course, Guy Brewster in London. All your own work.'

Flemyng looked genuinely confused. Amar didn't believe it. 'I really don't understand. I . . . I couldn't kill another human being . . .'

'Just abuse them and fantasize about it.'

Flemyng didn't reply.

Amar leaned in close. 'Tell me.'

Flemyng recoiled in his seat, backed right up against the window until he could push himself no further away. 'I don't know, I don't know . . .'

'I don't believe you. You're a liar and a manipulator. You tried it with me, you tried it with everyone. You're very good, I'll give you that. You got away with it for a long time, but you don't fool me.'

The tears started in earnest then. Great big self-pitying sobs.

Amar sat back, knew he would be getting nothing more for the time being. Maybe Flemyng had been telling the truth. Maybe he knew nothing about the deaths. And maybe he was lying. Back to square one.

The refreshment trolley appeared. Flemyng was still sobbing when a uniformed stewardess leaned across and asked if they wanted anything. Amar shook his head.

The girl looked at Flemyng, back at Amar. 'Is he all right?'

Amar tried to smile. 'He'll be fine. Just had a bit of bad news.'

'Can I get him anything from the trolley?'

'Nah,' said Amar looking from the sobbing heap of Flemyng back to the girl. 'He doesn't deserve it.'

She is still crying. 'He thinks he can do what he likes. I tuh — try to get away from him, I do, but he keeps catchin' up with me . . . they said I was a liar, I was manipulative. They never met him . . .'

Donovan rubs his face with his hands. Thinks. 'So. These black-outs. Do you really think you do something bad when you have them? Or do you think he just plays on that, gets you into such a state of panic that he can make you believe you've done something?'

She looks at her bandaged hands. 'I don't know, I don't know . . .'

'Well, assume he does,' says Donovan, trying to keep his voice calm and steady. 'Say he doesn't want you to be happy. So he, what? Plants things in your mind. Taunts you. Keeps you in a state of unease, never knowing whether he's going to catch up with you again? Does that sound right?'

'No . . .'

'Look, Anne Marie. I don't believe it's you. I've seen your psychiatric report. There's nothing in there to indicate that you would do that.'

She looks up. 'You've seen my . . .'

'It was in the background stuff you gave Wendy Bennett, yes. And I'm not even convinced that this psychopathic personality diagnosis you had all these years ago is correct.'

She looks at him, and, although still sobbing, it seems like her face has been lit by a small shaft of sunlight. 'Really?'

'For argument's sake, let's say it's him. Why would he do it?'

'He wants to make his point, that he can do what he wants with me,' she says in between sobs, 'So the boys have to die. An' . . . an' . . . he's workin' his way through to Jack . . . if I don't do what he says, he'll go after Jack . . .'

'So . . . if you know he killed all those boys and you know for a fact he's going to go after Jack, why haven't you gone to the police about him before? Told them everything?'

'Buh – because they might think it was me . . . because it might have been me . . . he says he always chooses boys who won't be missed. Says I could have done the same, they're kids nearby to where I've been livin' . . . Says there's evidence from each one that he's kept back. That he could plant on me if he wanted to . . .'

Her head goes down and she starts sobbing again.

'And you've carried this with you for years?'

Without looking up, she nods.

He sits back thinking about what to do next, how to approach what she's just said in the most delicate way. Mind made up, he leans forward again.

'Tell me his name.'

She shakes her head vigorously, hands still covering her face.

'Come on, Anne Marie, tell me his name. Please. Tell me his name then I can help you.'

She looks up at him then with a complete lack of hope in her eyes. 'You can't. Oh, you can't. He's too . . . No . . . I've got to go. Again . . .'

'You won't. Look—'

'I will. You don't understand. There's been a tabloid journalist askin' round. She's on to me as well. She tried to bribe Rob. Come on to him.' A ghost of a smile played on her lips. 'Rob just belted her one.'

'Well, that's . . . good, I suppose. Look, he can't get to you. We can get you protection from him.'

She looks at him, begging, like she really wants to believe him but can't make that leap of faith. 'No . . . I'll have to move . . .'

'No you won't. Listen to me, Anne Marie. I've got friends on the police force, they can protect you. I can protect you. Please. Just tell me the name of the man after Jack. The man who is making you think you're a murderer.'

She closes her eyes, opens them again. When she speaks, there's pleading in her voice. Worse than he has heard before.

'You've got to help me. You've got to promise to help me. And Rob. And Jack. Especially Jack. He needs protectin' the most.'

'I will. I promise.'

'And there's that journalist.'

'Don't worry about her. We'll get her stopped.'

She sighs. 'It's too late . . .'

'No, it's not.'

'Yes, it is. What about that boy who was killed last night?'

'What, you're saying he did that? He's here in Newcastle?'

She looks at him, speaks like a sinner seeking absolution. 'I don't know . . . he doesn't need to be . . .' *She looks down to her bandaged hands once more.* 'He can make things happen wherever he is . . .'

Donovan is about to speak but doesn't get the chance.

The bell rings . . .

24

'This could be it, Ray,' Tess Preston said, after topping up with Collins's painkillers, 'this is the big time.'

Ray Collins just grunted. He had been there before, the grunt said. No big deal. You get used to it. Or don't. Tess knew all this without asking because she was learning to interpret Ray's grunts. A real skill. Another thing she was getting good at.

They were in the car, heading towards the estate. Tess behind the wheel, elated. Walking on sunshine, walking on air. Or rather driving. Necking pills and smiling constantly. But she was feeling all those clichés and more. Even the plaster on her nose didn't make her look ridiculous, she thought. Just like Jack Nicholson in *Chinatown*. The guys back in the newsroom would think she was cool. And why would she want to look like Faye Dunaway, anyway?

She had written up her story, emailed it along with Collins's photos. Now they would get back to the Hancock, get some more external shots of the murderer's flat, sound out some neighbours for possible later reaction, maybe even get lucky and get inside the flat itself. That really would be a scoop. But apart from that it would be just background stuff, just making sure they were in the right place at the right time, ready to grab a ringside seat for when the story broke in the morning.

They approached the estate, Tess pleased with herself for remembering the way. Could almost be a local, she thought.

Then, seeing the sprawling dirty red-brick flats in front of her, changed her mind. She would have to be paid to live on this estate, she thought. Or any estate, come to that. And she doubted whether there was enough money in the world to make her. She put those thoughts out of her head. Because it didn't matter. She was going places. And soon.

'There's that kid,' said Collins, pointing out of the window.

Tess looked. It was Renny. Walking slowly along the pavement, kicking a plastic bottle, directionless.

'Looks lost without his mate, doesn't he?' said Collins.

Tess didn't know whether the words meant the photographer was concerned or whether he was just making a statement. Tess didn't think it was important either way.

'Shall we stop? Have a chat with him?' she said, already pulling the car over to the side of the road.

Collins gave only a grunt in reply. Tess decided to take that as a yes and put the handbrake on, wound down the window.

She leaned out. 'Hey, Renny.'

Renny looked up, and Tess saw fear in the boy's eyes. His body posture changed; he tensed, ready to run, eyes darting round quickly, scanning for possible exits. Then he realized who it was calling him and his body relaxed. A lot. So much so, thought Tess, that it seemed as if Renny didn't care one way or the other whether Tess spoke to him or not.

Tess popped the bottle in the glove box, crunched another little pill, got out of the car. Collins followed suit.

'How you doing?' said Tess.

Renny, with his eyes on the ground, shrugged.

Collins stood in front of the boy. Looked at him, got his attention. 'You OK?'

Renny shrugged again, caught Collins's eyes. Some kind of communication had taken place. Collins nodded, cigarette

in the corner of his mouth, as if he understood. Tess either
chose to ignore this or didn't notice.

'Heard about . . .' What was his name again? 'Your mate.
Pez. Harsh. Very harsh.' Slow down, she thought, you're
talking too fast.

Renny nodded. Said nothing. Just looked at the pavement, scuffed his already scuffed trainers along the paving
slab. Watched the plastic bottle roll into the gutter where he
left it.

'Yeah,' Tess continued, speech no slower, 'knifed like that.
Two in one week.' She leaned in close to the boy. 'Hey,
this'll cheer you up. Wanna make a bit more money?'

Renny looked up, suspicious after their last encounter,
was about to reply when he saw Tess's face. 'What happened
to your face?'

Tess smiled. 'Got into a fight,' she said with pride, knowing it would impress the boy. 'What you do around here.'

It didn't. He just looked at her with contempt. 'How do
I make this money? Will I get it this time?'

Tess ignored the look, took her recorder out, stood ready,
thumb on the button. 'You will. Just tell me how it feels to
lose your best friend. Give me a few quotes, something I can
use in the paper and I'll see you all right for a few quid. What
d'you say?'

Renny stared, said nothing.

Tess took his silence for interest at least, if not encour-
agement. She shoved the recorder in the boy's face. 'You see,
Renny, tomorrow, I'm going to reveal who killed Pez.'

Renny narrowed his eyes. Tess could almost see his mind
working.

'Oh yeah. And when I do, I'll need a few quotes.'

Renny still stared, said nothing.

Tess was on a roll, words tumbling out. ''Cos you see,
when I unmask Pez's, I'm also going unmask Calvin's killer.

And it's going to be huge. The biggest thing this place has ever seen.' She leaned in closer to the boy, completely invading his personal space, recorder right against his mouth. 'So, I think you're going to want to be there. Don't you? Want to say something now for the record?'

Renny looked like he was ready to kill. He backhanded Tess, who, taken by surprise, found herself unbalanced and stumbled backwards, recorder going flying. Renny then stalked off, as fast as he could. He reached a corner, turned to see the two of them still there and ran away.

'What is the matter with these fuckers round here?'

Tess got slowly to her feet, more surprised than hurt. She picked up her recorder that was still thankfully intact, looked at Collins, smiling, expecting him to share in her reaction.

Collins pulled his cigarette down to the filter, exhaled and casually flicked the stub at Tess. 'I thought you were OK. For a posh bird. But you're a special kind of cunt, you know that? And you're not having any more pills, either.'

Collins got back in the car, and without waiting for Tess, drove away. Tess opened her mouth to shout but stopped, frowned. What had she said? What had she done to annoy him?

Tess watched Collins drive away feeling confused. And it was her own car. She tried not to let that get to her. She would meet up with him later. She trusted Collins not to damage the Golf. Knew that whatever was upsetting him, he obviously wanted to be alone. And he wouldn't want to drive round in a posh bird's car for long.

Instead, Tess decided to walk round. Ask questions. She didn't think anyone else would try to damage her the way that Rob had. She was no longer scared of this estate, not today. She felt on top of the world, like bullets would bounce off her. That once the locals knew it was her who had outed the monster in their midst, they would just about venerate her.

She took in the atmosphere, looked at the locals. They all seemed so unhealthy. Overweight, a lot of them, but still looking undernourished. All kitted out in Primark's finest. And all with a lethargy, like they'd either been worn down or, and this was more likely, she thought, they couldn't be bothered to make an effort. Really, she should keep as far away from them as possible, just in case whatever they had rubbed off on her. Even if they were her readers, the very people who were going to make her famous.

Walking, she sensed something. A tension in the air, an expectancy. And not a pleasant one. Like waiting for a lynching. Angry faces, tense bodies. She was glad it wasn't dark. Whatever veneer of politeness daylight confers would be gone by then. She popped into a newsagent for a can of Red Bull.

And stopped dead.

The early edition of the *Evening Chronicle* was on the counter, the headline:

CHILD KILLER BACK AND LIVING ON MURDER ESTATE

She nearly dropped her Red Bull.

In a daze she picked up the paper, read on. It told how convicted child murderer, Mae Blacklock, was living on the Hancock Estate. It speculated in the loosest terms – Tess could spot a piece that had been scrutinized by the legal department when she saw one – that she might possibly be responsible for one, if not both, of the two recent deaths.

There were photos accompanying the article. The famous old one of Mae Blacklock as a child, smiling, the photo that resided in the public psyche as much as that of Myra Hindley. And beside that another photo, an older woman with a stern, forbidding face. Sylvia Cunliffe. And sure enough, as she read on, there were quotes from her. Plenty of them. Just the kind of quotes she had put into her own article.

'Bitch. Fucking bitch . . .'

By the time she had finished reading, she had worked out what must have happened. She wasn't stupid. But she felt like she was. As soon as she had left, Sylvia Cunliffe must have been on the phone to her friends in the local press. And did she have a story for them. It wouldn't have taken too long for them to look into matters, see who was leading on it the next day. Whatever, it had scuppered her own story.

She screwed the paper up, stood there in the shop not knowing what to do next.

'Hey,' said a Geordie Asian accent, 'you buying that?'

Tess looked down at the screwed-up newspaper in her hands. 'Have it,' she said to the man behind the counter.

'Hey. You pay for that!'

Tess walked out of the shop. The shopkeeper was out after her.

'Fuckin' bitch! Fuckin' scum! Why don't you fuck off back to London and leave us all alone!'

Tess felt something hard and heavy hit her between the shoulders. Bullets didn't bounce off her. She turned, looked. A full can of Coke. The shopkeeper was giving chase, his hands full of whatever he could find to throw.

Tess ran away. As fast as she could.

She no longer felt comfortable or happy. She felt miserable, coming down. She wanted to get out of the estate as quickly as possible.

And get some more pills off Collins.

The ringing bell is followed by a sharp rapping on the door. Donovan looked up as if woken from a trance. Anne Marie jumped too.

'The only people who knock like that,' she said, fear mingling with experience in her voice, 'are police.'

'Don't worry,' said Donovan standing up and making his way to the stairs, 'it'll not be anything important.'

Anne Marie clearly didn't share his opinion but she said nothing. Donovan turned away from her. He didn't share his opinion either.

He went downstairs, opened the door. DI Diane Nattrass was standing there.

'Howdy, sheriff,' said Donovan, masking his surprise as quickly and as flippantly as possible. Hoping he carried nothing with him of the conversation he had been having upstairs. Or nothing visible to Nattrass. 'What brings you round these here parts?'

'Hello, Joe,' she said, a trace of weariness in her voice. Whether from her work or his attitude he couldn't tell. He decided it must be a bit of both. 'Can I come in?'

Donovan stepped back, allowing entry. 'But of course. Always a pleasure and never a chore. To receive a visit from the law.' He smiled. 'Hey, that rhymes. Should go into poetry. I'll put the kettle on.'

He turned, walked away towards the kitchen.

'You need a receptionist,' she said, following him.

'It has been mentioned,' he said. 'Come on through.'

Nattrass was looking tired, he thought, more so than usual. But then the murders on the Hancock Estate were her case and she had every right to be. She was dressed in her usual long, brown overcoat that covered a dark, two-piece trouser suit, heels that were more to give her height with the men than any overt concession to fashion and a light-coloured blouse. Her hair was still cut in its no-nonsense style and she wore only the minimum of make-up. She wasn't an unattractive woman but Donovan knew she deliberately unsexed herself for work. It was a good ploy. Everyone took her seriously. No one messed with her.

'So,' he said, once the kettle was on, 'I presume this isn't a social call.'

Nattrass shook her head. 'No.'

'Not that it wouldn't be pleasant. It's been too long since we caught up.'

Nattrass nodded. Paul Turnbull, the ex-policeman Donovan had employed to investigate Matt Milsom had been her old partner. His death had cast a shadow between them. It always would. 'It has.'

'Should get together some time.'

Nattrass nodded. He knew she wouldn't just as much as he knew that he wouldn't. It was the kind of thing you were supposed to say. They both knew that.

He made the coffee, handed one to her. They went into the main office, pulled out two office chairs, sat down.

'Didn't you used to have a room where you could sit? Comfortably?' said Nattrass.

'That was the old place,' said Donovan, covering. 'Bit different here.'

She nodded, not quite taken in but not pressing it. 'Where's the rest of the gang?'

'On assignment. Things are going well in the private sector.'

'I'm glad they're going well for someone.'

'Always a place for you here.'

Nattrass managed a weak smile. 'Thanks but . . . I think I'm better off where I am.'

Donovan said nothing. She was alluding to Turnbull again.

He nodded. 'Right,' he said, face as blank and as open as he could make it. 'What can I do for you?'

Nattrass took a sip of her coffee, placed the mug on one

of the desks. 'I'll come straight to the point. Have you seen the *Chronicle* today?'

Donovan shook his head.

'The TV news? Local?'

Another shake.

'I didn't think so. Well I have. And you're not going to like it.'

'Why?'

'Because Mae Blacklock has been outed.'

Donovan sat back. He felt almost physically winded by the news. 'Shit.'

'Indeed. At the moment all they have is the information. They don't have her new name or address. And thankfully they don't have a photo. Although from what I hear, they're working on that.'

The journalist Anne Marie had mentioned. Things were moving faster than he had thought. Donovan's mind was racing to keep up. 'Why did you come to me?'

'Because as soon as this broke I did some digging. A couple of phone calls led me to the probation service. They gave me your name.'

He nodded, averting eye contact. 'Right.'

'So . . .' Nattrass looked round. 'Where is she?'

'Why?'

Nattrass looked at him as if he was a particularly stupid child. 'Because the Hancock Estate is going to explode like Guy Fawkes Night. So I'll have to take her in to protective custody, and her family, until we can sort out something a bit more long term.'

'Right.'

She locked her eyes on his like heat-seeking missiles. 'This is serious, Joe. Her life is in danger. And her family's life too. And possibly other people on the estate. This is no time to treat me to your awkward bastard routine.'

'I'm not being awkward,' he said, trying to think faster than he was speaking. He was conflicted and was trying to work through that conflict while he talked. He knew he should give Anne Marie up. Not only that, but tell Nattrass what Anne Marie was telling him. But that would ruin the trust he had built up with her. There was more she had to say and he doubted she would say it to a policewoman. Not only that, she certainly wouldn't go gently.

But on the other hand, it might just save her life. And Rob's and Jack's.

'What about the knifings? You still working on them?'

'Of course. But your name came up so I thought I'd better pay you a visit.'

'Don't you think Anne Marie had anything to do with those stabbings, then?'

'Did she? If she did, then of course I want to talk to her. And you had better tell me where she is.'

Donovan came to a decision. 'She's not here,' he said.

'Really,' said Nattrass, clearly not believing him.

'Really,' he said. 'We don't work together every day. You probably know what we're doing. Well, it's a very intense procedure. Not the kind of thing you can do day after day.'

Nattrass looked at him, unblinking, giving him the well-practised police stare that was supposed to break suspects down and make them confess. She – and other police officers – had tried it on him in the past and, although she was very good at it, he wasn't going to give in. He hoped.

'Honestly,' he said, his voice slightly higher than usual.

Nattrass broke off, realizing she was going to get no further. 'Fine, you stubborn bastard. Play it your way. But don't be surprised if I arrest you.'

'What for?'

'I don't fucking care. Listen, Donovan, this is no time to play cowboy. That estate is ready to go up. Two murders in the past week have put the national spotlight on them in the worst possible way. Then this. The *Chronicle*'s out, word's spreading. They've got a killer in their midst and they're very pissed off. Now if she isn't moved we're going to have a very bad situation on our hands. Very bad.'

'I suppose you've been to her flat.'

'No one in.'

Donovan thought, sighed. 'All right. Let me try to find her. If I do, I'll talk to her, see what she says.'

Nattrass realized this was the best she could hope for. 'I don't know why I came here. I should have just sent a uniform. Why I thought talking to you would be straightforward, I do not know.' She stood up. 'I'll see myself out.'

She did, but he still walked her to the door. Just in case she decided to make a detour upstairs.

He watched her go. Once he was sure she was gone, he leaned against the wall, breathed out a huge sigh, closed his eyes. Opening them and straightening up, he looked upwards.

Made his way slowly upstairs.

Not looking forward to what he had to say.

'I assume you heard all that.' He stands in the doorway looking at her. Sobbing is his only reply.

He enters the room fully, sits down on the sofa opposite her. She doesn't look up, keeps her face bowed, in her hands. 'OK. I'm guessing you did. Don't . . .' He searches for the right words. 'Let's get this sorted now. All of it. Tell me . . . tell me about him and I'll do the rest.'

She doesn't answer, just keeps sobbing.

His heart goes out to her. The world she had tried to create is crashing down around her. He has to do something. 'Look, tell me who he is, where he is and I'll get him stopped. Get him out of your life. For good. And we'll deal with the other stuff too.'

She looks up at that, her face red and swollen from crying. 'The uh – other stuff?' she manages to sob out. 'That's all it is, the other stuff? It's my fuckin' life you're talkin' about. An', an' my son's . . .'

'I know. I realize that. That's not what I meant. You know that. Please, Anne Marie, work with me here. I can help you. Tell me about him and I'll make sure you're safe. I promise.'

The sobs are subsiding slightly. She can't keep that intensity going indefinitely, no matter how upset she is. Donovan presses on. He takes hold of her bandaged hands, looks her straight in the eye. She has no choice. She has to look at him.

He hopes his sincerity will be understood. 'I promise. Tell me and I will help you.'

Her sobbing is fading away. She looks back at him. He sees that she desperately wants to believe him. He remains calm, holding her gaze. Eventually she nods.

'All right,' she says. 'I'll tell you.'

Donovan breathes a sigh of relief.

'But on one condition.'

'Name it.'

' I want to see Jack. I want to tell him.' She takes a deep breath, tries not to start crying as she exhales. 'About everythin'. But mostly about what I did. About who I used to be.'

Donovan is unable to disguise the worry on his face. 'You think that's a good idea?'

'I don't know. Probably not. But I'm tired of runnin'. Of hidin'. I'm just tired. I want . . . peace. I just want peace.'

'Anne Marie, this isn't the right time. You're distressed, you're not thinking straight. By all means let him know, but get this out of the way first.'

Her hands begin to tremble in his. 'You don't understand,' she says. 'I do have to do it now. Jack's a target. I know who's after him. I have to warn him, tell him why. It's the only bit of power he's got. Over me, over my son. Don't you see?' Her eyes were imploring. 'If I break that, he's got no hold on me. Ever.'

'And you can move forward. And we can deal with him.'

She nods.

Donovan sits back, lets go of her hands. It feels like letting a toddler walk unaided or releasing a bird and watching it fly. 'OK then. Give him a ring. Get him over here.'

She almost smiles. Instead she sighs. Her relief is palpable.

Donovan can feel it but he doesn't share it. He has a bad feeling about her decision. A very bad feeling.

25

Jamal's fingers were numb. In fact, he could barely feel either hand. He wished he was wearing gloves but hadn't had time to grab any. And now that he came to think of it, the wind was cutting through his jacket. But none of that was important now. He had to concentrate. He had to keep tailing the Audi.

He had been on it since it pulled out on to Brighton's seafront. Always a couple of cars back, but still well placed to keep following if Milsom made an unexpected turn or stop. He hadn't so far. But Jamal couldn't rule it out.

Jamal tried flexing his fingers while still gripping the handlebars. He threw quick glances to either side, trying to guess where they were headed. The fish and chip restaurants, hotels and bars were thinning out. They were heading out of town, he reckoned. That didn't sound good. If they got on to a motorway he couldn't follow them. If they went on the winding, country roads around the South Downs he would be too conspicuous. So he just bided his time, hoped for a break, or even a clue as to where he might expect to end up. Try and memorize the numberplate so at least he would have something.

He saw a roundabout up ahead, the right-hand turn pointed to the M23. The Audi signalled right.

'Aw no . . .' he said into his helmet.

He was going to lose them. No doubt about it.

But then something unexpected happened. Before joining the motorway, the Audi pulled in to a service station.

Jamal followed, scooting round the side of an automated car wash, hoping Milsom hadn't seen him. He pulled the scooter to a halt, turned off the engine, dismounted.

His legs felt numb from both the cold and being locked in the same position for so long. He shook out his hands, flapped his arms around his body to get the circulation started again. He opened his visor; his breath came out in plumes of steam. He risked a glimpse round the corner of the car wash. The car was at a petrol pump. Milsom got out, began to fill up with petrol.

He had checked the gauge on his scooter before pulling up. He could do with some petrol himself but he didn't dare risk it. So he could either run out of petrol or lose him on the motorway. Either way, it seemed he was screwed.

Milsom took a while filling up which Jamal interpreted as him going on a long journey. His heart sank further. Milsom replaced the nozzle in the pump, went inside to pay.

Jamal watched helplessly, as his one lead slipped away before his eyes and there was nothing he could do about it.

But then for the second time in as many minutes, something unexpected happened. Milsom came back out and gestured to the car. The woman who claimed to be his wife reluctantly unbuckled her seat belt, picked up her handbag, went inside.

'Must have had his card refused, or somethin',' Jamal said aloud to himself.

And he looked again at the car. The boy was in the back seat. Alone. Jamal had an idea. It was wild and reckless and desperate but it seemed like the only option he had if he wasn't to lose the boy.

Keeping his helmet on to perplex the CCTV cameras, he ran over to the car and opened the driver's side door.

'Afternoon,' he said to the startled boy as he got in.

The boy didn't reply, just looked at him.

Jamal checked for keys. Milsom had left them there.

'Oh you fuckin' beauty,' Jamal said, and laughed.

Locking the doors, he turned the engine on and put it in gear. Took the brake off.

'Don't worry, kid,' he said to the boy in the back, 'slight change of plan. You're goin' on an excursion.'

He was aware of Milsom running towards the car as he reached the turning for the main road and drove off as fast as he could.

He threw his head back, let out a huge laugh. He had no idea where he was going, what he would do next. But he had the boy. Joe would be proud.

Hopefully.

Jamal put his foot down. Didn't look back.

Jack saw his phone ring. He didn't hear it; his headphones were firmly clamped to his ears. School cancelled for the day he was in his room, trying to tune everything out, letting Fall Out Boy into his head. He had been thinking about them a lot, ever since Abigail mentioned she liked them. He had played several tracks, listening to them over and over again, trying to work out what it was she must like about them. He found them a bit ridiculous, like an underage heavy metal band, or something you would hear on the soundtrack of that old sitcom they kept repeating, *Friends*. But Abigail liked them. So they couldn't be that bad.

His phone flashed, vibrated. He took the headphones off, the sound of their cover of Michael Jackson's 'Beat It' bleeding feebly out, and checked the display. His mother. He debated for a few seconds whether or not to answer it. He doubted it would be good news. It usually wasn't.

But she was still his mother. And she obviously needed him. He answered it.

'Hi,' he said.

'Hello, son.' His mother sounded hesitant, nervous. He felt like a cloud had taken residence over his head. 'Are you busy?'

He said he wasn't.

'Good. Listen, I need you to come down to Albion. Now. There's . . .' She sighed. And it sounded like a similar cloud was hanging over her own head. 'There's something we have to talk about. Urgently.'

His instincts had been right. It didn't sound good. But he told her he would be there and hung up. He threw the phone on the bed beside him. 'A Little Less Sweet Sixteen' came from the speakers. He wished Abigail were here so she could come with him.

Reluctantly, he got off the bed, turned off the stereo, made for the door. As he walked past the other bedroom, he heard the sound of Rob snoring. He had been asleep all day, since he and his mother had been up all night. Talking. Not arguing, although it had started that way, but talking. He had cracked open his bedroom door and watched them, unseen. Sitting next to each other on the sofa, voices quiet but sad. Sometimes his mother cried and Rob hugged her. It wasn't the usual kind of argument or heated discussion, but something much sadder. Scott Walker had been playing softly, his mother's favourite, so he hadn't been able to hear anything. But he doubted it was anything good.

And now this. He tiptoed past the bedroom, down the hall and quietly closed the door on the way out.

Not expecting good news.

The train pulled into Newcastle Station; Amar pushed a very reluctant Martin Flemyng on to the platform.

'This is kidnapping, I'll have you arrested.'

'Yeah,' said Amar, trying not to yawn, 'so you keep saying.' He pointed to a pair of uniformed police officers patrolling the concourse. 'Look, there's a couple there. Why don't you run up and tell them that? And then I'll tell them who you are and what you've done, and we'll see who gets arrested. What d'you reckon?'

Flemyng said nothing.

'Didn't think so. But don't worry, you'll be seeing them soon enough. In the meantime, Martin,' Amar said, grabbing the other man's arm, 'let's go.'

'Where to?'

'To see an old friend of yours.'

The remaining colour drained from Flemyng's face.

Peta drove towards Newcastle as fast as she could. No radio, no music, no distractions. She wanted to think.

There was something niggling at her. She had tried to work out what it was all the way up the A1 but it had so far eluded her. Something to do with Tom Haig. Something he had said.

Or not said. Or the way he had said it. Or not said it.

Or something.

She relayed the conversation with Haig from the beginning, word for word, as well as she could remember it. Playing it over in her mind. Again. And again. Nothing came to her. But there was something. She just couldn't reach it.

So she tried not to think about it. Come at it from a different angle, think laterally, try to creep up on it by surprise. She thought instead about Donovan and his night out with Wendy. Unsure what to make of the situation. She thought of how Wendy had contacted him, out of the blue with the job—

And she had it. The thing that had been niggling her. How had Tom Haig found her mobile number? Neither she nor Amar had given it to him. So how had he got it?

Perhaps Flemyng wasn't the only one who needed further investigation.

She floored the accelerator.

'Hi, Jack. Come in.'

Donovan opened the door to Albion, Jack entered. The look on Donovan's face – taut, sombre – did nothing to calm his fears about this meeting. Donovan attempted a smile, but Jack could tell it sat uneasily on his face.

'Upstairs,' said Donovan, closing the door behind him. Jack walked slowly upstairs. He had seen a black and white film once about a murderer being sent to the gallows. The camera tracked him climbing the steps to the scaffold where he was hanged. That was exactly how he felt now. Condemned.

'Any trouble getting here?' Donovan had tried to make his voice cheery and open but he couldn't disguise the tension.

'No, it was fine.' That wasn't entirely true. Jack had felt as if he was being watched when he walked through the estate. There was a real tension in the air, as if something was about to happen. Something bad like a fight or a riot. He had thought he was imagining things or it was just him experiencing it, but Donovan's question made him think that maybe there was something more to it.

Jack reached the top floor. He went into the conference room where his mother was sitting on a leather sofa. If anything, she looked even worse than Donovan. Sitting up all night talking to Rob hadn't helped, but she looked even worse than expected.

'Hello, son,' she said. 'Come and sit down.'

She gestured towards the other sofa. Donovan slipped silently out of the room, closed the door behind him. Jack swallowed, waited.

'Listen,' said Anne Marie, 'I've got somethin' to tell you.'

It's important because it concerns all of our futures, and you in particular.'

She sighed. He waited. His body was so tense he could feel his muscles starting to ache.

'You know I have . . . episodes. Bad episodes. I wish I didn't but . . . there you go. And you know we have to move around a lot. Well.' Another sigh. He noticed her hands were shaking. 'There's a reason for that.'

'It doesn't matter,' he said, his voice small and reedy. It did matter, but he didn't want to hear it. Not now. Not ever. Because he sensed that once he did, it was something that would tear his world apart.

'It does,' his mother said. 'I never wanted you to know this, but I think it's time you did. Because someone else has found out. And they're tryin' to tell everyone else. And they're tryin' to force us out.'

'No . . .'

Another sigh. 'Yes. I wish it wasn't like that, but it is. I thought I'd be able to come home and settle. But we can't. You can't go home again. An' it's because of this.' She looked down at her bandaged hands as if expecting to find strength there. She looked up again, clearly decided she couldn't face him with what she was about to say, looked back down again. 'When I was young, younger than you, I did some-thin' bad. Really bad.'

Jack felt his heart hammering. It was hard to breathe. He didn't trust himself to speak.

Her head was bowed, eyes on her hands. 'I . . . killed someone.'

Jack felt the world slip away beneath him. His head began to spin. He blinked. Once, twice. Looked at his mother. She was looking at him now, as if in pain.

'Who . . .' His voice sounded like someone else's in his head.

'A . . . child. A boy. And someone's found out about it. And they still hate me for it. And they want us to leave.'

Jack's head was now spinning like he was on a fairground ride. He had no words, no coherent thought, to describe how he felt at the words.

'I . . . I used to be called another name. But that wasn't me. I am who I am now. It was . . . a . . . horrible thing to do. And I hate myself for it. I never stop thinking about it. I had a horrible time when I was a little girl. A horrible time . . .'

He looked at her, unable to speak. His mother started crying.

'I'm sorry . . . I'm sorry . . .'

Jack felt like he would collapse. The walls seemed to be moving in on him. He felt trapped, suffocated. He swallowed. His throat was dry. He needed water, he needed air.

'You . . . you . . .'

'I'm still you mother, son. I love you. I won't let nothin' bad happen to you. I promise. It was . . . I was a different person then. Sometimes you do somethin' bad. Everyone does. Well, I did the worst thing imaginable.'

Jack stood up. 'No . . . no . . .' He had to get out of there. Get some fresh air.

'Jack, please . . .'

'No . . . no . . .'

'Jack . . .'

A sudden thought came to him, knifing into his mind, cutting through his mental fog. 'The estate . . . there were two boys killed this week.'

Anne Marie reached out, tried to grab him. Didn't connect. 'I had nothin' to do with them, honest.'

He looked at her bandaged hands. 'Two boys . . .'

'It wasn't me . . .'

'No . . .' He had to get out. He had to think. He wanted

to scream, to cry, to run. He wanted to sleep. Curl up into a ball, let oblivion overtake him. 'No . . .'

He turned, made for the stairs and, before anyone could stop him, lurched down them.

'Jack!'

Anne Marie reached the top of the stairs, he heard her behind him, following him. He ran. Through the front door, out into the lane.

'Jack . . .'

He ran. And kept running.

'Oh God, what have I done . . . what have I done . . .'

She sits on the sofa. Looking like all the life has drained from her, just the crumpled shell of a human being remaining. Donovan sits down beside her. She doesn't move, doesn't acknowledge his presence even.

He waits. Knows she will start speaking again soon.

'Oh God . . .'

'It was a risk,' he says.

She says nothing.

'D'you want to go after him? D'you want me to go after him?'

After a long time, or what seems like a long time, she shakes her head. 'No. Give him time to think. We'll . . . hopefully we'll talk later . . .'

'OK. Listen, do you want to keep talking? Or would you rather have a break?'

She sighs again. Before she can answer, Donovan's mobile rings. He excuses himself to her, answers it. He walks to the other side of the room, away from her. Talks, hangs up. He comes back, sits down next to her on the sofa again.

'Well,' he says. 'That was Amar. He's on the way here from the station. He's bringing someone to meet you. I think it should solve a lot of problems.'

She looks up, a fearful expectation in her eyes. 'Is it . . .' She can't bring herself to finish the question.

Donovan nods. 'It sounds like we've got him. All you have to do is see him for yourself, we'll take him away and then that'll be it.'

She is still looking at him, desperately wanting to believe him. Fear overtakes her. 'No, he'll see me, he'll get me . . .'

'No, he won't. Amar will bring him in, you can see that he's *going nowhere and then we'll hand him over to the police. End of story. The spell will be broken. No more bad spirits.'*

She looks like she desperately wants to believe him but fear won't allow her to.

'I promise.'

She sighs again. Nods. Lets his words sink in, realizes he is telling the truth. And then the tears start.

26

'Thanks,' Jack said.

'What for?'

'For meeting me like this. When I called. I . . . I really appreciate it.'

Abigail smiled. 'That's what friends are for.'

They were back in the same juice bar in Eldon Square but everything else was different. The day was ending, the sky had darkened, the air harsher and colder. When they looked out of the window over to Eldon Square itself, the harmless goths, emos and drunks of the daytime seemed to have taken on a more sinister aspect. Shadowed and hunched and sodium-lit, they no longer sprawled, they patrolled, guarded their territory, warned unwary wanderers to stay away.

All around them the staff were trying to close up, their daytime shifts coming to an end. Jack was conscious of all this, but he didn't want to give up his time with Abigail so easily.

He had phoned her as soon as he had stopped running after he left Albion. His head was so messed up, he couldn't think. It was far too early to describe, even to himself, what impact his mother's revelation had on him. He had to talk to someone. Not even to sort it out – because there was nothing he could do to sort it out, it had already happened – just to connect. Abigail had been the obvious choice. And, of course, he wanted to see her again. Even under these circumstances. Under any circumstances.

He watched her sip her smoothie through her straw. Loved the way her cheeks went in, the way she swallowed. The enjoyment in her eyes as the liquid went down. She looked up, caught him staring. Looked away quickly.

She licked her lips, sat back, looked at him once more. He noticed something in her eyes. A distraction, a tension. Was it him causing that, or was there something more? Something she hadn't said?

He watched her. 'So, what about you? Everything fine with you? Your trip to Newcastle still working out well?' God, that was so lame. Why couldn't he come out with anything but lame stuff when he was with her?

She sighed, sat back, flicking her long hair out of the way. 'God, where do I start?'

He smiled. 'Wherever you like.' He hoped she would talk. That's what he needed. To hear her talk. To not have to think too much about his own troubles, lose himself in someone else.

'Well, I had a shock this morning. Just when I thought everything was going well, I bumped into my dad's girl-friend.'

'Where?'

'In the kitchen.'

'Oh.'

'Yeah. She was like, oh, you must be the daughter. I've just, you know, shagged your dad.'

He laughed. Abigail seemed taken aback at his reaction and he thought he had done the wrong thing again. But then she joined him.

'Yeah,' she said, smiling, 'when you say it like that it does sound kind of funny. But it wasn't at the time.'

'Are your parents divorced, then?'

'No, but they're separated. Haven't lived together since – for years.'

'Well, that's OK, isn't it? For them both to have new people in their lives?'

'I suppose so. It's just that . . . that's why I came up here. Mum's got this new guy. And he's OK, you know. She likes him and that. And he's good to me. But sometimes he gets all, you know, like, telling me what to do. Like, I'm your dad. I say, you're not. You're my mum's boyfriend. Don't act like my dad. And he gets all, like, upset and we have a row.'

Jack nodded. 'I know the feeling.'

'Right. Well, last week, she announces to me, well, they both do. You know, sitting down on the sofa together, me on a chair, them looking at me, smiling. Then they tell me. Mum's going to get divorced from dad. And they're going to get married. And I just blew up.'

Jack frowned. 'Why? You didn't think they'd get back together again, did you?'

Abigail puts her head down, her hair falling forward. She plays with her straw, swirling it round her glass, scraping the froth off the sides. 'Well . . . you kind of hope they would. And . . . well, this just seems so final.'

Jack nodded. 'But it happens all the time.'

'Yeah, but . . .' She sighed, still scraping at the froth. 'There's something else. Something I haven't told you yet.'

Yet. He liked that *yet.* 'What?'

'My . . . brother. I had a brother. Have, I don't know.'

'What, what happened to him?'

'He disappeared. He was out shopping with my dad and then . . .' She shrugged. 'He just disappeared.'

'God.'

'Yeah. We tried to find him, my dad spent years looking for him. And he couldn't find him. Not a trace. It was what split us up, really. What sent him away. Just, David not being there any more.'

'But . . . he still had you.'

'I know. And that used to make me so angry. Because I was there and David wasn't. And Dad went looking for David. Really angry. But he said to me, if it was the other way round, if it was me who'd disappeared, he would do the same. He wouldn't stop until he found me.' She sighed. 'But it didn't matter. I was so angry I couldn't see that.'

'And he never found him?'

She shook her head. 'And he says he'll never stop looking.'

'And now your mum wants to divorce him.'

She nodded. 'Yeah. And I suppose the thing that makes me cross, really cross, is that it means David's dead, you know? If she marries Michael it means that's it. That's the end.'

She looked out of the window, wiped tears from her eyes. Continued talking, eyes on the darkness outside.

'So I ran away. Came to see my dad. See if they could get back together again. One last time. And then I met her.'

He nodded. He wished there was something more he could do, even lean across the table, take her hand, let her know he was there for her. But he didn't. He couldn't. She turned back to him.

'Sorry,' she said. 'I shouldn't get like this.'

'Hey,' he said trying to smile. 'That's what friends are for, right?'

She smiled. 'You're really . . . thanks for listening.' She reached across the table, put her hand on his. His heart began to race. He didn't know what to do, whether to pull away, put his other one on top of it, grip hers harder, what. In the end he decided to just stay as he was and hope the smile on his face wasn't too soppy.

She ended it herself, giving his hand a squeeze and pulling away. She wiped her eyes again. 'God, I must look a mess.'

'No.' He looked straight at her. 'No, you don't.'

Their eyes locked. Then she looked away. 'So,' she said, 'how about you? Wasn't there something you wanted to talk about?'

'Yeah,' he said. And Abigail sitting there in the brightly lit café, after hearing about her troubles, his own and his mother's seemed to belong to a different world. 'It's a bit . . . complicated. Maybe . . .' He shrugged, tried to smile. 'Maybe it's not that important.'

'OK. Whatever.' She looked at her smoothie again then glanced round. The staff were cleaning tables, stacking up furniture. 'I think they want us out of here.'

'Yeah,' said Jack. What did they do next? 'Are you . . . where are you going now?'

She shrugged. 'Nowhere. I'm not in a hurry to go back to the flat in case she's there again. What about you?'

'Nothing,' he said. 'Shall we go for a walk?'

She smiled. 'Yeah, that would be great.'

They left their table, walked out into Eldon Square.

Unaware that someone who had watched them enter the juice bar and waited patiently outside on a seat all the time they were inside, was following them.

The taxi pulled up outside Albion. Amar paid the driver, made sure he got a receipt. The cab pulled away, leaving Amar and Flemyng standing there.

'Here we are,' Amar said. 'Journey's end.'

He opened the door with his key, pushed Flemyng inside.

'Joe? Hi, honey, I'm home,' he said in an exaggerated, camp American voice.

Donovan came down from upstairs. Saw Amar and his reluctant guest in the doorway. 'Come on in,' he said. 'We've been waiting for you.'

He motioned Amar to follow him upstairs and to bring Flemyng with him. On the way up, he says to Amar. 'I've told her what's happening so she knows what to expect. If we show him to her then get him out of the way, that should do the trick.'

'Fine by me,' said Amar.

They reached the top of the stairs. Donovan knocked. 'You decent?'

'Yuh – yeah.' Anne Marie's voice, through the door, was small, unsteady.

'OK.' He put his hand on the door handle.

'Wait, please.' Flemyng put his hand on Donovan's arm. 'There's no need for this. It's just dredging up unpleasant memories. For both of us. Why put her through this now? What do you have to gain from it?'

Donovan gave a tight smile. 'Nice try. But you're still going through with it.'

He opened the door. Anne Marie was still sitting on the sofa, a look of expectant dread on her face.

'Here he is.'

Donovan ushered Flemyng into the room, Amar behind him, ready to grab him if he made a run.

Anne Marie's face turned to a mask of horror. 'No . . . no . . . take him away. Not him, no . . .'

Donovan looked between Amar and Flemyng, then back to Anne Marie.

'No . . . no . . .'

'But, Anne Marie, this is him. Martin Flemyng. This is the guy.'

'No, it's not! Not him! He's not Jack's father . . .'

'What?' Flemyng tried to make a run for it. Amar grabbed him.

'What?' said Donovan. 'You never said he was Jack's father . . .'

'No, he's not the one. He's not the one . . .' Anne Marie looked distraught.

'Shit.' Donovan looked at Amar.

They had the wrong man.

Jack and Abigail were sitting at a table in Pizza Hut on Grainger Street in the city centre. They didn't know of many places to eat and this was one of the cheapest and also one of Jack's favourites. Abigail hadn't minded. She didn't know anywhere else either.

They had pooled their remaining money, realized that they had enough for a large pizza plus salad and drinks. That was fine, thought Jack. Anything to extend his time with Abigail.

'Do you have to go home soon?' asked Jack.

Abigail shrugged. 'Don't know. I'm waiting for my dad to call me. Find out where I am. We're still not speaking.'

Jack nodded. 'Right.'

'What about you?'

He shrugged. 'Same. My mum and I . . . we had a bit of a falling out today.'

'Is that what you wanted to say earlier?'

He nodded.

'What about?'

'Well . . .' He still didn't know whether to tell her or not. He trusted her, probably the only person he could think of to open up to, but once he said it there would be no going back. The words would be out there. And what would she think of him? Would her opinion change? What would she do? 'She . . . she just told me a bit of bad news, that's all.'

Abigail leaned forward, concern on her face. 'What kind?'

'Well . . .' Here it comes. Now or never, he thought. 'Excuse me . . .'

They both looked up. A man was standing at their table. Short, bearded. Quite old. Wearing jeans, a plaid shirt and a suede jacket. He looked genial, smiling, yet slightly apprehensive at interrupting them.

'Are you . . .' He checked on a piece of paper. 'Jack Smeaton and Abigail Donovan?'

They exchanged glances with each other. 'Yes,' said Abigail.

He smiled in evident relief, exhaled a great sigh. Smiled again. 'Thank God for that. I've been all over town looking for you both. Tried everywhere. Just pleased that you got hungry eventually. I'm sorry to disturb you when you're eating, but I've got a message from your dad. I work with him at Albion.'

'My dad?' said Abigail.

'Yes, your dad. Joe Donovan. He says he wants to see you both straight away. Back at his place. The office.'

They exchanged glances once more.

'Why?' said Abigail. 'What's wrong?'

'I think you'd better ask him yourself. He just asked me to come and get you, if that's OK.'

Abigail frowned. 'Why didn't he phone me?'

'He said that . . .' He rubbed his chin, looked embarrassed at what he was about to say. ' . . . that you didn't exactly part on good terms this morning. He thought you might have your phone turned off.'

Abigail shared another glance at Jack. That explanation seemed to have mollified her, calmed her fears.

'If you want to phone him, please feel free. But let's do it on the way. We've got to hurry.'

A spear of dread shot through Jack. 'Why? What's happened?'

'Nothing to worry about,' said the smiling man, giving Jack all his attention. 'There's been some . . . developments in what he's working on, that's all. And he wants you both there, where you're safe.'

Jack looked at Abigail once more. She looked as uneasy as he did. They both had fears and concerns and knew not to go off with strangers, even in their teens. But this man knew things no one else could, unless he was who he said he was.

'Well,' the man said, 'it's up to you. I don't blame you. Some guy rocks up, says who he is and wants you to go with him. Like I said, if you want to phone your dad you can do. Same with you and your mum, Jack. But you'd better do it on the way. We have to hurry.'

That settled it. Jack stood up. Abigail, still nursing doubts but trusting in Jack's judgement, did likewise.

Besides, thought Jack, the man was old, fat, cheerful and he didn't give out any serial killer vibes. How threatening could he be?'

'Get him out, just get him out . . .'

Amar bundled Flemyng out of the room. Shut the door firmly behind him. Donovan crossed to Anne Marie, sat down beside her on the sofa.

'I'm so sorry . . .'

She shook her head, eyes closed. 'God, I thought I'd never see him again. Never hear from him again. And then he walks in . . . What did you do that for?'

'But, I thought we had him. I thought, from what you told me that was him. You never mentioned he was Jack's father.'

She looked up sharply. 'I was comin' to that. It's not somethin' I go around tellin' people. But him? Jack's father? No chance. I wouldn't trust any kid with him.'

'Then, if it's not him, who is it? Who's Jack's father?'

'I can't tell you . . .'

Donovan was starting to get angry. 'Anne Marie, you can. You have to. Who is Jack's father? What's his name?'

She sighed. Hard. Looked him square in the eyes.
'His name's Haig. Tom Haig.'

Jack and Abigail were grabbing their coats. They had asked for the bill.

'Don't worry about that,' said the smiling man. 'The company'll pay for that.'

He took it to the counter, paid, rejoined them.

'So,' said Abigail, buttoning up her coat and getting her mobile out, 'what's your name?'

The man smiled again. 'My name's Tom. Tom Haig.'

He ushered them out of the restaurant.

'Tom Haig. Tell me about him, Anne Marie. Everything. Who is he?'

'Please . . . I can't do this any more . . .'

'Yes, you can. You have to. He's out there and we need to stop him. Look,' he says, 'Amar's taking care of Flemyng, making sure he's nowhere near you. He's called Tom Haig's number in London but got no reply. We have to assume he's here or on the way. Please. Tell me everything. Then we can stop him.'

'He's already here,' she says, her voice quiet again, like she no longer has the energy to breathe, let alone speak.

'What, you've seen him? Talked to him?'

She nods.

'Why didn't you tell me?'

She looks up again. Tears are pooling in her eyes once more. 'I tried . . . I said he phoned me . . . he makes me do things . . .'

'I thought you meant killing those boys, or making out you killed those boys.'

She puts her head down again, addresses the table. 'He tries to make me believe it's me, that I've done it. I have blackouts. You know that. He tells me what I do in the blackouts. Like the other night, I blacked out and when I came round my hands were bleeding.'

'You said you broke a window in the flat.'

She nods. 'I did. But then I heard about this dead boy on the estate. And I had bad dreams. And I started to think . . .'

He leans forward, takes her bandaged hands in his own. Speaks quietly. 'You didn't. That's not you. There are no such things as bad spirits, he just plants suggestions into your mind.'

Her eyes screwed tightly shut, she nods. 'I want to believe that but . . .'

'But what?'

'Last night. He called. Said I had to meet him. He knew where I was. And that I had broken the rules. So I had to pay.'

'Pay? You mean he was going to hurt you?'

'Pay. I mean pay. Money. Every time he finds me he wants money so he'll keep quiet. I haven't got much, but he wants it. Now he's heard about this book. So he wants the money for that. If not, he'll do terrible things. Let people know where I am.' She gives a bitter laugh. 'He doesn't need to do that now.' Her face hardens once more. 'But he said he'd already started.'

'What d'you mean by that?'

'That boy who was killed last night? He said that was him. He did it. But he's got evidence that he's going to plant on me if I don't get him some money.'

'OK. So tell me about him. Everything. And we can stop him.'

She takes a deep breath, her eyes closed. Lets it go, opens them. 'Right. Tom Haig. He was my probation officer, my first point of contact when I got released.'

'This was in London.'

'West London, yes. Horrible place. But he was supposed to look after me, see that I found a job, help me. You know the kind of thing. And I clung to him at first. I mean, I was so scared when I came out, I didn't know what to do. And he helped me. And I really liked him.' She sighs. 'That was then.'

'What happened after that?'

'Well . . . we started to see each other. I mean, we'd always gone out. For drinks, meals and that. It was all part of his job, socializin' me, he said. Gettin' me back into the swing of things. And one thing kind of led to another.'

'What was he like?'

'At first? Lovely. Really sweet, understanding. He used to look at you when you talked to him, and he seemed to really be listening to you. That made you feel special. I mean, he wasn't all that to look at, little and fat, really. But it didn't matter. He was kind *to me. The first person in years to be kind to me.' She sighs. 'Knew it would be too good to last.'*

'He changed?'

She nods. 'Yes.'

'In what way?'

She sighs again, thinking. 'I found out I was pregnant. At first I was terrified. I wanted to get rid of the baby. I knew it was his, it wasn't that. I was just scared, you know. Scared of what might happen. Of what I might do. Thinkin' of me mother, an' that. But he talked me into it. Calmed me down, said it would be a good thing, that he would stand by me. He'd be with me. And when Jack was born, that's when he changed.'

'All at once or gradually?'

'Well . . .' She screws up her eyes, thinking back. 'I don't remember. I mean, it's so long ago and all I think when I think of him is the bad stuff. Because all the rest of the time he was just acting. All the caring, Guardian-reading stuff was just an act. His true self started to come out. He hated his clients. They were weak, spineless, he said. He was a human dustman, clearing up other people's shit all the time. If he had his way, he said, he would have the whole lot of them sterilized so they couldn't breed any more. It would be no loss.' She starts to shake as she says the words.

'So why did he have a baby with you?'

'Power.' Her voice begins to break as she talks. She reins it in again, continues. 'He wanted power over me. I was a killer, he said. A real-life killer. And he wanted power over a killer. He wanted her to have his baby. Because then it would make me weak. Really weak. One of the spineless lot, he said, queen of the spineless lot. He used to do this all the time, go on and on at me, grind me down, make me hate myself, make me worry that I'd do something to the baby.'

'Did he hurt you? Physically?'

She shakes her head. 'He didn't need to. He used words. He controlled me with words. He wasn't the person I thought he was.

He was hard, horrible. Had these Nazi fantasies. Like the only way he could feel powerful was by bein' cruel to those he thought were weaker than himself.'

'Like you.'

'An' he was always askin' me, what was it like, how did it feel when I had my hands round Trevor's throat, what was I thinkin' when I cut him. All the time. Tell me, tell me, tell me . . .'

She starts to cry. Not sobbing this time, just tears flowing slowly and silently down her cheeks. She continues. 'He said anyone could kill. That didn't take skill. It was harder not to kill. That was when I started havin' these blackouts.'

'Sounds like they were stress-induced.'

She nods.

'Did you not try to get away from him?'

'I tried but . . .' She sighs. 'Where could I go? He was the person I was supposed to go to if things went bad. And then when I thought they couldn't get any worse, they did.'

'What happened?'

Her voice drops to a whisper. 'He killed a boy.'

'Guy Brewster.'

She nods. 'Came back afterwards full of energy. Said it was easy, anyone could do it. Told me how much he enjoyed it, what a thrill it gave him.' She spoke as if her mouth contained something harsh and bitter that she wanted to spit out. 'Said he'd done a boy so that if anyone asked around, he could say it was me. And he kept a souvenir, he said. Somethin' that could be used to implicate me. Just in case I wanted to tell anyone.'

'Oh God . . .'

'And that was it. I knew I had to get away. For me. For Jack. So I went to his superior, told him about the killin'.'

'You told him Haig was responsible?'

She shakes her head. 'No. I couldn't do that. Just in case. I told him I had to move away. Because of my background. Told him I'd been blackin' out, getting panic attacks. Told him it was for safety's *sake. And he agreed. Thankfully, he agreed. So I got moved to Bristol. And that's when I met Martin Flemyng.'*

'You've not had much luck, have you?'

She gives a weak smile. 'Not really. But I did meet Rob. Eventually. But not till I moved to Hull. He's been great. I know some people don't think much of him but he's been great to me. I know he's got his problems, but he really loves me. And he'll do anythin' to make sure I'm all right.' She nods, still smiling.

His mobile rings. He ignores it, concentrates on Anne Marie.

'So Bristol,' says Donovan, putting her back on track. 'Adam Wainwright.'

She nods again and the smile fades. 'Tom Haig caught up with me. Wanted money this time. I didn't have it. So I ran.' She sighs. 'He hated the fact that I got away from him. Hated it. That's why he did what he did. Followed me. To Colchester. To Hull. He would get my phone number, tell me what he was goin' to do. Keep phonin' and phonin', sayin' stuff, getting me into such a state that I would have another blackout, have nightmares. And he knew this so he would play on them, tell me it was me that had done it, keep on and on, so much so that I started to believe him myself . . .'

She shakes her head as if to clear it.

'Thank God for Rob.'

'And now Haig's found you again.'

Another sigh. 'He's found me again.' She looks directly at Donovan. 'Please stop him. Please.'

Donovan returns her gaze. Before he can answer, Anne Marie's phone rings.

27

Night-time on the Hancock Estate.

The *Evening Chronicle* had been published in several editions, the local news had been broadcast on radio, TV and the internet. Now everyone knew or was capable of knowing: Mae Blacklock was back in town. And, it was strongly implied, up to her old tricks.

Sylvia Cunliffe had been quoted everywhere, her undiminished bile and anger poured through every medium. The TV still wanted to interview her as the story threatened to become national. She insisted all interviews be done at the site of the latest murder, the Hancock Estate. Coincidentally, a hastily organized candle-lit vigil was going to take place outside the school gates where the piles of floral tributes still grew. That was where she would be interviewed, the TV people decided. The impact would be greater.

The vigil went on. Community leaders, religious representatives spoke. Pez's mother made a small appearance. She didn't stay long. She didn't feel able to. Once she left, the vigil broke up and a different mood overtook the crowd. As if they were only being polite for her sake.

The residents, they decided, had had enough. They were sick of the TV crews, the reporters everywhere. They were tired of seeing their estate portrayed as a place where lawlessness and criminality were endemic. But mostly, they were angry. At children dying. At killers getting away with it.

It didn't take long for these murmurs of unease and unrest

to gestate, hatch and then spread. Mae Blacklock, Mae Blacklock. Spoken over and over, like a mantra of ever-increasing hatred. A target for their anger. A legitimate one, they felt.

The police had done nothing. They were protecting her. Who was there to protect the children who had died? She had more rights than the victims. It was a liberty. And someone should do something about it. Show them that they'd had enough. That they weren't going to be ignored.

They tried making assumptions as to whom she could be. Came up with parameters. She had to be new to the estate, or relatively new, someone who wouldn't be known to them. Who might have a secret. Someone mentioned the old goth woman, her alkie boyfriend and her long-haired son.

And it all coalesced.

It was time to direct that anger. Time to show her that if the police weren't going to do anything, they – the inhabitants of the estate, the *angry* inhabitants – would. This was their estate. And they were going to reclaim it.

They came with hastily made placards, chanting, shouting. Fuelled on anger and alcohol, the cold, dark night the perfect cover. They were out in the open, clear about what they wanted. The child murderer out.

By any means necessary.

They found the block of flats she lived in. Someone knew which floor she was on. They all went up the stairwell, stood outside the door. Starting banging on it, shouting. No reply.

'She's inside, keep shouting,' was one such shout, rage's conviction overcoming the evidence.

They kept shouting, banging, hitting. The noise deafening. But she wasn't there. There was no sound, no movement, not even any light inside the flat. She wasn't there. They had done all this, and she wasn't there.

Their anger was unspent, still coiled collectively within them. It needed an outlet. They had to do something, make some kind of statement. Protest. One of the number had come armed with a washing-up liquid bottle full of petrol. Clearly prepared, he had done this kind of thing before. In the raging cacophony, he went up to the letterbox, squirted it through. Lit a match, threw that in afterwards. Risked a glance inside: it had taken. The hallway carpet had caught nicely.

They turned and, their anger gleeful almost to the point of orgasm, ran from the flat. They stood on the ground, out-side the block, watching as the flames took hold. Neighbours started to appear from the other flats. Came and stood on the landing. Panicked and ran once they saw the fire had caught.

Some ran away, some came and joined them. Some phoned 999.

The fire took hold, clouds of black smoke belching out.

It started to spread to other flats, began to get out of hand.

The fire starters could do nothing but watch.

Rob was still in bed, CD player blaring, AC/DC's greatest hits reminding him of his glory days. He was drifting in that space between waking and dreaming, the zone where the subconscious was supposed to sort out the real world's problems. It wasn't working for him. Things were still com-plicated. But the rest was doing him good. It was the excuse, he told himself, for not getting up. What with everything that had happened recently, a day in bed, trying to relax, get his head together, was just what he needed.

He was trying to come to terms with so much: Anne

Marie being exposed, them all having to move and, he was ashamed to remember, he had punched a woman. She was a journalist, yes, but still a woman. Although that was probably a good thing – it had stopped him from going further. If it had been a man he would have done a lot more damage.

There was an awful noise going on outside, sounding like someone having a huge party. He heard it over his music. He couldn't lie there any longer with all that going on so thought about getting up, making another cup of tea and maybe some toast, when he smelt burning. He knew he hadn't left anything on in the kitchen – all he had eaten all day was a bowl of cereal. So he knew something must be wrong.

He got out of bed and, wearing only the T-shirt and boxers he slept in, opened the bedroom door. Immediately he was engulfed by thick, black smoke.

Oh God, oh God . . .

He shut the door straight away, looked round, his heart hammering. Think. Think. The flat was on fire, what could he do? Phone 999.

He scanned the bedroom, looking for his phone. It wasn't there. He had left it in the living room.

'Fuckin' hell . . .'

He looked at the door. Smoke was starting to curl in under the bottom. He could feel the heat, smell it. He was starting to panic. He had to get out of there, had to get away. If he stayed in the bedroom, he would die. That realization galvanized him into action. He had to open the door, find a way out.

Water. He needed water. If he could wet something, put it over his face like they did in films, then he might not get burned. But there was no water in the bedroom. He would have to go to the bathroom for that. If he could. He grabbed a T-shirt from the dirty laundry pile, took several deep breaths, opened the door.

The heat hit him like a solid, yet moving, wall. It pushed him back into the room. He fought it, knowing he had to move forward, had to go through it somehow, had to escape.

Then another thought occurred to him: Jack. Where was Jack? If anything had happened to him, not only would Anne Marie kill him but he would never forgive himself. The boy's bedroom was next door, further along the hall. The flames hadn't reached there yet, just smoke. He put the T-shirt over his mouth and ran, flinging open the next door along. He peered through the smoke into the room, called out.

'Jack . . . Jack . . .'

No sign, no sound of the boy. He crossed to the bed, flung back the duvet. No Jack. Rob felt a momentary relief. The boy wasn't in the fire. That was something.

Rob went back into the hall again, looked round, quickly assessing his options. The fire seemed to be coming from the living room and that was the only way out. He opened the bathroom door opposite, turned on the taps and thrust the T-shirt he was carrying under the water. Putting a bath towel into the sink alongside it, he turned the taps full on, soaking them. When they were good and wet he pulled them out and, dripping, put the towel over his head and the T-shirt over his mouth. It was hard to breathe through the wet material but preferable to inhaling smoke. Breathing as shallowly as he could, he entered the living room.

The hallway leading to the front door was completely impassable. Fire had all but devoured it. He saw Anne Marie's Spirit House in the corner, the gaudily painted wooden construction that she had bought in some hippy shop years ago that was supposed to trap bad spirits in, completely aflame. It was useless now.

He looked round, panic rising within him once more. He was trapped. No way out, without getting burned alive.

He let out a scream. It wasn't fair, it wasn't fair, it wasn't fair . . .

Then stopped, tried to control himself. Think. There must be some way . . .

The window. It had a balcony. A small one, but a balcony, none the less. If he could just get out there . . .

He moved quickly to the window, flung it open, stepped out, dropping the T-shirt and savouring fresh air. He leaned out, checked both sides. No fire there. He looked over the rail. Fourth floor. A long way down.

He leaned further over the balcony. There was another one on the floor below, just underneath him. If he could climb over, lower himself down, swing in . . .

It was a risk. But it was better than staying in a burning flat.

Rob didn't mind heights. He was used to them after his years as a roadie with different bands. Shinning up lighting rigs held no fear for him – he had even done it when he was drunk and stoned and never had an accident. But that was years ago. When he was younger and felt immortal. Before he got fat and lazy.

He had no choice. He had to do it.

He pulled himself up on to the balcony railing, trying to get his balance. He could hear AC/DC's 'Highway to Hell' coming faintly from the bedroom. That gave him the faith he needed. A deep breath, then another and he swung himself over, holding on tight. He looked down, and tried to reach the balcony below. Lowered himself so he was hanging by his arms. He tried to swing his body outwards then in. If he could do that and jump at the same time, the force should carry him on to the balcony below.

He swung himself out and, heart hammering in his chest, let go.

His arm was outstretched, trying to grasp the rail.

He missed.

Rob fell through the air.

Jack was scared. More scared than he had ever been in his life.

Tom Haig had led them from the restaurant to an aged, white Escort van parked in a secluded side street just off Clayton Street.

'Here we are,' he said, still smiling. He opened the back doors. 'Bit of a squash, I'm afraid.'

Abigail took her phone out, began to dial. Tom Haig's expression changed.

'Who are you calling?'

'My dad. I said I would.' She put the phone to her ear.

Tom Haig glanced quickly round, checked there were no passers-by and grabbed the phone off her, throwing it as far as he could.

'Hey,' she shouted, 'what—'

'Shut it, you stupid bitch,' he hissed through clenched teeth, then slapped her face. She gave a gasp of pain then crumpled to the ground.

Jack watched stunned, unable to move, as if this was a film he was watching, not real life. Haig turned to him. Jack saw no trace of the smiling, avuncular old man in the restaurant. His eyes were hate-filled black dots, his lips were spittle-flecked and his face was red. He was breathing heavily, moving menacingly towards him.

'Your turn now, boy . . .'

Jack tried to move, but was too late. Haig punched him hard in the face. His hands came up and his neck snapped back. He went down too, joining Abigail on the ground. Haig stood over him.

'Just in case you get any ideas . . .'

He brought his heavily booted foot back, let it fly into

Jack's ribs. And again. The pain was immense. Jack had never experienced anything like it. He didn't know which part of him hurt most. He started to cry out. Haig bent down beside him.

'Shut it, you fucking monster.'

Jack, terrified, did as he was told.

He was aware that Abigail was stirring. He watched, helplessly, as Haig grabbed her and pushed her into the back of the van. She was as scared as he was, and went without argument. Then Haig turned back to Jack, pulled him up. Jack began to scream.

'I said shut it . . .'

A slap to the face kept Jack quiet. Haig pulled him to the back of the van then let him drop. He bent over as if pain was attacking his midriff, breathed hard, his face contorted. If Jack hadn't been in such agony, he would have thought about running.

With what seemed like a huge effort, Haig pulled himself back together, pointed to the back of the van. 'Get in . . .'

Jack, despite the pain, did as he was told.

Once inside, Haig crawled in after them. 'Turn round . . .'

Jack fell on his stomach, felt his broken ribs move. It was like someone had taken a knife to his insides. His hands were grabbed behind him as Haig tightly attached a pair of PlastiCuffs. He then turned his attention to Abigail.

'You going to give me any trouble?'

Abigail shook her head quickly.

'Good. Hands behind your back.'

Abigail did so, but pulled them away at the last minute and turned on Haig, aiming her nails for his eyes.

'Bitch,' said Haig, managing to move slightly as she raked his cheek. He struck out at her with his fist, landed a blow on her collarbone. She fell backwards.

Haig looked down at her and took out a knife from his jacket pocket. 'You want me to get creative? Eh? Do you?'

'No, please, no . . .' She was starting to sob now.

'Good. Now get on your stomach and don't try anything else because I'll fucking use this.'

She did as she was told. Haig attached PlastiCuffs to her too.

With them both tied and helpless, Haig slumped back against the wall of the truck. Jack glanced up at him. The man looked tired and he was still clutching his stomach. Breathing heavily, face a mask of horror and hatred.

Jack's emotions were cascading through him. He didn't know what to think, to feel, how to process what was happening. Who was this man? What did he want with them? How soon could he get help? Could he get help?

With another huge gasp, Haig pushed himself off the wall, looked at the pair of them. Smiled. It wasn't pleasant.

'Right . . . we're going to . . . take a little . . . drive . . .'

Jack, through all his pain and confusion, found his voice. 'Why are you doing this?'

Haig gave a little laugh. 'Because I want to.' Then a cloud darkened his features. 'Because I have to. I'm going to show your mother . . . who's in charge . . . I'm going to show her . . . show her . . .' Coughing stopped his words. He rode it out, regained his composure, spoke again. 'Don't worry. No one's going to . . . to save you. You're going to die. Because . . . I'm going to kill you. But, but . . . before I do, you're going to be, to be . . . famous . . .'

'But . . . who are you?'

Haig laughed again, his eyes lit by a dark, twisted light. He attempted a mock-Darth Vader voice. 'I am your father, Luke.' Then laughed again until a coughing fit stopped him.

And Jack realized that, whatever had happened to him so far, his troubles were only just beginning.

Anne Marie glanced down at the phone in her bag, then back up at Donovan, fear in her eyes. He shared her apprehension, but tried not to let her see. He failed.

'Oh God,' she said.

'Answer it,' Donovan said, his voice as quiet and as calm as possible. 'See who it is.'

She nodded, trusting him. 'He – hello . . .'

'Hello, Anne Marie.'

She took a sudden intake of breath, gasped, as if she was about to start a panic attack. Donovan knew without asking who it was. Tom Haig.

Donovan mouthed the words 'Keep him talking' at her and, once she had nodded that she understood him, ran out of the room.

He went downstairs into the main office. Amar had just shut Flemyng in the kitchen, telling him to stay there until they could decide what to do with him. He turned as Donovan entered.

'He's calling, Amar,' said Donovan. Anne Marie's phone. GPS. Get it traced.'

Amar rushed to his computer, sat down in front of it, moved the mouse and knocked the live feed from Brighton off the screen.

'Haven't heard from Jamal in a while,' he said.

'We'll worry about that later,' said Donovan. 'Let's get this sorted first.'

Amar's fingers moved over the keyboard. He brought up Anne Marie's number, started to trace the call. 'Keep her talking,' he said. 'Should take me about a minute or so if he's local.'

Anne Marie's voice came out of the speakers. 'I knuh – know it's you, Tom.'

'Yes,' said the other voice. 'And you don't sound pleased to hear from me. Well, you should be. Because I've got someone here with me. Someone you'll want to talk to.'

'Oh God,' said Donovan.

Amar's fingers played over the keys. 'Little bit longer . . .'

'No . . . no . . .'

'He's a fine-looking boy,' Tom Haig said, unable and unwilling to keep the relish from his voice. 'Well, he was. Still, he's a credit to you. Needs his father, though.'

Anne Marie tried to choke back sobbing.

'And he's got a girlfriend. Good lad.'

Donovan froze.

'Wuh – what?' said Anne Marie.

'Little Abigail. And Little Jack. What a lovely couple they make.'

'Fuck . . .' Donovan's heart was beating double time. His legs felt weak. 'No, no, no . . .'

'Now what shall I do with them? Hmm?'

'Got it,' said Amar. 'Scotswood.'

'Be more specific!' Donovan shouted.

Amar, concentrating, didn't take offence at Donovan's anger. 'The Elms,' he said. 'Tower block.' He frowned. 'Why a tower block?'

'I don't know. Keep them talking, see if he says anything else. I'm going over there.'

'I'll come with you.'

'No. You stay here. Anne Marie needs someone with her. And you've got to man the phone line.'

'But you can't go on your own. He's a fucking nutter.'

'I'll go with you.'

The two of them looked up. Flemyng was standing in the doorway to the kitchen.

'Amar's right. You need someone else with you. I know

you don't think much of me but I can still do . . .' He shrugged. '. . . something. Please. Let me help.'

Amar and Donovan exchanged a glance. They had little option.

'OK,' said Donovan. 'But you do exactly as I tell you. And don't fuck about. You got that?'

Flemyng nodded. 'Thank you.'

'Right,' said Donovan. 'Come on.'

He ran out of the building, Flemyng following.

'So, Anne Marie. It's finally come to this.'

She chokes back tears. Can't answer him.

Tom Haig continues. 'You see, I've been thinking. And I've come to a few decisions in the last few days. I don't want your money any more. It was never about that anyway. But it would have helped, especially now.'

'Wuh – what d'you mean?'

'I'll tell you. I'm dying, Anne Marie. Cancer. Stomach to start with, but it's spread to my bones, apparently. And there's nothing they can do to stop it.'

'Cancer . . .' A part of Anne Marie is elated at the news. 'So you won't be around to hurt me any more.'

He laughs. It is cut short by a coughing fit. He gets himself under control before answering. 'No, I won't be around any more. For you or anyone else. So I thought I would sort things out before I go. One last time.'

A shudder goes through Anne Marie. 'What d'you mean? What's sortin' things out?'

'The usual things people do in this situation, apparently. Seeing friends and family. Saying my goodbyes.'

She absorbed the impact of the words. 'Friends an' family . . . you mean Jack, don't you?'

'Of course. It's only right that a father should want to spend some quality time with his son while he still has the chance. Set him right on a few things.'

'Where are you?'

He laughs. 'Your old home. Right back to the beginning. Full circle.'

'What d'you mean? My old home? What old home?'

'In Scotswood.'

'*That was demolished.*'

'*I know. But not the one where you lived. The one where you killed. Where the person you are now was born.*'

'*No . . .*'

'*Yes. And what a view. Perfect for having a dad-to-lad chat with my son.*'

And then something happens within Anne Marie. Driven by her maternal need to protect Jack, she finds her voice. And when she speaks again, her voice is strong enough to overcome the fear she has of Haig. '*You're not his father. You've never been his father. You might have provided a seed that formed him, but you've never — never — been his father.*'

The vehemence behind her words shocks him. He falls silent for a few seconds. Anne Marie continues.

'*You've gone quiet, Tom. But then you don't like it when people answer you back, do you? You don't have power over them, control over them when they do that, do you? You don't like it.*' *Her voice gets stronger.* '*I'm tellin' you now. Let him go. An' Abigail. Let them go an' we'll say nothin' more about it. You can go. Just . . .*' *And here her voices wavers.* '*. . . just let them go.*'

He hears the hesitation, assumes it is weakness, pounces on it straightaway. '*Bitch.*' *He hisses the word.* '*You fucking bitch. Who the fuck are you to tell me what to do? Eh? You're nothing. You've got no power, nothing. You're helpless. Useless.*'

'*And what are you, Tom?*'

'*Better than you. I've spent my whole life clearing up after people like you. I've been a dustman cleaning up human shit.*'

'*I know, Tom. You've said that to me before. Lots of times.*'

'*Well, I'm tired of it. Tired of listening to weak, useless bastards and their weak, useless excuses for why their lives are so shit. Any excuse, so long as they don't blame themselves. And I've tried to help them. And are they grateful? Are they fuck. It's cost me my career, my health and now this. My life. Because this cancer is stress-related. That's what the doctor said. So it's your fault.*'

Anne Marie continued talking. She didn't stop to question where this new-found strength was coming from. 'My fault? Now who's blamin' other people?'

A roar of anger is her only answer. She waits for it to subside, holding her breath, hoping Jack is still all right.

'Why?' *he says once his voice is under control again,* 'why should you live and not me? Why should you enjoy yourself and have a life to look forward to, bearing in mind what you've done? Eh? You'd have nothing if it wasn't for me. If I hadn't sorted you out once you left prison, you'd have nothing. You'd be back inside by now. I gave you everything. Everything.'

'That's not how I remember it.'

'Then you're a liar as well as a bitch.'

'Tom,' *she says calmly. The calm surprises her. But she accepts it, works with it. Rationalizes in a split second what is happening. He is her fear. Her greatest fear. And now she is no longer running away. She is finally facing him and she is no longer scared.* 'Tom. What you've done is far worse than what I did. I know what I did was awful and I pay for that every day of my life. I'll never stop payin' for it. But I have to keep goin'. And I have to live with it. But there was a reason for what I did. Not an excuse to hide behind, a reason. Now you did somethin' far worse. You killed all those boys. And you don't care. And you don't have a reason for it. You just have an excuse. You think that makes you stronger? It doesn't. It just makes you weaker. Not superhuman, less than human.'

He is silent. All she can hear is his breathing.

She waits. Says nothing.

'I'll be in touch. When I've got something I want you to listen to.'

The phone goes dead in her hand.

'Tom? Tom?' *She redials, can't get through. She throws the phone down on the sofa, stares at it.*

'Oh no . . . oh no . . .'

28

Donovan was behind the wheel of the Scimitar, pushing it as hard as he could, on the way to the west side of the city, to Scotswood. He had heard the whole conversation, Amar having patched it through to his earpiece. Beside him in the passenger seat, Flemyng kept trying to talk. Donovan kept ignoring him.

'Thank you,' said Flemyng. 'For the chance to help, I mean.'

'Fine.'

'I mean, it's good of you. I really appreciate it. And I do want to help.'

'Good.'

'You see, I don't think I've got . . . once something like this gets out, and it will get out, I'm sure of it, I've got nothing to go back to. I'll lose my job, that's for certain. I'll be ostracized. And I've done so well recently. Kept my, you know, in check . . .'

Donovan barely looked at him when he spoke, keeping his eyes on the road ahead, his hands on the Scimitar's steering wheel. 'Listen, Flemyng, whether your friends won't talk to you any more because you like shagging kids and the university won't want you near students is not top of my list of priorities at the moment. I've got more important things to worry about.'

'Fine. Sorry. Right. It's just that . . .' He sighed. 'You don't know what it's like. What I have to go through. I—'

'Flemyng?'

'Yes?'

'You're here on sufferance, right?'

'Right.'

'So shut up. And suffer. In silence.'

Flemyng fell silent. Donovan pressed a button on his earpiece. 'How you doing, Amar? Got a better fix on the signal?'

'Think so,' the voice said in his ear. 'It's the one nearest the river, when you drive up to them off the Scotswood Road. I think he may have them on the roof.'

'That's what I thought. That thing he said about the view. Brilliant. Just what we need.'

'Should I call Nattress?'

'Might be worth a try.'

'Why there, though?' said Amar. 'Why a tower block?'

'Because Anne Marie, aka Mae Blacklock, killed that boy Trevor Cunliffe in a partially demolished house in Scotswood. They were putting up the tower blocks at the time. This was the Sixties when they were going to be the future of architecture. Once that street was demolished, they built the Elms in its place.'

'This Tom Haig guy's done his homework.'

'Yeah. But he's still a prick.'

Amar gave a grim laugh. 'I'll call Nattress.'

Donovan kept his eyes on the road. Nearly there.

Oh Christ . . .' DI Diane Nattrass stood before the burning block of flats and thought: As if my night couldn't get any worse.

The fire engines had arrived and evacuation procedures implemented. It was clear which flat had been targeted and once she found out who lived there, she could guess why. If Donovan had just given her up when she'd asked. She would talk to him later, and he wouldn't enjoy it.

The firefighters had the blaze under control. Thankfully it hadn't had time to spread and was contained in one area. Everyone in the surrounding flats had been evacuated as a precaution. And luckily there had been no casualties which, given what was intended, was near miraculous.

'Boss . . .'

Oh dear, she thought, I spoke too soon.

'Boss . . .' DS Stone, one of the junior officers on her team, came running towards her, out of breath. 'We've found a body,' he said, between gasps.

'Oh God . . .'

'Behind the flats. Looks like . . .' He paused to get his breath back. 'Looks like he jumped. Or fell.'

'Dead?'

'No, boss. Alive. Ambulance is there now. Paramedics trying to work out the damage.'

'Male or female?'

'Male.'

'How old?'

'Not young.'

Nattrass nodded. 'Jesus, those . . .' She composed herself. 'Thanks for letting me know. Get someone with him in case he comes round. Get a team of uniforms going round the estate. In fact, get everyone who's not doing anything to do that. I want people talking. I want whoever did this hauled in. I want an identity for that man. And quickly. And I want the fucking book thrown at whoever caused this. Make sure everyone understands that, right?'

He smiled. 'Yes, boss.' Breath regained, he ran off.

Nattrass looked again at the blazing flats as her phone rang.

'Nattrass.'

'Hi,' said the voice on the other end. 'It's Amar. Amar Miah.'

'Good,' she said. 'Has Joe Donovan decided he knows where Anne Marie Smeaton is?'

'What?'

'Is he going to hand her over to me for protection?'

'Er . . . no, but—'

'Then this conversation is over.'

She snapped the phone shut, returned it to her pocket. She was weary beyond sleep, functioning on caffeine and adrenalin. She wanted a long bath, a warm bed. She knew they were still a long way off.

Damn that bastard Donovan, she thought.

Tess Preston couldn't suppress her glee. The paper was still running with her exclusive, even if the news had been leaked by other media. But they had given her a proviso – they wanted an interview with Mae Blacklock. She had agreed, not knowing how to go about it, but determined to succeed. After all, she knew all too painfully, chances like this didn't come along too often.

The mob had scattered, naturally. Dispersed back to their ordinary lives, spending sleepless nights until morning when they had to cope with the guilt of what they had done. Tess smiled. Not bad, that line. She might use it. Alongside a little interview – anonymous, of course – of one of the angry mob. And for the good news: the police didn't have Mae Blacklock. She was in hiding, undoubtedly, but not with them. Her informants had told her. This was all good because she knew something they didn't. She knew the address of that place she saw her outside of, Albion House. She was sure Mae Blacklock was there.

She walked round the estate, keeping away from the police, watching the firefighters tackle the blaze. Collins should be around somewhere, snapping away. Despite the fact that they weren't talking, he was still a professional and knew a good story when he saw one. Didn't matter. They didn't have to like each other to work together. That wouldn't stop them getting paid. She wouldn't mind a few more pills, though. Adrenalin was keeping her going for now, staving off the comedown, but she knew it would happen eventually.

She walked away from the blaze, down a narrow, deserted alleyway. The estate didn't scare her tonight. There was too much happening, too many people around. She had summoned up courage to head to the dark heart of the estate, hoping to find someone to talk to. Flash a bit of cash, see what happened. They wouldn't hurt her. They wouldn't dare. She turned a corner, adjusted her eyes. It was very dark here, the crunching underfoot telling her that someone had taken out the streetlighting forcibly. She felt a stab of fear and hesitated, wondering who could live here. And in that instant thought about turning back.

When she was grabbed from behind.

She didn't have time to react, to turn around, even, the attack was so sudden. Her attacker was quick and ferocious. He punched Tess in the left kidney, which made her crumple at the knee, then twisted her arm so that she fell hard to the ground. Tess tried to cry out but as her body hit the glass-strewn tarmac, the wind was knocked from her and all she could do was wheeze and whisper. Once she hit the ground her attacker kicked her in the ribs. Twice. Tess clutched her side, rolled over. Her attacker bent down over her. Tess saw his face.

'What . . .'

It was Renny. And he was holding a very large, fierce-looking knife.

Peta pulled up in front of the Albion offices, turned off the engine. She looked round, expecting to see Donovan's car in its usual space but it was empty. She got out, went into the building.

"'S me!' she called out. 'I'm back.'

No one replied. She opened the door to the main office, entered. Amar was sitting at his desk. He looked up as she entered, his face grave.

'Where is everyone?'

Amar moved the headset away from his face as he spoke to her. 'Joe's over in Scotswood. His daughter and Anne Marie's son have been kidnapped.'

'Where?'

'Tower block. The Elms.'

She didn't need to hear anything else. 'Tell him I'm on my way.'

Peta ran back out of the door and straight to her car. Drove off as fast as she could.

Donovan dials the number, waits. He looks up at the tower block, imposing against the night sky. He knows the phone will be answered. He is counting on the curiosity of the man on the other end to respond to a number he does not know. He is right. The phone is answered.

'Tom Haig?'

'Who's this?'

'Joe Donovan. I believe you've got my daughter.'

A sound, somewhere between a sigh and a laugh. 'Where's Anne Marie?'

'She's on her way. You've got me first.'

'I don't want to talk to you.'

'Really? Then why did you send me that note the other night? Telling me about the dead boys?'

'Because you would have had no idea if I hadn't sent it.'

'So you wanted to get my attention. Well, you've got it. I presume you're on the roof? I'm coming up. If you decide to do anything before I get there, you're dead.'

There was doubt in Haig's voice. 'Are you threatening me?'

'No. Just giving you a statement of fact. I'm coming up. Be ready to let them go.'

He slides the phone shut, looks at Flemyng. Donovan's face is like an Ancient Greek theatre mask styled for revenge. Fixed. Unchangeable.

'Come on,' he says, and enters the building. Flemyng follows him.

29

Tess looked up, too stunned to speak, too hurt to move. Renny crouched over her, his left fist grabbing a handful of jacket, his right hand holding the knife to Tess's throat. Tess had never been so scared in her life.

'Please . . . don't . . .'

Renny sneered at him. 'Don't what?'

Tess closed her eyes. 'Don't kill me . . . please, don't kill me . . .'

Renny's eyes were lit by the kind of light Tess had often written about but never experienced first–hand. She hoped she would never experience it again.

'Please . . .' said Tess. 'I've got money. Is that what you want? I've got money.' She tried to get her hand into her pocket. 'Take it . . .'

Renny tightened his grip. 'I don't want your fuckin' money. Bitch. Cunt.'

'Then . . . what . . . what . . . d'you want? Tell me, and I'll get it . . .'

Renny leaned closer, hissed in Tess's ear. 'You were gonna give me up, weren't you?'

'What?'

'Don't fuckin' lie. You told me. You said it. You're gonna give me up. Tomorrow.'

Tess was genuinely confused. 'What . . . what are you talking about?'

Angered by Tess's words, Renny gripped her jacket even tighter. Tess winced in pain. The knife came closer to her neck. 'You know what. Don't pretend you don't.'

Tess said nothing.

'Calvin. You're gonna announce who killed Calvin tomorrow. You said. You told me.'

'Yeah, that's right. I am. But what's . . .'

'You think I'm gonna let you do that?'

'I don't know. Why . . .' And then Tess realized. She had made a mistake. A big mistake. The biggest she had ever made. She looked up into Renny's eyes. Saw in them the worst things she had ever seen. 'No . . . you . . . you killed Calvin?'

'Yeah. Little cunt. Dissin' me in front of all those people. Needed a fuckin' lesson.'

'And . . . and Pez?'

'Don't be fuckin' stupid. Pez was my mate.'

'Oh God . . . oh God . . . this is so wrong . . .'

Renny's breathing was getting harsher, faster. He was pumping himself up, getting ready to end it. Tess could tell. Tess thought fast.

'I wasn't going to name you. Honestly. I didn't know it was you.'

Renny was still breathing heavily. The knife glittered darkly. He paused. 'Then who were you goin' to blame?'

'Mae Blacklock,' Tess said as if it was obvious. 'The child killer. She's moved back here. The boy I asked you to look out for. His mother. I thought . . . I thought she did it. Did both of them.'

Renny stared at her.

'That's who I was going to say. Honestly.'

Renny's expression changed. He looked suddenly haunted. Like he had made a huge mistake and there was no way to make up for it. Tess noticed the change, tried to press forward. Talk her way out of it.

'Look, come on, Renny. Let's just forget this ever happened, yeah? I didn't hear it and you didn't say it. We get out of this alley, go our separate ways and that's the end of it, yeah? Come on, what d'you say?'

Renny sat back, loosened his grip on Tess. Seemed to be thinking. Tess decided to press the advantage.

'That's right, Renny. Let's just let it go, yeah? Get up like mates, walk away. And that's that. Yeah?'

Renny stood up. Tess couldn't believe it. She was going to live. She had talked her way out of it. She was going to live. Brilliant. Just wait until she wrote this up for the paper. How close she had come to death and how she had escaped. Yeah. Imagine the headlines for that one . . .

Renny was looking at her.

'What?' said Tess.

'I don't trust you,' said Renny. 'You're a liar. You'd get out of here and you'd tell everyone.'

Tess swallowed hard. It was like the boy had just read her mind. She gave him what she hoped was her most reassuring smile. 'Come on, Renny, don't be like that . . .'

She took a step towards the boy. And that was when Renny stabbed her.

Tess looked down at her stomach. She staggered backwards. Felt another blow. And another. And another.

Tess stumbled against the wall, looked down at her front. In the darkness her blood looked wet and black, like oil. She clutched her stomach, tried to hold herself together. Her legs felt weak, numb. They buckled. Without the energy to stand, Tess slid down the wall. She was starting to panic, the blood was pumping from her body.

She could barely think straight, only fight to hang on to life. Her vocabulary failed her. She couldn't describe what was happening to her. She watched Renny walk away, tried to put up a hand to stop him, to call out.

But she couldn't even do that.

She closed her eyes.

She had no time left at all.

Renny watched Tess die. Saw the life bleed out of her. And began to shake.

The first time had been righteous, watching Calvin die, that anger informing the stabs, telling him it was the right thing to do, that Calvin was paying for what he had done. Feeling more powerful, more in control of his own life with each blow. But this time it was different. He had stabbed a woman to death and watched her die. A woman who he might not have liked but who had given him money and done him no wrong. Well, she might have done if he'd let her live. Yeah, that was it. Renny held on to that thought, clutched it to him like a shield, hoped it would stop anything else, any contrary ideas permeating through. Failed.

The shaking intensified, as tears welled behind his eyes. He was scared, really scared. He looked at the knife, seeing it as if for the first time. Like it had just been put there. It was wrong. What he had just done was wrong. He felt physically sick.

He blinked the tears back, tried to focus on practicalities. Looked round. There were plenty of people on the estate tonight. Hopefully he could merge into the crowd, drift away. He looked down at his front. Saw the blood spatters arced across his jacket.

Shit. Maybe not. He had to get away. Quickly.

He turned and ran. Straight into the arms of two uniformed police officers.

'Hold him!' It was a woman's voice.

He turned, struggling. She was a detective, he remembered that much. The one that had come to their school after Calvin was killed. Now she was walking down the

alleyway towards him. He tried to pull away but the uniforms were too strong, their holds too practised. He felt
pain lance up his back as his arm was twisted almost to
breaking point.

She walked right up to him, stopped in front of him. 'I
am arresting you for murder . . .'

He didn't listen to the rest.

He didn't have to.

He pitched forward and threw up all over his trainers.

Donovan stood before the doorway to the roof of the tower
block.

'It's locked,' said Flemyng.

'Yeah, thanks,' said Donovan, turning the handle and
pushing as hard as he could. He felt the frame give. 'He must
have locked it from the outside.' He pushed again. The
frame gave some more. 'Hardly craftsmanship, these old
buildings . . .' He gave another shove. The door opened.

Donovan almost fell out on the roof. He managed to
pull himself up, not hit the hard asphalt. He looked round.
Figures silhouetted against the night sky, at the far side of the
building, right on the edge. He waited for his eyesight to
adjust, made out three of them, huddled together.

'That's far enough.'

Donovan stopped moving. Haig was on the edge of the
building, an arm round Abigail, Jack pulled towards him
with a knife at the boy's throat. Both teenagers had their
hands behind their backs. Tied presumably, thought
Donovan. They both looked terrified. Jack's body was
crumpled, his face agonized as if in pain. They both
looked defeated. Abigail's eyes pleaded with Donovan to
help her. He felt rage rise inside him. He had to do something.

His first impulse was to rush over to her, push Haig over

the edge, save the two of them. He stifled it. Knew it wouldn't work. He needed to be cleverer than that.

Instead, he looked round. Saw the lights of the city centre over to the left, Gateshead and the Tyne in front of him. The sky was cloudless. He swallowed down his anger, tried to work with it. 'You've picked a nice night for it, Tom. Bit chilly, though.'

'I said stay where you are.' Haig looked at the third man on the roof. 'Who's that?'

'Martin Flemyng,' said Donovan. 'Your replacement in Anne Marie's life. Better than you, but not by much.'

Flemyng started to complain. Donovan silenced him with a look.

Haig tightened his grip on Jack. The knife pressed harder on the boy's throat. 'So what d'you want?'

'What do you want, Tom? Why are you doing this? What are you hoping to gain?' Donovan moved forward slightly, hoping Haig wouldn't notice. He didn't. Donovan was shaking with fear and anger. He suppressed it. It wouldn't help. 'Do you want to talk?'

'About what?'

'I don't know. But let them go and we'll talk. About anything you want. The credit crunch, the fuel crisis, whether you think David Tennant's a good Doctor Who, anything.'

He pushed the knife tighter against Jack's neck. 'Don't fuck me about . . .'

'Then let them go,' Donovan said quickly, struggling to keep his voice calm and reasonable. 'Let them go. And we'll talk.'

Haig laughed, shook his head. 'I don't think so.'

'Then what? Why are you doing this?'

Haig sighed and for a second Donovan thought he was going to let them go. Just for a second. 'I'm going to die.'

'We're all going to die,' said Donovan.

'Not as soon as me. Cancer.' He spat the word out, his eyes pinwheeling with rage and madness. 'Fucking cancer. After everything I've done for everyone else. Cancer.'

Donovan moved forward another centimetre. Haig didn't notice.

'Anne Marie's . . . writing a book . . .'

'She is.'

'Why her? Ey? What's she done that's so impressive? So she killed a kid. So what?'

Donovan saw Jack tense at Haig's words, hoped the boy wouldn't do something stupid. He didn't. He was too scared to.

'I'm sure you'll be in there, Tom.'

'Oh, I'm sure I will. I'm sure she can't wait to put me in there for the whole . . . fucking . . . world to see. What'll they think then?'

'I don't know.' Another centimetre forward. 'What do you want the world to think?'

Haig pulled himself up. Abigail gasped. Donovan moved forward but Haig, brandishing the knife, his eyes wide and staring, made him stop where he was. Haig waited a few seconds then spoke again.

'I've spent all my life . . . working for other people. People who didn't . . . fucking deserve it, people who should have been left to rot. Some of them wrote books. Got TV careers out of it. Became famous. What did I get?' He screamed his next words, like a rabid wolf howling at the moon. 'What did I fucking get? Cancer.' He slumped forward slightly, regaining his breath. Continued. 'That's all. They'll be . . . they'll be remembered . . . and I get cancer. Well, this way, I'll be remembered as well.'

Another centimetre forward. 'Remembered as what, Tom? Someone who killed children?'

'Why not?' He spat the words out in rage and hatred. 'At

least it's something. I mean, look at these kids here. They're more important than me, aren't they? Don't pretend they're not.'

Donovan didn't answer.

'What I thought. You wouldn't have come if it wasn't for them, would you? Eh? No. You'll come to save them. But not me. Well, that's a shame. Because I've got nothing to . . . nothing to live for. When I've said what I want to say, when Anne Marie gets here, I'm going over that ledge. And I'm taking these two with me.'

Donovan's legs felt weak. He heard both Abigail and Jack whimper and cry. 'Don't do that, Tom. We can talk about this.'

'Fuck off.' Haig clutched his stomach as if a band of pain was encircling him. Got a grip. Straightened up. Thought for a moment. 'Five, isn't it?'

'Five what?'

'You need to kill five people to be officially classified as a serial killer, isn't that right?'

'I think so,' said Donovan, not liking this latest turn in the conversation at all. 'At least five.'

Haig smiled. There was no humour in it. Only madness. 'At least five.' He tightened his grip on Jack and Abigail. Laughed. 'At least.'

Donovan risked another move forward. From his peripheral vision, he noticed Flemyng was moving alongside him. He hoped the other man wasn't going to do anything stupid.

'So that's how I'll be remembered.' He stopped talking, his body wracked by a coughing fit. He kept the knife where it was. Jack closed his eyes as the blade bounced against his skin with each cough. Haig regained control. 'Tom Haig . . . serial killer. Might get a book written about me.'

'You might.'

'Will you write it?'

'I don't think so, Tom.'

Haig became angry again. 'Why not? You'll write hers, why not mine? Why does, why does . . . she get a book and not me?'

Donovan realized by now that Haig was totally unhinged. He had to say or do something to bring him back to rationality.

'OK, Tom,' said Donovan, 'I'll write your book.'

Haig looked at him suspiciously, eyes narrowed, expecting a trap. 'Really?'

'Yeah. Really.' Donovan swallowed hard. 'Just . . . just let them go, come over here and we'll talk about it. Yeah?'

Haig seemed to be mulling over Donovan's offer, his expression clear and open. Then his features changed, his face twisted once more. 'You fucker,' he said, panting for breath at the energy behind the vehemence of his words, 'I nearly believed you then. Give these up—' He squeezed the knife tighter against Jack's throat. Jack gave a whimper. '—let them go . . . you think that would work with me? Eh?'

Donovan had no answer. He doubted there was anything he could say that would reach him, affect him, make him change his mind from what he had planned. If words weren't going to work, he would have to stop him any way he could. He risked another couple of centimetres. Flemyng did the same.

Haig was still ranting. 'Bastard. And I nearly believed you . . . So tell me. Why should she be . . . be famous for, for . . . what she did?'

'Because Anne Marie has suffered,' said Donovan. He was exhausted. He didn't know how long he could keep this up for. 'Suffered. Her whole life. Her mother, prison . . .' He gestured to both Flemyng as well as Haig. 'The bad choices she made with men . . . all of her life. Nothing but suffering. She needs release.'

'Bullshit. She killed a kid.'

'When she was a kid herself. An angry, damaged kid. She didn't know what she was doing. She didn't know right from wrong or life from death.'

'So what? Boo fucking hoo. She's not the only one who had a bad childhood.'

'She was just a kid,' said Donovan. 'You were old enough to know what you were doing.' He risked another centimetre forward. Haig spotted it.

'What are you doing? Get back! Now!'

Donovan stopped moving. 'I'm trying to talk to you, Tom—'

'You're trying to fucking grab me! Now get back!' He waved the knife in the air before him.

Donovan noticed Jack tense. Not just from pain. He hoped that because the knife had been moved the boy wasn't going to try anything. He had to stop him. 'Jack,' he called out, 'stay where you are.'

Haig looked quickly down, put the knife back in place against Jack's throat. The movement caused Haig another bout of pain. It showed on his face. Donovan kept calling.

'Don't move, Jack, stay where you are.' He risked another step forward.

Haig looked between the pair of them, pain and madness in his eyes, tracing arcs through the air with the knife, his control slipping. 'I'm warning you, stay back . . .'

Donovan moved further forward. 'Tom, put the knife down. Jack, stay where you are, don't move.'

Haig looked between the two of them, confused now. Donovan moved again, as did Flemyng. 'Jack, don't . . . Tom . . . put it down . . .'

Haig, pain clouding his vision, didn't know where to look.

Then there was a sudden noise behind Donovan. He

turned. Peta had reached the door, kicked it open, and come on to the roof. She saw what was happening, stopped dead.

Haig looked over to her, confused as to what was now happening, who she was. The knife dropped, pointed downwards in his hand as his concentration fell and the pain took him over.

And in that moment, Flemyng was on him.

'Flemyng . . .!' shouted Donovan.

Flemyng ran forward from where he was standing next to Donovan and, before Donovan could stop him, was on top of Haig, his left hand outstretched to grab Haig's knife.

Donovan rushed forward also. He heard the sound of footsteps behind him, knew Peta was joining him. Jack and Abigail, freed from Haig's grip, stumbled out of the way, on to the roof, away from the edge of the building.

Donovan grabbed Abigail, Peta Jack. Donovan looked up. Flemyng and Haig were on the edge of the building, fighting for the knife. As he watched, Haig took a step backwards, unbalanced himself. Flemyng, rather than pulling him back, pushed him. Haig grabbed on to Flemyng for balance but only succeeded in pulling the other man with him.

'No . . .' Donovan tried to make a grab for Flemyng, missed. As he sailed over the edge of the building, Donovan was sure he had smiled at him.

Peta and Donovan went to the edge of the building, saw the two bodies hit the ground. They heard sobbing behind them, turned. Donovan moved towards Abigail, enfolded her in his arms. Peta did the same to Jack. Abigail kept sobbing.

'It's OK now,' said Donovan, holding her as tight as he could, 'I've got you. You're safe now. You're safe now . . .'

PART FIVE

THROUGH A LONG AND SLEEPLESS NIGHT

In the room is a table. At either side of the table are two chairs. On the table is a tape recorder. Two on one side, two on the other. She leans forward, introduces herself into the microphone.

'The time is 10.39 a.m. Detective Inspector Diane Nattrass. At my right is Detective Sergeant David Jobson. Opposite me is Christopher Renwick. And because Christopher Renwick is a minor he is accompanied by Jane Foreman, child liaison officer.'

She turns to the boy. 'So, Christopher. You've been read your rights.'

He nods.

'For the tape please, can you say yes or no.'

'Yes.' His voice is small, mumbled.

She looks at him as he speaks. Sitting in his paper suit, he looks like he has been crying. She understands. A night alone in the cells will do that to an adult never mind a child.

'And you understand them?'

He starts to nod, then speaks. 'Yes.'

'Good. Well, you know why you're here. You're charged with the murder of Theresa Preston-Hatt. You were found at the scene of the crime standing over the victim holding a knife in your hand and covered with blood. Your clothing has been sent to the lab for analysis.' She stops talking, looks at him. 'It looks conclusive. Did you do it, Christopher?'

He shrugs.

'For the tape is that a yes or a no?'

He sits for a moment, thinking. He seems to be weighing up more than just the answer he will give. Eventually he nods. 'Yes,' he says.

Nattrass sits back. 'Good. So you're pleading guilty, you did it.'

He nods.

'For the tape—'

'Yes . . . I did it, yes . . .' And then the tears start. He sits there, hands in his lap, shoulders hunched, seemingly getting smaller with each tear that falls.

'Right. Why did you do it, Christopher?'

'She . . . she said she would tell everyone what I'd done . . .'

'Why? What had you done?'

Renny, realizing he was about to incriminate himself further, closes his mouth. Nattrass leans forward.

'What had you done, Christopher?'

His only response is a shrug.

Nattrass sits back, opens the folder before her on the desk. 'Calvin Bell. He was a friend of yours, wasn't he?'

Another shrug.

'Yes or no. For the tape, please.'

'Yes.'

'Thank you. And he was killed this week. Stabbed. With a knife identical to the one that killed Theresa Preston-Hatt. Did you do it?'

'No.'

'Did you, Christopher? Because we're waiting for lab results that should be with us any moment and they will be able to tell us better than you.'

Another shrug.

'Do you watch CSI, Christopher?'

'Yeah.'

'So do I. Good, isn't it? Well that's where all of Calvin's clothes have gone. To our CSI lab. And the knife you killed Theresa Preston-Hatt with. And all your clothes. And you know how they always catch the criminals in CSI? Through lab results? Well, that's what'll happen here. So I'll ask you again. Did you kill Calvin Bell?'

He thinks for a moment. Then sighs. 'Yes . . .' He starts to cry again.

'Right. Good. Thank you for being honest. But why, Christopher? Why did you kill him? He was a friend of yours, wasn't he?'

Renny nods.

'For the tape.'

'Yes.'

'So why did you kill him?'

'Because . . . because he dissed me.'

'He . . . dissed you?'

'Yeah. He dissed me. Made me look small in front of my friends, you know?'

'How?'

'Well, I like told him somethin' that I'd done an' I hadn't really done it. But I wanted him to think I had an' he didn't.'

'What was it? What did you tell him?'

'That I'd been for a ride with one of the kids in their cars. The racers. In Tesco's car park. And I hadn't.'

'Why did you tell him that?'

''Cos . . . 'cos he's always . . . he's a good kid. Popular. Everyone likes him. He's, like, really brainy but not a boff an' . . . an' I just wanted to show him that I could do somethin' too. An' then he made me look small.' He shakes his head. 'An' I couldn't have that, man. I couldn't have that.'

'So you killed him.'

He nods. 'Yes.'

'Right.' Nattrass turns over a page in the report in front of her, looks up again. 'John Pearson. Pez. Did you kill him as well?'

Renny shakes his head. 'No.'

'Are you sure? You killed Calvin and Theresa Preston——'

'I didn't kill Pez.'

'Why not?'

'Because Pez was my friend.'

'So was Calvin.'

'Yeah, but I wouldn't do that to Pez.'

'You wouldn't?'

He shakes his head. 'Nah.' Then thinks. 'Well, not unless he really pissed me off.'

Nattrass sighs. 'Do you know the difference between right and wrong, Christopher?'

He shrugs.

Nattrass is about to pursue the matter when the child liaison officer reminds her that the boy needs a rest. Nattrass doesn't ask him to clarify his shrug for the tape. She looks down at the report once more, turns over another page. There is a report from social services, investigating allegations of physical and perhaps sexual abuse by Christopher Renwick's father on Christopher himself at the behest of a teacher at his school. Renwick senior was found to be very unhelpful and incommunicative and the investigation went no further. The situation, the report said, was being monitored but at present no further action was being taken. Nattrass looked up, back at Renny.

'Your dad's not here.'

Renny shakes his head.

'I believe he was asked but didn't want to come down.'

Renny looks scared as soon as the conversation turns to his father. He shrugs.

'Would you like us to call him again? See if we can get him here?'

He shakes his head. 'No . . . no, don't get him in here.'

'You sure?'

He nods. 'Don't . . .'

And then he starts to cry again. And the tears he has shed so far are nothing compared to the ones he is now shedding.

Nattrass closes the report, sits back. She thinks of Mae Blacklock. How the abuse she experienced was ignored until it was too late and manifested itself as murderous rage. Looks at

Christopher Renwick crying before her. Thinks how little has changed in the intervening years.

She leans forward to speak into the microphone. She concludes the interview.

There is nothing more to be said for the time being.

30

Anne Marie looked at the figure before her, lying in the hospital bed. She had cried rivers – oceans – of tears over him in the time they had been together. And now she wiped her eyes with a tissue, letting the latest watery emissions dry up.

She had come to the General Hospital as soon as Donovan had called her, Amar driving. Once there, a nurse had directed her to the waiting room and told her to wait. Mister Hutchinson was in surgery and she would let her know how he was as soon as she could. Anne Marie had pestered her until she had brought a doctor who then told her the extent of Rob's injuries. Neither his neck nor his back were broken, nor was there any sign of brain damage which were all encouraging signs, but his legs were broken, his ribs were shattered, one of them puncturing a lung which meant for the time being he couldn't breathe unassisted. Seeing Anne Marie's face the doctor added that he was in a good state and that, although it might be slow and painful, given the right kind of care there was no reason why he couldn't make a good or perhaps even full recovery.

There were police everywhere in the hospital, almost as many of them as medical staff. They had questioned her and questioned her until she couldn't think straight and then left her alone.

Hours Anne Marie had sat there, worrying about Rob. And Jack. He was in another part of the hospital. Donovan had contacted her, told her what had happened with him and that he was dealing with the police in Scotswood but he would be at the hospital as soon as possible. Jack and Abigail had already been taken there and their injuries were being treated. Abigail's were mostly superficial, but Jack had four broken ribs and they wanted to keep him in for observation in case of internal bleeding. He was sleeping now, comfortable, as the nurse had said. Expected to make a full recovery. Anne Marie tried to take what positives she could from it. She knew it could have been a lot worse. Haig and Flemyng weren't so lucky.

So as she sat in the waiting room, a plastic cup of something claiming to be coffee in her hand, certainly nowhere near as good as Donovan's coffee, she allowed herself to feel relief. With the police leaving her alone for the time being, she felt that, for the first time in more years than she could remember, she could relax. A little. If she could get beyond this then she could allow herself to experience something a little like hope. There was still stuff to get sorted, and she would have to move again, but if they could just get through the rest of the night, then the next day might not be so bad after all.

The door to the waiting room opened and a nurse walked in.

'Ms Smeaton? Your son's awake if you would like to see him.'

She didn't need to be told twice. She stood up, overturning the plastic cup of toxic liquid into the carpet, expecting it to sizzle.

'Sorry,' she said to the nurse.

'Doesn't matter. Come with me.'

The nurse led her to a ward. And there, lying down and heavily bandaged, was her son. She wanted to run forward, hold him, but she knew that would only make things worse.

So she stood there, trying to contain her emotions, hoping he understood.

There were tears in his sleepy eyes. 'Mum . . . I'm sorry . . .'

She frowned. 'What for?'

'Running off like that.'

'Don't be stupid.'

'I've been thinking. About what you did . . .'

Anne Marie tensed, not wanting to hear the rest but knowing, despite everything else that had happened, she wouldn't be able to move on until she had. 'It's all right,' she started to say but Jack stopped her.

'No, Mum. I've got to say this now. Because I've been thinking about it and we've got to get it said. Now.' He paused, took a deep breath, exhaled. It seemed to hurt him. She sat on the edge of the bed, held his hand. 'I just wanted to say . . . you were just a kid. What you did, you were just a kid. You didn't know what you were doing . . . you can't punish yourself all your life for something you did when you were a kid . . .'

And the tears started again.

Time passed. Anne Marie didn't know how long they stayed like that, but she noticed after a while that a figure was standing over her.

'I hope I'm not interrupting anything,' said Joe Donovan. 'I was just passing, you know . . .'

Anne Marie smiled. 'You OK?'

Donovan managed a smile. 'I'm fine. I'm just going to get Abigail and I thought I would see how you were doing. How's Rob?'

She told him. 'But they're hopeful. So that's somethin'.'

'Good.' Donovan looked round, clearly embarrassed. 'So. I think you might want to take a day off tomorrow.' He looked at his watch. 'Well, today, really.'

She nodded. 'Look, erm . . . this book. I've been thinkin'. I don't want to do it any more.'

'You sure? I would have thought now would be a great time to do it. Publicity, money . . . the chance to tell your story.'

'Well, I don't know. Maybe. But not right this moment. I don't think I can handle the past. I've had enough of that recently what with one thing and another. I think I'll just concentrate on the future from now on.'

'Whatever. Decision's yours.'

'And I think we might have to move on again.'

'You never know. It'll all blow over in a few days. Things'll be back to normal. People will forget.'

'Maybe they will, maybe they won't. We can't take that chance.'

'Right.' He thought for a moment, then smiled. 'But if you do decide to stay and you need a job . . .'

'Yes?'

'Well, people keep telling me I need a receptionist.'

She smiled. 'Thanks. I'll bear that in mind.'

She said her goodbyes to him, thanked him once again. As he was leaving, Jack spoke.

'Will you see Abigail?'

'Yeah, I'm going to pick her up now.'

'Right.' Jack became suddenly tongue-tied. 'Tell her . . . tell her . . .'

Donovan smiled. 'I will,' he said, and left.

Anne Marie turned back to Jack, smiled at him. And, fragile and shaken though he was, he returned it.

Perhaps things weren't going to be so bad after all, she thought.

Donovan walked down the corridor of the hospital on his way to pick up Abigail. He checked his watch. Nearly seven o'clock. The next day was starting.

He had spent the night giving a statement to the police. They hadn't looked on what they described as his vigilante actions very favourably at first but once he mentioned that he had attempted to call DI Nattrass and been rebuffed, perhaps sensing a possible lawsuit, they backed off. And that was just fine with him.

'Joe . . . Joe . . .'

Donovan turned. Wendy Bennett was running down the corridor behind him. Back in her jacket, jeans and trainers. She still looked good, though, he thought.

She caught up with him, out of breath and lightly perspiring and her chest heaving, all reminding him of how pleasantly they had spent the previous night. 'Joe . . . I'm glad I found you.'

'Right. They're down there.' He gave her directions to where Anne Marie and Jack were.

'Thanks, I'll see them in a minute.' She looked at him, gave him her biggest smile. 'Well. Hero.'

'Oh, fuck off.' But he couldn't help smiling.

'Seriously though, well done. I heard about what happened. Any problems, we're right behind you. The agency and the publishers. They'll be so excited now. Gagging for the book.'

'The book. Right. Anne Marie's thinking of not going ahead with it.'

Wendy looked gutted. 'Why? Now's the perfect time.'

'I told her that, but I think she just wants a bit of peace.'

Wendy nodded. 'We'll see about that.' And with those words Donovan saw the steel within her that must have made her good at her job. 'Don't go booking any more work. You're still doing this.'

'Right.'

'Right.'

They both stood there, suddenly embarrassed and tongue-tied.

'So . . . what happens next?' said Donovan.

'Well, once I've talked to Anne Marie and persuaded her to keep going I'll be on a plane back to London. I might have to renegotiate the contract in light of what's happened, but it'll be more money all round. Everyone'll be happy.'

'That's not what I meant.'

She nodded. She knew that. She kept her eyes downcast. 'I'm going back to London today. I don't know when I'll be back.'

'It's only fifty minutes away on EasyJet,' said Donovan. 'It's not the end of the world.'

'I know but . . .' Wendy looked at him. He saw things in her eyes that she wanted to say, things he both did and didn't want to hear, but couldn't find the words to express. 'Look,' she said, 'last night was lovely. Really great. But . . .'

'You've got a boyfriend.'

She nodded.

'And this was just an adventure. You wanted to satisfy your curiosity.'

'I didn't say that. That's not what I meant.' Wendy sighed. 'Look. I'm not good with things like this. Look. We'll still be, be working together. Let's . . . let's just see what happens, shall we?'

Donovan realized that was the best he could hope for.

'OK.'

She nodded, smiled. It was much less dazzling, more tentative than the ones he had become used to from her. She looked at her watch. 'I'd better get a move on.'

She kissed him. On the cheek.

'Bye.'

She turned and walked quickly down the hospital corridor.

Donovan turned and went in the opposite direction.

*

Donovan found Abigail in A & E. She was sitting on a plastic chair with Peta. Peta stood up when he arrived. She looked tired, he thought. They both did. No doubt he looked the same. He certainly felt it. He smiled. Genuinely pleased to see them. Both of them.

Peta glanced between father and daughter. 'Well,' she said. 'I'll be off then.'

Donovan thanked her and she left, squeezing his arm as she went. She gave him a smile in return, so full of warmth and concern that it made Wendy's absence easier to bear. Abigail joined him in watching her go.

'She's nice,' Abigail said. 'I like her.'

'Yeah,' said Donovan, 'I agree. She's great.'

Abigail looked at the retreating figure then back at him, frowning. Slightly worried and sensing something more in his reply. 'But she's not Mum.'

Donovan smiled. 'No,' he said. 'She's not Mum.'

'I saw your girlfriend before.'

'She's not my girlfriend.'

'Yeah, right.'

He looked at her. 'Yeah. Right.'

She gave him a smile again. He could see how fragile around the edges it was. But then she had been through a great trauma and needed some rest.

'Come on,' he said, 'let's see if we can catch Peta. Amar's gone home and she's headed back to her house. She can take you along, put you to bed for a couple of hours. You look like you could do with it.'

'What about you?'

'I'd better have a look in at work.'

She seemed about to argue but thought better of it. 'OK,' she said. 'That'd be cool.'

'Don't worry, Peta'll look after you.'

She nodded. They began to walk out of the building.

The morning was cold. Abigail snuggled up against Donovan's side. Still my little girl, he thought.

'You know,' said Abigail as they were walking through the car park, 'it was Mum I wanted to talk to you about.'

'I thought so,' he said. 'You don't have to do it now if you don't want to.'

'No, I do. Get it said and sorted.' She took a deep breath and continued. 'Mum told me she wants a divorce.'

'Right.' Donovan nodded. 'I thought it would be something like that.'

'She wants to marry Michael.'

'Well . . . she's been with him a long time. It's only natural, I suppose.'

She stopped walking, looked at him. 'But aren't you angry? If she does that we'll . . . we'll never be a family again.' Tears glittered in the corners of her eyes. 'We'll never . . .'

'I know he's not me, he's not your father, but he's good for you. And Mum. He's there for you.'

'But you could be . . .'

He pulls her away from him, looks in her eyes. 'Abigail, I would love to be. There's nothing I want more in the whole world than my family back together again. But you know it wouldn't work. Because there'll always be a space there. A ghost haunting everything. And you and your mum, and probably me, we'd hate it. And hate each other for it. Not at first, but in time we would. It would drive us all apart. Possibly forever.'

She kept crying, nodding.

'You're my daughter and I'll always love you. I'm always here for you. And I always will be. I'd love to come and see you and you can come and see me . . .'

She hugged into him again, sobbing into his leather jacket.

'Let's just hope next time there'll be no knife-wielding maniacs around.'

He felt her laugh among the tears.

'So don't tell your mother.'

She laughed again, clung to him all the harder.

He found Peta. She took Abigail back to her house to get some sleep.

Then he drove back to Albion.

He stood there in the main office, looking at the one active screen. It was still showing the same blue door. No news from Jamal. Donovan had tried phoning him but it just rang out and tripped over to voicemail. If he had more energy and felt less tired, he should start to get worried.

He rubbed his face, closed his eyes, suddenly aware of just how worn out he really was. He should go home, he knew that. But he would sit a little longer. Look at the screen, see if something happened. Try not to think of murdered boys that nobody cared for.

He went into the kitchen to make himself a coffee. A strong one, keep himself awake, when he heard the key in the front door.

'Hello?' he called out, peering into the main office.

'Man,' said a voice he recognized only too well, 'you would not believe the fuckin' hassle I have had to endure to get here. Straight up, blood, it has been mental.'

Donovan stepped into the office, smiled. Jamal came in through the main door, threw his key on the nearest desk. 'Jamal . . . I was getting worried about you.'

'Worried? So you fuckin' should be, bruv. I've been like Jason Bourne crossin' borders an' dodgin' the CIA to get here.' A huge grin split his face. 'But it was worth it, man.'

Donovan frowned. 'Why?'

Jamal stepped back. Donovan was aware of another figure in the doorway. Jamal ushered the figure in. Donovan froze.

'Joe,' said Jamal, 'meet your son. Meet David.'

The boy smiled.

Acknowledgements

Thanks to everyone who helped either through professional obligation, friendship, love, inspiration or some combination of the above: Mark Adair, Ray Banks, Mark Billingham, Tony Black, Ken Bruen, Sharon Canavar, Andrew Clark, Jay Clifton, Sally Cline, Steve Cook, Natasha Cooper, Alastair Craig, Jim Eagles, Mike Fenton Stevens, Lizzie Forbes Ritte, Kim Galvin, Fiona Geddes, Stephanie Glencross, Jane Gregory, Allan Guthrie, Claiborne Hancock, Robert Horwell, Maxim Jakubowski, Paul Johnston, Jennifer Jordan, Jon Jordan, Ruth Jordan, Ali Karim, Danuta Kean, Deb Kemp, Nick Kemp, Kate Lyall Grant, Angela Macmahon, Ken McCoy, Jemma McDonagh, Claire Morris, Jefferson Kingston Pierce, Steve Pratt, Sheila Quigley, Chris Simmons, Mike Stotter, Cathi Unsworth, Linda Waites, Sarah Weinman, Kevin Wignall, Laura Wilson, Mark Wingett, everyone at Borders Silverlink, Borders Team Valley, Waterstone's Sunderland and Waterstone's Newcastle, and special thanks to all the readers who have taken the time to write and chat to me, either at events or through my website, to tell me how much they enjoy my books. It's an old cliché but its true. You really do make it all worthwhile.

And next time, no cliffhangers. Just answers. Promise.